PENGU… BOOKS

THE PLEASURES OF MEN

…he London of the "Hungry Forties", not yet the pompous capital …m; rank, cholera-racked, clinging precariously to a squalid Regency … . . . *The Pleasures of Men* shares with *Wolf Hall* an ambitious, … concern with form combined with a pitch-perfect historical ear. …ating and disturbing novel is properly thrilling and extraordinarily …itten. Kate Williams is already an accomplished biographer; …sures of Men shows a soaring talent let loose' *Independent on Sunday*

…lly ripe, imaginative and gripping, with a spider's web of a plot and a …pine-tingling atmosphere of menace and suspense' *The Times*

…ce-ripper, part slasher, the elaborate plot moves along at a brisk clip with a nod to Sarah Waters' *Daily Mail*

…e murder mystery set in the corrupt heart of Victorian London' *Marie Claire*

… intelligent and hugely entertaining, *The Pleasures of Men* will add …ns to the ranks of queens of contemporary fiction' *Guardian*

…book, with sumptuous period detail and a narrative crammed with … speculation, this is the debut novel that Kate Williams was born to … sure-footed evocation of an era and a deft critique on repression' *Sunday Telegraph*

… novel as crowded with sensation as a Victorian parlour was with …For Catherine – bored, listless, starved of affection, locked away in …s house – even just imagining the handiwork of the Man of Crows somehow frees her imagination' *Scotsman*

'With a remarkable imaginative intensity that seizes attention from the start, this dark, disturbing story will not easily be forgotten' *BBC History Magazine*

'A dark story of murder and obsession' *Elle*

'This is a fast-paced thriller written by an expert on all things Victorian. Fans of Sarah Waters and Michel Faber will revel in this charged and colourful Victorian epic . . . Williams creates an extraordinary world with unforgettable characters and a dark heart. Highly recommended' *Bookseller*

'Not since Sarah Waters have I seen so much lesbian sex in a historical novel' Mariella Frostrup, Radio 4, *Open Book*

'A dark world of murder and betrayal ****' *Daily Express*

'Chilling' *History Today*

'Mesmerizing . . . Captures a city in thrall to a madman' *Lady*

The Pleasures of Men

KATE WILLIAMS

PENGUIN BOOKS

PENGUIN BOOKS

Published by the Penguin Group
Penguin Books Ltd, 80 Strand, London WC2R 0RL, England
Penguin Group (USA) Inc., 375 Hudson Street, New York, New York 10014, USA
Penguin Group (Canada), 90 Eglinton Avenue East, Suite 700, Toronto, Ontario, Canada M4P 2Y3
(a division of Pearson Penguin Canada Inc.)
Penguin Ireland, 25 St Stephen's Green, Dublin 2, Ireland (a division of Penguin Books Ltd)
Penguin Group (Australia), 250 Camberwell Road,
Camberwell, Victoria 3124, Australia (a division of Pearson Australia Group Pty Ltd)
Penguin Books India Pvt Ltd, 11 Community Centre,
Panchsheel Park, New Delhi – 110 017, India
Penguin Group (NZ), 67 Apollo Drive, Rosedale, Auckland 0632, New Zealand
(a division of Pearson New Zealand Ltd)
Penguin Books (South Africa) (Pty) Ltd, Block D, Rosebank Office Park,
181 Jan Smuts Avenue, Parktown North, Gauteng 2193, South Africa

Penguin Books Ltd, Registered Offices: 80 Strand, London WC2R 0RL, England

www.penguin.com

First published by Michael Joseph 2012
Published in Penguin Books 2012
001

Set in 12.97/15.25pt Garamond MT Std
Typeset by Jouve (UK), Milton Keynes
Printed in England by Clays Ltd, St Ives plc

ISBN: 978–0–241–95454–6

www.greenpenguin.co.uk

Penguin Books is committed to a sustainable
future for our business, our readers and our planet.
This book is made from Forest Stewardship
Council™ certified paper.

ALWAYS LEARNING PEARSON

The Pleasures of Men

'The sick . . . how much more they think of painful things than pleasant ones. The ghosts of their troubles haunt their beds.'

Florence Nightingale,

Notes on Nursing

Prologue

London, July 1840

Night comes late to Spitalfields Market, across the dump at the back used by the traders for the detritus of old vegetables and splintered crates. The stall holders pack up their apples and cabbages, gather their pieces of meat, oysters and bags of fish, the battered hardware and cheap clothes, down the last dregs of ale, then wrap their arms around each other for the short journey to the lights of Lely's gin house on the corner. I stay behind, near the dump, see the mass glistening as maggots slither out of the soft flesh of the discarded beef.

The first scavengers are the younger men, dismissed soldiers hiking useless legs, crawling up the dump and delving in their hands. Then women, babies swaddled to their breasts, picking off the heads from trout and cockerels and pulling scraps of pork from the bones. Huddles of rheumy children come next, biting off carrot tops and around potato eyes, licking at the old boxes, rubbing their feet in the last juice of the meat. And when all the others have departed, the old woman comes, baring her rotted teeth at the pile, her lifeless bosoms like dirty moons, pulling herself around the sides of the stack, racking herself with laughter.

At first, when she screams, no one hears but me. Not the seamen outside the gin shop, talking about money and girls, or the women in darkened red dresses and thin shawls, waiting along street corners, or even the scavenging children, fighting over their spoils in the corner of the marketplace. She does not stop. The sound hurtles over the walls until they seem to echo to her cries and so the children look up and the women hear, and the sailors put aside their bottles and soon real men come, significant, responsible men with dressed hair and long black cloaks, who never give those who work in the market or the scavengers a single thought. They look at the madwoman, rocking in the blood, and think that she is the one dying.

Then they see what lies behind her. A girl, her blue dress ragged ribbons around her legs. She has been stabbed twenty times, they guess, over and over until her skin lies like ruffled feathers over the darkening flesh. Her arms and legs have been bent back so she is all chest, and her pale hair has been plaited and thrust into her mouth. A blue ribbon and a feathered comb cling to the edges of her hair. Over what remains of her bosom, the killer has gouged a deep star. And then they peer further and see a one-pence coin, perched on the still warm core of her heart.

Abigail Greengrass shakes out her thick skirt as she leaves Davis's Milliners. She beats at the wool, as if by doing so she can throw off the dirt and cruelties of her day. The door bangs behind her and she does not care. She hates Mrs Davis and her simpering girls. She feels the wetness of the cobblestones touch the soles of her boots as she sets off towards Long Acre. Four builders at the pie shop whistle at her and she is not so tired that she cannot toss her head slightly and give a half-smile at the swarthy one at the front. Then into Long Acre and the crowds of people milling home, and her day returns: the bottom of her spine is sharp with pain from bending, her left eye is twitching and the skin smarts under her fingernail from when Mrs Davis pushed the needle there, on purpose she is sure.

The old witch. For the last two weeks, Mrs Davis has been making her sew in lining and mend holes, which means sitting at the back of the shop. Even though she was just as good at netting and embroidering as the others and ten times better than stuck-up Emily Warren, who Mrs Davis petted just because of her thick golden hair fit for pleasing the gentlemen and a face not so pretty that the peaches there would upset the ladies.

Abigail walks past the blazing shops and sees nothing. The rounded glass bottles glowing blue, green, red in the window of the chemist's she has regarded a thousand times before, likewise the toppling apples and pears on the stall next to the stationer's. She ignores the newsboy selling the latest gossip about the Queen's ladies-in-waiting, and the boot polisher, his nails blackened for life around the edges. Even the custard tarts trembling in the steamy window of the cake shop, dotted with raisins like stars around the sky, do not touch her eye. She sees only the inside of her mind.

Her mind turns over the spite of Mrs Davis as she walks up Kingsway and to High Holborn. The cuts in her heels catch slightly on her stockings and she does not flinch, for she likes the feeling of rawness, the heat that comes before the fissures widen and grow painful. Abigail crosses the road towards St Paul's and then trots along London Wall. Gathering her heavy skirts out of a puddle, she turns on to Bishopsgate and then Shoreditch High Street, rehearsing to herself how Lily, the front shop girl, said that a customer had asked for her, Abigail, to do the work personally and Mrs Davis had replied that the young lady in question was ill and offered Emily instead. She blows on her thin fingers. One day she shall have her own shop and Mrs Davis and Emily will come begging for work, and she will offer them a little simple stitching to do at home. *I cannot do more*, she imagines herself saying. *I have such good girls now*. Her mind wanders to glassy windows full of hats and to benches of neat workers bent sewing just for her. *Abigail Greengrass. Milliner of Distinction.*

She touches her hair and then the soft blue silk of the ribbon. The gentleman had come with a lady (some lady, Lily said) to pick out a hat, returned an hour later and said that if the young lady with the hazel eyes might accept a ribbon from the shop – any type – he would be pleased to add the cost to his account. Mrs Davis was out, so she came up. His eyebrows thinned at the ends and she imagined reaching up and touching the few stray hairs into place. Thanking him, she felt Lily's nudge and wondered – was this the beginning of ruin? The gentleman would come back for her and start taking her to the theatre where she would wear big flowers on her hat and everybody would think her fallen. She chose the blue and waited. But he did not come, and even sent a servant to the shop to collect the hat. 'Men are unaccountable,' said Lily, a word they both enjoyed. Still, months on, Abigail wonders. Well now, when he finally came for her, he would be too late, she would be the owner of her own shop, married perhaps. The young lady with the hazel eyes. And since yesterday, she had a better ornament, a feathered comb she'd found on the street near St Magnus the Martyr Church.

She turns into Boundary Street. As the gas lamps thin and the street darkens, she is not seeing, not thinking, caught in the trap of her mind.

A scuffle behind her. A footstep.

She looks ahead and the street is empty. Only the beginnings of the moon casting over the stones. The trail of pictures of Mrs Davis and Emily Warren disappears and she thinks only of where she is and the air around her.

The footstep comes once more, and then there is a

breath. Walking forward, she tells herself that there is nothing. So many times she has thought a man was too near behind when he was simply close by for no reason. She hears a cough and a clack of fine-sounding heels and her chest tightens. She moves more quickly. So does he.

God help me.

She will not turn. To do so would make him seem real, but if she walks and pretends she does not know he is there, he will melt away and she will be safe and she will never tell of this to anyone, never. Soon someone will appear, a man carrying his bundle at the end of the day, a ragged woman with two squalling children. She will go up to him or her, smile and stay beside them and take the route home that stays in the light.

Abigail walks on. So does he.

Stay calm, she tells herself. Only a few streets to her lodgings. Not far. She has not spoken to God since she was a small girl and her mother was dying. Now she bargains. *Let me return, and you can have anything. I will be in church every Sunday. I will make Joseph marry me. I will love Mrs Davis and Emily Warren.* Her mind tries to hold the image of a white-bearded man looming kindly in a yellowy tunic, just like the one her father wore for mending things around their rooms when she was a child.

She walks, faster now, hearing the man do the same.

Stop imagining things, she tells herself. *He's just trying to frighten you.*

She turns left and knows he will follow. The street is quiet. A few years back, the parish decided to knock down the homes and put up brand-new buildings, in which artists and the like could make paintings and furniture for rich folks. But the buildings were completed just as everything changed and all the money was lost and so they are empty, some already run over with rats. There is no other route she can take, save turning around. She passes the deserted blocks, their windows shining like eyes, hearing him behind her. *Nothing will happen. You are a lucky person – remember that. You have always had good fortune.* She moves slightly to the side of the road, and hears him do the same. *Happier thoughts*, she tells herself. That day with Joseph by the Thames. The times her father swung her over his head when she was small.

But all she can think of is her lodgings. Her room, left in a tumble when she hurried out in the morning, bed still unmade, her chemise thrown across the floor. Mrs Wornley hanging over the rails, her bangs catching her face, shouting, 'Not another instant for the coal money, my girl, it had better be tonight or you'll be in trouble.' She would do anything to be in her bed, trying to sleep while Nelly crashes around in the room above her, breathing in the stench of overcooked sprouts and suet, hearing Peter bump buckets of water up the stairs. How she had detested her tiny room, longed for something more spacious, in a better part of town. Now she wishes only to touch open the greasy door, pull off her boots, sit on the wobbly chair she found on a street near Holborn and know she is safe. *Then*, she tells herself, *you will laugh at how afraid you have been.*

And you will never take the short route back again.

Only a few more yards. First left and second right. Then all she has to do is cut through the alleyway behind the pie shop and she will be there. She moves to the black mouth of the alley. Hesitates for a moment, breathes. She is warm now. She thinks of Mrs Wornley, opening the door to her, peering as the yellow from the lamps floods out into the street. *Home*. She straightens, smiles to herself and moves towards the light.

1. City of Men

Two men in overcoats stand by our gate. My uncle would have me believe them working men, leaning and talking before going on. The dark one I have seen three times over the past week. He is so close that I can see the black flecks of hair at the edges of his beard and I imagine reaching and up and pulling at them, the rough brown skin resisting and releasing until there is nothing there but clean skin, like a child's.

Even as late as last winter, I saw many people from my window. Couples walking arm in arm, maids carrying milk pails, labourers shouldering baskets of bricks, old women shuffling past. Now July steams our street and all I see are men. Men saunter past my home and stop by the gates. When I pass in my carriage along the street, they watch. They lean against doors, look at my dress and brush my arm.

'Please *try* this afternoon, Catherine.' My uncle was pretending to adjust the Hogarth etching of Gin Lane on the wall so he did not have to look at me. 'It would not inconvenience you so very much to smile.' He stepped back and over the African death statue from the eastern part of the continent propped on the coal scuttle. 'Mr Janisser is a very wealthy man.'

My breath was rising. 'So you have said.'

My uncle batted at his dusty sleeve, turning to swirl his eye at me. 'Is that the prettiest gown you have?' I had grown so much over the past few months that even the pale yellow dress, bought not long after I arrived at Princes Street, was too short at the ankles. The green trimming touched the top of my boots.

'I shall sit. Buying dresses is difficult at present.'

He shrugged. 'Life must continue, my dear. We cannot live prisoners of fear. No one is going to trouble you. Always are the poor the victims. Well, I shall ask Thomas to take you out in the coach next week to a dressmaker.'

When my uncle's mind reflected back at me, I saw an old, unmarriageable woman, locked up in her small room, adorned in the faded dresses of her youth.

'I shall resolve to stop growing.'

'That would be wise.' The dark clock to his side struck and the gold man on the top began his slow turn. 'If you rose earlier, Jane would have time to help you arrange your coiffure.' His face was quite still in the hot air. 'After our meal, I wish you to return to your room and have her tidy your hair. And find a more becoming gown.' He raised an eyebrow. 'The pale lilac. Our visitors this afternoon are of consequence.'

He turned away and my eyes caught the large brown spot that sat in his cheek, like a bite that will not heal. He always combed his black hair very carefully off his forehead and he had no moustache or beard, so that his face, sun-scored with wrinkles, was bare to the world.

I longed to be back in my room with Grace, her hands flickering at my hair as she imitated my uncle and made me laugh.

'I have met your friends before.'

'The occasion would not be the same without you, my dear.' He reached out and the signet star ring glittered on his little finger.

I had to pour the tea for the South American mines man and his weasel face, but I didn't wear my lilac gown for him.

'Mr James Leith Janisser is the brother of our dear friend Mr Belle-Smyth. He is not in the most splendid of health.'

I would not give him the satisfaction of a reply. At the window, our neighbour Mr Kent passed and waved, his child face shiny in the warm air. I looked back at my uncle and a sly expression was illuminating his face. 'I hear that the younger Mr Janisser has a great facility for pleasing the ladies.' He patted his hand as if he were making a full stop.

Our house was three storeys and over a hundred years old, in Princes Street, in the eastern part of London. Most of the other buildings were crammed with families, thirty, even forty bodies in one house, tailors, furniture-makers, and weavers whose French I could not understand. They kept lit candles in their windows all night long. I grew up in Richmond, and came to this area once before, but that visit was all pain in my head and the streets I could not remember. When I arrived in the

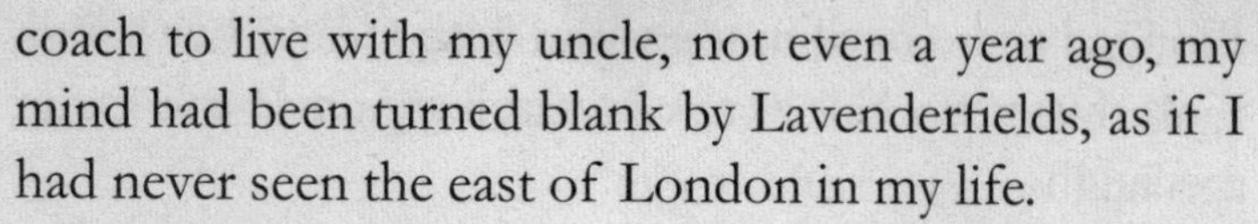

coach to live with my uncle, not even a year ago, my mind had been turned blank by Lavenderfields, as if I had never seen the east of London in my life.

I could not credit the noise, in those first weeks. All day and night, the shouts of men, the cries of babies, howling dogs and an endless clanging and crashing of wood and metal. The smell assaulted my nose, human sewage, rotting vegetables, dirty bodies and dogs, seeping into my chamber. I would turn the corner from the corridor into my bedroom and feel certain I could see the yellowish smog from outside drifting on to my counterpane. In Lavenderfields, the noise was made only by us inside. Outdoors was calm and quiet and all you could smell was grass. Number seventeen Princes Street was always invaded by the outside world. On those first nights I lay in bed certain that the grimy pigeons on the roof were about to come tumbling down the chimney and start flapping over my bed, the filth of the street falling after them.

Still, after a few months, I grew habituated to Princes Street, forgetting until I saw our visitors, pale and surprised at the door, that we lived in an environ many in London would revile.

I climbed the stairs to my small room. I dreamt that Grace was already there, waiting, her pale hair like a candle in the gloom.

'You need a gown for this afternoon, I hear.' I turned and she began to unbutton my dress. Her fingers were on my neck as she moved aside my hair. She smoothed the lilac over my shoulders and I wanted then to lean against her. Reach for her with the hands that only a year ago had been tied with rope.

'Trying again with the suitors.' I sat on the chair at the table.

'You must marry some time.'

'Never.' *I want to stay with you.* 'I wish we could take a house together.'

'I would like that.' She moved her hand under my hair and began to brush it. I smiled as she did so. I leant against the bosom of her dress and my skin turned to fire.

But there was no one in the dark room but me, the masks my uncle found in Africa that stared out from the walls, and the two little dolls that looked like hunters. I took my tangled hair in my hand and brushed it, then called for Jane to form the style.

The visit was as I expected. Constantine Janisser, skinny, slack-jawed, stretched out his legs in front of him like two long drains. His mother admired and his father sat too close, extolling.

'Our son had great success at school.'

My uncle nodded. 'Catherine received excellent reports from her governesses.'

Oh, all so polite! My uncle and Mr Janisser began, exchanging questions about business and family (two younger daughters finishing their education in Bath, and a niece living with them, eighteen and already affianced), and talked of the health of their relatives, the

Belle-Smyths. Mrs Janisser clutched for pleasant words about our ramshackle curiosity shop of a parlour. I poured tea, clumsily, and offered Mrs Graves's teacakes and shortbread biscuits on our best flowered plates. I smiled. How I smiled.

I found myself desiring an aunt. A motherly female presence to flurry our visitors with chatter in a way I could not. I imagined her warming the room with her words, freeing us of the silences that hung over our heads like icicles. But then, my aunt Cross was not comforting nor kind, and a wife of my uncle would have surely been the same.

Grace would tell me I looked well. But this man and his family would flee from me, and I hated that they could make the choice to do so. I had my mother's small nose and the green eyes a friend of my father said reminded him of paintings in Rome. And even when I was chained to the wall with it cut short, someone would say, *my but she has handsome hair. So dark! Surely some Indian blood?* Now my hair was blacker than ever, and since I had come to live with my uncle, it had grown down to my back. My appearance was not the problem. It was my manner. Anyone could see that I did not fit in, and every part of me was out of place, in my body and in my soul.

I wanted to ask my uncle, 'Why do you show me around as a potential wife?' A responsible father might enquire about my past.

I turned my head and saw the footman by the glossy Janisser carriage, upright, every sinew of his body tensed to show resentment at standing in Princes Street, where scrawny dogs scratched at the corners of houses and rainwater ran brown down the centre. I looked past him at the small face etched on the front wall of the opposite house, eyes, mouth, nose, and allowed the features to throb behind my eyes. Since every street in the east was controlled by a gang, Princes Street was fortunate, said my uncle, to be under the rule of the Malays. The collector came to our door for money twice a month and then we were protected.

Mrs Janisser reached out her beeswax fingers for a biscuit and ventured a declaration that the walls must be very strong. My uncle looked up and, as if his voice had been stoppered in a jug and set free, began to talk.

'I bought this house twenty years ago,' he explained. 'The value has much increased. But speculation was not my ambition. No. I was entranced by the history.' He held out his arms. 'I walked in and could immediately sense the past. Do you not agree?' Mr Janisser bit at his teacake. My uncle turned to open the drawer behind him. 'I dug these pieces of pot from the garden,' he said, holding them up to the light. 'Surely from the medieval age, would you not say? The thirteenth century, I think. Consider that family, cooking over a small fire, in fear of invaders. Or the inhabitants of later years in a black and white house on this spot, hearing talk of Queen Bess entering London, then others seeing their possessions aflame in the Great Fire.' Mrs Janisser was gazing at the African death masks on the wall behind my uncle's head. 'This house was built anew in 1720.

I picture the master silk-weaver stepping out of his brand-new door and taking a sedan chair to drink coffee in Covent Garden.'

I ran a finger over my teacup, wishing I could flick the china so hard that it would break. I thought the Janissers were probably tormented by the smell of incense. My uncle sent Jane for incense sticks from the sellers near the docks, in the hope that they would mask the damp. I was used to the smell, but I knew visitors were not. I hoped they were confused by it. I could not understand how a man as established as the elder Mr Janisser could have struck up any acquaintance with my uncle. The Belle-Smyths too, whom he had recently begun to visit. I could not see what they would want with him, even if he were as rich as they believed.

'Sometimes,' my uncle was saying, 'I feel I can hardly work, such is the weight of history here. I prefer to sit and absorb the intense mass of Time.' He sat back, quite satisfied. 'Your dress is of fine quality, madam. Spitalfields silk?'

I knew we were ridiculous to them, two oddities adrift in their shadowy, panelled house in a part of London no one would wish to visit. They screwed up their eyes at the Hogarth prints filling the walls, the lopsided couch bought in a market, the death masks and the table etched with astrological signs. They ornamented their white houses in St James's with choice pieces of Sèvres rather than lumps of Babylonian frieze, candleholders from India, Malian death dolls and pots from old China. Their bodies were gowned in fashion but my dress was puffed-out lilac and I had only an Egyptian necklace of green and blue beads that my uncle had allowed me to take from the pin on the wall. His black suit edged with velvet was not what a man would habitually wear, that I knew.

'Your collection must be a trouble to dust,' ventured Mrs Janisser, eyes on the Damascene warrior by the fire.

'Ah, madam, but when one acquires items of beauty, one cannot consider the housework they may entail. Regard this coal holder from Siberia. Mahogany and tiger skin, very ornate. The shopkeeper offered me his child instead, but I insisted.'

I looked at Mrs Janisser. If I married her son, I would wear those same high-necked gowns, fuss about parlour fittings. I would spend the morning perusing tradesmen's catalogues and the afternoon suffering a mild headache on the couch, until the time came for an overcooked dinner in a room hot with light. With child by Constantine, discussing choices for table for hours on end, no interest in what was important or beautiful in life. I would not hear it. I refused to. *That will not happen to me.*

'The fireplace induces my particular pride,' my uncle was saying. 'It was part of the original house and works splendidly. New is not always superior.'

My uncle could not tell them, of course, that our roof leaked, servants had to be paid large sums to stay, and our neighbours were not respectable. The richer silk-weavers had moved away to set up in the country and so the houses were cheap, and Mr Horace next door lived here because he could not find another rental after debtors' prison. The Kents, mother and son, came here from Chatham, so that the son could study art, they said, but Jane told me she had heard the elder brother was hanged. Uncle did not care, such was his love for History.

'I could not live without shelves,' Mrs Janisser said (we could not attach them to the panelling). 'And do you not find the interior dark?' At first our visitors were interested, and then after half an hour or so, the condescension bubbled up like water in a well after the leaves have been cleared. The Janissers were like the others. They, not we, were the explorers, they return confirmed in the happiness of the choices they have made.

She would not be discouraged. 'No air!' I could hear her think: a young girl shut up in this dim house, surrounded by old things. *Not normal.* 'Do you enjoy the fresh air, Miss Sorgeiul?' I gazed back at her in the expensive pink dress with blue lacing she hoped would make her look like a drawing in a magazine. I willed her to know that I was a long piece of silver and her thoughts would slide off me, unable to find a place to grip. *I cannot bear the rooms either!* I wanted to cry. I sat in the house and felt the history seeping over me, trying to get under my clothes, thick and hot as burning sugar. I sensed the people who had lived in the rooms pressing on me through the darkness and knew they wanted to take my thoughts for their own. I looked at Mrs Janisser, her husband, and Constantine, unextraordinary but so clearly from the land of the living, where lives were sunny, yellow, rose or blue like imported flowers, and there were always choices.

My uncle lied! It was not the charm of the lives that attracted him but the heavy weight of death. There was so much death in the house: the masks, the skulls in the cupboard, the swords that had cut off heads in India, and all the possessions of people long in their graves. He was the king of the realm, the ruler who remained. I could not escape so I had to make the masks into a consolation. They encouraged you to think that life was, if not painless, quick, when the truth was that the days stretch out for ever and all you had were endless hours to wait out.

But I could not say such things. Mr Janisser's gleam would slide and his wife would cough and the son might even laugh. And paying a social call to friends, to a high, white room where delicate teacups clink, they might declare, well, we visited Mr Crenaban and Miss Sorgeiul, and, why, she is strange. And someone, one day, might think of my name and a tale she'd once heard, and soon my story would be known to all, and I would be lost.

So I simpered at her. 'My uncle allows me to drive out whenever I wish. May I offer you more tea, madam?'

Mr Janisser fingered his teacake and shot his wife a quick glare. Within a minute, he had returned to describing the excellence of his son. Constantine Janisser was, we learnt, possessed of a rapier-like intelligence, honed at Westminster and Magdalen, and now fully displayed in his daily work at Janisser & Smyth, Investors. Within a few weeks of arriving, he had discovered a host of accounts left to rot, contacted the clients, and renovated every account, and one owner had since brought two hundred pounds to the business.

'Well,' I managed. 'Truly an achievement.'

'Yes, indeed.' He could not stop talking, he leapt in and off he went, veering through his first-born's virtues like a young deer hurtling past a river. I let the magnificence of Constantine's eye for detail pass over my head. Ever since their arrival, I had been fighting the desire to look back into my dream from the previous night. If I'd let the visions take me in the presence of others, they might have been able to tell. But a remark about Constantine's 'prospects' pushed me over and I gave in. I had dreamt that I was outside our house, alone on the street past midnight, night air wrapping around me. And, yes, just as my uncle had said, overnight thick violet flowers had appeared, clinging to the front of our house and those of the Kents and the Horaces. They sprouted from the cracks in the pavement and over bricks. There was a hot wind, a flower broke off its stem and the petals began blowing towards me. I felt myself back there, my heart on fire. I gazed down at my hands, imagined them scraping the dirt of the wall under my nails.

'Catherine.' I looked up at four expectant faces. 'Are you in agreement?'

'Oh, yes.' I smiled. 'Mr Constantine Janisser's attainments are truly impressive.'

My uncle narrowed his eyes. Constantine Janisser let out a low laugh.

'Catherine,' repeated my uncle, 'we were discussing the recent surge of criminal behaviour. Mr Janisser informed us that there have been four robberies close to his office. All the windows of the neighbouring gold merchant were smashed and the safe forced open.' Here my uncle lowered his voice, for money was worthy of respect. 'He lost six hundred pounds.'

'We were remarking,' Mr Janisser added, hard-faced, 'that each robbery was accompanied by the most curious acts. The culprits decorated the walls with daubings of animals and plants.'

Constantine Janisser sat up, his torso all of a sudden rigid. 'Yes,' he rushed, a fold of black hair trembling over his right cheek. 'I ventured there and thought them quite remarkable. I cannot imagine that they were produced by an inferior mind.'

I could not look away.

'You should see them, Miss Sorgeiul. I would strongly advise you to go.' There was a clatter of china from my uncle's side of the table. 'That is, if Mr Crenaban would allow.'

My uncle held his gaze. 'Miss Sorgeiul is a young lady of good family. She does not wander the streets around the Bank of England in search of paintings on walls.' I presumed he was hoping that their carriage would not take the route through Brick Lane on their return.

The air cooled a little. Then Mr Janisser spoke. 'No, no. Of course not. My son was forgetting himself.' He was eager to soothe and I felt surprise. Perhaps we were more in demand than I had thought. 'They said there would be moral breakdown after the financial crisis,' hurried his wife.

'I believe the paintings are connected to the wider crimes.' Mr Janisser junior stared at my uncle, as if waiting for an answer.

There was a silence. The elderly cuckoo clock chimed in the corner. It was time for the visit to be over. We all five of us felt relief.

Jane came with their wraps and moved towards Mrs Janisser while the men stood awkwardly. 'Certainly,' Mr Janisser suggested, still trying to please, 'this area is not inconvenient for the City.'

'But, sir,' Mrs Janisser broke in, 'the streets must be teeming with crime.'

'Especially now,' said Constantine Janisser, staring at the floor, his voice soft. 'After that girl.'

I felt my heart clench. 'What do you mean?'

Mrs Janisser shuffled on her fur and in one quick movement reached for my hand. 'I am very glad you do not go walking around, Miss Sorgeiul. I would be concerned.'

'I blame the Queen,' said Mr Janisser. 'A young girl is not strong enough to restrain society.'

My uncle moved over. 'This area is perfectly safe.'

'Miss Sorgeiul, did you not know?' said Constantine Janisser.

'We have had some problems receiving news,' I said, staring at him, willing him to say more.

'You would not wish to keep your coachman waiting,' waved my uncle. I saw how much taller he was than anyone else, as he loomed over the Janissers, pushing them out. They said their goodbyes, proposed we visit their house, and the dark door swung shut after them. My uncle took up the steel rod and began lacing the chains that kept us secure.

'Imagine their parlour,' he said. 'The same combination of gold and green cushions and curtains as in every other house in the street, copied from the magazines. Cheap cornices.'

'What did they mean when they spoke of crime?'

'All the latest furniture,' he mused.

'Mrs Janisser seemed fearful.'

'Ladies fuss. Now, I must leave you to your thoughts. My papers call.' I looked at his face and saw the boredom and – yes – anger fall from it like dust. He was all brimming pinkness, eager desire to hurry upstairs to his study, where he fled from me every day, and most of the night.

2. Swan Street

That night, Mr Trelawny came. I heard the tinkle of the bell at about ten, the heavy tread of my uncle down the stairs, whispers as they passed my door. I watched the shadows of the masks on the walls and listened to the cries from the street. I could not sleep while Mr Trelawny was in the house and yet I could not begin a candle to read, for I would not want him to see the light beneath the door and give any thought to me. He always rang, although he could use the spare key under the stone to unlock the back door. Sometimes, I wondered if he did so because he wished me to know he had arrived. I lay still, heavy with heat, listening for every sound, willing him to leave.

My uncle's house was comfortable in winter but in summer the walls retained the heat until the place felt swollen with warmth. When I first came to live there, I found the rooms small. There was a parlour and a dining room off the hall, a corridor on the upper floor and then my room, and my uncle's, and his study, which I was forbidden to enter. He did not even permit Jane to clean there. On the lower-ground floor was our kitchen and next to it a door that was always locked. My uncle declared it false, with no room behind. At the back of the house, a small garden, the jewels two flowering trees.

Thoughts hurried through my head: Mrs Janisser talking of crime, and memories I did not wish for. My leg was twitching. When the same had happened before, they forced me to lie still and take salt from their hands, but I knew now it was better to rise and walk a little. My room was cramped and there was little space, so I moved to pull at the door to the corridor. I opened it and there stood my uncle and Mr Trelawny.

'I could not sleep,' I said to them, pushing myself behind the door, as they stared at me through the gloom. 'I desired a little water.'

'Miss Sorgeiul.' A white hand snaked towards me. I felt the plump palm around mine and made out Mr Trelawny's cragged red face, the blotchy nose, the small, glinting eyes. He moved a little closer. 'Always a pleasure.'

'Mr Trelawny was about to descend the stairs,' said my uncle. 'You do not normally rise at night.'

'Bad dreams,' I replied, staring at Mr Trelawny, his baby-soft covering of blondish hair, the pinned-back ears, and his precise cravat and suit, at the neatest angle, such a contrast with the roughness of his face.

'About what, pray?'

'The crime. Robberies and flowers on walls.'

My uncle patted my shoulder. 'An unfit interest for a lady. When Mr Trelawny has left, you may go down for your water.'

When, finally, I heard the door slam, I crept to the shutter and peered out of the small holes. I watched his bent back shuffling slowly away, until I was quite sure he had gone.

In 1820, the mad old king died, his terrible son came to the throne and Princess Victoria passed her first birthday. Two thousand men planned to invade a city in the north, and the longest winter in history froze over the Thames. And I was conceived in February, a cold month. I knew nothing of my birth. I used to wonder if very little children could remember the moment when they came into the world, but there is surely no memory without words. I had never been near enough to a young child to ask.

My mother, then, in the large bed, covered in the patchwork quilt, crying with the pain, the doctor talking to her. And I sprang into the world. Was I red and screaming at the wrench or impatient for life? Did I wail or settle to the nurse's breast? I could not guess. There was no one alive who could tell me.

I remembered a corner of our garden, at the front, near the house, where my father grew tropical trees, their leaves heavy and tinged with yellow at the tip. My mother wore long dresses for parties, violet and blue silk following her as she walked. My brother, Louis, and I begged my father for a dog, but he would not allow it. We played soldiers under the arched stained-glass window by the stairs.

The house in Richmond was large, handsome and quite new, and you would declare it the ideal home for any family. Now, every day, I tried to forget it. I hoped that the size and shape of the rooms, our possessions, would fade from my mind, and so the green rugs in my bedroom, the vases in the parlour, the cool surfaces of the kitchen would become nothing, cleanly replaced by Princes Street, my home for ever.

In Richmond, we had nursemaids and a governess, two maids for my mother's dresses alone. At Princes Street, there was only Mrs Graves, Thomas and Jane, whom I could not bear because she was not Grace.

At the beginning of this year, 1840, I walked into the parlour, and Grace Starling was there. In her grey dress, her hair looked yellower than ever, as if she had come straight from an egg.

'You and Starling met at the Belle-Smyths', I believe,' said my uncle.

She curtsied to me and I saw the top of her head, hair neatly parted over the thin skin. My leg twitched as I thought of her mouth at my ear. *Tell me.*

'I thought you would need a maid, my dear.'

I could not speak, as if the air between us was like china that could break. Those Belle-Smyth girls, their hands on her.

'Very pleased to do anything for you, miss,' she said. Her fingers in my hair, her nails tipping my cheek.

'Thank you, Uncle,' I said, overwhelmed.

She followed me upstairs and offered to put my room in order. I had so few things, I could not imagine what a maid would find to do for me. She said she would dress my hair, as she had done at the Belle-Smyths'.

'I told you I would come to find you,' she said, and then her fingers stroked quickly at my face. I was an orange without its skin.

'I looked for you. Where did you go? Miss Edwarda said you were occupied with other duties.'

She shrugged. 'I was elsewhere. Let us not think of it.' She brought her hand to my shoulder.

'But you must miss their grand house, surely?'

She shook her head. 'The Belle-Smyth girls were not kind.'

My mind curved. 'What did they do?'

'I will tell you another time.'

The second day, she asked me to read to her from the newspaper. 'I wish I could read, miss.' When she moved away from me, I touched my face, as if my fingers were hers, dropping light.

My uncle read newspapers and left them in a pile in the dining room, so there were pages everywhere from *The Times*, the *Chronicle* and even magazines, the *Gentleman's*, and twice I found the *Englishwoman's Domestic Companion*. He had once told me he loved the feel of the paper, could hardly pass a newsboy without buying. I picked up some pages and took them upstairs.

'There is so little news,' I told her. I wanted the old papers for the months I had been away. I wished to read of the Princess coming to the throne at just eighteen, the coronation at which they dived for coins, her new life in the palace. I had come out of Lavenderfields believing old King William was still alive. Only a few months older than I, the Queen ruled a whole nation, everything she did reported. She was tiny, they said, with a pretty voice, like silver drifting over gold.

Grace told me she had gone out to join the crowds near St James's to see the Queen married. She said she hardly saw a thing as the carriage passed, the man in front of her was so tall, but two women next to her fainted because they had glimpsed Prince Albert. She curled my hair around my head and told me of the Queen's twelve bridesmaids, all attired in white, like swans. She said she and her sister, Flo, had stayed with the crowds until two in the morning, when a man had tried to grasp her around the waist and Flo had beaten him off.

March news was not interesting: Lord Melbourne and the Jamaican planters, renovations to the palaces, unrest in the mines. 'No stories, are there, miss?'

And then, in May, with the wave of heat and the crash of the stock market, everything began to change, and London seared with temperatures like those of India, shops closed, and there were stories of the poor eating rats for food. We fell on the reports as if we were starving too.

'At least I have work with you, miss,' she said.

Poverty, heat and disease filled every page. I held Grace's hand as I read.

'The newspapers this month say we will be poorer for ever on account of the crisis,' I said to my uncle, when I felt courageous.

He shrugged. 'You should not read such stories.'

'I read that even the banks need money from the

government.' America would supersede us, said *The Times*. Britain was in the dying embers of its power.

'A female can make no one afraid. She hides in her palace.'

'Perhaps her innocence protects us.' Grace had thought this.

Have you lost all your money? I wanted to ask. At the beginning of the year, he went every weekday to his office, somewhere near Bishopsgate. But by May he spent every day in his study. People like the Janissers thought him rich, but I wondered how he could be, with the jewel discovery in Africa that had not come to pass and the South American mines man who had taken so much.

'Their child will save us,' he said. 'The Queen will produce a son, and he will rescue us with his strong blood.'

I told this to Grace but she snorted. 'She shouldn't have married Albert. No money to his name, no wisdom. And her cousin.' Now the country was in distress and it was the Queen's fault for not remaining a maid. She caressed my face and I felt the smoothness of her finger against my cheek, the whorls dancing over the skin, and forgot I had been afraid.

Grace was always looking at things. Almost as soon as she came, she was picking up ornaments and plates and books and holding them up to her eyes. Every object we had attracted her. In my room, she would find the African masks and run her fingers over the wood. 'What are these, miss? Do you know?' She asked where my hairbrush had come from, and liked to hear the story of the dresses bought for me, curling my yellow ribbon in her hands. She took the dolls, which looked like hunters, off the walls and made their legs move. She played with the empty birdcage in the corner of my room. 'So curious, your uncle's things, do you not think, miss? Why would he have little people holding spears?'

Our house was to her a cabinet of curiosities to be touched. In the parlour she ran her hands over the bureau of his books. Most were on accounting, history, geography – but she found others that had no colour on the spine. *Memoirs of a Courtesan*. And another, *Innocence Broken*, and then others about similar subjects. 'Odd books. Makes you wonder what he has upstairs.' We read them, marvelling at the heated scenes until I could not bear to think of my uncle's hand on them and asked her to put them away.

We were in new worlds of glass figures or death masks. She felt the contours, held them to the light, and wondered over the past of such things. 'Tell me, miss,' she said. 'Tell me stories for them.' And so I did, tried to, for by then I would have done anything for her.

Halfway through May, I was lying in bed and waiting for Grace to come. After a time, I rose, pulled on my dress and walked downstairs. My uncle was in the parlour, staring from the window.

'This city is truly alive with crime,' he said, without turning. 'Look. We are all beginning to steal from one another.' A group of women were outside, pulling at each other's shawls and hair.

'Where is Grace, Uncle?'

'She has not come. Just as well. We do not need her.'

'No!'

'Niece, your blood is beginning to heat. I think you are well enough without a maid. You are not Miss Belle-Smyth, as you keep telling me.'

'But where will she go?'

'She will find another position, soon enough. Niece, calm your face. You should not excite yourself in your delicate state. Think of her. It is safer for her to live in a house in St James's than here.'

'Is that where she is?'

'I do not know. And I cannot tell you. She did not say. She may have left London.' He walked to me. I expected him to stand in front of me but he passed by. 'I will go upstairs, Niece. I advise you to put Starling out of your mind.'

'I am sure she will come.'

But she did not. Not the day after that, or again. I told myself I had accepted she would not return, that she did not want me, she had found another girl to work for. *How can you not need me the way I need you?* I wanted to cry.

'And your verdict on the Janissers?' my uncle said. We were at lunch two days after their visit. It was the first time he had spoken to me since I had seen him with Mr Trelawny. I put my spoon next to my plate of milk pudding and looked at him in surprise. 'Visitors are visitors, I suppose.'

'And Constantine Janisser?'

'Of little interest.'

In the garden a squirrel scrambled over the blue-flowering tree.

'He is a highly esteemed young man.'

'So you have said.'

Until Mr Trelawny began to come in March, my uncle used to talk to me at meals and ask me questions: how had I slept? Did my head still give me pain? Had I any appetite? We would discuss my favourite foods, my thoughts about the weather, and he would ask about my dreams. *She is normal*, I supposed he might say to fathers of suitors. *Her favourite food is the strawberry and she likes to read. She dreams of flowers and fish and girls with long hair.* (I lied: I dreamt of other things.) Just like any other girl. But after Mr Trelawny, we began to sit silently, our lives and thoughts ticking like two clocks on opposing shelves. He spent his time in the study, while I sat in the parlour.

Since Grace had left, I had been trying to write about life in our new city. They told me at Lavenderfields to cultivate an interest, and I detested embroidery and my hands were too awkward for paperwork or watercolours. I learnt a little piano while living with Aunt Athelinde, but then the doctor forbade me to continue, for fear the playing might inflame me. I tried to write poems about the sky and trees, but they were always weak. After Lavenderfields, I had no more use for the beauties of nature, for I was altered and thought only of my shame. After Grace left, I began to write of the crime. She had been so occupied by it. I hoped that she might return and be impressed by my book. *Tell me stories*, I heard her say.

I took up my uncle's old newspapers and read them for myself. When I read a book, the pains in my head would seep into me as I reached a slow chapter, but the newspapers were different. The stories were short, vivid and the torment stayed at only the sides of my mind, threatening but not arriving. I felt a usual fear instead: of men breaking into our house, thieves attacking my uncle.

I became a little pleased with some of what I had written. I thought that Grace would enjoy it. But since the week before the visit of the Janissers, we had received no newspapers. My uncle said there were problems with trade.

'I would have thought you impressed by young Mr Janisser,' my uncle was saying.

'No.' *Grace. Come back to me*. The squirrel was still crawling over the tree.

'You are a proud young lady.' He gave me a chill look. 'I have noticed you have been picking at your fingernails lately. I rather think you have been distracted.'

'I have been thinking about the increase in crime. I wish I could see a newspaper.'

'The newspapers are not fit reading for a girl of your –

fragility, Catherine. Anyway, there is little of interest, I assure you. Ministerial debates, the failings of Viscount Melbourne.'

'I would like to see one, all the same. I am perfectly well.'

'Thus you should give yourself up to more ladylike *pensées*. Such as the new dress you have an appointment to buy at the end of the week. Later, when I return from Regent Street, I shall tell you what the ladies of fashion are wearing.' He raised an eyebrow. 'I hear primrose is sought after.'

I wanted to push my plate away and cry out at him, but I held tight to myself until the moment faded. 'You,' Nurse Griffin said to me once, 'you make your desires clear. Whatever you wish for, you should compose your face to the converse.'

'Shall you be paying your usual calls, Uncle?' I smiled.

'Correct. The stationer, the picture gallery, and I shall visit the gunsmith.'

'May I accompany you?' He was beginning to shake his head. 'I think the outing would benefit me. Perhaps I have been inside for too long. I would like to see the fashions for myself.'

He shrugged. 'Perhaps so. We will visit the Janissers soon and you will need topics of conversation. Ready yourself, my dear. I shall depart in two hours.'

He reached for a walnut from the bowl on the sideboard, tipped it on to his open palm. I thought he was about to take up the silver nutcrackers resting by the bowl but instead he clenched the nut in his palm, pressed, and I heard the shell break. He unfurled his hand, eyeing me.

My face was hot and I could feel the blood tumbling around my heart. *I am not afraid*, I wished I could say, but the words would not have been true.

'A trick I learnt in South America.' He held out his hand to me and I stared at the cracks of shell and the nut, snapped in half. He tipped the pieces on to his plate. 'I made you start, did I not? I saw shock in your face and your shoulders moved.'

I shook my head.

'Indeed? Well. I would remember. You cannot always expect to find knives when you need them.'

I held up my skirts and left the table, telling my heart to stay. At the top of the stairs, I stood still to breathe, away from my uncle's eyes. I looked up and there was Jane, tapping her way out of his room. I had thought her downstairs, helping Mrs Graves.

'You look pale, miss.' Her wide face, pitted with smallpox scars, the hair under the cap thick, brown but streaked already with grey, even though she was surely not many years older than I. 'Anyone would say you'd taken fright.'

I shook my head. 'I am a little tired.'

'No one would be surprised, if you had. I'd think I should be afraid, walking back from here every night.'

I coughed. 'What do you mean?'

'That girl, miss. You know.' Her uneven face shone out at me, as I held tight to the banister.

'I do not understand.'

'Did you not hear? Some milliner, I read. They found her near Spitalfields Market. Murdered.'

'Dead.' Mr Janisser's voice. *After that girl.*

Jane lowered her voice and leant in close. Her nose quivered. 'Worse than that, miss. Quite torn apart. Terrible, they said. The newspapers are calling him the Man of Crows. They say he will strike again.'

I am very glad you do not go walking around, Miss Sorgeiul.

She bobbed her head. 'Abigail, I read her name was. Seventeen, from the north. I must go downstairs, miss.'

I held the banister. She brushed past me as her heels clicked down. 'As I said, I should be afraid.'

3. Spitalfields Market

'Count,' they said, so I did, over and over, two hundred, one, two, three, four times, and I heard the sounds of the road, and I did not stop counting. Again. I sat up and counted. Numbers. Solid, reliable. Numbers did not invent things or kill. One. Two. If I counted, I told myself, Louis would come back. Three. Four. It was like sheep. If I went through the numbers, I would awake and the *dream would be over*. Four hundred. A thousand. The numbers we used to make sense of our world. *Let them make sense of mine.*

And then my eyes opened.

I lay on my bed in Princes Street, my mind scraping and flashing. The girl, the milliner who died, her body in Spitalfields Market, chased by the Man of Crows. Her death was a precipice and I had thrown my mind over the edge. I tried to pull my thoughts back, think of anything, even the Janisser family, but I could not keep my thoughts from the blood. The butterflies I hoped to imagine in their wood disappeared and I threw myself into blackness. My uncle cracked his nut in his hand. I was not in my room in Princes Street, but at home in Richmond, and my mother cried out.

'The only way to live,' said Dr Neville, 'is never again to mention what happened. For you want to live, yes?'

I turned on to my side and wished I could cry out, but my uncle would hear. Happy thoughts, dogs, cats, shells, rainbows, were of no help to me.

The young milliner, walking, afraid, and then dying alone. I might have gone to her for a hat and exchanged friendly words.

'Catherine,' called my uncle, up the stairs, 'we will depart within the hour.' I gathered myself, looked in the mirror and tried to see my face. And then the words left my mind. My hairbrush was not there. I had seen Jane put it back on the bureau that morning. But it was not anywhere near, nor had it fallen to the floor.

I had to admit it: I was losing my things. In the previous week, I had been unable to find the spare lace for my corset and a pot of beeswax. I could not see how I might mislay items in my tiny room, and indeed until then I had never lost anything, other than a pair of gloves last winter on our visit to the ice sculptures at Hyde Park.

My thoughts had been worse since Grace left. The lost things were the proof: they were taking me over. I was becoming again what I once was.

I had been sleepwalking again, surely. If that was so, I was truly lost. The evil was returning.

Please come back, I wanted to say to Grace. *The demons fly once more.*

'I shall not wait,' my uncle called. I put my hand on the mirror. My cheeks were patchy, my eyes reddened, but I did not care. He was accustomed to seeing misery on my face.

I made my way down, and at the base of the stairs, he touched my hand. 'Young ladies must try on so many styles before they go out.'

'Jane told me a girl was murdered nearby.'

He held his gloves. 'Thomas awaits us, Catherine.'

'Why did you not tell me?'

'I do not know, my dear, why you would be interested in such a morbid matter. The mere outcome of a lovers' tiff, I imagine.'

'Surely not. I heard they were calling him the Man of Crows.'

He tipped his head. 'Indeed. A pun on the collective noun, a murder of crows. He left her so mutilated that she looked a little like a bird. Although probably not a crow.'

'I –'

'Now, come, my dear. This is no fit interest for a girl of your disposition.'

He closed the door. Thomas helped us into our coach and I sat back, my mind slipping under its own weight. We were about to depart when our neighbour, Mr Kent, walked into our path, his arm propped over three thick books of art. 'Good afternoon,' he cried. His mother gripped his other arm; she was dressed in black as ever.

'Such a cheerful young man,' murmured my uncle. 'Hardly affected by the losses of his family.'

'Where do you go?' Mr Kent called.

'A few errands in town.'

'You should take care, sir. Miss Sorgeiul. That killer, they say, is on the loose.' He looked in and caught my eye.

His mother gave a weak smile, grief etching her face

as ever. His expression was calm. 'I would not let Mother go about these streets until he has been apprehended. And I hardly trust the authorities to find him, blunderers that they are.'

'I have no interest in this criminal. Good day, sir.' My uncle gave the signal to drive on.

'I doubt he will make anything of his painting,' he said. 'He should study law.' We drove past the stables of hot, kicking horses, leaving Mr Kent meandering across the road. I wondered if the urchins at the corner might thrust him into the mud. My uncle had said he was interested in painting fairies but I could not see him ever finding magic. I never heard a sound from their house, although there were often bumps from Mr Horace on the other side. I imagined the Kents, living in stillness, creeping around in a house full of fallen dust.

The carriage lurched through the city and towards Regent Street. I stared out at the new world in front of me, shops nailed over with boards, beggars by fires outside St James's Church, pie-sellers standing idle, a ruined carriage untouched near Pulteney's on the corner, and weeds sprouting between the cracks in the road.

'It is much changed,' my uncle conceded.

'The streets are so quiet.' I glanced across at him and felt afraid of him and his big brown face. 'Do you know anything about the milliner who died?'

'Catherine, I wish you would apply your mind to subjects fit for a young lady.'

'But even the Kents are concerned.'

'It will be shown as nothing, my dear.'

I turned to the window. A woman held up a sign begging for food.

'We are all the poorer,' he murmured.

Last year the man had come with a plan for a South American mine, then left us with a few brown-edged maps and such debts that my uncle had to sell the six Chinese vases he said dated from the third century. He asked me to supervise the auctioneer's boy while he stayed upstairs because he grieved his loss. I did not miss them, ugly bulbous things.

Thomas turned the horses. The stationer my uncle favoured was still holding on, even though the barber and the cake shop on either side were boarded over. We descended from the carriage, my uncle pushed open a door and a man with an eyeglass behind the counter looked up to greet us. My uncle demanded to see different selections of paper, while I gazed at the drawers over the man's head, imagining the different colours inside. Abigail had walked through Spitalfields, her eyes afraid. Younger than me, but already dead.

'Did you hear of the murders, sir?' said the shopkeeper. 'There will soon be another young lady slain, I am sure.'

'Sir?' My hands moved.

'I would ask you not to discuss such matters,' returned my uncle.

The shopkeeper bowed. 'I offer my apologies, sir.' He caught my eye and shook his head. 'I forgot myself.'

Swan Street, a place I had never seen, dark and empty

of souls. Abigail walking through, her dress dragging over the ground. A man comes in front of her and smiles. *I only wish to help you*, he says. *Let me.*

'Are you quite well, Niece?' My uncle was staring at me. The stationer was pretending to busy himself with the paper. I looked down and my hands were white with the effort of holding the counter.

I forced myself to return his gaze. 'Yes, Uncle. Merely a headache.'

He turned back to the piles of paper.

Abigail's skirt flickered through my mind and I realized *I had not been in my head.* With those thoughts of her, I had been free of my darkness. *It had left me.* A pale grey opened at the corner of my mind, began to swell into blue. The cloud bubbled and burst into turquoise and gold. The Man of Crows.

It was the first time I had been truly released from the chains of my thoughts since Grace had left. The gold turned red and danced into my eyes. Standing in the stationer's shop, the dirty windows streaming heat at my dress, I understood. The Man of Crows had taken away my dreadful thoughts.

I held the counter as violet, gold and blue fired through my mind. *Your delicate state*, my uncle had said. My missing hairbrush, the ribbon, the sleepwalking evil coming towards me, I could be free of it, by thinking about the Man of Crows. I had fallen low since Grace had left. The violet turned green and up seeped words. I would throw myself into the Man of Crows, be bound up in him and his atrocity and find release.

I thought: I would know how that moment was for Louis. To know his hours were to be taken away. I would experience the terror he felt, know that I used my evil to escape.

The man takes Abigail and grips her as he reaches into his cloak for a knife. 'Do not fear,' he says. 'I mean no harm.'

And I would find him! *A girl of your fragility.* Others were too much of the world to recognize him, but I was darker and crueller and more wrong than them all so *I would be able to see him.* Mr Kent was right. The officers were searching blindly. How could they know a man of such evil? But I had seen the blackness. I could find him, and then, once I had helped the city, people would think me good, and I could be free.

'Niece, you are pale.' My uncle was staring at me. I could only shake my head. 'I thought the outing would be too much for you. Let us depart.'

I told my heart to calm. 'May I buy a little paper, Uncle?'

'For what purpose?'

'For sketching.'

'But this is not drawing paper, my dear.'

'I know, but surely better than none.'

'Many ladies buy their supplies for sketching here,' piped up the man. 'With the shortages, we must take things where we can obtain them.'

We debated the quantity, variety and the amount, money crossed the counter and finally we departed the shop and handed our packages to Thomas. The violet and turquoise came back, sparking again and spreading in my mind over a hundred sheets of paper, white light in the corners, gold pattering from the margins. I clenched my hand and knew I would follow the Man of Crows with words.

Everybody would ask, 'But how did you know? The finest minds were puzzling over the Man of Crows and you found him.'

'It is very simple,' I would tell them. 'A case of understanding the victims.' That would be me, free from my dark thoughts, the person who had found the murderer, admired and rich, in a house of my own.

We journeyed to seek out the gunsmith's. There, my uncle touched different sizes of gun, ran his finger over barrels, discussed handles, bullets, ranges. The younger assistant sidled to me and said, 'We do not often see ladies here,' as the sun broke through the windows on to the glass fronts of the cabinets, and my mind swelled wildly through the Man of Crows. The door closed on the guns and their cases, oddly patterned with flowers, and I was decided.

Back in the parlour, I sat down with the bundle of paper and told myself that I should begin to think about Abigail.

In my bureau stood the books any young lady might display: the works of Miss Burney, Miss Edgeworth, Mrs Barbauld. My collection of Miss Tonno's sermons rested behind the glass. *Evelina* was the first book I had bought with my uncle's allowance, Miss Burney's naive heroine and all her mistakes.

What did she think, Miss Burney, when she sent her book out to be read? I had bought many of hers. I wondered if she was concerned over the warm scenes. People read the book across London, in fine drawing rooms while they waited for tea, by the light of a candle in their chambers, in coaching inns between journeys and on trips to the seaside, because they could not stop or they heard the story was fashionable or simply to while away time. Some did not finish, others cut straight to the end. Pages were torn, stained with milk or dotted with preserve, scribbled on with notes about haberdashers or grocers; copies were lost in parks or shops. Perhaps Miss Burney cared nothing for ripped pages. Instead, she gathered up the acclaim and her money and launched herself into an independent life.

But Miss Burney could not write of killings. Of course not. She had no idea of the darkness that held itself inside certain people, those who did not wish to please others but to destroy them. Unlike me.

I returned to the table and picked up the pen. I wrote 'The Man of Crows' at the top, underlined the words. Then I stared. I stood up to look out of the window. The men were still working on the road outside. Time passed and I sat with the African masks and the Siberian coal scuttle. My fingers were still. And then, moments before the hour of dinner, the image came into my head of Abigail leaving her milliner's shop at the close of work. Jane banged plates in the kitchen and my uncle moved across the corridor upstairs in preparation for descending and the words began flooding through me.

I crouched over the paper, scribbling, feeling as if I were writing with her. She battered on the doors of my mind, burst through, and I was writing of her journey back to her lodgings. Throughout dinner I scraped at my plate and forced myself not to kick my heels.

Jane cleared our plates and I hurried back to the parlour, and under the dirty light, the words soared. I scrawled until my hands were burning, and as if I, the pen and the paper were one thing, pulling off my ring because the thin silver was a barrier between my finger and the page. I felt her unwashed hair catching at the sides of her face, the cramp in her back from bending. I was not Catherine Sorgeiul, untidy, silent, queer, but the possession of the story, swept up in its arms and forced to write. The words sparked the room with flames and my arms were hard wire. *I am free of you*, I said to my uncle in my mind. *I am new*.

I have read that when you die, your life appears before your eyes. And the future, all those dreary, habit-filled days, assume the colours of romance, beauty, unlimited possibility. But those few times in Lavenderfields when I thought myself on the edge of leaving this world, on the brink, I saw nothing of my life, past or future, but felt only my body and my heart, reaching for another world. And I knew Abigail had felt the same. First she fed her wolf of anger, thinking of the fires of her day, and then he grasped her shoulder, took up all her thoughts and after that there was nothing but white.

I put down my pen. *But then what does he do?* In a moment, the heady, sick feeling I had felt as I scribbled was gone. The exhilaration was there, on the curve of the letters, laughing. *You cannot go further*, it said. What did he do to her as he killed her? I could not think. Above me, clouds were moving, drifting, changing, while I stayed the same, a lumpen mass.

I walked to the window, peering behind the shutters. The workers digging up the street had not progressed in their travail. The pile of rubble had hardly mounted and we were surely no closer to having a drainage system, as we were to have by the end of the year, connected to the cesspits. Usually, I would have seen the group of ragged children playing at the corner, the girls my age who wore their hair loose and laughed, looking for labourers, and washerwomen carrying their wares. But in the street I saw only workmen with bricks, and the few women were hurrying, apart from two, who were talking on the corner, clutching each other.

What does he do to her? Grace would know.

Your delicate state. My uncle promised me, when I came, that he would not make reference to what I had done. But he had come to do so more and more. I told myself I could not expect kindly treatment after what I had done. It was coloured dark and red, and then it flared, like a tiger, and took over my mind. My brother was next to me, and the men who were telling me to count, and I was begging in my mind but I did not have the courage to stop it, any of it. The smile of Mr Gillibrand. *You brought us here.*

That night I woke when I heard the latch and Mr Trelawny skittering his baby feet into the hall. I lay awake, hearing my uncle descend the stairs, and then the whispers as they talked. I yearned to throw every piece of furniture against the door, and block up all the windows, so I could pretend he was not in the house, rubbing his lizard hands over the banister and brushing his dirty coat over my door. They padded past my room and my body begged to scream.

I lay on my bed, the air close and hot around me, telling my beating heart to still. There was the bell of the nightsoil men coming to clear our cesspit and I supposed the hour was about three. The holeman shouted as he was lowered into the mud and my mind began to rock and turn, skewing into the dark thoughts.

4. Albemarle Street

'I wish you had a lady to accompany you to such occasions.' My uncle stood at the foot of the stairs and passed my wrap. He could scarce conceal his excitement that I would be gone from the house for two hours or so. I was invited by Mrs Belle-Smyth and her two simpering daughters to a tea party at their home in Albemarle Street. When I received the card, the day after the trip to buy paper, I sent a note to say I was unwell. I was so engrossed, so caught by my thoughts that I saw myself as unbound from such fripperies, too important for such ways of eking out my life. But, nearly a week later, unable to write, there seemed little purpose in remaining at home. In fact, I could not bear the thought of another day spent in our parlour, staring at the masks on the wall, failing to write any word of use.

I could hardly believe the fire that had taken hold of me on our return from the gunsmith's. But on the succeeding days, I had barely written a word. Instead I slept until ten or twelve in the morning, worked through my daily tasks as I always did, and even thought of retrieving my embroidery. And because I was so idle, my mind began spooling, the awfulness returning, first a tinge of scarlet at the sides of my head and then a full flood of red across my face: the hospital, my brother, my parents, the thoughts I promised to prevent myself thinking, and I knew I should do anything to stop. And I was still losing things. I could not find the yellow ribbon for my hair. The demons were returning.

So, I had no choice but to attend the party, which previously would have inspired me to scorn. I could not find the Man, and so I should spend my time with girls who thought such gatherings the highlight of their lives. I retrieved the yellow dress from the closet and at its touch remembered visiting the dressmaker with my aunt Athelinde, the seamstress pulling pieces of cloth against me and tutting over my too-long legs and arms.

Jane came to help me dress and tried to talk of Abigail Greengrass, but I shook my head. She teased my hair into ringlets with her untidy fingers and my new hairbrush, and I was grateful for how such matters filled the waste of my morning.

'Enjoy yourself, my dear,' said my uncle, patting my elbow. I picked up my gloves in clean hands (no ink now) and climbed into the carriage. My seat rocked as Thomas whipped up the horses and we set off for Albemarle Street. We trotted through Spitalfields and out on to the wide road of London Wall, and I told myself: *This is where you belong.* You must go to parties and discuss dresses, play a little music and embrace the trivialities of life, and soon you will have become sufficiently intimate to be introduced to a brother or a cousin. He will admire your shrinking delicacy and eventually ask if he might request your hand. Then the rinsing your hair in vinegar and pushing on the pressure points of your face, spending days being pinned by dressmakers and learning how to drop the chin when you talk will have been worthwhile. You will have achieved your ambition and your life can begin.

From the window of the carriage, I saw Regent Street falling apart. The spire of the church at the top of the road had collapsed into itself, and the stones were strewn across the road. The stained-glass window at the front was entirely broken in and some panes had been taken. Men in rags clustered around a fire and a dog pawed rubbish by the door. There were no women to be seen. The city was afraid and poor, people were dying, but in the houses of St James's life had to continue. For what excuse would there be, thirty years later, if someone were to ask, 'Why did you never marry?' and we replied, 'Oh, the country was sinking into disaster and a man was murdering in the east. 'No. We must darn our dresses and smile. For if we did not, what would we be saying? That there will be no future.

I arrived at the heavy blue door, already late. A pinch-faced maid with hair tucked into her cap did not try to hide her smirk as she showed me into the room. Eight young ladies and six mammas looked up, holding delicate plates adorned with flowers and taking cakes too big for a child. In the cracked mirror in my room, I had thought I looked well, but there, in front of them all, my delusion fluttered from me. I was untidy, outdated, and sure to say words that would prove me ridiculous. The girls wore pearls and silver, but my cross and the bracelet from my father had been taken from me at Lavenderfields. I had only the string of Egyptian beads that looked well pinned against the dark wood of the parlour but added to my strangeness at a tea party.

Mrs Belle-Smyth bustled out of her chair. 'Welcome, my dear.' They thought I was to be left wealthy. I might have had black hair growing too long and flecks of brown in my green eyes, but to them I was a bright shop window full of coins and handsome furniture, a house that stretched back with long, cool light, and expensive stays in spa towns. Even the Belle-Smyths, a patriarch who owned a bank and a wife who came with a great dowry, were not immune to the new poverty. There were fine cracks running over the white ceiling rose in the centre of the room, like those in teeth, and the sash window to the front had a splintered frame. Yes, there were the trappings of wealth: the room that could accommodate twenty seated (and forty for drinks, they will never hesitate to say), the mirror sufficiently grand for Marie Antoinette, the gold frame decorated with curls as neat and heavy as those of a Botticelli heroine, the Sèvres figures in graceful poses on the mantelpiece, insouciant, like girls pretending not to worry about who might ask them to dance, and the mahogany furniture so heavy that I wondered how they had ever eased it into the house at all. But there were economies: the flowers in the vase were bowed after three or four days of display, a few candlesticks were empty, and a leg on one of the chairs was held together with string. The embroidery resting on the table was hardly finished: perhaps the girls could no longer afford to send their work to seamstresses to complete the difficult sections in silver and gold.

I sat in the pale blue chair Mrs Belle-Smyth indicated and felt the cushion sink under my weight as I listened to her talk. Unlike her icy daughters, she was a woman of perpetual motion. Her face jiggled with energy and her skirts flowed colour and crease. Even in sleep, her eyes surely flickered with distracted thoughts. 'We were just discussing the latest pieces of work by Mr Dickens,' she rushed. 'About Little Nell. Have you read the story, Miss Sorgeiul?' Her leg bounced under a sea of navy bombazine.

'I found there to be many distasteful scenes,' said Mrs Heather, mamma to insipid Ellen and seated in the chair across from me. 'Excessive.'

'Indeed.' I gave the young lady next to me a smile that I hoped would make her think of sugar mice and roses.

'Miss Grey,' said Mrs Belle-Smyth. 'Miss Grey, Miss Sorgeiul.'

The girl had frizzed hair around her small face and a tiny waist encased in green chiffon. I looked at her and she gazed back, but I broke first. 'Do you enjoy Dickens, Miss Grey?'

She bent her head. 'I find I have little time to read.' Her voice was so quiet that I hardly caught her last word. On her ring finger, a diamond glistened like a glassy wart.

'My niece is engaged,' slipped in Mrs Belle-Smyth, her mouth swallowing the sentence. 'To Mr Prior of Nether Grange. You have heard of him, I am sure?'

I touched my cold cup. 'I have not.'

'I am sure you have, my dear. Mr Prior has a house in West Eaton Place and an estate in Lancashire. My niece will have much occupation as the chatelaine.'

'Yes,' said Miss Grey, quietly. Her vowels were slower and rounder, as if they were not formed through teeth, and I supposed she must come from somewhere by the sea. I wondered if she was subdued through her own desire, or because she was pushed down by the Belle-Smyths, whose bodies and voices always took all the sound and light in the room. Then she turned away and the girl next to her began talking about dresses.

I sat silent, conversations twitching around me. I wanted only to return to Princes Street. I was a shabby fish ill at ease in the large glass bowl, bumping past the false ferns, cutting my dirty fins on the shells that scattered the sand at the base.

I could not bear the noise in the room. I wanted to hold my hands to my head and run to the door. In December, I had come here, Grace touched my hair and I thought I had found a friend. The memories beat at my mind. The other, pretty fish approached, nibbling and picking so that each time the shabby fish turned, lumbering and hopeless, another sank in her teeth.

'A scone, Miss Sorgeiul?' A maid stood above me. Mrs Belle-Smyth gesticulated at me, her chin quivering.

I shook my head and she pouted. 'Our cook has a very light hand.' I felt the air tremble between us – she was but four feet away. I began to stretch out my hand. Then I noted that Miss Grey had no scone on her clean white plate and I withdrew.

'Perhaps later, miss.' She contracted her eyes as if I were coming towards her with a screw. Out of the corner of my vision, I caught Miss Grey shaking her head.

I looked over at the elder Belle-Smyth daughter, Miss Edwarda, nineteen. Like me, she lived in a critical time: if a girl was not married by twenty-two, she would be lost. I could hardly credit how she had changed in the past months. Previously, you would have thought her a girl from a fashion plate, with a fine nest of yellow hair and a figure like two glasses placed end to end. But, like all of us, she had breathed little fresh air in recent months: there were blotches across her cheeks and her eyes were pinched and wet. Her dress was bunched up a little at the waist, as if she were swelling. Still. She had her delicate hands yet, even if they were redder than they had been, and although her lips were peeling, the shape remained sweet, as if someone had taken two rose petals and crushed them together. She met my eye, and I blushed and looked down, hoping she thought I was admiring her, not wondering how she could be so changed. I looked around the room at all of them – us – testament to the importance of keeping things going, even though fathers declared masseurs an unnecessary expense, the creams to soften the face were a little adulterated, and the air was so much hotter and dirtier than before that grime lay over our skin in a thin film. As even the finest blooms in Covent Garden had lost the brightness they once possessed, so we were all a little ragged at the edges and there was no expectation we should become less so. I imagined Mrs Belle-Smyth declaring she was willing to reduce the cook's expenditure that week, so Miss Edwarda might have another pair of gloves. I hoped that Miss Grey had not agreed to a long engagement.

Miss Edwarda glittered, still. Wherever she sat or stood, she seemed to be cutting into what was around her. I thought of Grace and wanted to weep.

The three next to me were murmuring of embroidery. Did they not wish to say, *What is happening to us?* The city was crumbling under a sun burning like an angry eye and a man was killing. People were dying and we could talk only of sewing.

'How is your uncle, Miss Sorgeiul?' enquired Mrs Belle-Smyth.

I told her he remained in good health. She asked after his business. I replied that profit proceeded well.

'I hear you have lost your cook.'

True. Last week, Mrs Graves had given notice to my uncle, declaring she no longer felt safe. My uncle told me that he had offered to add to her salary by a quarter but she had refused. She would not even suggest a replacement, he said.

I held my hands to stop myself pulling at my necklace. 'Our maid, Jane, is fulfilling Mrs Graves's duties and my uncle is seeing cooks.'

She gave a slender smile, and I read the message she meant to send: *Who would want to work there?*

'You had a visit from Mr Janisser,' she said, scooping up a raisin with her forefinger.

I nodded, wanting to flick the raisin from her finger to the floor.

'You have settled with your uncle so comfortably.'

I inclined my head. All the conversations around me appeared to have stopped.

'He was very preoccupied with his work,' she added.

'I am sure that Mr Belle-Smyth is similarly attentive to his occupations.'

She narrowed her eyes. 'Cake,' she said. 'We have more cake.' She swivelled in her chair. 'Those girls! Where are they? Black, summon them.'

The maid ambled from the room, without particular effort. We sat quietly.

'You will play for us after the cake?' Mrs Belle-Smyth said to Miss Grey, her voice scrambling the words. 'And then you, Lucinda, dear.'

Miss Grey fingered the lace on her sleeve. 'Thank you. I shall be pleased to do so.'

We waited, all of us folding our hands in our laps. I looked down at the impression in the rug at my feet and wondered why they had moved the chair. And then there was a high sound from somewhere far back in the house. I looked up and saw that Lucinda had heard it too. Red stains flowered on her face as she tried to compose her features into calm. Mrs Belle-Smyth, I realized, had dropped a few spots of tea on her skirt.

Outside the room, I heard shuffling and murmuring. Two, three maids, I could not tell. The door moved slightly, then closed again. Mrs Belle-Smyth straightened and looked ahead as the noises continued, like tiny mice running around a room. A door opened some way off, and there was the unmistakable sound of a sob. Then a catch of breath and the door slammed. Footsteps. It was as if we were all turned to stone, but then – finally – Mrs Belle-Smyth spoke.

'The maids are slow.' She showed her teeth. 'My cook's sponges are beautifully light. I hope they will not have sunk.'

'I expect they have heard about the murder,' said Miss Grey.

Her aunt shot her a glare but Miss Lucinda was already leaning forward. 'What murder?'

'You mean Abigail Greengrass,' I said, a little too loudly.

Miss Grey's eyes widened. 'No, another, Sara Shell, I believe her name was. They found her close to a church near Hoxton Square. St Agatha's. Not so very far from your home, I believe.'

'What happened to her?'

'Lucinda!' said Mrs Belle-Smyth. 'To the piano, my love.'

Lucinda stood up and Miss Grey leant towards me. 'They write,' she said, holding her skirt, 'that he reached for the heart this time.'

The air in the room was so still that I could feel trembling in the haze. And then Mrs Belle-Smyth came with her plate and put herself between Miss Grey and I. The strains of Miss Lucinda faltering over the second movement of Mozart's Fourth filled the room.

5. Bishopsgate

As a child, my father fell in love with a fossil in the window of a shop near the British Museum. For as long as I could remember, he would travel away three or four times a year and return after a week or so, his bags full of stones. The maids and, later, my brother and I would clean the curves with brushes small enough to use on the teeth of dolls. He displayed them across the house on shelves too high for us to reach. He set some in gold and silver chains, for my mother to wear around her neck.

He promised me that when I was older he would give me a silver bracelet. 'Maybe you shall wear such jewellery as a bride,' he said, an idea that seemed to me impossible. I spent hours trying to discover how I would appear as a young lady. I came closest when I stood in front of the mirror, put a piece of net over my head, and looked at my face through the holes. I suspected I had achieved a mystery that might show adulthood. But I could not really believe in the future. I thought I would always be a child. The change, the growth, belonged to my body alone; the rest of the world seemed still and I could never imagine those around me having once been young. We lived in a house of aged things and I could not see time at all.

When Louis was seven and I nine, we became consumed by a passion for mud castles. We stacked up the turrets and decorated the doors and windows with shells and broken saucers. As the castles grew, we wanted things that shone and glittered, frivolous, expensive. We used my silver chain, with the cross, to harness a horse made of sticks. Then we stole my mother's necklace.

She was writing letters in the parlour and my father was out. We crept up to her room, opened the door into calm whiteness and tiptoed to the dressing-table. The box was open, jewels dropping over the sides, like a medieval treasure chest. We touched the box and fingered the rings. Then my brother spied the chain and pulled out the pendant, a large curled fossil in a bright gold setting. We smiled, like the thieves we were, and took our treasure downstairs to lodge on top of the castle. In the course of the afternoon, the fossil became a monster that invaded the castle and took the princess hostage, only to be slain by our favourite warrior and turned into a part of his shield. Evening fell, we were called to dinner and we left the fossil in the mud at the front of the castle, a sleeping behemoth comforted by chains.

We ate, the evening passed and we forgot about the castle until we woke next morning, rain heavy on our windows. I tore down to the garden in my nightdress. Louis was there too, his hair wet, his hands scrabbling through the muddy earth. Our castle had been washed into sticks and stones, slipping away into the mud through the flowers.

All day we searched, and found nothing. That evening, my mother asked my father if he had moved her necklace. Louis and I looked at each other, started to speak, and he confessed. The memory hurts. Instead of shouting, my mother sat calmly and said that she understood the temptation: she had surely taken objects and lost them as a child. My father declared that he would look in the morning and no doubt the fossil would be found.

The lack of a punishment worked better than if they had thrown us into our rooms, for we both felt great guilt. I prayed in church for the necklace's return, and we clubbed our small savings together to buy flowers for my mother. 'I know I have not been angry with you,' she said, 'but I find you easy to forgive. I never knew my own parents and my childhood was lonely, but I think you yourselves feel what you have done.'

How wrong she was, how deluded, about me. If she had punished me for that and other transgressions, would I have been different? Kinder, better-behaved, more normal? And now they are all gone and I am the sole member of the family, the worst and blackest, for there is no justice. I am alive and alone, and all I do is scribble about the murderer, he the newspapers call the Man of Crows.

'I think you should stop this writing.' My uncle stood at the doorway in his coat and black gloves. He spoke calmly, as if he were asking me to pass him a plate at dinner.

I touched my papers. I had not heard the slam of the

door as he came in and I wondered how long he had been there. 'I am not writing, Uncle. I am merely making a few notes to myself.'

He took a step towards me. 'I presume that is the paper you bought recently. I wondered the purpose of your interest. And now you are scrawling wildly.'

I covered my paper with my arm, feeling cold inch up my back. 'I record my thoughts about the day. The warm weather. The scenes outside.'

He shifted slightly in the doorway. 'Really, my dear. But the moment you returned from the Belle-Smyths' party yesterday, you rushed into this room and began writing. And now you are here again this morning. That would indicate a degree of urgency beyond describing the weather.'

'I saw some particularly beautiful clouds on my return.'

'Was there talk of Starling at the party?'

'No.' I shook my head.

'Well, she is forgotten, then.'

He fingered the African mask on the wall, cupping his hand around the teeth. 'When you came here, I asked you to write in your book about the day, your likes and dislikes. That should be sufficient for you. Or are you neglecting the discipline?'

I felt my cheeks flame. 'Not at all, Uncle, I derive great pleasure from the book. This is nothing more than a few scribbles.'

'You should devote your time to more worthwhile pursuits. Still-life watercolours, perhaps. You liked to draw as a little girl.'

He was right. I could remember drawing for him before his travels: him stepping off a boat on to an island of yellow sand, surrounded by blue sea, like Robinson Crusoe.

'You might paint this vase and some foodstuff from the kitchen,' he was saying. 'Like the Dutch masters.'

'I do not think I can draw any more. Anyway, I have my embroidery.' I usually tried to pull out the frame when I heard him approach, but I had been too slow this time.

'I do not think you have been attending to the embroidery.'

I looked down at the blue stripe melding into the green in the material of my dress and did not answer.

'Niece, I have observed that your behaviour has been different over the past few days.'

'I feel perfectly in health.' I wanted only to lean closer over my paper, so he could not see.

'You seem to me changed. You had no report on the tea party.'

'I do not know why you are so interested in the Belle-Smyths. They are dull.

My dear, we have lost our train. I was talking about you. You appear giddier, distracted.'

Outside, the men were still working on the road, piling up the rubble for others to break into pieces. Women used to stand and gossip on the doorsteps, holding their babies, or the younger ones nursing their cut hands after drawing shuttles or thread. No more; the women hurried along, holding their children close.

I took courage and shuffled blank papers over my writing. As I did so, he came nearer. He reached down and lifted my right hand into the dryness of his palm. 'You will pick at your fingernails, my dear.' His blackened nail at the edge of my skin. 'It is not becoming. Look at what you have done to your ring finger.' He was correct. I tugged at my fingers when I was not writing and the skin had become raw and pulled, like upended soil.

'You have also let your hair grow too long. It is unruly and the ends fall out of your style. We should have it cut.'

'I like it.' I would not let him. It had not been cut since Lavenderfields and I would not allow him near it.

He stroked the pad of one finger. 'You came to me to get well and that is what you should do. Perhaps you should attend church.' I could smell ash and wood and I wanted to recoil from his hand.

'You do not.' Churches were for families. There, the good waited for the day when they could be perfect after death, and would not welcome me. I once went with my parents to a great church away from our house to watch their friend conduct his first service as bishop. I emerged as if light and full of kindness. I could not imagine ever feeling so again.

'Yes, but I am a grown man. You are young and you should not be cynical. Well, I suppose I am not so very aged. I was only five years your mother's senior. But generations separate.'

'Indeed.' I wanted to reach out my hands and push him from me.

He clipped his cane. 'I will bring you something, Niece.'

He trotted out and returned a minute later, carrying a silver pot and a cup on a tray. 'Cocoa. They tell me the remedy is particularly good for young ladies at this time of year. Your feet grow chill when your body overheats and the cold rises to your mind.'

'My feet are not cold.'

'You will enjoy the taste.'

I sipped at the cup. The drink was sweet, with a bitter tinge.

'There! You should drink this every day. I shall assume the particular task of bringing the cup to you. I should delight in the duty.'

I wanted to throw it to the floor, but instead I passed it to him. He gave me an arch look. 'We shall make you strong.'

'So I desire, Uncle.' If I smiled at him sufficiently, perhaps he would leave.

'You and I should attend church one day.' He toyed with the cup in his hand. 'We could attend St Agatha's. A handsome building.'

I would go with him to the place near where Sara Shell was found? I looked up at him, trying to hide my confusion, and he touched his forehead.

'I think we often forget in our modern world how much the martyrs gave for us. They chose to die for their beliefs in such appalling ways.' He passed another finger over the right eye of the death mask. 'I think of St Catherine, her body upon the wheel, suffering great terror. Do you know how St Agatha died, my dear?'

I shook my head, trying to thrust the image of St Catherine on her wheel from my mind.

'Nor I. Still, they were rather similar. I remember the lessons at school. The Romans were more imaginative in the torments they imposed than the modern man.'

He smiled briefly and looked down into the cup. 'The day passes. I must leave you. We will discuss this writing again.' He stepped back. 'Is Jane in the kitchen? I desire to speak to her. The upkeep of this house is deteriorating.'

My blood swelled at his every word. But what was the alternative? Lavenderfields. I would become like Miss Elm, who had lived in such places all her life and did not wish to be in the world outside.

My legs twitched and my eyes hurt but I would not let a tear fall. I listened to him walk away and down the stairs to the kitchen and the false door, with no room behind it.

I did not wish I was back in Lavenderfields, never, but life outside was confusing, and there was nothing to prevent you thinking. Miss Grey's ring, my uncle looming, telling me to stop, Abigail turning a corner into the dark way. I stood and told myself to *stop these thoughts.* I passed my nail over the bureau, piercing the cracks made by years. Some people have furniture that is clean and new, without history. It sits in their rooms, waiting for the imprint of lives. Ours was new once, on sale in a shop. Passers-by admired the clean curves until it was bought, perhaps by a newly married couple. They kept their new furniture until the time around them crumbled, with their initial joy, and the piece was sold on, to an old lady in need of a display case for china or a scholar wanting to house his books. My uncle spotted the curved legs and delicate doors on a market stall, brushed off the dust and fixed the broken glass, pleased by the out-of-fashion look that made the thing cheap and unwanted.

My uncle and I lived with furniture scratched over with other people's frustrations and delights, the shelves bearing the dirt of hands, the lock unsteady from the old lady's nervous fingers, the wood pierced deep by the fog of other lives. Old pictures on the wall, ancient rugs, mismatched French chairs from different houses, and the burnt-red sofa from Italy. Even the hook where I hung my Egyptian necklace was not new. We lived among all these people, and their old dead lives hummed around me. I heard their voices, unclear and shortened, as if I had my ear to a glass bottle and they were huddled in the base.

I stared at the newspaper I had begged Jane to find. Sara Shell, twenty-four, found near St Agatha's Church, horribly attacked. I stood in the parlour and tried to think of the Man of Crows. But he could not live in a house like mine, or even in a busy part of town, like Holborn, where there were too many people to notice if you ventured outside. Such evil could not exist in comfort, a parlour and a kitchen, supping on beef and vegetables for dinner, tidying his belongings before bed, finding holes in his shoes. Someone like him would live on a wire, free from coughs and indifferent meat, chimneys spitting dust, cool and apart in close-shuttered rooms.

Then I heard my uncle's heavy footsteps, creaking down the stairs and past the parlour door. I stood at the window and watched him stroll out into the wide world, content to leave me behind. I was suddenly brimming with anger at my dark life. Even though I knew there was nowhere for me to go, I wanted to chase after, grasp him, and beg him to set me free.

6. The Girl in Hoxton Square

'I am Mr Sand,' said the moustache man, lolling by the fire. 'Hello, Sally.' He was so tall and smart and precise that he looked like a story creature come to life in our room where rainwater seeped down the side of the walls and the brown rug was eaten with holes – Johnny found it in the street.

'The gentleman is come to see you, Sally,' Ma said. 'He is interested in your lovely eyes.' She was twisting her apron so it caught on her thumbs.

May, two months before my eleventh birthday. I was playing skipping with the other girls when Johnny came to tell me that Ma wanted to see me – quick smart and try and do something about your hair. We hurried home – and there was a man in our front room, his gangly body wedged between Boppy's cot and the wall. He looked, I thought, a bit like a grasshopper in a suit, very old, even though, really, he had only six years more than me.

'Well?' prompted Ma. 'Greet the gentleman.'

'Can she curtsy?'

Johnny gave me a shove. I bobbed to the floor, trying.

'Not bad,' said the gentleman. 'I might even be convinced that you were decayed gentility.' He bent down to my level and I smelt peppermint and wet wool. 'Well, my pretty. Take a holiday with me? To a beautiful house where a princess might live, and all the lovely dresses you might ever want? You will have your hair in a high pile, a proper lady.'

I shot a look at Ma. Surely she wouldn't allow that, being as I was the one she liked the least. But Ma was nodding, bumping off a grin like Mother Brown at her stall. 'Wouldn't that be lovely, Sally?' The grey hair behind her ear looked like dry wool.

The gentleman touched my hair, which was dark and thick and a beauty, everyone said so. 'I would be most honoured if you would come with me, Miss Sally. If you do not like it, you may return at any time.' He smiled at me. 'As soon as we arrive, I shall give you a big cake. Do you like strawberries? I thought so. A strawberry cake.'

My face turned pink.

'So. Will you come with me?'

I nodded, trying to think of strawberries.

But then it would have signified not a thing if I had said no. Either way, whether smiling or agreeing or screaming and begging to stay, the same would have happened. I would have been bundled into the hot plumped carriage and clattered through the dirty streets and then arrived at a house in which no princess would ever have lived. Instead of ladies-in-waiting and feasts on silver platters, I was pulled up the stairs by an old woman with moles on her face to a room where a man who said he was a doctor made me lie on the bed. Sand held down my legs and the woman my arms and he prodded until I cried out, and the woman said, 'She is exactly right.'

And whatever I could have done, I would still have been picked off the bed by Sand and felt him stroke my hair as he carried me out of the door and down the stairs, into a room swathed with scarlet, strange pictures hanging on the wall. 'I'll bring you some sweets,' he said, as he put me on a red coverlet, puffy with embroidery and slippery cold on my skin. He did – pink sugary things shaped as hearts.

'Where is the cake?' I begged.

'It will come,' he said. 'Soon.'

But instead of a cake, they brought me a man, old, old, old, who smelt of the damp stuff under the stove. When he opened the door, I cried out and the woman with moles pushed in front of him.

'Dearie,' she said, warm like Ma, when she had been at the gin, 'this gentleman is going to give you a kiss. He is a very nice man and he likes ladies like you. He knows you are away from your mammy and he just wants to be nice to you.'

The man moved up the bed and I watched his chin shake. I pushed myself against the wall. 'I want him to go away,' I said, trying hard to speak clearly. Really, I wanted to scream and shout and cry.

'But he can't,' said the woman with moles. 'He can't go away.'

I thought of Sand, his cool, wide face, the scratches of beard at his ears. 'I want Mr Sand.' And then the idea gathered. He would help me and look after me and stop this, stop it all. 'I want him!' But the woman with the moles was moving forwards.

'Dear child,' she said, stroking her palm with one finger. 'He only wishes to be kind to you.'

'Don't be like that, dear,' the woman said later, when the man had gone and the doctor was there again. I kept my hands over my face. 'Just think what awaits you. The great world of love.' She patted the bedclothes. 'Mark my words, you'll feel better in the morning. And Mr Sand might come and see you.'

So he did. He brought me a paper bag of sugar mice and told me how pretty I was. He said I wouldn't have to do this for much longer, just until I was grown-up and then he'd marry me. We'd have a big white house together and I could wear beautiful dresses and go out in the carriage to buy cakes whenever I liked. And so I loved him. I loved him when I was eleven and every year after that. One afternoon in April, when I was nearly fourteen, he came to visit as usual but instead he began to kiss me and touch my back. And then he made love to me and it was different from the others, for it was me he saw, not just a body, but the secret hidden me that those men could not find, and that I knew was there. He found it. He saw.

And now I am Mrs Marianette's best girl. I have my regulars, I earn well, I dress in heavy red silks and satins, style my hair like a lady, and the men who visit me tell me they envy me my life – nothing to do all day but lie there and look pretty. We live like gilded birds, in our overheated cage, primped and preened, the envy of many, beautiful, untouchable, but bored, trapped, hopping from our perch to the floor of the cage and back again, for there is nothing else to do.

It has been my life for so long.

When did Sand stop loving me? I cannot pinpoint the time. Falling out of love is as hard to track as falling into it, I suppose – you are already halfway in before you comprehend you have even begun.

Had he long fallen away from me when Jenny Anders appeared, lithe, lissom, yellow-haired, humble, adoring? Was it a case of, if not her, anyone?

'I can't understand it,' he said to me. 'She is not as pretty as you or clever. So why?'

I was beside him in bed at the time. I stroked his back a little. It felt hard, like marble.

'He'll come back,' said Polly. 'Crawling back, even. You're so handsome. And what's she? Nothing.' That was what most of the girls in the house said (apart from sour Alice who spat, 'You can't have everything').

'And he had such a good life with you,' said Polly. She meant: Jenny could never earn as much as you. They didn't know, of course, that I'd been telling him I wanted to retire, to set up home with him. And, he said, his feelings had changed, and he and she are gone somewhere together, and I have nothing but that house – and dozens of men wanting to take his place as my master.

'You might as well choose the best,' said Polly. 'Just don't fall in love with him this time.' She patted my hand. 'You can't work without one.'

'I don't know why! They do nothing. We lie on our backs and they take the money.'

'Yes, that's all they do. They spread the word about you, chase the payments. If the customer doesn't pay, Mrs Marianette can't chase him. She gets Mr Sand to do it.'

'Well, I think I could manage that.'

'Just you try.'

We were walking along Liverpool Street, on our way to see the Outdoor Magicians playing near Chapel Hill Church. As the two most senior – and high-earning – girls in the house, we were allowed to walk out on our own, one afternoon and one evening a week. Polly wanted to see the new show. They always included something topical, and this time they were going to play on the Crime Crisis that we read about in every newspaper. I'd never seen them before – I had spent most evenings with Sand – but, as the other girls said, I had to find new experiences. So, dreading the crush of unwashed people, the noise, the vulgarity of the show and the men who would reach for me, I agreed to go.

'Come on, dreamer,' said Polly. We were heading towards a crowd. 'Pick up the pace. We don't want to lose each other.'

I don't want to lose you, was what she meant. It was my first time out alone, without him. I had spent every free evening with him. He had taken me to the theatre, or to the Fox and Grapes at the end of Greek Street, or to a pie shop where we ate the hot pastry and meat and licked our fingers afterwards. Or sometimes we just walked around, looking at the shops and the houses, planning where we might live. I looked at the people surging forward. I wasn't with him any more, I was with them, and part of the great anonymous life, someone who no one knew or cared for. The tiny things I did every day meant something only to me. We walked in and then, when a fat man wedged himself between us, I let go of her hand and the crowd carried me forward. At the baker's by the station, I leant against the wall. He filled my head, smiling, walking, holding out his hand – and he was with her.

'Don't see it as the end,' said Polly. 'See it as the beginning. Really. Now you are free.'

I dropped my cheek against the bricks. I was too old for new beginnings, at twenty-four.

'You have to think of yourself and what you would like to do,' June had said. But I had nothing to think of other than his hands on her and what I could have done differently.

I brought my hand to the wall and pressed my face against the roughness, forgetting the crowd. I felt as if I could hear the very earth, right at the heart where – a gentleman once told me – there were layers of hard rock and a burning core. I wanted to let that core touch my face and tell me that the freedom I had was a blessing, not a curse. I did not have to go back to Mrs Marianette. I could stay out all night, with no one to watch or complain.

And that was when it struck me. How to hurt him most. I would devalue my own currency. I would do what no gilded-bird girl like me ever would: the act that if Sand ever caught me at, he would beat me. I would earn the first piece of money that had not passed through his pinching fingers. I knew where to go – all girls did. I picked up my skirts and hurried up Old Street, then turned up Rufus Street into Hoxton Square. There, girls hung off every spare corner and spot, like sugar sweets on a tree. I headed for an empty space of railing by the park, just vacated, no doubt. I'd have someone before she was back.

'Oo, there's one slumming it,' said a girl as I passed. They called out, 'Lady Muck.'

'Dirty duchess.'

'Steal that, did you?'

I positioned myself and the girl next to me started singing. 'I'm just a poor girl, wants to be rich.'

I looked out. While they were all occupied in staring at me, I could find my client. I swung my skirts at the trail of men lining their way around the streets. I gave one in a dirty brown coat a smile, but he walked on. A sailor I tried did the same. A young one who looked like a scholar glanced away when I caught his eye. The girl next to me laughed softly. 'Keep trying, dearie.' She reached out for the student and he caught her waist. After a few words they were off to the back of the square.

I touched my hair. What was wrong with me? I was more beautiful than any other woman there, and better dressed. Perhaps they were afraid of me, or thought I was a spy. But I couldn't leave, not in front of those girls. I brought my hand down and smiled. I would succeed.

And then, as if I had been answered by some higher power, he appeared. A tall man in a long cloak and high boots – the clothes of a different class. I should have trusted! A man who would be a usual client had sought me out. I lowered my eyelashes and thrust out my bosom.

'Good evening, sir,' I called sweetly. I would show those girls you could still be a lady, even if you were on the streets.

He didn't answer, but came close to me and caught my hand. His palm felt dry and cold, a little plump. I couldn't see his face under the hat, but I smelt dark wood and iron. 'Would you like me to walk with you, sir?'

He nodded.

I had to think. 'I have just the place, sir. Do you know St Agatha's Church?'

He made no reply, but tugged at my hand. I walked off, to the whistles of the other girls. I was brave and strong and beautiful. I didn't need Sand, not at all. Once I'd proved to myself I could do this, I could do anything. I could set up my own establishment, going into houses and giving advice to the courtesans about dress and hair. I could even be an actress. Or work behind the scenes on costumes. I smiled up at the man as we set off. I felt the eyes of the other girls on my back and slipped my arm through his, pressing close to the rough wool. Walking towards the trees, I could almost feel the burning core of the world floating in the sky. There it was, warm and waiting to embrace me. My new life. *Come*, the angel said.

Sara Shell.

7. Bloomsbury Fields

My hands were cold, as if they had been buried in damp soil. 'He caught her, he held her,' I wrote. And then I could go no further. Just the day before, I had been crabbed over the papers, unable to write the words pouring into my mind, every moment away from the table a betrayal. Now the page glared back at me, mocking.

I pulled up my sleeve and touched the birthmark on my forearm, just at the tip of the vein running up the tendon in the middle. It was large and brown like a cameo without a bracelet. My mother had told me the colour would lighten as I grew older, but it had not. My brother had a birthmark too, a small brown spot on his right shoulder. I had read since that such marks are caused if the mother sees something that creates extreme fear in her, and then touches that part of her body. So, with my brother, something must have caused her slight terror, but with me, great fear. His mark might have been caused by a door opening at night for no reason, or a strange man following her in the street. Mine was something more awful.

Young ladies should not stare at their arms. We should devote our time to delicate pursuits – needlework, music – even girls splashed over with evil like me. I looked at the writing on the page and wished I could throw it to one side. Other girls might go to their room to sort their jewellery or their belongings. *But mine were disappearing.* My hair ribbon, the beeswax, the hairbrush and, the previous night, my copy of *Camilla* had not been where I left it. I knew: if I could not write, nothing could protect me from losing my things – and sleepwalking. And when I began to do so, what would happen to me? I would bring torment once more.

The door opened and Jane padded in. 'Mr Crenaban left instructions with me. He said Thomas is waiting for you so that you may visit the Foundling Hospital.'

I stared at her.

'This morning, he said.'

'But he instructed me that I could not go out–'

'I have my orders. Come, take your wrap.'

Jane opened the door, and I stepped into the hot air. 'Enjoy your visit, miss.' Every day her tone was a little more mocking. I drew my wrap around me. Outside the gate the men were still working on the road. As I came towards them, one with a fuzz of black hair smiled. I felt my face flush and the stones of the pavement heat my feet.

'Give me your hand, miss,' Thomas offered, his hat askew. I held my shoulders and understood I was trembling. The man had me in his eyes. 'Come along, miss.' Thomas was so old I thought he must be seventy or more.

I put my hand in his and pushed myself into the back

of the carriage. I would not look out. I would keep my eyes closed until we arrived at the hospital. The leather steamed in my face and my eyes felt black.

It had been my uncle's suggestion that I should visit the Foundling Hospital. 'A young lady should have charitable interests,' he said. 'I am sure you will find it beneficial to meet those less fortunate than yourself. I feel it is of great advantage to you, my dear, to see children who have been weakened by their poor start in life. For, of course, strength lies in families.'

I dropped my head, then. What I did not have.

'And you will encounter other young ladies. The Belle-Smyth daughters are assiduous visitors.' Perhaps my face had shown how little I thought of them for he cleared his throat and looked at me, his eyes cold. 'They are charitable young ladies.'

I had been afraid that first time. Even though I knew it was an occupation that should improve me and make me good, my heart trembled when Thomas helped me out of the carriage and all I could see was the door of an institution where they locked every window, like Lavenderfields. It soared over my head, the great building, and I could think only of bolted doors and children unable to escape.

I was sent to join a group of young ladies. They were chattering like birds, and I stood apart. An older man came with two others, introduced himself as the rector and talked about how the orphans were left by their mothers and would have starved had the hospital not taken them in, given them an education, prepared the girls for domestic service, the boys for trade.

Then, he said, he would take us on a tour. I found myself shaking as we walked along the corridors. And then the children sitting at their desks made me afraid. I felt wrong above them, looking at them as if they were plants in a forest. The young ladies were chattering and pointing. Their voices pulled through my head on needles.

He said we would each be taken to speak to a child. I saw my hands trembling and the air was dizzying. The little boy in front of me shrugged as the rector moved away.

'Do you have lots of money, miss?'

I shook my head. I supposed he was about ten or so. His hair was cut short, but I thought that surely it must once have curled.

'You must do.' My uncle was wrong about weakened children. This one was strong.

The other girls were talking and discussing. I thought I should try to ask him about his lessons.

'What use is lessons? Only here for the food we put in our bellies. Do you have meat every day, miss?'

I nodded.

'Told you so. You have money.'

The other girls would have told him he was being impertinent, I supposed, or perhaps that money would come if he worked hard, but I could not. He was right. I had money when he did not. Who was I to speak to him, with all my sin? I could only sit and stare at him, while all the other girls were talking around me. He smirked at me and his blue eyes said, *How strange you are.*

I opened my eyes and Thomas was turning. The streets were deserted, only delivery boys hurrying to and fro – because no one dared go to the shops, I supposed. The park was overgrown and there were no nursemaids with children or ladies arm in arm. Thomas slowed when we arrived at the hospital. The large gates were closed. Two men stood outside, holding sticks.

'No admittance,' said the taller, loudly.

'It is ladies' visiting time at the hospital,' I heard Thomas reply.

'No longer. New rules, since last week. No visitors.'

I put my head to the window. 'What has happened?'

'Nothing, miss. The rector decided that, with a murderer on the loose, we could not allow anyone to enter the hospital. I am afraid that even mothers are not permitted to leave children.'

'But you can hardly think this young lady is the Man of Crows.' I had scarcely heard Thomas speak so many words.

'No, indeed.' At this, the guard gave a smile that made me shrink. 'But I have my orders. No visitors.'

'Until when?'

'We remain closed until the man is caught, I believe.'

'Well,' said Thomas, turning the horses, 'it is a foolish plan not to let in young ladies. How could they harm a soul?'

I leant my head on the side of the carriage, as we drove away from the park and the giant house with the ornate windows. We came to a halt and I started. 'No point going in there,' Thomas was shouting. 'Closed even to lady visitors.'

I looked out and there were the Misses Belle-Smyth, descending from a carriage, Miss Edwarda stepping out first in pale blue. I had to do the same.

'Miss Sorgeiul,' she said, touching her golden hair. 'You also came to visit. We knew you were a lady of charity. But the hospital is closed?' She shone, her gown glittering against the dry, overgrown grass and the brown-leaved trees.

'No admission, but for staff. Since the crime.'

'But of course. The murders in your area come closer to us all.' Her fingers were long and thin, like flutes. I could say nothing, so she continued, 'Are you not afraid, living there? He could be near you.'

'My uncle is sure he takes only poor girls.' The words were stiff in my mouth.

She moved closer to me. 'But how can you know? Have you not been through the city, where there is no one to be seen? Everyone is afraid of him.'

'It might be catching,' said Miss Lucinda. 'Other men might begin to do the same.'

'I could not think it.' They were tormenting me, I knew, but still I could not break away from their words. I was held to them with strings.

'It is a rare pleasure to see you out, Miss Sorgeiul. You were so reserved at our tea. Although, perhaps, as I believe, you prefer the company of servants.'

'You found Grace friendly?' Miss Lucinda chimed in.

'She was a good maid.'

'One should not be too close to servants. Do you not agree, sister?'

I could feel the heat of the carriage through my dress. 'I should depart.'

'Oh, no, Miss Sorgeiul. Come with us in our carriage. Our father would be so pleased to meet you.' She extended one grey-gloved hand and touched mine. 'He has heard so much about you.'

'My uncle expects me.'

'Well, if we cannot persuade you, Miss Sorgeiul, we must hope for another occasion. Be sure to keep safe in your streets. And do tell us if you see the Man of Crows. He must be quite celebrated over there.'

'Home, please,' I said to Thomas. I climbed into the carriage and sat back as he stirred the horses. I would not look out and see them mock me.

All the way into town, I heard their laughter tinkling. As we turned towards home, I closed my eyes and saw nothing but the gates of the hospital. I thought of the children inside, their hands on the windows, begging to be let out.

If we had waited outside, then perhaps the Man of Crows would have come. He would remain in the grounds and then, when night fell, scale the walls and push his way through the windows. There, in the upstairs dormitories, he would reach out and place his hand over the mouth of a girl. *Come with me.* She cannot scream as he holds her in her nightdress, past the snoring matron, down the wide stairs and out of the door that he cuts open with his knife. Only ten or eleven, perhaps, training as a maid, and now taken by the Man of Crows, kicking, for that is all she can do.

Then the other children begin to wake and they see she is not there and the door to their room is open. The matron sleeps still, and they creep out, one by one, down the shadowy stairs and then, after hesitating for a few minutes, one of the older boys leads the way out of the open front door into the dark gardens. They run to scale the gates, all of them scrambling up the iron railings, holding on to the decorative swirls, pitching themselves over the top. On the other side, the older child signals, and so it is without speaking that they run off in different directions, hundreds of them hurrying through the streets, scurrying into corners, hiding in the alleyways, dozens and dozens of children running from the rector, and lessons and good works and lady visitors, to live with horses in stables, to huddle under huts together, to walk through the streets in the daytime and take what they wish. Two boys remember the Belle-Smyth girls and think of their house, so they creep to St James's, scale the walls and find themselves in a house that might be theirs, full of shop-bought treasures. They scuttle through it, taking silver, ornaments, plates, then scramble out of the back door and run into the night.

They are free, every one of them, except the girl caught

by the Man of Crows. She lies in his arms, breathing only a little, as he smiles at the moon and takes a knife to her heart.

'We're there, miss,' called Thomas. I stared out at Princes Street. The men were still working on the road.

Thomas helped me out. 'The horses are restless, miss. It's the heat. I shouldn't leave them. Would you be able to walk to the door?' I nodded and watched him loop the reins into his hand to take the horses to the stable. His grey beard tipped as he did so and then I watched his bent back moving slowly away. I shook from my head thoughts of children dying and stealing.

I meant to go in, straight away, before the man working on the road caught my eye once more. But then I saw two men coming around the corner, with baskets and spotted handkerchiefs, a trail of cats behind them. I had not seen cats' meat-sellers for weeks. I stared at them, men from another world. They must know about death. Cats' meat-sellers took the horses from mines and cabmen and tied bloody rags around their eyes so they would not see the axe. Then they skinned them, cut up the meat, boiled the bones to take up the fat and used it all to feed cats stalking around the sofas of old maids in houses too big for them.

I gazed at the one with pale red hair. Men like that must come to smell of blood, I thought. It must seep under the skin and stay there for ever. He turned and threw something at me. I looked down and saw a bloody piece of meat sliding off my toe. There was a bubble of laughter from the children at the corners as the men walked away.

And then, in a moment, one of the cats from the line behind the sellers darted towards me, jumped up and grasped my palm with its teeth. I cried out and shook my hand. It stared at me, amber-eyed, then turned, waved its tail and ran after the sellers. I stood in the middle of the street, my hand bleeding, alone. Then I walked to the door. *Everybody sees my evil.*

Jane opened the door. 'Why, that was swift, miss.'

'The hospital was closed.' I wanted to push past her.

There was a rustle and my uncle emerged from the parlour. 'Why return so early, my dear?'

'The Foundling Hospital was closed because of the murders. Nobody may enter. The guard said it would stay closed until the Man of Crows was found.'

'Curious.' He paused. 'I imagine they worry he will lie in wait for the young girls who leave their babies there. Of course.' His eyes smiled. 'Those girls creep up in the dark to leave their babies, then hurry away – they are easy to catch.'

'I shall go upstairs.' His pupils were shining. I did not like him thinking of girls leaving their babies in the darkness.

Onlookers

I have become intrigued by these recent murders. As a gentleman of property and status, I would normally dismiss such matters as belonging on the front of cheap magazines. But this man, he they call the Man of Crows – I deem him extraordinary.

I suspect I am in possession of a second layer of perception. I see right to the heart of things when others are baffled. Sometimes I have to bite my tongue in company when they puzzle over a certain question, such is the violence with which the answer reverberates through my mind. I have become used to the mistrust that genius inspires.

What interests me about them? The way they are left. Throats cut, their hearts torn to the air, bodies ruined. But, most of all, I think of the hair. Each girl left her place of work with her hair gathered up in pins in the usual style. And yet they are each found with their hair in a long plait, like a little girl's. The question: is he responsible, or does he compel them to rearrange their own hair? I cherish the belief that he performs this task before he slays them. He asks his victim to take down her style. Shivering, she perhaps tries to smile or tell him about her family, to seem more human to him. Or perhaps she tries to argue. Futile, all. He curves his hands around her neck and up for the hair.

He reaches to the top of the curls and unpins each one, allowing them to fall across her face. Then he pulls out the pins at the back, one by one; they tumble over her shoulders and land on the dirty ground.

She stands there, hair heavy around her shoulders, half crooked because the shape of the style remains. He steps back to admire his work. She shivers again, contemplates screaming. But nobody heard her before so why would they now? And the sound might anger him, prompt him to pull out a knife. So she stands, the sound squashed in her throat. She waits. The waste water drips off the walls around her and he inches closer. He touches her hair, perhaps her cheek, and asks her to move forward. Then he asks her to turn. She moves slowly, trembling, feeling her skirts trailing in the water. She stares at the wall, waiting to feel him pull at her clothes. Instead she feels his soft hands (fine and well cared-for, not the calloused paws of a working man) folding her hair back over her shoulders. He uses his palm to smooth the strands over the bones of her back, working his fingers through the small knots as he does so. Then he reaches up to touch her skull and put his hands around her hair, just at the base of her ears, and parts the mass into three skeins. He runs his hand over the hair at her temples, first left and then right, to make certain there are no strays to spoil the line. Then he takes the right skein and lays it over the middle one, pulling slightly to ensure the plait is taut at the crown. Then what has been the right one becomes the middle, and he folds the left over that, so that each submits to the dominance of the other in turn. He continues, wrapping the hair over and over, until he reaches the end, always slowly.

Of what do his soft hands remind her? Perhaps her mother, plaiting her hair in the morning. Even if she never knew her mother, or had one who was a gin-soaked madam selling her out, she cherishes a vision of a different mother. A kindly woman who styles her daughter's hair before school, running her hands over the silkiness and ending with a kiss on her freshly washed crown.

No kiss for her now. Her possessor seals the plait with a piece of ribbon and lets the weight fall against her back. He turns her around. She has become a little girl.

And then what? His touch has been light, kind even. He is perhaps simply a man with a queer obsession for hair who wishes only to plait it and let her go. She thinks of saying she will not chatter to anyone, and indeed what is there to tell? *I will keep your secret*, she thinks of saying. Her life is close in front of her. She could reach out a hand for her future, as if the days were an apple, the hard exterior skin red with sugar.

He holds out a hand. 'Come,' he says. 'Come forward.' She does. Her plait heavy over her shoulder, she steps forward, out of her light and into his own.

There are men, all over the country, thinking about these deaths. Men in coffee shops and counting houses, following the atrocities with interest, imagining themselves like the killer. I hold my hair in my hands, pondering how they must think of the girls. Women hide, afraid of what occurs outside, while men walk the streets, watching.

I was woken the next morning by a knock on the door and Jane's reddened face.

'Miss,' she said, hushing her voice, holding out a paper, 'look at this. The new edition.'

I could just see a picture of a girl on the front. I sat up and reached out my good hand.

'I should be afraid, don't you think? All these crimes and I walk here every day.'

'I am sure he would not come to us.'

She toyed with the paper in her thin fingers, and a smile that was not kind played on her mouth. 'You feel no fear, miss.'

I tried to be firm. My hand throbbed. 'I hardly leave the house. Perhaps you could speak to my uncle. You could stay here if you felt afraid.'

She tossed her head. 'Stay here? In that kitchen full of I don't know what? I don't think so, miss. I have a family. My mother needs me.'

She threw the paper on to the bed. I reached out and saw a girl on the front page. And then a title. I read in haste. Another one: Jenny Amber, sailor's wife, found by the docks. I looked down at the picture of her, frills at her neck, hair bundled away.

'Walking back and forth every day, that's me. You sit inside and no one can touch you. The next one will be a girl like me, you mark it, miss.' She turned on her heel and slammed out of the door.

I stared at Jenny Amber. And then the answer came to me, in one moment, like a note in a song you could not get right all the times before. The brick wall I could not touch, the questions I could not answer, the scene that hid itself from me. *What he did next.* The breeze, the colour was so easy that I could laugh. How could I have thought that I could feel anything, sitting in my parlour as I am? *I must walk out.*

You sit inside and no one can touch you.

I knew. I must follow their route, go where they had been. I could not know them if I eked out my days in the parlour and left it only for tea parties. I would take the purse, all the money that my uncle gave me and I never managed to spend, and walk through the dirt and puddles and rain, like Abigail and Sara and this third one, Jenny, if only for a few hours. I would feel the dirt on my face, smell the street and find him.

8. Virginia Road

That night my mind burnt with plans and I could not sleep. I decided I must trace the route in daytime for safety, return in the darkness. Even though I lived without a governess watching me, my uncle forbade me to walk out alone. If he did not accompany me, I must be taken by Thomas, whose clear grey eyes followed me everywhere. I had no choice but to disobey him, skip out in the afternoon, when Thomas had taken my uncle to town and Jane was fussing in the kitchen.

The next day was impossible. A man came to look at the chimneys, scattering dust across the carpet. My uncle returned home for lunch and spent the rest of the day going from room to room. On Wednesday, there were men outside from early morning, debating the road we are promised. Thursday was washday and Mrs Letts came to knead our clothes in the wooden tubs behind the kitchen door and starch my petticoats on the board propped by the wall.

Five days passed, my hand healed and still I had not escaped. I realized I would have to go out at night, when my uncle was occupied.

That afternoon, I asked him, 'I presume Mr Trelawny visits us this evening?' We were in the parlour, trying to hang a print that kept tipping to one side. He grunted and nodded.

At night, the streets would be thick with pickpockets, robbers and women who would cut my throat for my handkerchief. How could I, who had never entered the park alone, wander streets of gin houses and beggars?

I knew I must. If I did not trace the streets, I would not be able to write the book, discover the Man of Crows and set everybody free, myself, the other girls, the city, even. He would not attack me. As my uncle said, he was a man who craved poor, lower-class girls. And, most of all, I could see evil, recognize terror, and that would stay his hand. Still, there would be other men. A hundred sharp eyes like Thomas's, following, watching, seeing. A lump gathered in my mind.

'A nail, Catherine,' said my uncle. 'Please pay attention.'

I am losing things, I wanted to cry out. *I cannot find my beeswax or lace or hairbrush.*

'The print looks well, Uncle,' I said instead. 'Shall we right the neighbouring picture?'

After two hours, I was permitted to return to my room. Under my bed, I had stowed a map stolen from the parlour. My uncle collected them, as he amassed so many items, all bundled together in a box at the back of the bureau. In my room, I stared at the faded paper, tracing the way she had taken to Swan Street, from Covent Garden to London Wall. I knew I could not go as far as Holborn, there would not be time. I would be in Spitalfields and then north past Bethnal Green Road, which divided her world from mine. I could not quite imagine I would be there, out in the open, following her, not stuck in this hot house, my heart tight, my uncle padding across the landing.

That night Mr Trelawny arrived early – at nine. I did not wait. I was already wearing my plainest brown dress and I had my purse. I seized my old cape and gloves, scooped up the map and ran down the stairs. I wished I had a lucky charm to take with me, but the Egyptian necklace was, like everything else in this house, the possession of my uncle. I removed the bar, opened the few chains (my uncle did not lace up the door entirely when Mr Trelawny was there), clicked the door shut behind me, and then I was outside.

The street was busy with people and the warm, thick air struck my face. I clutched the gatepost, and then I began to walk. I gathered my cloak around my face and hurried to the end of the road, past the bundles of rubbish and the tumbledown houses where candles shone for children sewing all night or forging coins in acid. Red and gold curved into my mind and then began to explode. I told myself: *You have succeeded.* I was embarking on the real London, the place the rich never knew. I was crossing between the worlds, like a spirit.

All those people in town, pretending to be in fear of a man who will never come to them, just to give consequence to their drab lives. 'Draw the curtains,' a woman might exclaim to her maid. They were prisoners to their own thoughts. Back in Princes Street, Mr Trelawny and my uncle fingered papers in the study under candlelight, talked over their matters, and believed I slept quietly in my bed. The Belle-Smyths slumbered, their hair on silk pillows. And I was alone in the street – unafraid.

Mr Trelawny and my uncle would be together for the next three hours or so – and that time was mine. I had to hope that church bells would ring to tell me the hour. I hurried through the hot air, not allowing myself to stop. There was no watchman on Princes Street to see me – the parish would not pay. I passed stables, the horses kicking their hot hay, then turned left by the Red Man, went quickly past the Three Bells, then more streets, across the road, behind the church and then down, down to the beginning of the underworld. I was so seized by excitement that I realized I had forgotten to look at the flowers they said were painted on the house at the end of Princes Street.

I walked swiftly along Church Street and towards Bishopsgate, holding my skirts out of the mud, listening to the noise. Even so late at night, the streets were crammed with traders, and everywhere I heard shouts for oysters, bootlaces, nuts, a pennyworth of hot eels. A butcher called to me with fresh lamb, another man held out a box of turnips, a candle thrust into one at the front. A fried-fish-seller leant close, with a tray of brown lumps around a pot of salt. All of this bustling life lay around the corner from home and I'd had no idea. Piles of vegetables were stacked in front of each house and other things I could not imagine anyone needing: old kettles, snapped umbrellas and what looked like the broken end of a bed. Tin saucepans shone next to little towers of plates, and chestnuts glowed over a flickering fire. I tried not to look, meaning to give the impression that I passed along the same way daily, as if huddles of women in shawls, picking out potatoes, and two shoeless children, their breeches sewn together so they could not escape, were nothing to me.

I turned past the stalls and the people up to Redchurch, and then I was in the street they said harboured dens of thieves.

I was only sure I was there because of the map and the reports in the newspapers, but standing on the street, I decided that those writers had never been where I stood. How could anyone come here and not faint with the smell? It was intolerable, soaked in old fish, shoes, mud and worse, a smell that covered my body, filled my nose.

The taste of dirt was terrible too, hanging heavy and thick in my mouth. And the darkness: we were so close to the main street yet it was blacker than the inside of a glove. People were brushing my arm, rubbing against my back, pushing me on, all strangers. I had never been in a crowd, felt their hands on me. *Do not be afraid.* I went with them, trying to think of myself as a stick floating in water, eddied around with grass and leaves. Slowly my eyes became accustomed to the gloom and I saw that everywhere there were people. Women sprawled in corners, rags scattered over them, men crawling, heaps that might have been blankets or children, and dogs dragging their legs through the filth. Everything I saw was as if it had never had colour, had always been a dirty grey or brown. The colour of death.

I dropped my head and resolved not to look. I moved forwards because that was what Abigail would have done. She had stepped through the small streets outside her milliner's and ended here in this awful place. But, I reminded myself, to her it was home. Perhaps she knew some of the people she passed – waved at a shopkeeper or patted a dog. Maybe. I continued on, trying to keep my face straight when I splashed into a dirty puddle. I told myself that I trod on dirty vegetables and perhaps bits of meat, although it felt like pieces of bone. The smell seared my nose. I was overwhelmed, every sense, my eyes straining through the darkness, my nose full and sharp, my ears battered with the shouts and the cries, and the hopeless, hollow wail of the dogs, and I could not open my mouth for the grey, gritty taste of the air. The street was attacking the rest of me too. My shoulders bowed under the weight of it, my stomach turned, my heart pulled tight like a violin string. I tried to walk quickly, but the air was pushing under my dress, winding its grimy fingers around my hair.

The air was dirty. If I made myself think about the air of the place, the dirt, then I would not mind the people around me pressing closer. I was being brushed, nudged, touched and, I was sure, the touches were more purposeful than before. Perhaps they could guess that I was someone in the wrong part of town. I had been seized and pulled in Lavenderfields, but never touched like this, followed. *You should not be here.* The dark wrap around me was not enough. I pulled the material tighter, and at that moment I made my mistake. I looked up and realized I was surrounded by men. They walked in front of me, their elbows jostling at my sides. I felt hands brush against my legs, my waist. I could feel them, their breath hot on my neck, on my back, sweet with the smell of decay. Men, their mouths full of rotting stumps, their tongues black, a lifetime of dirt in their throats. They were breathing it on me, hissing and spitting.

The mud splashed through my boots to my feet and my toes curled. Where had they come from, these people? I imagined them crammed into the ramshackle houses around me, where rags filled the panes in the glass so there was no light, four, five families, children and women and men and even animals all together, breathing in each other's dirty air, nothing to eat but dry bread, and the babies sucking rags. Three streets away, I knew, was the George Street rookery, where the most wicked of all plotted their routes into the west of the city. I read that they seized children from the streets around here, burnt off their legs and sent them begging. I looked at a dirty window above me and wondered if inside the house children of six and seven were bundled together, their fingers scorched by hot irons as a torture, their eyes pinched from staying up all night, dreaming unhappiness as their masters counted the coins, purses and ribbons they had accrued in Oxford Street and St James's. A small boy hurtled past me. I clutched my skirts, felt shame. They were poor and destitute in these houses, and I lived with money. These men and women did not have enough to eat, to drink, could not read or tell the time, and never saw anywhere but these streets and the damp insides of these poor falling-down houses. *Abigail.*

I told myself over and over, *You know the way home.* But sickness was rising inside me. I wanted to throw out my hands, run back to Princes Street, throw myself into bed and listen to Mr Trelawny padding about. My mind broke and the thoughts I had been trying to push away came back. 'Stop!' I said. The word came out loudly, but no one turned. *You cannot go back, not now.* And I knew that if I did, the thoughts would always be there and I would be less free than I had been before.

I told myself to be Abigail. *Think of her, not yourself.* Of what did she think? Of course. She was exhausted by work, worn down to her very bones. I had read about the tiredness caused by such work, how you could barely place one foot in front of the other, and your body died a little more each day. I thought of the nights when I could not sleep, then had to stay awake through the next day, and I imagined living like that always – as life must have been for her. She thought of little other than how she wished for sleep. Perhaps next time, I thought, I would try not to sleep for two nights, so I would be more like her.

Abigail trudged on, her mind untidy with thoughts, not seeing. I imagined her small of stature, with nimble hands, pale hair tied up, brownish eyes and heavy eyebrows, thin body tied up into a workaday dress.

I supposed she must have arrived here from the north at Charing Cross, clutching her money for the apprenticeship, surrounded by a crush of people, feeling so far from the cold cottage in the countryside where her sisters tended the pot above the fire and sheep stumbled over the bracken outside.

I turned the corner and stared into blackness. The people were thinning out and there was less noise than there had been in the other streets. My feet felt lighter. And then, all at once, I was following *her*, Abigail, rather than a hundred faceless people I could never know. A woman sloped in front of me, a baby across her back. My mind was sparking again, as if the grey mass of Spitalfields had never been there. I put my hand on my bosom to try to slow my breath and I could feel the skin, thinner and more alive, right through to my heart. *I am here.*

I walked hastily, not looking around, and turned right into Virginia Road. A shopkeeper there had been the last to see her. Around the corner, over Swan Street, and there was the alley where they thought she had died. I walked a little closer and saw that the bundle slumped in a corner was an old man, bottle clutched in his hand. He coughed and lifted his head. One eye flickered. He could hear, of this I was sure, so I decided he would be my sentinel. He would hear if I cried out and, since he was so drunk, begin shouting himself.

I held my breath and looked around the place she had come to and not left. I could walk to the end and she never would. I moved forward into the darkness. Then I stopped. The spot where she was killed. I looked around and waited to feel. I wanted a sensation in my heart, to see my life in another's hands. I needed it to gather me up so I could confront my life and be all *essence*.

I felt nothing. A gin-seller shouted his wares in a nearby street and I could hear men fighting. I touched the wall but nothing changed. *Abigail was here*, I told myself, but the words echoed back to my mind.

Why could I not *feel* her? I bunched my hands into fists and pushed them into my chest, over my dress. I felt myself slide into the old routine, hearing the chant that I would find myself saying over and over, like a child with the alphabet. I could hear Dr Neville instructing, *You must stop*, but all I knew was that I had come here and now I did not feel anything. I looked at the wall and wondered if a minute had passed.

I closed my eyes, hoping that would help. I tried to forget myself and think of her. I breathed in the air around me and begged to be part of the dirt. I pulled my cloak about myself, thinking of her dirty grey shawl, one she had had for years that she scrubbed at in her lodgings every night. I told myself I was not wearing my brown dress and the petticoats underneath, but thin underwear, and a skirt so cheap, so old, that the hot wind shivered through the breaks in the stitching. I stepped forward and felt the warm water of the next puddle spread over my foot. I wanted to look up at the sky but I told myself I could not for she had not. I moved forward again, holding the wall. I tried to be her, thinking, *I am nearly home.*

Then, at once, there was a break. A shudder in the air. I stopped, and it was as if time had halted too. I heard a breath and the tap of a foot. I understood. Somebody was behind me. I could hear him, as if the air were circling around his head. I took a step forward and heard his shoe break a puddle. My heart swelled and exploded. He could be two feet behind me or closer. *Calm*, I said to myself. I took another step. So did he. *Keep your pace.* In a moment, I had been emptied of thought. I was alone, in an alleyway, and there was no one to see me.

I walked, he walked. Then I stopped, and his heels scraped to a halt behind me. My uncle told me once that the way to scare off a tiger is to turn, scream and throw anything you have. If I did so here, he would jump at me *because I would have seen him.*

A bright sliver hit the wall. The end of the alleyway. There was a house beyond, lit in the window. Images struck my mind: a family gathered around a fire, smiling children, a room of light.

Behind me, he took one step. Fear swamped my mind and I could not scream. His shoe struck the ground and echoed.

I could bear no more. I grasped handfuls of my skirts, took one breath and launched myself forward. I tore on. My heart was in my mouth, my breath was short and I could not hold my skirts, but I kept running, running, hearing my feet on the ground. He could catch me in a second. I pulled my skirts higher and I ran, faster than when I was trying to escape from Lavenderfields and they came and pulled me back. I ran, splashed, heard my feet, and my heart filled up as I moved towards the light.

The house was not a bright family home, not at all, but a gin shop. I burst in, not caring, stumbling on to the wet straw. Men stared and moved towards me as I straightened. I dropped my head and hurried to the man at the bar. This place, which would before have terrified me beyond measure, now seemed safe.

There was dirt over my face and in my hair, and my dress was awry, but I knew I must appear respectable. 'May I speak with your landlord?' I said to the man at the bar, trying to stop my voice trembling. The man might come in, the knife hidden, and catch me in the crowd.

'Upstairs.' He shrugged.

'Will you call him?' He eyed me, put down the glass he held and turned for the stairs. I looked at the spotty mirror behind the bar and ignored the laughter of the men behind me. I could hear women too, cackling, surely at me.

After ten or so minutes had passed, a broad red-haired man lumbered to the bar. 'What?' He squinted at me.

I held out my hand. He looked. As he came closer, I touched my hand to his. The shillings I was holding grazed his palm. 'I have lost my way,' I said. 'I was visiting a sick woman and took a wrong turning.' I tapped his hand with one of the coins. 'I need you to find your most trusted men to escort me to a cab. Strong men. I shall give them fifteen shillings, of which five are for you.' I lowered my voice. 'I am sure they will pass the funds to you.'

He gave me a half-smile. 'I don't doubt it, miss.' He sidled off, flicking a dirty glass on the counter as he did so. Then he was snapping his fingers and talking to a grimy boy. The child ran off and returned with two heavy-set men, who looked like brothers.

'No need to be afraid with these two, miss,' said the owner. 'No one could get close.'

We left, the laughter rolling behind us, and walked out into the street. I did not look. They took my arms and we turned around corners, over and through a closing market, hurried by a collapsing house and then went into a main street where carriages passed. I gave them the money and soon I was huddled in the back of the cheapest conveyance I had entered in my life and the driver was hurtling through the streets. I sat against the dirty velvet and hugged myself. My skin was sparking, my eyes sheened with newness. Every part of me was alive and begging to be felt.

9. Grace Starling

I hated them when I was maiding. Those girls, creeping fingers, waiting eyes. I set down the silver salvers of those cakes they picked at like sparrows, crying, 'Oh, no, I cannot,' when I knew they had shunted themselves into the kitchen before the guests arrived, begged heavy scraps from the cook: fists of raw pastry, still floury, bowls of icing, bread dough sprinkled with sugar, making us turn our backs so we couldn't see. And, oh, the Belle-Smyths, Miss Lucinda and Miss Edwarda. Ten or so years ago, they were occupied in making the life of their governess a misery, putting frogs in her desk, pins on her chair and stealing her letters. As young ladies in their teens, they turned to me.

Miss Edwarda started it.

November, when we had frost on the panes, she began to demand a glass of lemon and water at four every day (two, if company were expected). My task was to take it to her. After the first few times, she began to fuss.

'Could you put it there, on the table, Starling? Yes, that's right, near me. No, a little further away. Oh – I don't know. Where would you think?'

'I think on the table, miss.'

'Yes, yes, you are right. Put it there.'

It proceeded like this, four times. Then on the fifth,

when I bent to put the drink on the table, she leant back on her sofa and gave me a gentle smile. Then, she extended one small foot in its silvery blue shoe, tapped on the side of the glass and pushed so that it fell to the floor. I looked at her, knelt to pick it up, rubbing the rug with my apron. 'Thank you,' she said. 'What is your name?'

Most girls rushed through their words, breathless and fast. She circled her mouth around each letter.

'Starling, miss.'

'I mean your first name. What you were *christened*. If you were christened, that is.'

'Grace, miss.'

'Grace?' She dwelt gently on it. 'Grace.' Her hand moved over my leg, on the wool of my dress. She extended a finger. 'Such a pretty name.' My face heated as I felt the tip of the nail. 'For you, a servant. Do you wash, Starling?'

I held the glass and my eyes popped.

'Well? Do you?'

'Yes, miss.'

'All over?'

'Of course, miss. Shall I bring you another glass of water?'

She shrugged. 'If you wish. But make sure that it is you who brings it. Do not send another.'

Outside the room, carrying the second glass, I tried to harden myself, pull in at the stomach so I would not feel anything. But when I went in, she had her back to the room and she was staring out of the window. 'Just put it on the table,' she said, so firmly that I knew I should depart.

The next day she was friendly again, asking me questions about my family and telling me that the grey of my dress brought out my eyes. We carried on like this for a few weeks – some days she would flicker her eyes at me and smile, others she would criticize. *I can see dirt under your fingernails. Go back and clean them before you presume to serve me.* Or, *I suspect you have thick ankles under your dress. Common girls like you do.* Never the same insult twice. *I asked you to bring it to me in a blue glass. Don't you remember? Are you stupid? I think you must be stupid.* I never knew which Miss Edwarda to expect, or how to arrange my face before I entered the parlour. In front of her mother and father, she behaved just as a young lady should to a maid, hardly noticing me and quite unable to tell me apart from Jones or Carter or any of the others. In her hour for hot water and lemon, everything was different.

Then she began to come to find me. The first time was a Tuesday morning, when I was carrying the water down from the bedrooms. She must have finished breakfast early. I was halfway down the stairs and she was standing at the foot.

'My, you are laden. How *do* you manage to carry that?' She curved her mouth around the words. 'You're always so *very* busy.'

I stepped further down the stairs, keeping my footing. No matter how many times I did it, I was still afraid of falling. I think she saw fear in my eyes.

'One step,' she said. 'Two steps. How very likely one is to trip. And then both jugs would smash – and no one would ever know that it was not your fault.'

Presumably, I prayed, someone would arrive in a moment. Jones passing with a tray or Carter on her way to relight the fires. Mrs Belle-Smyth might come looking. Miss Edwarda was shorter than me, and surely I was stronger, but I was afraid of her. There was something about her small wiriness, something hard and sharp – she might seize me and pull me and stab me full of thorns. But I couldn't go back. I had to go forward, every creak and crack of the stairs bringing me closer to her. The other sounds of the house mocked me. She gave me a half-smile and I knew she would not say anything now, that she would simply watch me coming down and wait.

Three steps up from her, I was so close that I could smell the lavender water, the hair pomade and a slight sweat that must be beading under her dress. I stood on the step and waited.

'I suppose you wish me to let you pass.'

'If you please, miss.'

'But what if I wish to pass you? Then *you* would have to move aside.'

I nodded.

She continued: 'You would have to squeeze to the side and then make yourself smaller, just so I could pass you. There isn't much room on the staircase, is there?'

She might have walked back into the corridor, where we could pass easily, but instead she moved forward slightly, her lips parted. I could just glimpse her two front teeth. The jugs weighed heavy, pulling on my arms.

'So?' she said. 'Make yourself small.'

No! I wanted to shout. *I will not! Go back into your pale dining room or sunny parlour, away from the servants' staircase, and leave me alone.* I turned my face to the wall and pressed my body against it.

'There is not sufficient space for me,' she said silkily. I pressed in harder, the jugs rigid and wet against my arms and chest. 'Keep trying.'

The dirty wood of the panelling filled my nostrils and I felt the sharp splinters crushing against my cheek.

'Still not enough.' And then a light touch on my back. I could feel her fingertip, lying on my dress. 'Surely you want to help me?' came her voice, hot and low in my ear, and at the same time her hand snaked to my behind.

'Of course, miss.' I knew then what she wanted. I crushed myself against the wall, and she moved past, and pushed herself into me, her hips into my backside.

When it was done, and she had moved up two steps, I heard her clear her throat. I looked up at her, still serene, quite calm. 'So,' she said. 'We succeeded.' She raised her finger to her lips, then moved her hand towards me. I thought she would touch my mouth, but instead she pushed it at the tops of my legs. 'How satisfactory.'

If the boys came creeping into your bed (and they always tried, in every place I've been), you could scream and shout and put them in their place, and the cook might hear, and usually you wouldn't be dismissed: the family would think he wouldn't try it again so there would be no maids with child in their house. The boys didn't usually care much for they got it from maids in the street – or paid for it if they hadn't the courage. The girls were stuck at home – and it was us they wanted. In my first house, Miss Gertrude was always pinching; in the second the mistress called me up every night, saying she had a terrible cold and asking me to rub her huge lollers with cure (you had to say no a few times, because she wanted to have to beg), and now the Belle-Smyths. It hadn't taken Miss Edwarda long to catch on to me.

That was the start. Soon she was plucking at the top of my leg when I walked around the corner, or begging me to take her hand and help her because she was too faint to rise. When I attended her in public, she would declare that I was *dirty* or *untidy* or *so clumsy*. Usually, Mrs Belle-Smyth would turn to whoever happened to be visiting at the time and praise Miss Edwarda's attention to detail.

Attention to detail – oh, there was plenty of that. She would catch at my thigh, run a finger over my bosom or lick her lips at me when no one was looking. One evening, a few weeks after she had pushed past me on the stairs, she called me to her to help her dress.

I stood at the door and tried to stand straight and unafraid. The bed, the floor and the chairs were strewn with gowns, hats and gloves. 'I told Mother,' she said, sitting at her table and talking into her mirror, 'that I was sick of Hall's pinching fingers. I said to her that

I was sure you could dress my hair in a greatly superior fashion. And if not, it could not be *worse*.' She turned, and beckoned slightly with a finger. 'I told Mother that I saw something in you. Po-ten-tial.'

I stopped near a heap of shawls.

'Well,' she said quickly. 'Come.'

I bent to pick up a dress.

'Don't do that! Come to me.'

I did so and she put out her hand for my face. 'We have time before the dinner,' she said. 'You do not need to worry about making mistakes.' And then she brought her hand slowly down my cheek, over my neck and on to my breast. She circled her hand dreamily, as if she were playing with the surface of water.

Where had she learnt such things? Who taught her the words to use? Maybe someone had done the same to her. Or, more likely, it was guesswork, and she was as trembling and nervous inside as I. Perhaps all I need have done was laugh in her face, ask her what she thought she was doing and toss some cruelty at her. Jones would have done that. But I didn't. I believed her and I was afraid, and by believing her, I made it real. I thought this as she moved her hand down, slowly, so slowly, to my waist. Then she lifted her hand away, and looked into my face, and that was when I realized I was lost, for I wanted her to put it back. Finally, finger by finger, she did, and once it was flat against my hip, she moved it over to my thigh. 'Well,' she said, more gently than she had spoken to me in a long while, 'aren't you going to touch my hair?' And I did. The room smelt hot and sweet and suddenly felt smaller than a chimney. I put my fingers on her crown, feeling the strands under my hand. I did not think I had touched another girl's hair since Ma and I used to do my sisters' every morning, working through them together. Hers felt like the inside of foxgloves.

Do you like butter? I found myself thinking. My second sister, Effie, used to ask us on the three days a year Ma walked with us in the country. Effie held the buttercup under my chin to see if it reflected yellow on me.

Miss Edwarda put her hand on my shoulder and pulled me on to my knees. I remember thinking how very much stronger she was than I had thought. Or perhaps I was weak.

I did like butter, the few odd times when there was a scrape of it on something Ma brought home from the shop. At the Belle-Smyth's, I became bold. When the cook was not there, or her back was turned, I would run my finger over the butter pat and bring it to my lips, soft and yellow and salty. I savoured it, filling my whole mouth with its creaminess.

So it went on like that, from day to day. I put up Miss Edwarda's hair with my ill-working fingers, so much clumsier after what she'd made me do to her. Then she made me fumble, pick and unpick as I laced up her corset and pulled the gown tight around it.

'You don't know much about dresses, do you?' was all she said.

'No, miss, but I can learn.' A little too pert, such was my faith in my new power.

'Perhaps you can.' But the pleasantness didn't last through my confused efforts to attach her collar, put on her jewellery, tidy her hair again and smooth on some pomade. She chivvied and complained, very loudly, which gave me hope she was doing it so her mother would hear and think that all was as to be expected.

'Hmm,' she said, regarding herself in the mirror. I didn't think my handiwork too bad. She picked up her silver clasp in the shape of a dragonfly and began to walk to the door. 'Tidy this disorder,' she tossed over her shoulder, then slammed the door, taking with her the smell of heat and the taste of butter. I would have liked to dwell on the clothes a little, but I had too many duties downstairs still undone, so I had to move quickly, taking each slippery, silky dress, folding it and tucking it away.

Perhaps I was supposed to hate what she did to me, but instead I came to like it, not always, but at least some of the time. Her touch was lighter and kinder than I had found men's to be and it was easier to kiss that part of her than have something driving into the back of your throat until he decided he'd had enough. And it did not always occur, an uncertainty I did not dislike. Sometimes I would go to her before dinner and she would simply tell me to put up her hair. I liked dressing hair, twisting it into three thick lengths, propping the horsehair pad against her head and winding the hair around it until it made a full crown. I pulled at the few strands at the front to frame her face. I put on her dress, mended the tears, tidied her nails and cleaned her ears and her teeth. I decided there was nothing in it, this lady's maid business.

So the work I liked, and what came before. What I didn't wish for so much were the games, because those you couldn't guess. Sometimes I would walk in and she would tell me to take off my clothes, there and then. I would stand there, shivering, and she would run a finger over me. '"Ring a ring a roses, a pocket full of posies,"' she sang under her breath, as she pushed one, two, three, four into my dry skin.

That's a plague song, I wanted to say, but I knew that the way to make it all end, stop quickly, was to pretend it did not hurt, be practical and smiling, for soon she would turn me around, kiss my cheek and the nice things would begin.

I began to hug it to me. Hall, who had dressed her before, spent her days with Mrs Belle-Smyth. Until one day when she came to the kitchen where I was loading the tray for tea and spat at me.

'She has been dismissed,' said Mrs Evans, after the door slammed, and it was then I understood who Miss Edwarda had used before me. I mentioned Hall's name the next day to her while tidying her hair, and she hardly flinched. That was something I knew then too: she could forget.

With Hall gone, I was Miss Edwarda's maid all the time, taking care of her clothes, and dressing her in the evening. I expect they thought it an excellent way of saving money because they didn't appoint a new maid in my place, and it wasn't as if the other girls would take on my duties. I was at the house's command for most of the day, and from the evening onwards, I was hers.

I felt as if there were two of me. One could be doing what I did every day, dusting the ornaments, tidying the rooms while they had breakfast, serving meals, loading the tea tray, and the other was someone quite different, a girl pulled about and falling, taken over by nothing but thought, and then, more shameful things, begging and pleading, demanding. My duties, more and more, would wind into my evening self: the soft silk of the gowns wrapping themselves around my hand as I reached for her, the hairs on the back of her neck so delicate as I ran my hand up – and kissed the naked skin beneath. And the waxy cream she gave me to smooth on her was a delight. I covered each leg in turn, first the foot, massaging it in slowly, then moving up to the ankle, gently stroking the bone on the side until she moaned. I let my fingers spread up to the calf and to the knee, until she was leaning back and sighing, not looking at me at all. I tapped my fingers up the skin of the thigh, circling every mole and the little pimples she said were caused by too much oil under the skin – they would go, she said, if I massaged her correctly. I tracked the raised blue veins with my forefinger and rubbed the roughish skin at the side of her rump. Then, when she was arching her back, moaning and running her hand over her bodice, I took my hand and the cream to the softness inside her thigh, and from there I moved my fingers towards the part of her that only I knew, that every time surprised me with its slight ugliness, and made me think of what it would be like to go deep under her skin.

I thought it then: *I will make you mine.*

10. Silk Street

It was the middle of July and the city was heating every day. In the morning, white air burnt the street. I felt the light streaming through the glass of my window, throwing fire across my face. I could not imagine the sky ever growing chill once more. The farmland past Chiswick was brown with the sun, the newspapers reported. The pigs and cows must be taken out further to Oxford, if London was to be fed. The Thames was sinking low and sometimes boats could not pass. The old were dying, we were told, and dogs expired of heat behind wealthy houses. Pumps ran dry. Visitors fainted on arrival in London and foreign ambassadors would not take posts in the city, for fear of disease. The doctors declared there would soon be another bout of the water sickness that had laid waste to so many seven years back.

I was hot and tired in my dresses and I dreamt of rain. In churches, they begged the heavens to open and feed our crops. I woke in sheets that were like flames. The floorboards razed the soles of my feet.

I watched my uncle bring his cup to his dry mouth. When visitors such as the Janissers were with us, he sipped delicately, conscious of his hands. With me, he gulped and slurped, eager to complete his meal and clamber to his study.

He turned his eye to me. 'As I have said, I believe you have not been writing in your book lately.'

I nodded. I had hardly touched the pages.

'Might you tell me why you have desisted?'

I bowed my head. 'I think perhaps I am not in such need of the book, Uncle.' *Last night I was wandering around with men and you did not know.*

He had given me the large brown notebook on the day after I arrived. 'Niece, I believe it would be a great discipline for you to write daily. You might describe your activities during the day and perhaps your thoughts about what you have seen and heard. You might explore your plans for the day to follow. I feel sure it would quicken your recovery.' He laid his hand on my shoulder. I was dizzied by his care, then, and how he had given me a home.

'I would take it as a great act of kindness if you were able to do so,' he continued. 'I know little about how to please young ladies. And you and I have so much time to make up. So, if you would write in the book, I could read and learn how to be a better friend to you.' He touched my hand. 'That, Catherine, is my cherished hope. I wish us to live as if you had always been here with me – or at least, ever since.' He broke off as my face flamed. 'There. I gave you pain. I know so little about young ladies.'

That night I had tried. I wrote down my thoughts about my room and my new life in Princes Street. I described the rose-coloured bedspread he had bought for me and the two dresses, leaf green and sky blue (he said his dear friend Mrs Belle-Smyth had advised him on the fashions for young ladies). He declared that she had shaken her head at the dingy room adorned with death masks and African dolls, so he had bought figurines of shepherdesses from Liverpool Street Market and put a bunch of fresh tulips in a vase on the table (after I had met her, I came back to my room and put the shepherdesses under my bed). Most wonderfully, he had also purchased a box of books. 'I remember your father telling me that you always had your nose in a book.' At Lavenderfields, we were never allowed books for they were deemed too stimulating.

I supposed he had merely asked the bookseller for a box and not asked after the contents, for there were novels: *The Romance of the Forest*, *The Castle of Otranto*, some I had never heard of, and then a small leather-bound volume with gold writing, *The Murderous Innocents*. Most young ladies would have been forbidden such a work, let alone such a one as I. The doctors commanded my aunt Athelinde to keep me in a 'realm of light', flowers and ponies and dolls. She tried, poor lady, but I wanted to pull the petals from the flowers, provoke the ponies into biting me and twist the heads off the dolls. For hours fat doctors told me to forget, waving chains at my eyes or rubbing my legs, and all I managed, as I grew older, was to think of my darkness when adults could not observe. In *The Murderous Innocents*, the young heroine was seized by a baron and taken to a murky castle in the countryside. As she began to wander the castle alone, she became sure children had been slaughtered there. I imagined the author as a tall, cold woman dressed in red or violet, living in a house that could almost have been a witch's lair. I read the book over and over, stowing it under the bed, in case my uncle came into my room.

I did not write about *The Murderous Innocents* in my journal, of course. I knew better than to do that, after those hours with the doctors. Girls and women should have empty, cheerful minds. I took up my pen and felt as if I were writing a story of my own. I would pretend to be a very different Catherine Sorgeiul, not strange and sorrowful with a mind full of disordered thoughts that made me cry out at night, but sunny with the contentment I found in life, thanks to the kindness of her uncle. I would leave the book outside my room and he would take it to read and replace it outside my door in the morning.

He was gratified by my words. 'Our Queen writes in her journal every day,' he declared. 'She began at the age of thirteen. You are like a queen, my dear.'

I pretended to smile, hoping a little that the words might come true and I might become the normal girl I professed to be. He read the pages so closely that he would ask me questions during the day. Did I really like strawberries? Why not asparagus? Which girl at the tea party had I found most appealing? I did not like his questions, but at least, with him, I had whole hours to myself: my uncle and aunt Cross had tormented me, and in Lavenderfields I was tied to the bed. I had to feign sweetness for he could send me away.

I had lost the only object I kept from Lavenderfields: a small cup from the collection they used to heat and place on my back to take the blood. I retained the scars and I wanted the cup too so I had stolen it. Now it was gone. Even though I was writing, my things were still disappearing.

'I am sorry, Uncle,' I said. 'I shall try to write once more.' I supposed the Queen did not always tell the truth in her journals.

'I am content.' He picked up his teacup once more. 'You are a good girl, Catherine. I wish you to be happy.'

I detested that word, *happy*: vapid and bare, a falsely smiling face. He had spoken similarly in the months after I had first arrived. Then I had thought he cared.

Last night, I was walking through streets you shall never know.

'How is business, Uncle?' I tried.

He looked at me over his cup. 'Reasonable. Even though travel is difficult.'

Thomas had left us the day after he and I returned from the Foundling Hospital. He told my uncle he wished to remain at home to ensure the safety of his wife and daughter. Although we still had the carriage and horses, there was nobody to drive them, and my uncle had to use public cabs.

We were about to sigh ourselves into nothingness once more when Jane arrived at the door. 'A young lady to see you, miss.' My face must have shown my surprise. 'Shall I show her in?'

'The lady's name?' asked my uncle.

'Miss Grey, sir.'

'Really?' I sat up.

'Is she a friend of yours, Catherine?'

I nodded, trying to pat strands of my hair into place. I was wearing my plainest blue dress and wished I had sponged off the stains as I had meant to do that morning. My uncle smoothed his hair.

'Well, show her in,' he said to Jane. 'And bring more tea.'

Our door opened and Miss Grey arrived, dipping slightly as she moved through the low doorway, hair frizzier than it had been at the party, face just as flushed. The floral skirt of her dress flurried around her. I had read once that the fashion for flowers on clothes began in the sixteenth century when ladies would embroider material to reflect their knowledge of plant medicine and midwifery. I could not imagine anyone turning the flowers on Miss Grey's skirt to any kind of use, for they were the type to exist for beauty, blossoming pink orchids, winding ivy, and leaves the size of hands.

'Miss Grey,' said my uncle, standing. 'How delightful to meet a friend of my dear niece. And you are a cousin of the Janissers, I believe?'

She swept her skirt under her and sat on my uncle's rickety chair. The legs were too low and tipped to one side but she kept herself upright, as if she were the stem of a glass.

I smiled at her. 'I am gratified by your visit.' Her expensive dress soaked up all the light, and the air was hurrying to settle around her, leaving us exposed. *Why are you here?* I looked at her thin lips and her eyes like black dots and nothing gave me the answer. The demands of being a young lady. All the industries in the city devoted to making our gowns and dainty shoes, binding our books, polishing our necklaces, hewing the wood for our pianofortes, boiling sugar in vats for sweetmeats to tempt us. In the streets where I walked last night, children burnt their fingers in acid to make the metal for our bracelets, women lost their eyesight to stitch our boots. Whole houses of people poisoned themselves to make us beautiful.

Jane arrived and I poured the tea. My uncle started to ask polite questions about the Janissers. Miss Grey's gaze flickered around the pictures, the ornaments, the falling furniture, her face surprised and her pupils huge, thanks to the gloom. I sat back. Perhaps I seemed to her a giant female spider in the midst of a dew-dropped web. Then she turned to me. 'I enjoyed our conversation at the Belle-Smyth's, she said, one long-fingered hand on the twisting green of her lap.

I thought again that her vowels must come from the coast, pale cliffs dropping into the sea. 'The tea party was pleasant.' What would our society be without that word? Mr Tilney's tirade in *Northanger Abbey* flittered in my head: *This is a very nice day . . . you are two very nice young ladies.*

'We received a visit from the Janissers,' declared my uncle. 'How happy you must be to live with your cousin.'

'Indeed.'

'And you are also the cousin of the Belle-Smyths. How fortunate to have such an extended family.' His eyes dropped to her ring. 'My niece and I have only each other.'

She nodded. I wondered if Miss Grey was loved by the Janissers or merely tolerated. I supposed she had been sent by her family in the country to live in town and find a husband.

'My aunt, uncle and cousin passed a pleasant visit.' She looked at me archly. 'An impression was made.'

'I am sure scant compared to the impression Miss Grey must always make.' My uncle turned to me in anger, but as soon as I had said the words, I regretted each one. *You must learn to live in the world*, Dr Neville told me. *Feign.* She looked at her hands, folded in her lap. Perhaps, I was struck, she was an orphan, like me.

'Tea, Miss Grey?' The shortbread Jane had brought was lumpy. The flour was adulterated, I supposed. 'Your cousin is a gentleman.' This took me some effort to say.

My uncle began to say the same, praising his work at Janisser & Smyth. I gazed down at my hands. The dirt of the street was still under my nails. I brought my hands to my nose – and remembered when I had become all fear.

I looked up and my uncle was standing. 'That was the door, my dear. I believe Mr Trelawny may be here.' He turned to Miss Grey. 'Mr Trelawny is a great friend of mine, and also of your uncle's. I know how much he would like to meet you.'

Mr Trelawny and Mr Janisser? I stared at my uncle,

but had no time to think because as soon as the door closed she pitched forward in her chair.

'I wanted to ask you,' she whispered, hurrying as if water were pouring between us. 'Grace Starling. Edwarda's maid. She is here, yes?'

'My uncle sent her away. I do not know where she is.'

'I am sure you, too, visited her for hair. She was an artist on the face, I think.' She gave a wry smile. 'She made me almost pretty.'

'She never styled my hair.' I held hard to the wood.

'Really? Ah.' But she did not dwell, she rushed on. 'I wanted to speak to you. I do not think she is a good maid. I do not think any of them are good.'

'I found her satisfactory.' My scalp prickled as if Grace's hands were burrowing in and pulling at my hair.

Her eyes widened. 'You talk to people too much, Miss Sorgeiul.'

We looked at the door. I could hear the rumble of Mr Trelawny's voice outside.

'What do you mean?'

She leant forward again. 'I saw your face at the tea party. You are interested in the murders. You show it.'

I could not speak. I looked at the window. Mr Kent was passing and he raised his hat. I thought he would burn his fair skin if he continued wandering in the afternoons.

'Forgive me, Miss Sorgeiul. I remember her little hands twisting my hair and her questions. "Are your parents from London, miss?" She was one of those maids, I could tell, hunting out secrets.' She looked at me delicately. 'Surely she must have asked you.'

'I never noticed.'

'Miss Edwarda was always too close to her. Did you not think?'

There was a bang from outside, footsteps, voices, and we both sat up. She raised her voice. 'Anyway, a magician and his assistant have ceased performing their usual illusions. Instead they play out the deaths of the girls. They perform at the Egyptian Hall in Piccadilly, so it is quite respectable. You should come. Tomorrow afternoon.' She blinked and I noticed her long eyelashes. 'My cousin will be there.'

I shook my head.

'I very much wish you would, Miss Sorgeiul. I have no friends in Miss Edwarda and Miss Lucinda.'

Her smile was gentle, but still I could not agree. Grace danced behind my eyes. 'I have an engagement I cannot break.'

'If you change your mind, send a message.'

The door opened and my uncle came in with Mr Trelawny. He walked up to her and seized her hand. 'Miss Grey, I presume,' he said, his voice snaking low. 'What a pleasure.'

I saw that she wanted to snatch her hand back. I wished I could thrust him from the door.

'Have you come far, Miss Grey?' he was saying. 'What an appealing dress.' He moved his hand towards the fabric. 'I am so very fond of flowers.'

'I must depart,' she said, the distaste open on her face. 'My aunt expects me.'

'So soon?' he lisped.

'Thank you for the tea, Miss Sorgeiul, Mr Crenaban.' She shook out her dress and then she directed her gaze to my uncle. 'Tomorrow at five, my cousin Janisser and I plan to see a show at the Egyptian Hall.' She dipped her shoulder and I watched him follow every move with his eyes, as if he were drawing her. 'I hope Miss Sorgeiul might change her mind and agree to accompany us.'

There was a silence. 'A kind invitation,' he pronounced. 'Would you come for Miss Sorgeiul in the Janisser carriage?'

'My cousin and I shall discuss the matter.'

She nodded, and left. Mr Trelawny sloped to the window to watch her leave. 'A pretty young lady. And she is engaged.'

'So I believe.'

'Her aunt and uncle must surely be sad to lose her, do you not think, Miss Sorgeiul?'

'I really do not know.'

He was touching the window-pane, almost pressing his face against it. I made a movement to leave but my uncle was still beside the doorway, where he had stood to usher out Miss Grey. 'So you have refused an invitation. What is your reason?'

'I do not wish to attend.'

'We cannot always live as we wish, Catherine. We will

discuss the matter further tomorrow.' He looked at his friend, still hunched at the window. 'Come, sir.'

Then, finally, at five o'clock, I thought I might be able to record the events of last night. I took out my book from behind the bureau and sat at the table. I held my pen, but the words were cold.

On the previous night, when I had come back and thrown myself into bed, I was pure, with nothing in my mind but me and him, together in the alleyway. I became for a moment only fear, and that was what they were, Abigail, Sara, Jenny and the others he would find.

I put my head into my hands and tried to ignore the sound of Mr Trelawny and my uncle moving about upstairs, scraping their chairs and banging doors. Perhaps if I climbed upstairs to my room and lay on my bed, my mind might rest. I crept up the stairs quietly so they could not hear. The door had blown open, which was rare. I closed it and pushed the chair against the knob. Jane had made the bed but I wondered if some of my thoughts might still be there, huddling in the woolly stiffness of the blankets, burrowed in the cushions bought on the advice of Mrs Belle-Smyth. I lay back. And then I became aware of a low hum. I closed my eyes but the sound remained. I realized that it was coming from under my bed. I scrambled off and found a full-grown glossy cat curled up by the pot, looking at me with eyes the colour of amber beads, entirely black, save for a white streak over his forehead. He must have wandered in when Miss Grey arrived. I reached out to touch him and he recoiled. Perhaps, I thought, he has been mistreated and is hiding here.

'You are safe with me, Mr Cat,' I told him. 'I shall give you a name. Crispin.' I'd thought of Crow, but that seemed cruel.

I lay back on the bed and closed my eyes. *Come*, I said to the Man of Crows, as Crispin purred. *Come to me.* I started to imagine my route to the alleyway, down Calvert Street and Paisley Street, through crowds of people who looked like dead souls. But other thoughts came instead. Grace flashed through my mind, touching my shoulder, smiling. And her words: *Your uncle is friendly with Mr Belle-Smyth, is he not? I wonder what they discuss. You must miss your family. How young you are to be an orphan.*

I asked her how she had come to me.

'I met your uncle at the house of Mr Belle-Smyth. He was very eager to talk. He said I should come here. Interesting words he said about you.'

Her hand on mine, tracing her name. Such tiny things, little movements, only ten or twelve at most, and I had given up so much. *Where are you?* Walking the same streets as the Man of Crows. My mind tossed black.

11. Lavenderfields

As a child, I used to like to stand near the stove and watch the hot saucepan, hanging in the cook's way. When you heat water, nothing happens for a while. The bubbles begin on the base of the pan, so small you can hardly see them. And then they grow larger and rise until they are bubbling hard, cannot be stopped and the water will never quite return to what it was.

'I cannot stand any more of it,' said my aunt Cross, lifting her hand from the couch. 'My nerves will not bear it. What she does to little Tommy.' She laid her hand over Uncle Cross's. 'Anthony. You must think of the welfare of your own child.'

I detested my cousin Tommy, a plump redhead good only for hiding my hairpins. After my aunt Athelinde in Oxford had fallen ill, I had come to my only other relations on my father's side, Uncle and Aunt Cross. Tommy left a frog in my dressing-table on the day after I arrived. After that, his campaign was incessant. I presume he had practised on the housemaids before me. He put pins on my chair, jam under the table to catch my knees, and dirt in my books. The first few times, I pretended not to notice, hoping he would desist. When I told my aunt, she called me a liar. He intensified his activities, then, busying himself with stealing my things, taking the ribbons from my bodices or dropping pots and boxes on my bedroom floor. Mice burrowed in my drawers, lice licked at my hair pomade and once I found a host of spiders in my shoes. He blamed on me everything that went missing or broken in the house.

My aunt Cross disliked me. She said I was sly and cold, and could not be trusted. And then there was my past. I had no innocence. I would pollute Tommy. Uncle Cross agreed. He came to me one morning. 'There is a doctor you should see,' he said. 'He would help your headaches.'

I cannot stand it, she said, and so began the round of doctors. I recall their rooms: the pale plum edging decorating Dr Smithson's walls; Dr Kelly's green curtains; the painting of limpid women in medieval dresses over Dr Hazell's desk; and the dolls propped up on Dr Eyre's shelves that his daughter had grown out of but he could not bear to throw away. It was the ceilings I remembered most of all: I lay on my back for hours, staring at cracks running out of the cornices or bumps in the plaster while they poked and prodded, asked about my childhood while they squeezed my arms. So many doctors, each producing a different version of me. I heard my aunt and uncle discussing their reports. Dr Smithson judged me insane. Dr Kelly thought I was confused and should take a cold bath every morning. Dr Hazell recommended I be tied and bound in a jacket each day, and Dr Eyre believed me overeducated and in need of a husband. In the end, my aunt chose the one best suited to her.

One Wednesday morning, I was called down to the

parlour. Two large women sat on the ottoman, side by side. One had a red face that looked as if it were carved out of scone dough. The other was younger and her more delicate features made her appear – oh, how deluded I was – kinder.

'Catherine,' said Uncle Cross. 'Miss Smith and Miss Welsh.'

'Good morning.' The elder woman – Smith – nodded. And then, as if a bell had rung, they moved towards me. Smith seized my arm and I gasped. Welsh did the same and, in one swift movement, pulled my elbow behind my back. I threw my head up and cried out as the pressure of their hands pushed me to the door. And then I saw my aunt's face. She was not horror-struck or protesting but creamily content, her hands resting lightly on her skirts, the corners of her mouth turned up in a cool, incipient smile.

'Good girl,' said Welsh.

I remembered fragments after that. I knew – as Dr Neville said – that I should not remember at all, but I could not help myself. I scratched at my wound, confusing repetition with investigation, control. The yellow green of burnt summer grass outside as Smith and Welsh dragged me along the drive. The carriage doors as they slammed on me, then the hoofs of the first horse, the cold leather of the seats and the dark blot – blood? – on the wood frame next to the covered window. I cried out, screaming, hammering on the walls, begging them to stop, that my uncle did not wish it. I probably kept it up for less than half an hour.

Dr Johnson said that the prospect of death concentrates the mind. This was, for me at least, not true. No great thoughts came into my head, no insights, no notions of the world. There was only numbness. I sat there, stared at the leather walls and wondered how long I had to wait. I briefly thought of a Gothic castle, as Mrs Radcliffe might write about, but really I imagined I was destined for a school for girls who had been a little difficult. I should have known my aunt Cross better.

Smith opened the door of the carriage and said, 'Now, you had better behave nicely and come quietly or you don't know what we will do.' She turned to two men at the side. 'This one's not a screamer. She can walk.' I emerged into the dull September light.

My first vision of the house: grand brown brick set back against a long range of grass. It was almost beautiful. At the front, women in white outfits supported – what? Things. Hunchbacked, dirty-looking things with threads of hair over haggard faces.

Now I reached down for the cat but he evaded my hand. I was alone with my thoughts.

'Come, miss, quicker than that.' Then the door and a cold corridor, both nurses holding tightly to my arms, pushing me along, until we reached a room where they propelled me into a red-leather chair. A doctor prodded me in all the usual places but with none of the unctuous words, such as, *Does this give you pain, madam?* He put a finger into my mouth and to the back of my throat. Next, Welsh and Smith were holding me in the bath, scrubbing at my hair.

Then the days rolled, one after another, into one. Pills in the morning and at night, three brown, two white, took my mind away on a cloud and hid the dreams that flayed my soul.

Dr Neville was right. I should not think of it. The screams of Miss Brent and the moans of Miss Angel – soon my mind was wandering in circles and I felt as if I were doomed to return there. I would do anything to prevent that, marry Janisser, anything.

And then Grace Starling danced through my mind, throwing her skirts behind her. 'Did you think I liked you?' she called. 'I only wished to make you afraid.' A church, too high to reach, arched over my eyes.

I woke to sunlight streaming through the breaks in the shutters. My head was heavy and I could barely put my feet to the ground. I called for Jane, but there was no response. I set off along the corridor in my nightdress, stepping carefully to avoid splinters. By the fifth board, my head was falling on my shoulders and my eyes were dizzy. I leant against the wall.

I moved towards my uncle's study so I might prop myself on the heavy frame of the door. But as I dropped against it, the wood gave a little. I stared at the panels, hardly able to credit it. The door was unlocked, a sliver of light bending through.

'Uncle,' I almost whispered. 'Are you there?' There was only silence. I walked to the banisters. 'Uncle?' I edged to the stairs and called for Jane. There was a soft heat at my legs and I looked down to see Crispin weaving around my calves.

I called for Jane once more. 'Do you know if my uncle is at home?' There was no answer. I hurried down to the kitchen, opened the door and saw that her coat and shoes were not there. She had not come. The one day she was ill, she had sent a note with her little brother, so she must be late and on her way. I did not have much time. I closed the door and went back up the stairs. They had left me alone – and the house was mine.

At the top of the stairs, Crispin waited for me, purring. I held tight to the banister and looked at the open door. In eight months, I had never entered the study, never seen so much as a crack behind my uncle as he closed the door. The floorboards sighed with the weight of the house as they always did. I pushed the mahogany panels and put my hand on the wall. The curtains were closed and I did not dare light a candle.

I moved forward and tried to take in what I saw. I had always imagined an orthodox kind of study, a large desk by the window and shelves of books – a little like Dr Neville's but without the couch. Instead I felt as if I were in a shop of old things. The shelves were heavy with leather books, jumbled with ornaments, stones and glassy rocks, shapes of golden wire, little dolls, glass globes. The confusion muddled my eyes. I had heard about proposals for an underground store for London's museums, a vault under the busy carriages of Holborn filled with the items for which they did not have space on the shelves, rocks and statues cluttered together, like bodies in a graveyard. Except the items owned by the museums were precious, and my uncle had odd-looking things that did not look as if they were worth much at all. He had wandered Africa, India, China, picking up stones at bazaars and masks made of wood, bargaining for them in exotic languages, giving them to his servant to pack up and send home – and for what? To adorn a room at the top of his house that only Mr Trelawny saw? I turned away. The walls were covered with prints I could not make out and the floor was bare, some of the boards upended. At the sides of the room there were large globes and then an open-sided bookshelf, full of glass bottles. Over the fire hung a heavy black cauldron. A red *chaise-longue* touched one wall.

In the centre, a desk was covered with maps and splayed books. Crispin jumped up and perched on the edge. I moved there, put out my hand and felt the dryness of the paper. I looked at the marks of roads and houses and understood I was looking at a map of the area nearby. I reached down and traced Virginia Road and Swan Street and touched the spot of the alleyway where I had been, for it was not marked on the map.

I fingered through the maps. Each one was of London, folded to the section in the east. The places I had gone. Swan Street, Spitalfields, St Sepulchre. Then I saw a cross on Swan Street and wanted to take my hand to my mouth and bite my nails. *They were watching the Man of Crows.*

I moved my hand down, and under all the maps there

was a large book, leather-bound and old. I touched the spine and flecks of gold spittered to my finger. This was what they really cared about, I could feel. I walked to the door and listened, but there was no sound of anyone. I returned and carefully pulled the maps from the top until I was touching the cover. The room was so silent that Crispin's purring was as loud as a lion's might be. I opened the book and a puff of grey dust smoked into the air and dropped to my face and chest. I turned the first heavy page and looked down at lines of symbols and signs, swathes of black ink, some coloured blue and gold. I thought a little of monks illuminating letters and turned the next page. The letters again. My head throbbed. *Something is going to happen.* On the fourth page, the symbols were punctuated with figures of stick people. A stick girl wandered at the bottom of the page. The paper was so heavy that I had to use both hands to turn the pages.

I was turning towards what looked like a large portrait of a woman's face, when there was a sound from the door downstairs. I threw the book closed, put the maps back in order and hurried to the door.

The bottom stair creaked. I rushed for my room, pulling the door to behind me. Only when I had flung myself on my bed did I realize that Crispin was not with me. I had left him behind.

12. Piccadilly

'An intriguing trick, do you not think, Miss Sorgeiul?' Constantine Janisser's mouth was very close to my ear. He was as awkward as ever and a fleck of soap had lodged in his hairline.

'Indeed,' I managed. We were sitting in the Egyptian Hall, watching the show, and I did not like it. I was only there because, afraid of my thoughts, I had sent a message to Miss Grey that I would accompany them. Jane still had not appeared, so I called from the back room to Mr Kent, bent over his roses in the garden, to ask if his mother might send over her maid. Emily was a sweet-faced girl with quick hands. I sat at the show in my second-best blue dress and the Egyptian necklace, with my corset pulled very tight.

I had not been to the theatre or a show since I was a child. I had read about the Egyptian Hall, and my father had described the place to me for he came here to see Napoleon's carriage, just after the war. The building I had seen in pictures was grand and imposing, the heavy pillars standing out on Piccadilly with their guardian gods, the ornate decorations covering the walls. This place was hot and cluttered, paintings of the Pyramids and men on camels, splintered seats and threadbare curtains over the stage. It, too, was suffering the shortages: the reddish paint on the pillars was peeling, the false mummies were rubbing clean of paint. Over the centre of the stage a statue of Anubis soared too high for us to see if he was losing his gilt. Under him, the Golden Prince was performing.

In the carriage on the way there, Miss Grey had told me that the show was deemed quite terrifying. I could not say that I agreed.

A tallish, dark-haired young man in long red and gold robes stood at the front, propped up on high heels and waving his wand. The show began when he sprang out of a burst of white fireworks and announced that once upon a time he had performed ordinary tricks, such as sawing a lady in half, but the current crisis in the city had given him a project of greater urgency.

'Everyone tries to understand the awful deaths,' he shouted. 'Judges, lawyers, people who believe themselves sleuths. But the way to discover the truth of what has been occurring is to explore the crimes through magic.' He stepped back and flourished his arm. 'Tonight I am the Man of Crows!'

Constantine was looking at me so I stared ahead, trying to appear as if I were suffering boredom. The bad thoughts, those that had most colour, were pulling through my mind. I was surprised to feel Miss Grey's hand pat my arm.

A slender girl with brown hair and the type of face that would look well in a soap advertisement flounced out of the side stage in a long, unfashionable dress. The magician pronounced her his Cleopatra, found in Egypt dancing around the Pyramids. 'I am Abigail Greengrass,' she cried, in a reedy London voice. 'I am a milliner's assistant on my way home.'

'Just look at her,' called the magician. 'Beautiful, young, her whole life ahead of her. The Man picked on her for no reason. He could have chosen anyone.' He flurried his cape. 'Ladies! It might have been you.'

I turned around and saw that every eye was upon him, agog and fascinated. 'Does he really do this so very often?' I said to Miss Grey. 'He has drawn such a crowd.'

'The show is apparently very successful. Is it not, Cousin?' Each time she spoke, she directed words to him.

My corset was a little painful and I wanted to cough. 'I cannot see why.' The magician pattered on about the hot bricks in the streets, the mist in the sky, the dark stars, and I stared at the painting of the Pyramids on the nearest wall. He would tell the story of Sara Shell, he declared and began speaking as his assistant feigned terror. He added the names of some other girls that I knew were invented – simply excuses for his Cleopatra to wear wigs of different colours and change her dress. At the interval, Constantine hunched off to fetch us refreshments while Miss Grey and I perched on a small bench under a picture of a temple.

I wanted to seize her hand. 'I have been thinking of what you said about Grace Starling.'

She shook her head with a little smile. 'Let us not speak of it in a place of resort.'

'No one will hear.'

‘I do not think a discussion wise.’

‘I suppose you are right.’ She probably thought that she was always listened to, living with the Janissers. ‘Are you truly interested in this?’ Next to the puff of her brown silk sleeve, she was wearing a bracelet of violet stones, amethysts, perhaps. I wondered if it had been a gift from Mr Prior.

She shrugged. ‘Not really. The magician has charisma.’ Her pale hair was curled, rather than tangled and puffed, and it looked pretty, made her more so.

‘Did you see magic shows as a child?’

‘Never.’ I decided she did not wish to discuss her family. Perhaps they were not in the country, as I had once thought, playing ball on rolling hills near the sea, but had died in a respectable kind of fashion, maybe in the sinking of a pleasure boat one Sunday afternoon on the Thames. A smartly dressed man passed and tipped his hat. ‘Good evening, ladies.’ We did not answer. Perhaps the murder on stage inspired everyone to boldness.

I looked down at her hands and her ring. I could not resist asking, ‘Did you think of coming here with Mr Prior?’

‘No.’ She did not look up. Her sadness glimmered in the silence and I felt immediately cruel. I did not like to answer questions, yet I had demanded one of her and caused her pain. I looked at her stroking the violet stones and tried to think of what I could say to return her to feelings of friendship.

‘I was so very pleased to receive your visit,’ I said. ‘So few people come nowadays. I think they are afraid of the crime.' For that, I received a nod. I forged on. 'Perhaps I do not always welcome visitors as I should.'

'My comb looks well,' she said, touching a turquoise ornament propped in her frizzy hair. A long feather came out at the side. 'I like it very much.'

'Yes.' Presumably, she was trying to turn the conversation. A plump woman squeezed into a pink-striped dress shuffled past carrying three dripping ices. I could see that the line Constantine had joined was very long.

Miss Grey started to speak and coughed. Her face had reddened and little bumps had sprung up around her nose, caused by the heat, I supposed. My mother had a maid who suffered from the same complaint. She touched the bracelet once more and I thought that I had hurt her by asking about Mr Prior. I thought of her living with the Janissers, always the poor relation, making way for Mrs Janisser to stand by the fire, and I felt heartless and unfair.

'I wondered –' I began, but she interrupted me.

'Who was that gentleman with your uncle? Is he a colleague in business?'

'Mr Trelawny. No – or, well, perhaps they once were. They are friends.'

She was looking straight ahead and I could not see her expression. A small curl edged around her ear and the drop of the pearl earring. 'What is his occupation?'

'I do not know. I have never asked.' I would not like to feel a hole put in my own ear.

'He has a family of his own?'

'Well, I cannot say. I know very little about him.' I had

thought him simply a friend of my uncle. My uncle's only friend, really.

'He is peculiar.' She paused, looked at me and began to rush her speech. 'Miss Sorgeiul, forgive me, but I feel I must speak. Your uncle does not seem to attend much to your wishes. Surely your situation cannot be happy.'

I stared at her in wonder. *Do the Janissers care very much for you?* I wanted to ask. Then a shadow leant over us and there was Constantine, bearing two ices about to turn into water. 'I took such a very long time,' he fretted. 'There were many people waiting.'

Miss Grey bowed her head. 'I was speaking to Miss Sorgeiul about her uncle's friend, Mr Trelawny. I have never met anyone like him.'

'Indeed? I have not encountered the gentleman. I tell you who is a perplexing one, though. That neighbour of yours, what is his name?'

'Mr Kent.'

'When my parents and I paid a visit, he was standing outside his door, holding feathers. His face did not show the most intelligent of expressions.'

'He studies at the Royal Academy. My uncle heard he was trying to paint fairies. I suppose he uses the feathers.' I looked as hair flopped over his forehead and his long eyelashes, and put down my ice. 'This is too wet to eat. We should return to our places. Quite a spectacle awaits us, watching her fall over and spread herself with red fluid – again.'

We settled back into our seats and Miss Grey clutched her ice. Two new people were sitting in front of us – a large, grey-haired woman and a man in a tall hat. I would have to crane past it to see.

'Now for an interlude,' announced the magician. He brandished a box in the air and passed it to his assistant to place on the table. She waved her hands back and forth.

'This is the box of change,' he called. He brandished a piece of red silk and drew out a gold coin. 'Regard.'

The assistant held up the box and showed us the sides, the top and even opened the back to prove it was empty. She handed it back to him and he placed the coin inside. 'Behold!' he cried, as he drew the box to his bosom, and dropped over it a cover of red silk. Then he shook his parcel, shouted some odd-sounding words, and a man from behind the stage slid a cover over the candle burning in the centre. He began to shout again, crying words in a fast, high-pitched voice. The man returned, relit the candle and our magician flourished his hands, threw off the red silk and gave one shake of the box. It fell quite open and up flew two large white doves.

I heard Mr Janisser cough as the birds fluttered and landed on the outstretched hands of the assistant – one on each. The magician clicked his fingers and they flew to him. He moved his arms up and down slowly and the birds stayed with him, as if they adhered to his nails. I watched him, caught by what he was doing, hardly feeling Miss Grey shift at my side. He opened his arms, bent forward slightly, shook his dark hair and looked out at us. I felt that his gaze was directed at me. I wanted to give my hand to him. Then he clicked two free fingers, looked upwards and the birds soared off his hands, crossed over his head and flapped down into the box, held by the assistant. She closed the lid and passed it to him. He shook the red cloth over the top and called out the words. He turned, pulled off the cloth – and the box was gone.

The crowd gasped and he bowed to us.

'That was impressive,' pronounced Constantine. 'No seeing how he did it.'

'I feel afraid of him now,' said Miss Grey. I imagined her as a little girl, playing on the sands with her brothers and sisters, expecting to live with them for ever.

'I hope that the next trick is similar,' declared Constantine, as we burst into applause, 'although I suspect we may return to the previous routine.'

He was correct. The assistant emerged, dressed in white, covered herself with red stuff and fell over, screaming. 'Abigail Greengrass,' intoned the magician. After a brief pause, she pretended to be Sara Shell, wearing a satin dress like a dancer's with a shiny red rose at her hip. She fell, covered again with red liquid, and he jumped forward, waving his hand. 'I shall show you the girls to come,' he cried. 'I shall reveal to you your fate, if you too find yourselves in the wrong part of town.' He started to set the scene, describing hot, dim streets, damp walls, girls struggling home, wading through mud, manure on their skirts. Then the assistant sauntered out on to the stage in a pale dress. We watched him follow her, creeping, holding a knife. 'I am the Man of Crows!' he shouted.

'I do not believe I can stand much more.' The heat of the hall was pressing on us and my back hurt from sitting straight. 'Surely there is a tea-room nearby, Miss Grey.'

'I have heard there is a very impressive finale,' Constantine replied, not looking at me. 'He first suggests that the whole city bears responsibility, for not protecting the women, then acts his own execution. He hangs himself so convincingly that one believes he is truly dead.'

'He hangs himself?' Miss Grey's allergy-reddened face was pained. 'Surely such a thing is not possible. It cannot be allowed.'

'He has the noose and the hood. I expect he simply does something clever and does not tighten the noose too much. Apparently, the trick is very dramatic. Ladies faint.'

Her cheeks grew pinker and I felt for her. 'We both might faint,' I declared. I felt her stiffen slightly beside me.

'Indeed?' he said. When he looked at me I felt jolted. 'I believe that this finale is what makes his show so famous. The executioner becomes the executed, as it were. I am spoiling the surprise for you, ladies.'

He was pleased with himself to be able to impart such information. His eyes were light under his thick eyebrows.

Miss Grey was still red and confused, and more bumps were emerging on her cheeks and under her eyes. 'But what of these people here?' she was saying. 'There are *children!*' Her arm twitched in its brown silk.

'My dear cous, what do you propose? I tell those lumbering elephants they may feel afraid. I doubt a thing has ever frightened them in their lives. Do be reasonable.' He turned to me. 'You are not so easily frightened, Miss Sorgeiul, surely.'

I opened my mouth but Miss Grey broke in: 'Oh, her!' she said, her voice low and angry. 'Why should she be afraid? I do not believe she thinks of anything but death.' She stood, picked up her skirts and hurried off, pushing her way through the people who jostled her and looked disapprovingly at her cousin and me.

'I have offended her,' I said to him.

'My poor cousin.' He lowered his voice. 'Her engagement with Mr Prior has ended. My father closed it yesterday evening.'

How cruel I had been. 'I am sorry. I thought the prospects a matter of pride to your family.'

'So I believed. But my father has made the decision.'

I wondered if he thought Miss Grey poorly treated by his family. 'There is no chance of a reunion?'

'None, I think.'

On stage, the girl was crying out again. I thought of Miss Grey, hoping to be married, and now what? I wanted to ask if she had many suitors, but he began putting forth polite questions about my uncle. I almost felt as if I should offer him a confidence, as he had given to me, but I could think of no words that were safe. *I am full of sin*, I could not say. *I detest your cousins. I suspect my uncle's business is unsuccessful and I worry he will lose all his money*.

Perhaps my confusion showed on my face for he asked about Princes Street and the size of the rear garden. I told him about the old oak tree. He began asking about parks, and whether I took walks – the assistant was falling on the stage and screaming – when Miss Grey returned, wiping her nose, her face more inflamed than ever. She held her dress stiffly. I saw she had expected we would follow her. I had been thoughtless.

'More girls are dead,' I said quickly, before Constantine could speak.

She gave a weak smile and the red spots on her face faded a little.

'The grand finale approaches,' he said.

'I shall not stay,' she declared. 'I do not wish to see a man hanged.'

'Did you ever see a public execution, Miss Sorgeiul?' said Constantine. 'We were forbidden to. My father dubbed the practice disgraceful.'

'I never have,' I lied.

'My father was correct. Imagine having to die in front of strangers.'

My uncle Crenaban had taken me to an execution when I was six or seven. In those days he was often calling to see my parents, and Louis and I would delight in how tall he was – he almost hit the ceilings. He would take my brother and me to the fair or the British Museum and to walk in Hyde Park. Louis went to school, and my uncle continued to take me out. One day we walked to St Paul's and to the City. We arrived on a grassy patch outside some high walls where families were sitting with picnics. I begged my uncle to buy me a gingerbread man from one of the stalls. He picked me up, set me on his shoulders, and I saw a wooden frame, then three heads.

'They do not tie the legs together,' he said. 'I believe they should, for sometimes a taller prisoner can succeed at putting his feet down either side of the trap door.' Then he swung me down and hurried me away. The crowd gave a great scream. I understood later that the place had been Newgate Prison and the people were waiting for the men to fall and begin kicking for their lives.

Not two months later, my uncle departed for overseas and visited, as my mother tended to say, if anyone asked, 'Japan and China and heaven knows where else.' I suppose he was quite young then, twenty-nine or thirty. He returned when I was nearly ten, his arms heavy with bundles of dried fish and odd flowers. We had our old uncle back. Sunday teas began again. He was more wrinkled than before, full of stories about ships and curious animals. He took me out alone, on Saturdays and sometimes on Wednesdays too – to a tea-room and to the great shops, but also just to walk around the park and watch the ladies on their horses. I felt quite grown-up. He escorted me home and then he would stay to eat with my parents after I had gone to bed.

After four or five months of this, in October or so, I was lying upstairs in bed when I heard my father cry out. I could not hear the words but the raised voice of my father and my mother's weeping came through the walls. And then there was more shouting and the sound of something dropping to the floor, my mother screaming and the front door crashing shut. I got out of bed to run to the window, but then I heard my parents start up the stairs so I pushed myself under the covers and pretended to sleep. My father tossed open the door and his face was small with fury, like that of a tiny baby who believed he had been left alone. My mother was holding his arm. 'Be reasonable, John,' she was saying, tears splashing down her face. He threw her off and strode to the bed.

I looked at him, not pretending to be asleep, frozen in fear. My father was so mild that everyone said my mother was the one in charge. But his face was so angry that I cowered, sure he wanted to hit me. He came to the side of my bed and I thought he was about to grasp my hair. My mother hung on him, begging him to stop.

'You will never see your uncle Crenaban again. Do you understand? If he writes to you, you will throw the letter away and tell me. If you see him in the street, you will ignore him and you will tell me. Do you understand?'

I meant to speak but the words would not come. He reached down and pulled my arm from under the covers. 'You will obey me!'

'Of course she will, John,' my mother gabbled. 'Catherine is a good girl.'

'Is she? Will she obey?' he shouted. I thought the walls must be shaking with his rage.

I managed to nod. 'Yes, Papa.' He stood for a little

while, looking down, and I thought I saw his face soften. That was when I made my mistake. 'So I shall never see Uncle Crenaban again?'

He seized my arm, anger flooding his face. 'You shall miss him, shall you? You shall miss your conversations?'

At this, my mother rose up. 'Stop, John. She is only a child. Let us go downstairs. She does not understand.' While she was speaking, she was manoeuvring him away from my bed and he began to walk with her. He did not look back as they closed the door.

Next morning, my father was not at breakfast. My mother was quiet, her eyes shadowed, and we did not speak. Nothing was said and our life continued as it had done, without my uncle, until the day that Dr Neville said I should call a terrible stroke of fate, but I could not, for fate is the fault of nobody and what I had done spread dark wings of pain over all.

From time to time, since I had come to live at Princes Street, I had thought of mentioning those afternoons we spent walking around the park or visiting the British Museum. But my uncle seemed different and those days like another time, other people. We spoke as distant relations, which I knew was as I deserved, considering what I had done.

'Miss Sorgeiul.' Constantine touched my shoulder. 'We are due for a dramatic scene.'

I looked at the stage. There stood the magician, flashing his gold and red cape, his black shoes shiny with polish. 'These young women,' he shouted, 'are like the sacrificial victims of Ancient Greece and all women in history put to death for our desires. Ladies and gentlemen, this is true. Yes, sir, you, in the top hat at the front row. Yes, madam, respectable lady in the fine blue dress, you destroyed Abigail and Sara and Jenny and the others who shall come. We all killed them because we do not protect our females. No! We let our young ladies wander the streets. Miss Vine here. I discovered her in Egypt, but I would never allow her to wander the streets of London unaccompanied. Yes, you might keep your daughters close and look after them now that a strange man is questing through the streets, but what about all those other girls who must walk out to work? They have no choice.' The man and woman in front of us were shifting, disliking the direct address. Then he silenced them. He reached upwards, something in the roof opened and grey feathers fluttered down over Miss Vine.

Drums rolled as she was carried off. Then he flourished his way to the back of the stage while two men in black pulled out a bench with a long thin box on top and began turning it and fussing over the lid.

'Behold, the place of death,' cried the Golden Prince, coming forward a little. 'And now she who will die!' The girl emerged from the side of the stage in what looked like a nightgown. The orchestra was playing lugubrious music and she began to dance, propping herself on tiptoe and sweeping out her arms.

'How old do you think she is?' I said to Constantine, watching the dress pull over her arms.

When he answered, his voice was thicker. 'Sixteen, seventeen. Maybe.'

'Do you think she is his sister?'

'That I doubt.'

I turned back as the music dipped and one of the black-clad men appeared onstage with a set of steps. The magician moved to the box. 'Here is the moment of truth!' The girl stood on the steps and smiled. He shouted, 'No! This cannot be.' The music stopped. 'We must have a volunteer. Ladies!'

In a second, he had jumped off the stage and was standing between the first two rows. 'Dear ladies,' he beseeched. 'Why not?'

Miss Grey nudged me. 'What do you think?' she whispered. 'We could volunteer.' She had a light in her eyes.

'I thought you despised tricks.'

'I know, but – still.' She seized my wrist and was tugging me up but Constantine moved around and pulled down our arms, holding our hands to our knees.

'What are you doing?' he hissed. 'Are you trying to make a spectacle of yourselves?'

Miss Grey broke away. 'It is only a show.'

He was still gripping my fingers. 'If my father discovered, he would never let us out again.'

'He would not find out.'

'Of course he would. What an idea.'

Miss Grey turned to look at the stage, her face drawn and her back straight. She leant to me. 'Next time we will come without him,' she whispered. I smiled at her, thinking how changed she was from the Miss Grey who had said she had no time for books.

Hands were waving in the audience and the magician selected a plump girl in a too-tight mauve dress. He led her up to the stage where his Cleopatra swathed her in a long red cloak.

'What is your name and where do you live, madam? Speak up.'

The girl in mauve declared her name was Millicent Wood and she lived near Chiswick. On further prompting, she told us that she had two younger sisters and was only just returned home after school in Surrey. 'I hope,' she said, head lowered shyly, 'to see more of London and attend concerts.'

'Poor girl,' sighed Miss Grey, very quietly.

'I am particularly fond of Mozart,' mauve Millicent said, when he asked her further. Her voice was soft, as if she were looking at something pretty every time she spoke.

'And would you like to marry, Millicent?' enquired the Prince. 'Or shall you become one of our great bluestockings?'

Millicent looked confused. Every girl must have a husband, but if we were to express this wish, we would be seen as strident and masculine. No, we must attend to be asked and wait for a man to reveal to us what we had not understood: that we wished to be a bride, all along. I saw the indecision in her face.

'I shall accept the future God has laid out for me,' she said finally. 'But I would very much like a home of my own.'

'Good answer,' said Constantine. I wanted to knock his leg with my arm.

The magician bowed and gestured to us. 'I am sure that you will gain your wish, Miss Wood.'

He turned to us. 'Now, Miss Wood will assist in our final trick.' Beside him, she was trembling. 'Our young lady shall show us the truth! Miss Wood shall lie in this box and we shall cut her into four tiny pieces. And then put her back together again!'

'I had not heard that he took a volunteer for this trick,' Constantine remarked to Miss Grey and me. 'My friend said he used the girl.'

Miss Wood lay down and the orchestra began the same dreary air, but much louder. The magician pranced and the sound swelled to fill my head. The girl passed him swords and he brandished them around the box. The music rose and he pushed one through, quite near the end. The woman in front buried her head in her husband's shoulder. Miss Grey clutched my hand.

'Are you pleased you did not offer yourself?' said Constantine, but then his voice softened a little. 'Do not worry. It is only a trick. She will pop up again in a second.'

The magician was carried away, whirling around as if a new spirit were in him, plunging another sword into her middle and one through the bosom. Miss Grey's hand was crushing my knuckles. I felt the dry patches on her palm and the rough skin just under the base of her fingers. The music ceased. The Golden Prince came to the front of the stage and threw open his arms.

'I seek one more volunteer,' he cried. 'I desire a sure-handed young gentleman to help me with the swords.'

A man at the front stood. 'Allow me, sir.' His thick black hair was so long it touched his back.

'A quick volunteer. This is the most wonderful audience I have ever had the pleasure to encounter.'

The Cleopatra girl stood at the front, reached out her hand and beckoned him towards the steps. Once he was on the stage, she handed him two swords and propelled him gently to the box.

'What is your name, sir?' called the Prince.

The man bowed his head. 'William Whitehead. I am a clerk in the City.'

The magician looked out at us and I sat up for his eyes were very bright. His skin shone. And then he cast his eyes down to the sword.

'Place the sword here, Mr Whitehead,' he said, pointing. 'Gently, now.'

William Whitehead stood there. I decided he was unsure and did not wish to do what was asked of him, but he was too shy to change his mind. He wished to depart but could not. Instead, he took a sword and aimed to push the tip at the spot the Prince indicated, his arm shaking a little. The music rolled, Cleopatra spread her arms and the Prince handed him another sword. This one was to go through the area where Millicent's head would be. Our volunteer was quicker the second time and thrust in the sword, hard. The music was deafening. We applauded and William Whitehead stepped away, his face pale, pink spots on either cheek.

Then he was forgotten. Onstage, the black-clad men twirled the box around and the Prince held his hand above the girl as she reached up and spun a little, on one foot. Perhaps she had hoped to be a ballerina, not a confidence trickster's assistant in the Egyptian Hall, waving her hands towards a wooden box.

Miss Grey's fingers gripped the edge of my palm.

'And now the finale,' he cried. He came to the front, ready for our applause. 'Miss Wood, entirely safe, not slightly harmed.' The girl moved to the steps, I supposed to help Millicent stand. The black-clad men took up position at either end of the box. The orchestra rolled the music so loudly that I wanted to clamp my hands over my ears. I wondered that the Golden Prince was not quite deafened. 'One, two, three,' he cried. 'Magic!'

The music halted.

The men lifted the top off the box. Cleopatra smiled out at us, bent and put her hand down to help Millicent out. We saw her face freeze and whiten. The black-clad men followed her eyes, and the one at the top end dropped the lid, so the corner hit the box and then the whole box was almost toppling off the stand. She began to scream, high and terrible, worse than anything I had ever heard at Lavenderfields, a cry like an animal beginning to die. The younger black-clad man was holding his head, stumbling to the side. The assistant staggered off the steps and held up her hand, clutching the wrist, and the skin was covered with blood, not the red liquid they had used earlier, but real, unmistakable blood. The Golden Prince stared at her.

‘Stop it!’ he croaked, and that was like the magic word. Until then, we had been sitting still like children in rows, hoping that if we were quiet, the horror would go away. As the curtain dropped, someone at the front began screaming and then the cries spread, as if there was a disease.

13. Newspapers

In the month before the murders had begun, two newspapers had appeared. *London Daily* and *Whitechapel News* were devoted to the East End. They wished to compete with *Criminal News of London. The Times* and the *Morning Chronicle* announced such sheets fodder for maids, with their feet propped at the fire, and coach-boys loitering outside theatres. I disagreed. In the Egyptian Hall, I stared at society ladies squeezed into rich gowns of pink and blue satin and I could see that they read the papers too. In drawing rooms, chambers and studies across the city, we were all reading *Criminal News of London*, relishing the horror that others endured.

Until recently, *Criminal News* had told of angry footmen, vengeful housemaids, robberies and suspicious falls. Then, as the summer broke, the talk was of the fights between gangs at the docks and near Liverpool Street. Two weeks previously, the editor had declared on the front page that there was so much crime in the city that the paper could not keep up to date: he would publish every few days 'as demand decrees'. Now Jane brought me the newspapers behind my uncle's back and every page was occupied with the Man of Crows. Each edition bore a picture of a victim and listed the girls across London reported missing. So far, not one from the lists had died at his hand, but I, and everybody, I suppose, expected their predictions to come true.

The curtain fell, the screams began and everybody started to shuffle to their feet, so much more slowly than you could ever imagine. About a month after I arrived at Lavenderfields, there had been a fire alarm. The nurses ran through with bells, untying those in the C beds. We sat there looking at each other until the matron shouted and we finally clambered out to hurry to the door. We were the same in the Egyptian Hall: we waited, time stopped, and then we began to move. I felt Constantine take my hand. The *Criminal News of London* ran in my head. Tomorrow's edition would bear a picture of us on the front, weeping, running to leave the bloody body behind. 'Dreadful Death at the Egyptian Hall'.

Miss Wood, pale in her mauve dress, lying in the box. The assistant touching her hand as she arranged her hair on the cushion inside. I supposed the side was padded too, so Miss Wood's head did not press against splinters and dirt. She had lain down in the dark and softness, like a fairy princess in a bower, watched by hundreds of us. She heard us clap and cheer, and the magician crying out above her as the music rolled. The arms of the velvet embraced her as she registered hands on the box. And then, as the music soared, the swords. Surely, surely, the sharp ends stilled her in shock and she lay there, without sense, until they cut her heart and her soul flew into the dirty air of the Egyptian Hall.

'We must hurry, Miss Sorgeiul.' Constantine wrapped

his palm around mine. I wanted to pull away and find the thick-haired man who had plunged in the sword. We were pushed forward, I crushed between two fat women who smelt of lead. I turned my head to look back and saw nothing but clothes. I had to take my chance before the door thrust us into the street and Constantine led Miss Grey and me to the carriage. Knowing them, they would wait outside for hours if I were left behind, so I let a man thrust forward and separate us. Then I pushed ahead, until I was out of the dark door and free.

'Miss Sorgeiul.' A hand touched my shoulder. 'Let me help you.' I turned and saw Mr Kent. He had lost his hat and his pale hair was dishevelled. I realized I must look similarly untidy. He held out his hand. 'Miss Sorgeiul. Have you become separated from your friends?' A man rushing past pushed me towards him and I found myself on my neighbour's thin chest. I apologized, propelling myself backwards, my face hot. 'Are you hurt? The Egyptian Hall is most hazardous.' He reached down for my arm. 'May I?'

'I am not in need, really. I must meet my friends.' I wanted to push him away. *Why are you always wandering around?*

'Let me be of assistance, Miss Sorgeiul.' Hair fell over his face. His wide eyes would have been handsome, if they were not overhung by his heavy brows, thick and pale with hardly a space between them.

'Thank you, sir, you are kind, but I must find my companions.'

'I will assist you.'

I tried to disentangle my arm. 'Thank you, but I am well.' A man's elbow crashed into my back. Constantine and Miss Grey were surely due to appear at any moment. I had to leave before they caught me and bundled me into the carriage, where I would spend the journey listening to him drone and watching the red patches flare on Miss Grey's face.

'Let me at least escort you to Princes Street.' He leant closer. 'We live in perilous times. Ladies should not be alone.'

'Oh, Mr Kent, I am not afraid.' The street was brightly lit, there were people. 'Thank you, sir, but I must depart.'

He loosened my arm and looked at me. 'Danger encompasses us. The threat cannot be seen but it exists.' He reached down and, in one quick movement, he had taken my left hand in his and was tracing a figure on the palm, circling and touching the crossing lines. The pattern he created jolted through me before I came to my senses and pulled away. His blue eyes stared back, innocent.

'Please pay a visit to my mother one day,' he said. 'She would be gratified to see you.'

'I shall, sir. Thank you. Now, if you will allow me, I must find my friends.'

'Keep safe, Miss Sorgeiul.'

I hurried on and did not turn, in case he was watching me. At the corner of the road, I saw a hansom cab and hailed it, imitating the men I had seen doing the same. I asked to go to the docks, near Wapping.

'Closest is St Katharine's Way, ma'am. Not a quick journey.'

We pushed through Charing Cross and up towards Holborn. My dress felt almost unbearably tight and I watched the streets dizzily. In a carriage, somewhere, Constantine and Miss Grey were starting back towards Cheapside, Miss Grey sobbing on to her brown silk, he shaking his head over the perplexing nature of it all. And Miss Wood was being taken from her box, wrapped in black cotton, put into a carriage to be taken to be prodded on a table by doctors, washed by the old women who specialized in bodies, and laid in fresh soil. Her younger sisters, dreaming on soft pillows, unaware. The Hall was empty: the magician taken by the watch to a gaol, his assistant too. The Tower loomed as we passed the Thames. Anne Boleyn there, declaring herself no witch, but still her head rolled and the King did not care. I climbed out at St Katharine's Pier, paid the man, and then I was in a main street, stacked high with rubbish. *Look as if you know*, I told myself, and began to walk.

Every greying doorstep was occupied, fidgeting children or thin girls with their legs stretched in front of them, bathing in the hot, dirty air. I could smell the docks: men's sweat, salt and the sour filth of the river. Two small boys without shoes tottered under boxes of stores for the ships. I walked a little farther and there were sounds of a ship coming in: the heavy thud of wood against stone, shouts and scuffles as men lined up to pull off the bundles and crates. I supposed they were carrying parcels of silks and jewels and gold, ready for girls like the Misses Belle-Smyth. 'Cargo coming down!'

I felt the sharp cobbles against my feet and looked up at the sky. Jenny Amber had died here. *The Times* said she was nineteen and had come with her husband from Portsmouth, but the authorities had not been able to discover if she had other family, and her husband, a sailor, would not return until next year. *Criminal News* declared that while her husband was away she had earned money the 'way she could'. I walked past the Gun Wharf public house, the shrieks and clink of glasses slipping past me. She and her husband had moved into rooms nearby, he took a ship – and then? No money. Not a penny until he was back in port, and what was she to do before that? I wondered if she had worked at the Gun Wharf. So many men eyeing her, making offers, and when there was no word from her husband (how could there be? He could not write) and she had not the funds for her lodgings, she began to return their smiles. Who had been the first? Say an Irishman, down for building work and not planning to stay long. He was only a little older and his eyes looked kind. Surely, she thought, being with him would not be too bad. She suggested twopence and he agreed, readily enough, and so, she understood, she could earn more from ten minutes with him than hours behind the Wharf's sodden bar. That night, he waited outside for her. At the back of the gin palace, she propped herself against the wet wall and pulled up her skirts.

Then it was more times with him, and as the other men who came to the bar began asking too, she started to think: why work? The publican might dismiss her soon enough, since most nights she ran away quickly, not helping the others scrub the bar or wash the glasses. One evening, she waited in the shadows for the men coming in and out. They all knew her and, for a month or so, she took two or three each night, all pleasant enough, some giving a few pennies extra.

Then, after one man had left and she was back in her usual spot, another emerged. All she could remember later was that he had been taller than usual, but otherwise there was little different about him, except he hardly spoke and did not smell much of drink. He asked her to take him to her dark place, but many did. Only when they were walking did she think she had become less cautious, for at first she would have done that only with a man she knew. Then after he had taken it out of her, he hit her. She remembered staring at him. The next fist was harder and she felt her head burst. That was when her legs gave way and she found herself collapsed against the muddy wall, weeping now, begging him to stop. He began to kick her with his hard boots and she found herself covering her face with her hands, curled up, back against the wall, trying to bury her head in the wet ground, feeling the softness of old waste against her face and hair, no longer pleading.

There was a pause. She did not look up, waiting for the next blow. Another kick, but not so hard this time.

'Don't come here again,' he said. 'Ever. Or worse will

happen.' Another kick came, against her knees. She curled up tighter, and heard his feet tapping away on the stones. Free. She lay there, feeling as if her whole body was turning into a bruise. She did not want to get up for if she did, then she would know how much it really hurt.

That was how she came to miss so many teeth from the back of her mouth, have an arm that fell limp at her side. Worst of all was the torn eyelid, which meant her eye was always half closed. So – with that – she was not pretty and could not ask for the same sums of money. She began to work the open streets for less.

I had reached the Fox and Grapes, which the *Criminal News* said she frequented. I stood there, watching the shadows of men and women, through windows thick with steam, laughing, drinking as if the Man of Crows did not exist. Miss Vine in her white dress screamed out in my mind at Miss Wood's dead face. An old woman in the doorway gave me a gap-toothed smile and held out a tray of baked potatoes, their heat curling into the air.

When had the Man of Crows first seen her? Had he trailed her before? I supposed he probably followed his prey a few times, thinking of what he might do. Some girls he decided against. Others, he did not find again. He had seen Jenny Amber, followed her – had he used her? Yes. He had taken her to the dirty alleyway and pushed her against the wall until he had had what he wanted (my face flamed when I wrote such things), and then, while she was straightening her skirt, he took out the knife.

I turned the corner into the mouth of the alleyway near the back of the place where they had found her. Had it really been like that? Just because she was a sailor's wife and they could not find another occupation for her, did not mean she took men for money. Maybe he had simply followed and attacked her. But, still, when I looked around those streets, I did not think she had been the other type of girl, someone like Abigail, walking home from her work in a shop. She had been with him in that alleyway, so near to the river. I looked at the wet walls, old bricks dotted in the puddles on the ground, and thought that she had probably brought others here, and touched them until they were begging and crying for more. Tired, cold, wanting gin, she had hurried them by stroking and speaking into their ears about wanting and pleasure. For maybe they were as weary of it as she, and were thrusting into her against the wall, cold and bored, wondering how much longer it would take, blaming her for not clutching hard enough, vowing never again to do it with such a bit of dirt. In their hearts was not a feeling of escape but dread at the shame of not managing it with a cheap, half-eyed girl like her, and the desire to pull back her hair until she coughed, wipe the smile off her face.

But the Man of Crows was not like that. Of course not. He did not need to despise her or imagine because every push into her took him closer to his goal. It was sweet joy, this delay, a putting-off of the moment when he would grasp her and she would look at him in disbelief, half thinking he was joking, expecting him to loosen his grip, slap her quickly and be done with her. Then as he moved in close and pinned her to the wall, she was too shocked to scream. How he loved that moment. It was better than pleasure, far superior to the plateau before the break. In what was called the act of love, you were not fused; indeed he had never felt so far apart from a woman he had been with in that way – using each other like children clambering over frames, striving for release, moving to that moment when you forget everything about the other person and she could be anyone. That deed was commonplace, something to be despised. But when he leant and seized a woman's throat, he knew he had her all. It was so very different from the usual moments of passion for the woman could not hold anything back.

I read in a novel of my uncle's that the appeal of love lay in entering an unknown world. There is something in another's life that invites you in and you hope your doubts and sadnesses will fade in their light. So I knew I could not love Constantine Janisser. There was nothing in his life I desired. Jellies, menus, charity drives and Sunday outings to the park in my third-best dress. Every part of it was obvious and familiar and the life I would lead with him would be more constrained than anything at my uncle's. The Man of Crows was different. He did not wish to be a part of those women but to possess them entirely. He reviled them, those girls, even though he knew that his hatred was a validation they did not deserve. They existed on the surface of things, he knew, parasites on greater beings. But still it infuriated him, how much they were able to live.

I walked through the dirty streets and could not believe how he was rushing into my head. I had searched for him for so long, and there he was, open in my mind. I could not see him, not yet, but I could feel him, sense his motivation. He was young, I was sure, quite handsome, and – what? I passed a group of women shrieking with laughter on the church steps. One in a deep green dress tossed back her bright hair and raised an eyebrow at me. And that was when it occurred to me: he had been betrayed by a woman. The handsome did not always win their desires (or that was what the unbeautiful, like me, told ourselves).

My murderer in the early days, a young, serious student. I chose a name: Frederick. He stood very tall and thin with dark hair, of that I was sure. He had moved to London from his family estate in the south and lived alone. He began to walk the city and fell in love with a beautiful woman he had seen at a concert, entranced by her large eyes, the loops of hair curling over her tiny ears, and her violet dress, fit for a queen. He had sent over a note and she had replied in delicate handwriting, suggesting he visit her rooms in St James's the next day. When he arrived, she touched his hand and introduced herself as Françoise.

'You may call me Fifine,' she said. 'My French mother always did.' She asked about his studies, served him tea and then, once, when she was enquiring about his travels, shyly touched his knee. He left the room feeling as if there was no boundary between him and the air and the birds above.

'This Fifine sounds like a *poule de luxe*,' said Marsden, his desk partner at lectures. 'Find a nice girl. Or, if you must have a whore, get a cheap one.' He talked about a girl named Betty and her friends. Frederick let him. How could a man like Marsden understand?

Fifine was intelligent, for a start. They discussed literature and she was entirely conversant with the latest trends, even timidly soliciting his opinion on authors noted in the *Quarterly Review*. Mrs Ferrier, he told her, was quite overrated. He brought her roses and little jewels and wrote short poems she declared better than Wordsworth's. When he entered her parlour, he saw her eyes soften. The streets outside were covered with grime, but all he could ever touch on her satiny skin was clean.

I couldn't feel sorry for him though, not really. He fell in love with a courtesan because she was beautiful and expensive, spent hours lavishing herself with creams and oils, receiving visits from the best hairdressers and dressmakers. Although he could not pay for any of this, he liked to enjoy it, and then became angry with her because she would not give up her money. Then he called her immoral. I reminded myself that I could not think like that. I must think like him, the truly devastated lover with whom Fifine had dallied when she was unoccupied and then had made wait.

He soon came to realize what was supporting his

world of love. One day, he was visiting her with one of his poems when the bell rang. She sent him into an antechamber, and there he had to sit while she arranged her dress. He heard her begging another man to take a little wine, sit beside her, tell her about his business. She gave a tinkling laugh and then the door to the upstairs rooms closed hard.

'It is only conversation,' she said. 'They are kind friends and they bring me little presents, that is all.' She gave him a dazzling smile and he knelt to kiss her hands. But when he was not with her, he wondered how you might tell if a woman was lying. One day, he decided to take matters in hand. He was tired from having drunk too much the night before and the weariness made him angry. On the way there, walking the cobbled streets from his lodgings to the high shops of St James's, he felt a heavy resentment firing his heart. How often he had had to sit in the next room while she flirted. She should not treat me thus, he told himself. He would tell her she must devote the whole afternoon to him – and after that, as much time as he desired.

He arrived at her stucco porch and rang for the maid. When the door opened and Gardner's pinched face peered out, he was seized with hatred. How he detested that woman, the shrivelled sprout of her head and her sagging body. She looked at him with eyes of contempt and tugged open the door. 'You may be admitted,' she sniffed, 'only for a few minutes. Madame is arranging her hair.' She opened the door into the parlour. 'No smoking,' she pronounced, as he seated himself on one of the velvet chairs. 'And no fire.' He stretched out his legs as she closed the door and felt himself grow light. *Things were going to change.* Everything in the room agreed with his intentions. The flowers, the vase, the bureau, each one jumped out at him as something to be remarked, thought over and named anew. In only a few minutes, Fifine would come, beckon him, and he would put his hand into her soft skirts. He stood up and walked to the sofa, touched the green silk. Here he would take her and kiss her, and when she was lying on his chest, stroking his skin, he would tell her that matters between them would be different.

There was a rustle behind the curtain and Gardner emerged.

'Madame will not be ready for at least another half-hour. Perhaps you might return later.'

'I have waited long enough.'

'Madame feels you might be easier if you were out, rather than here, sir.'

'You have admitted me. You cannot send me away.'

She narrowed her eyes, repulsive. 'Very well. You shall wait. But not in the antechamber. You must take another room.' She pushed back a thick curtain at the side. He walked past it and through a door, which closed behind him. He heard a key turn in the lock. He backed against a shelf and his fastidious nose revolted against the sweet smell of perfumed cotton.

As his eyes grew accustomed to the gloom, he saw shelves springing with female paraphernalia: boxes of pins, pots of powder and cream, and dozens of pairs of shoes, all broken in some way, torn across the front or missing a heel, or without their ribbons, and a few on which the fabric was completely worn through. Why did she keep such things? His mother was the same: she threw the buttons into her sewing box rather than ordering them by size. When Fifine was his, he would not let her behave so.

There were voices outside. He had been so absorbed in horror at the detritus around him that he had not realized people had entered the room next door. They were whispering, but he could catch Gardner's sour tone, and answering her, he realized, was a man. He moved to the door and strained his ears. Something was said about money. Gardner remonstrated. The man replied.

Frederick felt a chill tingle over his spine. The man outside was not discussing money because he was selling fine silks and jewels. They were debating Fifine's price. The voices dipped again and the man coughed. Gardner said something. And then – well, he could guess. She would shuffle out and Fifine would enter, a vision in feathers and lace. She would sit beside the man on the sofa, giggle and touch his knee. Then, Frederick supposed, after a little time, she would lead him to her room.

He heard her flutter in, the rustle of silk as she sat. But instead of giggling and offers of wine, he listened to low rumbles from the man, another rustle and then she gasped, as if someone was seizing her arm and bending it behind her. She gave a breathless cry. 'Oh, sir! Please.' His heart twisted. The man disrespected her so much that he would take her on the sofa, when anybody might walk in. He was heaving her skirts over her head – or perhaps even pushing her to the floor and making her go up on all fours. Frederick was enticed and hated himself for it, but he could not stop. Soon, he was straining to listen for every sigh, every catch of breath, moving with them.

Then he heard a harsh slap and Fifine's cry. And again. The man was hitting her. Frederick clenched his hands and began to push at the door. He could leap through and save her. He seized a hairpin from a box, unbent it and began to pick at the lock. But then he heard her cry, 'Oh, sir, that was wonderful.' The man hit her again and she cried out in French. She had said she spoke only to him in her mother tongue. He pushed the pin into the lock, working into the little spaces at the side, driving at them until the whole mechanism tensed and released. He flung into the room and the monster they made looked up, ugly and flurried, his face distorted, her moan cut short. He would have liked to throw pennies at her and say they were all she was worth, but he could not speak. He stood and stared, and as the man began to rise, he rushed out of the room and down the mahogany stairs, tears weighing at his eyes.

In the street, the carriages careered around him and his heart heaved. People were shouting but their words were as nothing. He heard only Fifine's laughter, echoing behind him.

That night, after gin and cards with a man he did not know, and a drunken woman pushing herself at him, he made a resolution. He would live only for pleasure and use people for experience. He would be like Fifine, cruel, untouchable, giving pain, but immune to its thrust.

After four days of laudanum and gin in his rooms, he made up his mind. He donned his hat and gloves, walked out of the door and to Dover Street. Then he wandered along St James's and Piccadilly, left, right and then around again, hoping his route would become clear to him. He arrived in Brewer Street and there understood what he desired. A gaggle of girls flitted on a corner outside a public house with smoky windows. He flicked his eyes over their bright lips and garish dresses, pleased with how his desire for them was cool and easily forgotten as if they were fruit on a stall. And what was Fifine? Under all her paint and folderol, she was no better than these half-dead street whores. The blonde with a waist looked not unlike her, and the scraggy brunette had a good swell of bosom under her shawl. He nodded to the blonde. The thin ones were easier to hold, and there was vulnerability in her eye. She saw his glance and stepped from the others, picked up her skirts and started to move towards him, holding out a pale hand. He caught her wrist and noticed that the ribbon around her neck had two wrinkles just below the corner of her jawbone. He would see to it that those were smoothed.

She led the way, he manoeuvred her against the alley wall, and she stood there, docile, as he thrust into her. He had chosen correctly; she was pleasingly obedient to his commands. From time to time, he thought he heard her gasp. With Fifine, he had concentrated on every movement, listened for each breath she took. This one was not worthy of such attention. Pushing into her was like using an animal, he thought, as he breathed in the meaty smell of her neck. Fifine was always scrupulously washed, but when he gripped this girl's waist, he felt sure layers of grime were shifting under his fingertips. You paid girls like Fifine to be clean. They remained in their rooms and occasionally took an airing in the carriage. The grime of the streets never touched them. All you could feel on their skin was the faint dust that might have drifted in through a window when the maid opened it to beat out the carpet. But this girl had been roaming the streets, trailing her feet over the mess from dogs and rubbing her hands on walls spattered with sewage. The rest of her would be fouler still, pulled about by hundreds of men, filled with their leavings.

'Tell me it's wonderful,' he said to her. 'Say, "Oh, yes, sir, do it again." '

She did so, her voice dull, and he pinched her ear to make her breathe as he wished. He thrust into her, knowing he was forging through so many other men's leavings, driving the remains of his predecessors into the boundaries of her sex so they might make a solid, clouded wall around him. He shot all those other men's liquids into her flesh, so only his remained. Really, he thought, girls like her were no more than corners that dogs might water.

'I want to see it,' he said, adjusting his cloak. 'Show me.'

She was leaning against the wall, fiddling with the material over her bosom. 'See what?'

'Pull up your skirt and show me.' He wanted her to sit on the cobbles, open her legs so he could see what he had done, how he had left her red, raw and marked.

She shook her head.

'I insist.'

She began to edge along the wall. He looked at her and, as he did so, he almost imagined himself as her, staring up at him, and he made his demeanour more terrifying. 'I have paid you, have I not?' He admired the wet glitter in her eyes. 'So,' he said. 'As I requested.' He enjoyed watching her face as she came to understand that she had no choice. Her hands moved to the front of her skirt and began to raise it. She gazed up at him, the wetness becoming a film. He doubted she had ever looked as beautiful as she did then, and he was pleased that he was the only one ever to see her thus, so finely attractive.

'I cannot wait.'

She slid down the wall. He watched her and listened to water drip over the bricks. She collapsed on to the ground, legs ungainly, hauled up her skirt, a thousand birds flew out, and a bright, fast sweetness overwhelmed him, pulled at his heart. This was the moment he had been waiting for. How long? Years.

Frederick picked up another blonde the following night and then the next. Every time, fear tingled at the corners of their eyes, and then – oh, how willingly they submitted. And yet each one gave him less satisfaction, and took him further away from the first. He looked at the tenth woman, quivering as she held her skirts aside, and felt nothing. The wetness in the eye, elsewhere, was much the same. The feeling he had experienced with the first dirty blonde had become painfully elusive, and there was nowhere the cool wash of dominance that had made him feel like a king. These women were hardest to possess, much more so than a drawing-room powder-puff. They cared not what was done to their bodies, as long as they were paid, and because they had no interest, they could not be hurt. You could drive into them, over and over, and still they were impossible to catch. He was rather pleased by the thought and wondered if he should turn it into words for one of those special newspapers. He stifled the idea. Writing for publication was vulgar.

He must have collected and forced about a dozen girls. Then – the date was etched on his mind: Wednesday, 8 July – everything changed and he found, finally, the moment of joy.

14. Ordinary Street

He had begun to notice in the course of using these low-class girls that one feature often remained fine. Like a flower growing in a dung heap, as if God had allowed her to preserve a single part from the ravages of poverty. The girl he had taken the previous evening had had remarkably pretty lips, with their own neat outline, like a doll's, and the one before a surprisingly high bosom. With this girl, Jenny Jane, it was her hands. As he haggled with her over the price, he noticed she had pretty fingers and slender, straight-sided nails with half-moons at the base. He touched her palm, 'You have the hands of a musician, miss,' and saw the light of pleasure in her eyes. Women were easy creatures. One compliment, and they became your toys.

On the walk to the alleyway behind the Prince of Wales (a public house he had used before), he'd asked her about herself and she'd spun the usual lines, down from the country to work, dismissed as a maid, and no position to be found. He played his role, the young client, not too jaded as to be wearied by her tales, not so inexperienced as to offer help, encouraging, tutting, inserting innuendoes between the cuts of her accent.

They arrived in the alleyway, and he steadied her

against the wall in the usual way. Then she put her hands on her hips.

'I know what you want, mister.' Her voice was louder than before. 'The other girls talk. And, let me tell you, you're going to have to pay. I'm not to be pushed about for your pleasure and no money at all.'

He was shocked to see aggression in her eyes. Where did these young girls learn such bitterness? Next time he was debating the expansion of education and someone declared that learning taught discontent and envy, he would suggest that the unschooled were worse – animals in touch with nothing but their brutal, feral selves. She tossed her head. 'A guinea.'

Unbelievable. Surely even Fifine would not demand so much.

'Quite impossible.'

She tipped herself against the wall and twitched her skirt across her feet. 'Well, then. You won't see, will you?'

'Two shillings.' As soon as he had uttered the words, he regretted them. She would tell the other girls and they would expect the same.

'I said what I said.' Could he detect a note of fear in her voice? He strained for it, hopeful. If so, that was what he had to edge for, pull out of her as if it were a skein of silk trapped in her throat.

'Two shillings.' He moved closer, wanting her to feel the heat of his breath on her skin.

She began to pull at her skirt. 'Mine is a very pretty piece,' she said. 'And I assure you it is very ready, sir.

Oh, yes. You can see it all if you like – for as long as you wish. For a guinea.' She leant her hand against the back wall and shrugged. 'Otherwise I can go, sir. And wish you luck in finding another girl. But I tell you this, I have seen those of other girls, and mine is a beauty, just like my mother's. And of course' – her voice dropped slyly – 'you, sir, are something of an expert.'

All the time, she was swinging her hips and worse, still worse, touching her fingers to her lips and trailing them over her chin and down to her bosom. Such unendurable pain.

He tried to quell the rising heat in his body. 'I have three shillings only, no more.'

'Well, sir, perhaps you may be able to return with the rest.' She took her hands from her skirts and straightened. 'I won't take up any more of your time.'

She began to edge past him, and as she did so, his nostrils filled with the smell of her: the grease of her hair, the decay gin-rotted on to her teeth and, he was sure, the slimy sugariness of her other parts. The scent held tight to his nose, as if winding round the inner hairs. He felt possessed by it and supposed this was how dogs must feel, taken up by a smell, forced to follow it, wherever it led them. He reached to grasp her arm and was surprised by how thin and – yes – birdlike it was, as if it could be caught and crushed in one.

'Don't,' she stuttered. 'Please.' Her voice quivered.

He looked at her and made to touch her shoulder. What on earth did she think he was about to do? Then he had the answer. His body was trembling, but with desire. It seemed to him later that he had never felt longing of such freshness. He reached down and, in one quick motion, ripped at the front of her skirt. She made an attempt to push away his hand and he gripped her wrist. She looked at him, her eyes wet with fear, and at that moment he felt the sensation of full renewal course through him. The heat of the close streets melted away and he was standing in his own cool, light room at his parents' house, the last time when everything had been simple, clean, coherent.

He clutched her shoulder. Her body flexed and he saw she was about to scream so he pushed his hand over her mouth and thrust her harder against the wall. She tried to bite his hand and he propelled her back, reached down for her skirt. She began to grab, kick and try to lash out, and he almost detested himself for wanting such a vicious little cat. He rammed her to the bricks and tried for the skirt again, but she pushed and kicked until he had to bring up both hands to stop her breaking free. He wondered how long she would take to still. He wanted to talk to her, tell her to be quiet, but he thought that if he did, she might feel less fear. His wish was that she would be stiff with terror, aware that her whole life was dangling on the edge of his desires. She bucked again and he stared at the dirty bricks. Slowly, he brought his right hand from her shoulder and pressed the palm against her throat. The flesh relented, as if he were entering a wardrobe and parting soft coats.

He drove his hand harder and savoured the

gratification – still sweet, although less of a surprise this time. They were both actors, he thought, playing familiar roles, and he wondered if she thought the same, for her body seemed suddenly conscious of what he needed her to do. She grew still and he felt her limbs soften, as if ready for him to consume. She would become an iced cake when you took it into the sun, falling in your fingers. At this thought, he began to feel hotter, the warmth rising in his body, for yes, that was what he was now, a man who had just bought one of the cakes glistening in a baker's window, taken it outside, pushed his finger into the top, felt the mixture disintegrating, and instead of being disgusted, throwing it on the fire and demanding one that had just been made (Pray, why did you leave it in the window, surely you knew, sir, what would happen?) he became delighted at the soft relentingness of it all, and he began shovelling it all into his mouth, not taking the tiny bites you might with a fresher cake, but curling his teeth and tongue around the syrupy mess, crushing his hand around the base.

He pushed harder, gripped his fingers around the flesh of Jenny Jane and heard high, tight gurgles of pain. Below, her legs were flexing and she was banging her back against the wall. She had been in the shop window too long, growing hard and stale in the sun and now she was crumbling in his fingers. The heat in him had begun the process and his role was only to conclude it, to hold and grasp until she sank into his hands, became nothing. She was beginning to make less sound.

He pushed harder on her neck, holding tight and digging in his fingers as her legs kicked, as if she were a baby on her back. He felt the gulping of her windpipe, the beating of the pulse, and pressed harder, delighted by the wealth of little animals, tiny things, under his hands. He thought of his mother holding up her bronze hair for the maid to fasten, exposing the back of her neck over the silky edge of her gown. How trustingly people do such things, hold up their hands, show their necks and reveal everything, thinking that no one wishes to give them hurt, appealing to each person to be a protector, expecting a touch that bears only kindness.

She was silent and he thought from the roll of her eyes that she had taken her fill, but he held on for a little while more for good measure. He drew his hands away and she slid to the ground, dropping forward like a rag doll. He reached down quickly to touch the heart. Nothing. In a heap by the wall, she looked smaller. She would probably be soaked through. He straightened and caught his breath. He had been panting. The air smelt of hot sugar.

He looked down at her again, crumpled in the dirt, and knew he could not leave her thus. People would know her – they would recognize her – and maybe some of those upstart jays would remember she had gone off with him, a respectable man, recall his face (for money, it was always for money) and damn him for ever.

The graininess of the air scratched his nostrils. There was a smash of wheels outside – and fear lit in his heart. And then the answer came to him. He would have to do something to the body. He must alter the form, make the skin other than it was. Up to this point, he had been himself in every action, discovering parts of himself that he had hardly known. Now, to cover his deed, he must become someone else, a man who might mutilate for amusement. He had to think – what would he not do at a moment like this? He watched her blood colouring the dirty water. She was a slumped doll and there was no inspiration for him there. He had rather enjoyed thinking of her as a foodstuff. Maybe, it struck him, that was the way to continue. He would have scooped the cake into his mouth, greedy for sugar, but well, if he were someone else, what would he do? He remembered a friend of his sister who was always fiddling with her food, pushing slices of pie around the plate, scraping her fork through potatoes. He thought of the girl's long hair hanging as she prodded her vegetables – and came to an idea.

He must play with her. He had to make it seem as if the slayer were not him, but someone so strange that none of Jenny Jane's friends would be able to imagine or place him. He had to do something so alien that people would judge him a man beyond comprehension. The whole city would wonder over his identity. It would be rather like acting. He had been rather good at plays at school.

The escape would all be a question, he declared to himself, of letting his old self flow out and allowing another to replace it. He stood there in the alleyway, trying to rise above the awful stench coming from the warm floor, and breathed deeply. He tried to imagine his soul streaming away, a bright blue mist of poison, and saw a new colour replacing it: red violet, perhaps. He was rather enjoying the sensation, he had to admit. He felt the new colour tingle into him, stretch into his hands, and then yes, yes, arrive in his mouth, slip under his tongue and into his throat. It tasted hard, unyielding.

He looked down at the girl. She was crushed in such an unfamiliar shape, bunched up and squat, as if she were all bosom. The red violet sparked over his mind and wrapped around his heart. He stood up, puffed his chest and felt the colour speed about his shoulders and through his arms. It was like melted steel, he thought, burning the inside of his body. Its energy must be taken and used before it was too late.

He held his arms – and tried to let the new self flow. If he wanted people to believe this the work of a madman, he would have to become thus. He had to let in fragments that would take over his mind. Anger, violence, blood, terror, evil. Yes. He thought of the other animals that lived in alleyways and drains. Rats mired in dirt, their tails close to tangling around each other, scurrying across the glimy stones and spreading disease with their loamy feet. Could she be a rat, heavy and foul, belly scraping the ground? No, too bony. A stray cat, prowling through the mud, shaking a flea-ridden tail? No. He looked down at her again, lumped on the ground, arms and legs protruding. A bird. She was a filthy dead sack of a bird, beak hanging open, spindly legs splayed, wings bent back on themselves. A pigeon, even. He hated pigeons. There was always one in the flock missing some of its scabby toes. No rat could scurry as far as a pigeon flies, spreading disease from its dirty nest in the east to the calm west, just like this soiled girl. She had probably done that, trailed out to sell her wares in Covent Garden, trying to pretend she was a Mayfair type, and only when they had finished having her and she let her accent slip did they understand what she really was. Old soil, used and trodden over a hundred times. London was cleaner without her. He stood up and let the image of her sear around his body, feeling the dirty bird flit into his arms and legs, understanding, recognizing that this was something spectacular that could create excellence and order in an untidy world.

'Danny!' A woman's voice echoed just outside the entrance to the alleyway. Her feet tapped out two steps, then faltered. 'Where are you, dear?' Her words were like a warm almond, tempting. 'Danny? Are you in there?' The hotness of her was seeping into his flesh. He extended his foot to push the dirty heap closer to the wall, but it would not budge. Still, he reasoned, she could enter looking for her Danny and then, when his hand touched her, she would not have time to see what lay at her feet. He moved to the entrance of the alleyway and tensed his body to receive her. He reached the edge, backing along slowly – and he could almost hear the shallow in–out of her breath. He would be able to touch her soon and this thought, unexploited and real, glimmered like an unburst raindrop. He breathed, gathered himself and leapt out for her pulsing mass, unable to see her face, but that mattered nothing for he would have time to explore the features when he had her on her knees.

Then all he saw was speed. His hand on the wool of her arm, her intake of breath, her scuffle of feet, him pushing her against the wall, and then her screams. It was nothing like the actresses onstage, whose cries were deep and emotional. Hers were not graceful at all, but so strangled and glottal you would think she was a dog mating, not a human female on the brink of great change. He grasped her waist, wanting to slap her into playing her part better, but then he felt her being overtaken by a kind of deep strength. It shook her body and she pulled against him, jolted, and then, in a moment, tugged free. He clutched at her throat but gained only a handful of shawl, and then she was hurtling away. The shawl bunched on the ground. He debated chasing her. It would be easy enough to catch her. But he would be leaving the first, before he had taken his thing with her right to the end. He could have another girl like her. They came cheap.

He knelt down to the shawl, and something bright caught his eye. A necklace, perhaps. A memento to remember her. He fished in the wool, touched the glimmer and saw the thing was not a necklace but a knife, a kind of meat knife. Perhaps she was a butcher's girl. But then, surely, he would have been able to smell blood, for butchers had their hands so deep in flesh that whenever they sweated the smell of death poured out. He held the knife to his nose and breathed in lightly, taking in the tang of metal and her scent of fear. Where had the knife been? Next to her breast or in a pocket, hanging against her hot parts? That he could not smell. Next time.

He held up the knife so the metal caught light from the clouded-over moon. Behind him, the body was dragging him in. He turned and walked towards the dirty heap, putting his hand on the wall, feeling his nail scrape against the brickwork. It was hardly human, that thing lying there. He crouched and touched the skin of its face. Still warm. A slimy desperation oozed out of the hair. He felt hatred steam in his chest, and then he knew what to do. He held out the knife, lifted it over her chest and began to slice at her corset. Then in one quick movement, he found himself cutting at her flesh.

I stood there, holding the wall, feeling the image of him breaking into her clothes. All the walking and thinking had taken me along the river, past the Monument, along Bishopsgate and Bethnal Green and into Swan Street. When I was living with my uncle and aunt Cross, I used to creep downstairs to my uncle's library, find the whisky bottle and drink straight from the lip. The first time, I had woken thirsty from a bad dream and come downstairs. Wandering along the hall, I heard a noise from the library. As I flattened myself against the wall, I heard my uncle's heavy footsteps and I saw him pass. He trudged up the stairs and I edged towards the library, feeling the waxiness of the endlessly polished wood beneath my feet. I opened the door into his room of books, merely because I knew I should not, and breathed in the smell of his cigar and the dying fire. On the table, glowing, was a decanter of golden liquid, the stopper lying to the side. I crept over and ran my hand across the glass, fingering the slitty depths of the diamonds. I wondered how the stuff would feel as it stole down my throat. I picked up the decanter and raised the lip to my mouth. Sweetness seared my skin. I let the liquid touch the back of my tongue and swallowed. I drank again and my head spun a little, light and dizzy.

Was that how he felt, the Man of Crows, clandestine, iniquitous, unobserved? I steadied myself against the wall of the alleyway, ready to throw myself back into the nightmare of imagining what happened when he began to cut.

I stood, breathed in the smell and knew: *he had been here*. I had felt him on me. This time I was not afraid. I was strong and tall, like a giant. I thought of those people staring up at the magician, pretending to be in fear of a man who would never come to them. Well, I did not share their arrogance. He was not looking for me. I had come here tonight to be a little closer to him – and discover. *For I can find him in a way I do not think anyone else can*. My brother was dead because of me, and not through an accident like drowning or falling. If I could do that at eleven, what might I do now?

I held the bricks and edged in, my feet tripping in the dankness. I heard my breathing but nothing else. I tried to block out the sounds of the streets, hoping my eyes would adjust to the murk. I wanted him to come to me. *Who are you?*

The air slid around me. I tried to ignore the smell. I would not be made afraid.

And then I heard it. A bright, hard sound like a heel clashing against a wall. I looked up at the walls of the alleyway. There was someone behind me. He – I knew it was a he – took a step forward and I heard his heel touch the ground. Then he breathed and I could almost hear the sigh touch the air. He wanted me to know he was there. It was him, I knew it. My breath pooled in front of my face, a witch's cloud. I heard the heel again. And then a sigh. I looked to the side and saw three gloved fingers curl themselves around the wall.

That was when I broke. My hands had moved to my skirt, and my feet had launched me forward, out of the alleyway and into the empty street, certain he was watching me run before he made a few swift steps and caught me with his hands. I turned left, cursing the tightness of my sleeves and the width of my skirts, looking for lights, people, telling myself to keep going, *not much farther*, until the streets were bright and wide and the people around me looked as if they might fear murderers, never be one. I threw myself into a street of men, and towards one in a smart coat and hat. I said I was lost and begged him to find me a cab, hoping he might take me for a lady's maid or similar. He looked at me for a moment and then called to another man and asked him to go for a driver. I wanted to hold his arm but if I did so, he would think me peculiar and mad and perhaps push me away. I clutched myself.

The man helped me into the cab and I wanted to grasp his fingers and pull him in. We set off slowly, so slowly, and I knew the Man of Crows followed. My heart crashed in my ribcage. I conjured scenes: he overturned the carriage and pulled me out, and no one stopped to help because they thought him my saviour. Or, when I descended at Princes Street, he reached out a hand to seize me and drag me – to where? Some place I could not imagine. And the thing that made me most afraid was that I might not need to be forced. Instead I would move of my own free will. He would draw me after him, just as he had those other girls. I would see him and could not help but join him. In front of the cab that had brought me to safety, and the house where I lived with my uncle, I would walk to him and let him take my hand.

15. Family

From the age of five, I had terrible dreams. Monsters flew through my mind and dragons tore out my soul. I woke not knowing if I were alive or dead, my face wet with tears. I screamed in the night, and most mornings my parents found me lying in a corner of the house or halfway out of my door. I could not remember walking. They took me to doctors. I sat in wood-panelled rooms and felt old men's hands on my head and eyes, looked at pictures and cards and answered questions. There were different recommendations. Do not eat before bed, sup lightly before sleep, rise early, slumber in the day, open the curtains, open the window, close the window. I was given pink, blue, yellow pills, liquids pale yellow or brown, salves to rub on my chest.

I grew to feel as if I were two people. In the daytime, I proceeded as any girl, walking out with my governess, taking lessons, eating in the nursery with my brother, attending tea parties and dancing. At night, I became all misery, my mind cut through with blood, dead bodies, animals rearing. Along with all their pills and suggestions, the doctors nearly all said the same: 'She shall grow out of her affliction.'

The dreams grew more dreadful as the years passed. The monsters and dragons were joined by thoughts of revenge. I attacked everyone: my governess, a man who had pushed past me in the park, a little girl who had taken my piece of cake at a party. They all died at my hand.

The first time I dreamt about my parents was after my mother had told me to eat the vegetables on my plate and my father complained about muddy boot marks in the hall. That evening, the night pictures were all hatred. I took a monster, pushed him into my parents' room and blocked the door with chairs as they cried out and battered to escape. I opened the door only when there were no more sounds and stroked the monster as I stared at my parents' ragged bodies.

I began to imagine that I destroyed them. I took a knife from the kitchen and plunged the blade into my father's heart. My mother screamed and I stabbed her too. Such dreams I could not tell the doctors. I lied that the dreams had gone and pretended I had outgrown my terrors.

One July night was particularly hot and another dream took hold of me. I swung in the grasp of the pain. I was falling and crying, afraid, and then my brother cried out behind me, I caught him, pushed hard at him, and he dropped over an edge. He stretched up a hand. I held back and he fell.

I woke up, but not in my bed. I was in my brother's room, holding a pillow above him, about to put a hand on his face. He was awake, gazing up at me. The door slammed open behind us. My mother seized me by the waist and pulled me from the room. Within two days, I was living in a place for children with darkness, bears and flowers painted on the walls, coloured pills in the morning followed by simple lessons and then doctors. Uncle Crenaban had recommended the establishment. After a few months, the chief doctor told me I was cured and my parents came to collect me. My mother could not look at me, she said, and within a week I was sent to live with friends of my father in Cambridge, who gave me a room at the top of their house, a visiting governess with pretty hair every morning, and meals with them in the evenings.

When I was nine, I was allowed to return home as the doctors had declared me well, if I continued to take the coloured pills.

'You will prevent your improvement if you recite to yourself the events,' said the doctors. I could not stop.

They gave me a new dress and a ribbon for the hair I did not have and sent me home in a carriage. A maid came to meet me at an inn outside London. She was sharp with me as she tipped me into another carriage, one I did not recognize. Our house was smaller than I remembered, but someone had covered the front with flowers. I could hardly see the bricks. There was a blue plant creeping up the front, pink flowers bubbling from a box on the windowsill, and yellow blooms stretching from a high flowering bush over the upper windows. In the old days, I had drawn our home as a gingerbread house, every window made of cake and icing in colours of cochineal and green, but now I had a house of flowers: petals and leaves and rich yellow hearts covering the rooms of my shame.

The same magic had been worked over the front garden. The beds spilt coloured blooms. Pink and red roses baked in the hot sun, a plant with large violet flowers sprouted over the wall and yellow summer flowers spun around every corner. Another maid opened the door, showed me into the parlour, and there were my parents. My mother was surrounded by flowers too: behind her sparked a great vase of tulips, their black prongs hanging towards her hair.

'Good morning, Catherine,' said my father. 'Have you been keeping well?'

My mother stood up then and tried to hold me. 'You have been away so long.'

'The doctors tell us you are completely well.'

'Yes, Papa. All well now. The dreams have gone.'

'Well, that is good. Louis is at school. He will come back in a few weeks' time. For now, you and he will always be accompanied. And then we shall see. In the meantime, you have a new nurse, Nancy. Now perhaps you would like to go to your room. You must be tired after your journey.'

Nancy took me upstairs and on my bed sat a large doll, with black hair and great brown eyes. 'She is a present for you, miss. You must give her a name.'

'She is my doll. I will call her Catherine.' It was as if I had been ill with a disease that a good child might catch, lung weakness, perhaps. I was filled with a feeling of light and sun, sure I could be new, like the doll.

But then the dreams came back, more terrifying and cruel than they had been before. I was always killing somebody, nameless grey people I had never seen, sometimes our maids, people who had come to visit, friends. Most often, I had my parents in my hands. I thought of hacking them with an axe, thrusting a knife deep into their hearts, stabbing them with a hot poker from the fire. I told nobody. I took the coloured pills. Still the dreams came.

My mother suffered from headaches. They would come on in a moment. She said they were like a colour spreading across her forehead, which started pink and ended a bright, bloody red. We became used to the signs of one beginning. Her face would turn a little pale and her walking would slow. She said later that it was as if bells rang through her mind and her whole head had become a tower, echoing, and the ropes swung through her. Then her eyes would flutter. That was when the lights came in her pupils and we knew we had lost her for the next few hours, sometimes even days. Her headaches became more severe as we grew older. One day, with me, she fainted in the middle of a shop off St James's. After that she was nervous of leaving the house with me. With my father or Louis, she felt safer.

And so the three of us had come to be in Spitalfields. There was a merchant Mama wanted to visit. She had heard from a friend that the cloth he sold was particularly fine, went straight to the Court, and never to any dressmaker or haberdashery. We had not been east before, and we took the carriage, staring from the windows at the newness of it all – the bustle, the dirt, the crowds. The coachman stopped outside the address, and I sat downstairs in a small dark waiting room while Louis escorted my mother upstairs. They returned, some time later, with armfuls of material.

When the old man opened the door for us, the carriage was not there. Instead, the street came upon us, the grime, the dirt, animals and people.

'Probably forced to drive to the end,' said the old man. 'They move them on sometimes from here. My apologies, ma'am.' He offered to escort us farther, but Mama shook her head. We were too proud.

And so we set off, my mother wearing her bravest face, keeping her skirts clear of the mud. A child caught at her hand. She shook him off and clutched Louis's arm. We arrived at the end of the street and the carriage was not there.

'Left,' said Louis. 'I am sure that is the way we came. That way takes us towards the main road. The carriage must surely be there.'

We walked through the people and past houses that looked as if they were about to topple on us, and Mama held our arms tightly. Every person looked the same. An old woman thrust out her blanket at us and Louis swerved. Children laughed at us, loudly. And then I felt my mother's grip loosen. Louis and I turned at the same time and her face was going pale.

'Don't, Mama,' said Louis. 'Don't be ill.'

But she was bending and her eyes were fluttering.

'Please,' said Louis. 'Mama, you can't.' He pushed her upright. 'Please.'

Her eyes were full of fear. 'I cannot avert it.'

'No one will help us. No one. You must try.'

'I cannot. It is coming.'

'So what shall we do?'

'Please, Mama,' I said. 'Help us.'

Her eyes were almost closing. 'Ask your uncle to come,' she said.

'But we do not know where he lives, Mama.' Her eyelids fluttered at me, and then she fell back into Louis's arms. He staggered under her weight. I helped him bring her to lean against the wall of a house and I crouched beside her, holding her head to keep her upright.

'What shall we do?' I said to him.

'We will have to wait until she recovers.'

A stone fell close to us. I turned and two children were laughing. 'I feel afraid here. Let us return to the shop.'

'We cannot leave her. Perhaps a kind person will help us.' His voice shook slightly. He sat beside me, and put his arm through mine. 'Mama will wake, I am sure.'

I do not know how long it was that we sat there. We looked at the ground or each other, anything to avoid the gazes of those who passed. People stared at us, children mocked, a dog sniffed at our feet. It felt like hours.

'Good evening,' said a man. His voice is etched on my mind. I looked up and there were two men standing over us. The one who had spoken wore a long coat and I could see only a mass of dark hair and two bright eyes.

His squat companion was mute, holding a smoking stick to his pipe. 'You have chosen a strange place to seat yourselves. Surely another spot would be more pleasant.'

I looked at him and I knew that he was not the saviour we had hoped for, even though his clothes were fine.

'Brother and sister, I presume?' he said. 'How friendly.'

Louis stood up. 'We are only waiting and then we will return home.'

The pudgy one coughed. 'Of course.'

'Where do you live, young sir?' said the tall one. 'Not near here, I would imagine.'

Louis shook his head. I could hear a woman selling violets just behind us. There was a kind note in her voice. If only she would come closer and send these men away.

'We are quite well, sir,' said Louis. 'Thank you for your interest.'

'Ah,' he said, turning to the pudgy one. 'It seems to me that the young man wishes us to go. Do you not think, sir?'

'Perhaps so.'

'But it might be difficult for us to do so. Mr Gillibrand and I have need of a young person, you see. Someone like you.'

He bent a little and I smelt onions and something I now suppose was wine. The small man puffed out a ring of smoke. 'We have rather an urgent need.'

'For what?' asked my brother.

I thought he might need a young person to play with his children.

There was a light as the other one took another smoking stick from behind his back. I saw a scarred face and a black hat with a dark red band, adorned with a diamond-like stone. The man lit the end and then I saw the hand of the one in front of me, which had been on my face. The skin bore a pattern, like a figure of eight, with the teeth and eyes of a dragon.

'You are just the people we like to meet,' he said. 'Pleasant young people.'

'We are only visiting,' said Louis. 'I do not think we shall return.' His voice was tight. 'We have no money. Even our mother has little.'

The tall man near me laughed. 'It is not money we desire,' he said. 'No. I need a person. A young person. Do I not, Mr Gillibrand?'

'Quite so.'

Mr Gillibrand took a step towards us. His pipe bowl glittered, reflecting a plume of smoke. He tapped the side. I supposed he was flicking ash on the ground.

'I do not think we can help you, sir,' Louis said.

'Our reasons why we require a person are complicated. The issue at press now is – which one of you might we take.'

'We must think,' said his companion.

'Ponder.'

'What would you say, young lady? Who would we need?'

And that was when the terror happened. I was tired and cold and thought only of returning home. 'I wish you would go,' I said.

There was an intake of breath. The pipe quivered in the dark. My words had made them angry. Until then they had been merely playing a game with us and would probably have left.

'Well,' he said, 'let us be celeritous. The young lady commands. So, Mr Gillibrand. Which one shall we take?'

The flame caught his face. I saw the hat, the scars, the dragon on his hand. 'Let us see,' he said.

'You can have neither of us.' We would be brave and stand up to them. They would leave us and we would return to Richmond. I thought of the big tree in the centre of the back garden with the swing, and Emma, the maid, making biscuits for us. We were halfway through our game of Noah's Ark and I needed Louis to be Noah.

'My dear.' I felt a finger on my arm, light. 'But we must have a child. Which pretty young person shall we have?'

'We cannot assist you, sir.' Louis's voice was braver than mine.

The other snuffed his pipe, and there was only darkness. 'One of you must come.' He touched my arm again. 'Let the lady decide.'

And then I felt Mr Gillibrand come close again, his breath on my face. In one quick movement, he took the chain of my locket in his hand and pulled it from my neck. He stepped back. 'You invited us here,' he said. 'You wanted us to come. Did you not, miss?'

'Maybe you dreamt of us,' said the other.

'So now you must decide.'

'Me,' I should have said. 'Take me.'

Instead I looked at the man and said, 'Take my brother.'

16. Walls

I slammed the door of Princes Street as if I had been chased there by demons. The wind was blowing so wildly that I was sure my uncle would believe the banging only hard rain. Candles blazed in the hallway – for Mr Trelawny, I supposed. I pulled the chain across, hurtled upstairs and dropped on to my bed.

I lay on the coverlet, my breath short, staring at the shadows on the ceiling propped up by its own four walls. How miserably confining I had thought them! Now I felt only terror that the walls might be thin like paper and the Man would put his fingers through and find me. *I have seen you*, he might say as he reached around his hand. *You are mine!* I had to tell myself that I was safe. The door was closed, every window was locked and shuttered and he could not penetrate. For so long I had told myself that if I died, the world would be freed from my cruel soul. And yet, lying there on the bed, my heart pounding, sodden gown crumpled under my legs, I thought only that I wished to cling to life.

A creak outside my door, and I wanted to cry out. I covered my face with my hands, shifted slightly and felt the wetness of my skirt pool under me. The dress was probably ruined, the silk stained with water. I liked this thought, a comforting normal idea that a young lady might have after a rainy walk in the park. If I left myself much longer, the corset too would dampen and ruin. I heaved myself upward, swung my legs to the side and noticed Crispin, his amber eyes glowing, standing under the table and turning a little. I reached down to him but he shied away, began turning once more, following his tail.

I lay there and told myself to hold on to what I could see: my room, the yellow and blue quilt, the bowl and jug on the mahogany side table, my trunk of dresses. On my first night from Lavenderfields, I had cherished the size, the solidity of the walls, the heavy furniture, the window. *This is mine*, I had thought, *I cannot be found here.*

I reached around to try to undo my dress. Without Jane to help me, the pearly buttons slipped from my clumsy fingers. I pushed at one with my nails, as if that would help, and fell back on the pillow. The wind was punching at my window, shaking the loose upper panes in the frame. Tomorrow I would tell Jane and my uncle that someone had thrown water at me in the rush at the Egyptian Hall. I pushed the wet mass of my skirts aside and reached down for my boots. I was untying the first when there was a beating at the door.

'Catherine?' My uncle. 'I feel sure you are awake.'

I sat quietly, hoping the pummelling of the wind would cover my breathing. A shutter banged and he raised his voice. 'Catherine, my dear. I know one cannot sleep in this wind. There is a matter I wish to show you.'

'I was sleeping, Uncle.' If I emerged, he would smell

the street on me. 'I was so tired after the show I fell asleep in my clothes.'

'Well, then,' the door opened a crack, 'you are quite fit to emerge, my dear, do you not consider?'

One of the African masks on the wall grimaced in my eye. 'What do you wish me to see, sir?'

'A matter of interest on the street.'

'Uncle, it is late. We cannot go walking outside.'

He opened the door wider and the whole of his face eased into the crack. The light from his candle sparked over his eyes. 'Was the show satisfactory?'

I sat up straighter. My corset dug into my ribs. 'No. A girl died.' Miss Wood cracked in my mind and a tear of blood fell from her eye.

He raised an eyebrow. 'So I have heard. Crisis seems rather to follow you, Niece.'

'There was a great panic. I caught a cab home.' I hoped he could not see me in the gloom. My hands were spattered with dirt, my hair was disordered, and there were surely streaks of mud on my face.

'What courage! I suppose many ladies were afraid.' His eyes were wet in the waxy light.

'Mr Kent was there. He was intent on helping me. He said there were hazards for ladies.'

'Wise words.'

'I do not know why people attend such evenings.' In the grey, with Crispin scuttling under the bed and my uncle slowly pushing more of himself into the room, the show was fragments in my mind, all blood. 'I cannot understand why they would.'

'Do you not, my dear?' The whole of him was through now and a hard, rusty smell filled the room. 'I have gained the impression that you have been a little – unsatisfied recently. Yearning, perhaps, for more than your daily routine here can afford. And who could blame you? It is a dull life for a young lady as – well, vibrant as you have proved to be.'

'I am perfectly content, Uncle.'

He advanced towards me and his shadow fell over my trunk. 'Ah, but one cannot remain in the place that is easiest all of one's life. One must make changes from time to time. Come, my dear. Our expedition shall not take long. Dressed as you are, I can hardly believe you will sleep. You will only toss and turn.' His largeness made my room look small, the ceilings too low.

I swung my legs to the side, wanting to prevent him approaching any closer. 'I come, Uncle.'

At that, thankfully, he withdrew his face. 'I shall attend you outside.'

He closed the door behind him and I scrambled to fasten my boots. When I emerged, he took my arm, his fingers clawlike, so he had to crowd behind me on the narrow landing. The light was slipping out from under the door of his study. Mr Trelawny, I supposed.

'Jane did not appear today,' he said, as he unlaced the front door. 'Very unlike her not to send a note.'

I followed him into the close air of the street. 'Perhaps she has taken after all the other maids and left us.'

He moved in front of me to lead the way past the

piles of rubbish in the road. 'You did not dress yourself, Niece?'

'No. The Kents sent over their maid. I shall do tomorrow. I can learn.'

'Bracing, is it not?' he said, into my ear, steering me to the right. I splashed into a puddle and he tapped my arm. 'So many hazards for ladies.'

Three gloved fingers curved around the wall, and the magician's assistant cried out.

The street was deserted. Even the cats prowling around the rubble from the road had slunk off elsewhere. A house was on fire somewhere nearby, for the yellowness shone through the smog above us. Other than that, it was as if Princes Street had been covered with ash from a volcano and we were the only ones still alive.

We turned the corner and he stopped. 'See, Catherine, dear,' he murmured. 'Here we are. Look up.'

He uncapped the candle and the light blazed into my eyes. I stared up at the side of the house and saw the flowers, painted across, curving out over the bricks, reaching to the roof. They were violet, just as Mr Trelawny had said, but brighter and more garish than I had expected. I had imagined them like blood, a colour which in certain lights could blend into the dingy side of the wall. These were as if drawn by a child, blobby round petals rimming a showy yellow heart. They were wet and shiny, as if they had only just been painted, even though my uncle had told me about them weeks ago. Their thorns twisted upwards as if a rescuer for Rapunzel might climb to the top.

'Regard the stems.' My uncle coughed. 'So skilfully intertwined. Very representative, do you not judge?'

I dragged my eyes down from the glistening paint of the petals to the tangle of gaudy green. I thought of myself in my room, sitting on my bed, while those flowers were spreading their sticky colour over the hot wall at the end of my street. Fear crept through my heart and I wanted only to be back in the house.

He gestured to me. 'Let us move closer, Niece. How do you think they came here?'

'I cannot imagine.'

'Flowers are of such interest. They generate in such an interesting manner. Pollen to seed, reseeding. Breeding plants from the same seed and crossing them can create the most beautiful hybrids.'

I said nothing. The sword thrust into Miss Wood.

'There are similar paintings over other houses in the city.' He was peering at the stems, his back stiff.

'Yes, Uncle.' I thought of Constantine Janisser's voice, his burning eyes. 'I have seen sufficient, Uncle. It is a little cool.'

'Are you quite certain, my dear? I believe I remember you suggesting you wished to leave the house with more frequency, in only – was it – May?'

'I am perfectly content, sir.' The fear was clutching me now, and I pulled my wrap close. 'Surely Mr Trelawny attends you.'

He nodded. 'Ah, yes. Mr Trelawny. Let us return.'

There was a crack of wood and another sound, like someone clearing his throat. I looked to the side but the street was empty.

'I thought I heard a cough.'

'I heard nothing. Come.' I turned and felt his hand on my back, propelling me forward. He maintained his hand thus all along the street. The Kents' house was dark, save for one light shining in an upper window that I supposed was a maid's. I could feel my uncle's gnarled palm through the wool of my shawl. He moved me to the front door. Only there, in the hall outside the parlour, did he let his hand fall.

'My dear, I believe your heart is beating at speed. You should sit in here for half an hour. It is not wise to retire when excited. You might have peculiar dreams.'

I ignored his raised eyebrow and nodded, attempting to look calm. I felt fear behind my eyes, tugging at my hair. I wanted to return to my room, slam the door and climb into bed, far from the murderer, flowers painted across walls and this city of death.

My uncle opened the door for me and I saw that someone had lit a fire.

'I had just made Mr Trelawny a special fruit beverage. I am sure you would wish for the same.'

I do not want your drink! I wished to cry. I said nothing, for I was afraid he would think of taking me outside again. I spread my hands in front of the fire, hoping to burn away the terror creeping through me. *Make the thoughts stop.*

He walked from the room and I reached down to a piece of coal on the hearth, feeling the heat inch along the lines of my palm and up into the whorls of my fingers. I shook my head, trying to push the blood and the flowers from my mind, moved my wet skirts to the fire. The material had barely warmed when my uncle returned, the door creaking as he walked through with the cup. I did not thank him.

I sipped the bright red drink, tasted currants, oranges and a bitter undertow.

'Retire as you please when you have finished.' He lingered with his hand on the doorknob. 'I feel we have grown a little distant recently. Tomorrow we should sit and have a proper discussion. I am intrigued that your headaches do not seem to have returned.'

Head pains had racked me in hospital. When I had come to live with my uncle, I found myself free from so many illnesses, the dry patches under my eyebrows, the ache at the side of my foot. The headaches had stayed, though, and even grown worse until I thought I might come to suffer from them like my mother. I sipped at the cup again and tried to remember the last time I had felt one.

Then I recalled – and my mind tipped. I had to stop and tell myself never to think so again. I sat quietly, emptied my thoughts as Dr Neville had taught me, opened my eyes. At this precise moment, I told myself, Constantine Janisser and Miss Grey would be tucked up in their rooms, sleeping innocent dreams. 'Miss Sorgeiul,' they said, on their return, sitting in the parlour.

'Why, she is strange.' They comforted themselves that such a freak incident would not happen again. Miss Grey gave her brown dress to the maid and laid her head on the pillow. I was alone, with no one but my uncle. The magician opened the box and there was Miss Wood.

I took a little more of the drink and let the warmth slip down the back of my throat. The fire was hot on the front of my dress. I hauled myself to sit at the table, telling myself I should take the half-hour or so to calm my nerves, then retire to bed. I pondered retrieving my manuscript from behind the bureau, but my uncle might enter and find me scribbling.

I looked at the window but could see only the shutters. If they were open, I supposed, I would see myself in the glass, half reflected, a kind of ghost. But I would not open them: what if eyes outside were looking in at me? I knew such thoughts were the product of fear, but I could not prevent them catching my heart. I pulled the first book I could reach from the bureau and found Miss Burney's *Evelina* in my hands.

The heroine was just entering Vauxhall Gardens when the door opened once more. I turned to see Mr Trelawny's lumpy face peering at me.

'Do I disturb you, Miss Sorgeiul?'

Did he also wish to discuss paintings? 'I was merely sitting.' The standard response of a young lady, not troubled by interruption, always prepared for visitors because her occupations were never of consequence.

In her bed in Albemarle Street, Miss Grey turned over and put her hand under the pillow.

'I came to say – good evening.'

'You are leaving us?'

'No, no. Not quite yet.' The fire flickered as he manoeuvred himself into the room. The air cooled. I watched his shadow splay over the table as he shuffled forward.

He cleared his throat. 'Your uncle is occupied. I thought I might come downstairs.' He wrapped one arm across his chest and pulled at his sleeve. Then there was silence and I listened to the fire. I thought it must have been about two o'clock in the morning. All across London, people were sleeping, children crammed into beds, men top to toe, women holding each other for warmth. The Queen dozed, rats and mice scuttling under the fine silks of her hangings, while her ministers slumbered over papers and glasses of port. Only those caught by fear were still awake: guards watching for robbers, women waiting for husbands, children hot after bad dreams. They – and us, the inhabitants of number seventeen Princes Street.

A log snapped in the flames. He coughed. 'How do you keep these days, Miss Sorgeiul?'

'I am well, sir.'

There were still no sounds from upstairs. Was my uncle sleeping? Mr Trelawny leant back against the closed door. 'I am glad to hear that.' He rubbed at his hair. 'What do you drink?'

'My uncle made me a fruit cup to help me sleep. I did not want it.'

'Ah.' His face was so strange, craggy and covered with blobs.

There was a creak from upstairs. I looked at Mr Trelawny and his face was flushed. In one quick movement, he was over by my table, so close I could feel his breath on my cheek. 'Miss Sorgeiul,' he hissed, as I tried to stop myself recoiling. 'Miss Sorgeiul.' I pulled my hand off the table in case he wished to perch his crabby paw on it. 'I did so urgently want to say to you –'

I looked up into his pale eyes. 'Yes?'

There was another creak from upstairs. Mr Trelawny turned to me and his words fell in a tumble. 'You are well now, yes. But if you were ever not, Miss Sorgeiul –' I nodded. When would he go? 'Yes, if you were ever not, I would wish it most heartily you would know you could rely on me. We are lightly acquainted, I know, but this is a dangerous world, you are a young girl, and, and . . . if there were ever anything you thought might harm your health, I would beg you to come to me.' He slid a crumpled piece of paper on to the table. 'My address. Any cabman would take you there.'

I put my hand over the paper. The fire flickered on his face and he seemed ready to say something further. The floorboards upstairs creaked once more. 'I shall depart.' Then, in one quick movement, he sprang towards me and clasped my hand. 'Whatever anyone might tell you to do, consider carefully. Think hard before you obey.' He leant forward, so close that I could see the bloodshot rivers wandering from the tear ducts in his eyes. 'Young ladies,' he said, a snaky tinge to his voice, 'are often too wont to say yes.'

And then he was shambling his bent back out of the door, creaking up the stairs and into the study he shared with my uncle. I stared at the sunken chair, imagining Miss Grey sitting there, the flowers on her skirt dancing in the light, but my mind was burning with the street outside, my uncle and Mr Trelawny upstairs. *Please*, I wished to cry, *let me sleep*. My mind was burnt with Miss Wood, the street, my uncle – and now Mr Trelawny. What had he meant, 'Whatever anyone might tell you to do'? No one spoke to me. I saw nobody, met nobody, other than my uncle's friends, and I would never go out again after tonight.

I waited for a few moments, finished my drink, and then followed Mr Trelawny's way upstairs. I tried to undo my boots but the strings were too much for me, and I threw myself into bed fully clothed. I could hear Crispin purring but my arms were like lead and I could not move. Only my mind was alive, it seemed, wild with blood. *Make the thoughts stop*. Miss Wood looked up and three gloved fingers curved around the wall.

I woke in the dark to feel a headache starting. This time it was scarlet, beginning as a pale pinkish colour at the edge of my temples. I lay there and felt the soreness thicken. Then, as it filled the front of my head, the ache grew darker and warmer, and soon I could feel it careening through and there was nothing but pain.

17. Grey Eagle Street

Professional fire watchers wait on alert to hear about a blaze. I had read about how they make their livelihoods from rushing to the place of a fire. They love the collapse of wood into flames, the smells of hot wax and charred wool. Then they begin to gather up the possessions of the family under cover of the panic or offer the bereft accommodation at a high price. I had used to think this something terrible. I could not even imagine hurrying to stand by the Thames and watch the Houses of Parliament burn, as my aunt and uncle Cross had, six years before.

That night, while we walked to the flowers, the house a little way distant flamed. Pots, pans, the daughter's blanket, the father's shoes, all burning. Glasses shattered and the cloth body of a doll sputtered in the flames. In the road, people stood watching, thrilling to the danger, relieved it was not touching them. This is what you have become, I told myself. You are watching the murders like people staring into the fire, eager to taste the misery of others. And now, with the show, the fire has come close to you.

Without possessions, you have nothing to show who you are. A family who had been burnt from their house would be like me when I had arrived at my uncle's house with not an object to display for my nineteen years on this earth. Less than a year later, I had stories and now these fears – flowers, darkness and a dirty alleyway with a hand on the wall.

'Count,' he said to me, as they pulled Louis to them. 'Count to four hundred three times and then begin to count to a thousand. Do that four times and then to five hundred, six times. If you do not do this, you will die. We will leave a curse, and if you do not count, it will tell us, and then we will return and kill you. As I said, Mr Gilbrand is very quick. Four hundred three times, and then a thousand four times, five hundred six times. No rushing.'

I tried to grasp Louis's hand.

'No, Catherine,' he said. His voice was tight again. 'I shall not be long, I promise. I shall return and everything will be as it was. Tell Mama I shall return soon.'

'You would do well to listen to your brother, miss,' said the man. 'Now, remain where you are and count. Tell me, how many?'

'Four hundred three times, One thousand four times.' My mind stopped.

'Five hundred six times,' said Louis's voice, desperate. 'Please, Catherine, you must. Do not forget.'

'Oh, yes,' said the man. 'The curse will hear. And then I will know.' He gripped Louis's chin. 'In fact,' he said, 'I was forgetting. The curse is a strong one. It will watch as you count. And then it will remain with you all your life. Indeed, perhaps it has always been with you.

Perhaps you are the curse. You brought us here, after all.'

'Count, Catherine,' said Louis.

'I shall be watching you,' said the man. 'Your life is mine.'

I sat there, next to my mother, and I counted, four hundred, five hundred, one thousand. I counted over and over, for my mind was so muddled that I forgot the numbers and had to start again, begging the curse to forgive me. I must have counted them at least ten times. When I stopped, I did not know what to do. I could not scream.

'Why are you counting?' said my mother. I opened my eyes and she was staring at me, holding her head. 'Where are we?'

'Louis has gone!' I cried. 'Two men came and took him.'

She raised her hand and brought it hard to my face.

The bells were ringing eleven when I awoke to banging on the door. My uncle had departed, and the house was so much as usual that it was as if last night had never occurred. I walked downstairs and looked through the hole in the door to see Emily, the maid from the Kents'. Upstairs she sighed over the ruined blue gown and helped me into the moss-green dress, too hot for summer, but there was no other.

'I take a pleasure in doing for a young lady, ma'am,' she said, combing out my hair. 'All I have is a gentleman, and Mrs Kent is not one for fashion. If you were to find Jane did not return, I would be pleased to come in her place.'

'I do not think that Mrs Kent would wish to lose a maid such as you.'

She shrugged. 'They would like to share. Mr Kent told me he was uncomfortable at the thought of you being without a maid.'

'That was considerate.'

'I do not think that Jane will come back, miss. I saw her. She told me she was afraid.'

'We are all afraid.'

'Have you heard about the show at the Egyptian Hall last night, miss?'

'Yes.' A hall full of fear. In gaol, the warders threw food at the magician, laughing.

'I have never been there. The newspapers say there was meant to be a false lid and sides to the box, but somehow they were not there.'

'I imagine the death was a tragic mistake.'

'Or someone took the false lid away. That's what I heard.' She pulled hard. 'Have you ever visited the Hall, miss?'

This was how people must be across the city, excitedly discussing the scandal. I could not bear it. 'Never. I have no desire.'

'The magic man will hang all the same, I warrant.'

After Emily had left, I went to the parlour. I sat at my desk and tried to write down the alleyway and the man. I looked at the ink. The magician screamed and Miss Wood looked up, covered with blood. *Stop*. I looked at the shuttered window, and caught the cracks of white light through the panes. 'I should be afraid,' Jane had said to me. The Hogarth print over my head was of St Giles, people crammed in, celebrating, fat and dirty in the years when they had no cleanliness at all. I supposed Jane lived in a very different house, a warm fire, the baby playing with a ball of wool on the sofa. Now she would not come to us. 'I will not walk that way again,' she had told her mother. 'I do not feel safe.' My thoughts ran through me, scattering fear, making my hands clench, and I could not call them to order.

The door opened, and my uncle's head poked through. 'I have purchased a mutton pie from a cook-shop. Let us take a meal in the parlour.' He passed me a plate. 'I imagine there will be less meat than usual, thanks to the shortages. And indeed they have filled the lack with potato, I see.'

I watched him cut the pie with a knife, and I could not credit it. Last night he had been so strange, and now here he was, cutting pieces of pie as if we were on a picnic. Then he looked up, and the silver of the knife reflected on his cheek.

'I do not understand,' I said. 'Jane is always so punctual.'

'I will send a messenger. If she will not return, I shall demand a replacement. I expect she is unwell. I have heard that the water sickness is taking hold once more. Do you remember, my dear, last time, when the Houses of Parliament put up curtains covered with lime to protect the Members? Very wise.'

'I worry she must be lost.' I picked at my portion. The pastry tasted to me of metal, but so many things did these days. It was probably the water.

'I doubt it. Enough of her. Do you think your friends Mr Janisser and Miss Grey would enjoy the pie?'

'I hardly know.' Jane circled in my head, wandering St Giles.

'Miss Grey visited you. She wishes for friendship.'

'I do not know. Uncle, are you not concerned about Jane?'

He put down his fork. 'I was talking of Miss Grey. But if that subject does not suit you, let us talk of something else.'

Then he began asking me about my dreams. I told my usual lie: that ever since I had arrived in Princes Street, my dreams had been benign.

And then, abruptly, he dropped the knife on to the bureau by the window and made to walk past me. 'My dear, I must depart. I suspect I will not return before nightfall, but do not fear. When I return you will be asleep, I feel certain.' He patted my hand. 'I shall prepare you another drink before I leave.' He closed the door and the Egyptian Hall returned to my mind.

Journalists wrote about the murders in the *Criminal News of London*, and then there were other shows – but out of all of us, Miss Wood, the magician and Mr Whitehead were the ones to be caught. I saw him open the box and his face was crossed with surprise and fear. Miss Vine screamed as she saw the blood on Millicent Wood's dress. The murderer was still there, laughing at us all, breaking free of our fingers and casting off our words.

What must it be like to hang? The moment when they seize the lever and the floor falls from under you. I had read about those too terrified to put down their feet on the boards – the men had to force them because if you bunched up your legs you would only take longer to die. The magician sits in a cell, the heat of the bars burning his skin.

Stop it. I emptied my mind as they had taught me and forced myself to calm. I touched the surface of the hot cocoa, looking at the patches of darker brown congealing on the top. So many days I had spent listening to Jane shuffling overhead or bumping the broom down the stairs, declaring her a distraction from the words I was trying to write. Now I yearned for the sound of her feet, and her heavy sigh as she hauled the jugs of water to the kitchen. I had never wondered very much about her. I had liked to hear the bang of the door when she left in the evening, but I'd given little thought to her journey home. I was not even sure of her age.

'I should be afraid.' I pushed her words from my mind. She was at home, surely, playing with her siblings, helping her mother with the sewing for the family. 'You sit inside and no one can touch you.'

Across London, in St James's, the Belle-Smyths were perhaps taking tea with Miss Grey, Miss Edwarda trying not to irritate her reddish hands as she tapped her silver spoon on the china teacup, all of them listening to the story of the Egyptian Hall. Miss Sorgeiul, they smile, well, something odd was bound to happen if she was there. Miss Lucinda pokes Miss Grey. You had a lucky escape from her. The way she sits there, biting her nails, pulling at her hair whenever anyone tries to make her say anything.

Miss Wood's sisters are in her house, touching her books and music, looking up at the dresses she will not wear. The unfinished drawing she had thrown away and the near-empty glass of tea on her bureau: all precious now. They want to go back to the moment when she was drawing the picture, hold her close.

Girls sit over tea, leaf through novels, finger embroidery, wait for fathers and brothers to return, their hearts flour-soft, attending the touch of men. For them, time is measured out, significant, the harbinger of change that cuts the day into periods to dress, embroider, take up their music, dine and sleep. They are fortunate. Abigail's brothers and sisters wait in their cottage in the north, their minds crossed with memories of her. Her sisters burn their hands in the fire, her sweetheart tries to find interest in work and gin as friends tell him he must. The mother stands surrounded by the sheets and chemises she takes in for money, and her tears drip on to the grey cotton. She fills her tub with water, delves in her hands, but cannot scrub, for her mind is run over with the baby that came from her body, a little girl learning to knit, sewing for fine ladies, and were they not all so proud of that? Sara Shell's friends share gin and dare not touch her clothes. Jenny

Amber's husband hears the letter read to him and cries out in fury, locked away in his salty prison.

'The pain will leave you,' a woman at market tells Abigail's sister. 'One day you will wake and find only acceptance of Fate.' But when the pain is departed, what then? At least its sting is something real. When the hurt is no more, then you have to admit it: she is lost for ever.

I did the same, touching the scar of my brother over and over, not wanting to lose sight of the final scenes of him, for if I let them slip, the last part of him would be gone. But the more I held them the more they left me, and although I could repeat the final event in my mind at will, the weeks before turned to mist. I told myself it would have been easier if I had owned some things of Louis's. At Lavenderfields, what I had was taken from me: his school geography book with his maps of India, a doll he made for me from scraps of wood, and a drawing of a robin he had given me. My uncle would never talk of him to me. 'You must look to the future,' he said.

I shook my head, to try to send away the thoughts, and moved to the window. The afternoon was becoming evening; I could tell even though it was still light – men carrying vegetables to set up their night stalls, and the day shift of labourers walking home. Two children were playing with some rags they had rolled into a ball.

If I died, *if I were killed*, my body would be taken and there would be nothing but the things I had left behind. My copies of Miss Burney's novels and *The Murderous Innocents*, the yellow gown, the lilac dress for visitors and the everyday blue, the green-and-blue-striped and the brown, almost all ruined now, the Egyptian necklace, my hairbrush and pens, and people would look at them and say, 'Yes, that is Miss Sorgeiul.'

'No!' I would say. 'Nothing I ever owned has been enough to contain me. My heart has been more than the dresses and ornaments and books.' But I look at my uncle's pictures, his African masks, the stick topped with silver and the velvet suit, and I think: Yes, that is he. Miss Grey is her brown dress, the pearls at her ears, Constantine Janisser his too-shiny shoes, and a few manuals of business. Their clothes and books and vases draw a thick line about them that turns them straight and flat on the page. They wish to take their outline from their belongings; they buy such things with care because there is nothing else to show their souls. I had thought that I would capture myself in my manuscript, the pages dancing with my thoughts and investigations and insights into the violence of the streets, but, no, it is mundane and quiet, and the words do not sing but rest in lumps on the page, immovable, like sadness.

But, then, if I died, who would care to look? Miss Wood's sisters weep, Abigail's family grieve, but I have only my uncle and I do not know if he would mourn me. I have committed a great wrong, and I cannot expect anyone to think that the world would not be a happier place without me. I suppose my uncle would pack up my things in a box, send it to a market stall, return the Egyptian necklace to the pin on the wall.

*

My mother hit me in the dirty street and then everything after that blurred.

'He is dead!' she cried at me. 'You have done it. I always knew you would.'

With her cry, there were suddenly people, official-looking men who came to help, men who had not been there before. The watch was called and men set out to search for him. We were bundled into a carriage with an officer. Back in Richmond, she locked me in my room. More men came and asked me questions.

I heard my mother cry, 'Bad blood. She always wished him to die.'

My father arrived home. He did not speak to me. The maids brought me food and took my clothes for washing, but I stayed in my room. I heard my father's voice, but I did not see him. I heard my mother weeping, terrible hollow sounds that I tried to push to the back of my mind.

I heard talk of a funeral, that they must accept he was dead. A woman's voice, very calm. My father crying. I became confused from the days in my room. Perhaps she had been right and I had dreamt up the men as a lie, and had really sent Louis through the streets to his death.

Locked away, I sat by the wood and pressed myself against it. I wanted to feel the splinters in my skin. Then, when I had been in my room for about a week, I did so, the door buckled against me and I realized that Emma had forgotten to lock it after she left. I pushed gently and there was the hall. After so many days locked in my room, I could hardly believe I was out in the house. I walked softly, so they would not hear. Louis's room I could not bear, but I wanted to walk to my mother's and see from there the road at the front. I wished to see people and perhaps a horse, stand there next to her box of jewels and her furs and look out at the world. I padded softly to her room, to the door, and pushed.

There was a loud rap on the front door. I lifted my head and saw a shining carriage on the other side of the workmen and their great hole. I walked to the door.

'It is the Misses Belle-Smyth,' Miss Edwarda called out clearly. As I unlaced the chains, I heard a laugh and a breathy sigh. And there they were, bedecked in pale silks, feathers in their hair, as if they were going to a dance, two fairies in the filth and the grime of Princes Street, the kinds of figures Mr Kent painted. Behind them children battled over a dog, but the sisters stood erect, no fear in their faces.

'You have come here alone?' I told myself to think of the darns, the let-down hems, but all I could see was grandeur, as if the patched-up girls at the tea party had become quite different, made rich. I pulled at my frayed sleeves.

'Papa offered us the carriage,' said Miss Edwarda. How could her pale feet even touch the dirt of our step? 'We came to return your visit.'

'Please come in.' Then I understood why they were staring at me so. 'Our maid is away at present.'

Miss Edwarda nodded, and I held the door open. They followed me into the shade of the hall and I wondered if the smell of the meat pie still hung around the walls. I heard one trip on a nail and thought they must be looking around them, their eyes twitching at the dark pictures on the wall and the masks. I pushed open the door to the parlour. The last light from the window dropped over the rug from Persia and the Chinese statue. 'Please sit down.' I would have to collect the tea myself, like a little girl making tea for her dolls. I left them staring at the statues while I went downstairs, rubbing at my skirt, put the water on to boil and got out the tea things. The water flickered, like their words, I thought, as they gazed around them and pointed at the masks, the clutter by the fireplace, the panelled walls, when they knew only white and mirrors and high ceilings like cakes.

I carried up the tray as Jane would have done and heard them hush as I entered the room.

'I am grateful to you for paying me a visit,' I said, every word hard and stiff. 'It is a little way to reach me here.' *What do you want?* Behind me, their carriage must have been shimmering in the midst of our hot street.

Miss Edwarda shrugged and smiled, her mouth bulging slightly as if it were full of chocolate limes. 'We wished to see your house. And it is such a long time since we have spoken, Miss Sorgeiul. There was so little opportunity at the tea party.' Her eyes nestled under her brows like two dirty fruits.

'My uncle is not here at present.' I passed them the tea and can say nothing. The clock ticks and a man outside shouts to another to bring over more soil.

'How are you keeping, Miss Sorgeiul?' said Miss Lucinda. 'You look well.'

'I have not been unwell.'

'You have seen our cousins more recently than we. Miss Grey and Mr Janisser.'

So I had been right. Constantine Janisser and Miss Grey had returned with their story of Miss Sorgeiul, how she had been so afraid, *and she is so strange.*

'You went to a show, I believe.'

I nodded.

'And there was a dreadful incident upon the stage. We were quite shocked to hear of it.' Miss Edwarda waved her hand, as if it were a fan. 'Unfortunate for you to attend your first performance in so long and then such a tragedy take place.'

Let me alone and do not torment me, I wanted to cry. *Set me free.* They were pulling and pushing at me and I did not know what they wanted, but I felt the fear weaving through my veins towards my heart and I thought they wanted me.

'We live in dangerous times, do we not, Miss Sorgeiul?'

No! I want to cry. *You do not. I do, and everything about me is fear and horror and danger and it always will be.*

'Such a shame for you, coming to live with your uncle, and then these begin.' She sips her tea. 'You must feel afraid here.'

'I rarely leave the house.'

'The man who commits all these crimes must live nearby, surely. Otherwise why leave the victims here?'

'I cannot guess.' The bones inside us are all the same, white, crumbling, like the skeleton Dr Neville had in his room. I feel mine rising in the flesh and begging them to go.

'You must receive so few visitors.'

'But our maid Starling gave you a little companionship,' chimed in Miss Edwarda.

'She did not stay long.'

'Indeed. We heard your uncle dismissed her. Quite right. We asked her to leave, also.'

My blood paced. Miss Grey's questions. 'I found her a good maid.'

'Oh, indeed, Miss Sorgeiul. She was no worse than any other maid in terms of duties. We had to dismiss her because she was always looking for secrets.' *Miss Grey saying the same to me. Have you lived long in London?* she asked. Miss Grey who, I thought, had grown friendly to me and now I knew from their faces that they had been laughing at me together. *How strange Miss Sorgeiul is.*

'Mama suspected that she might begin to threaten the other maids. Really, under all those smiles, she had a cruel heart, you know.'

'Better a plain girl, a simple girl, slow but honest, we know that now,' added Miss Lucinda.

'Did she ever ask you such questions?'

Every bone was tearing and crumbling inside me, and the ones in my feet were bursting, begging me to walk.

'I do not recall.'

'Nothing? She was always so clever.'

'I am sure she asked you about your family,' said Miss Lucinda.

Where was my uncle? Where was Jane? Why did not the glassy eyes in the masks glitter on the wall, throw open their mouths and send them away?

'There would be nothing to tell.'

The feather trembled slightly on her bosom. 'There are always stories of families. Yours were lost at sea, your uncle said.'

'Yes.' There was dirt from Princes Street in her hair, of this I was sure, the grime from the air and the dust sprinkling, and perhaps when she returned, however much she tried, she would not be able to brush it out. The magician reared up in my head and Miss Wood cried out.

'That could be seen as odd in itself. The whole family take a voyage and leave you behind? And then they die. How lucky for you to escape such a fate.'

I could say nothing.

'Where were they travelling to?'

'Africa.'

'Where?'

'I do not know.'

'Strange. I feel sure your uncle told us India.'

The blood on the sword, the girl on the stage. 'It was Africa.'

'How odd to be mistaken.' She leant towards me, the lace on her gown like a net. 'But, Miss Sorgeiul, we wish to be friendly to you. We want to know more about you. Your uncle has told us that you were particularly fond of your brother. We never had a brother, although we would have liked one so.' She held out her hand. 'What is it like to have a brother, Miss Sorgeiul?'

'I was very fond of Louis.'

'So Mr Crenaban tells us.'

And then I could bear no more of it. I stood up, thrust back my chair. 'I am sorry, but I have just remembered. I have an appointment I must attend.' Miss Edwarda's eyes flashed at me, and her teeth showed under her lips. 'You will excuse me.'

They did not stand. 'But our conversation was just beginning.'

'We shall have to continue another time.'

'We wanted so much to know about your brother.'

'There is nothing to tell. If you would excuse me.' I stood and stared at them and hoped that all around me, the masks and the statues and the warriors with their swords, were staring too, that together we were like Wellington with his army, massed, refusing to let anyone past.

Miss Edwarda rose and tossed her hair. The feather trembled. 'Well, then. If we are not welcome at your home, we shall indeed depart. I shall tell my father what came of our overtures of friendship.'

I nodded. 'My regards to him,' I said.

'One might think you preferred our maid Starling to us.'

'What happened to her, Miss Belle-Smyth?'

'Who knows? We have no interest.'

I moved to the door. 'Thank you for your visit. I wish you a pleasant journey to Albemarle Street.' *Never come again.*

I unlaced the front door and held it wide for them to flurry out into the street, taking their slippers and their feathers and their gowns into the mire, past men who stared and women carrying their children on their backs. I pushed the door shut, and did not watch them into their carriage. I did not care. I wanted to will the men to throw out a new hod of dirt and it to catch their dresses, dropping over the silk like paint, and then Miss Lucinda to trip so that her slippers became spattered with detritus and mud.

Off they go! They swelter in their hot carriage out of Spitalfields and the wheels dip into the cracks in the road. *Dangerous times.* Then, one crack too much: the whole delicate, shining thing is overturned, falls on one side. Neither dies, of course, protected by their fine coach and its soft leather inside, and the silk cushions they brought to protect their backs. The coachman is not so fortunate, his head split open on the road, his blood running and blistering on the hot stone. Miss Lucinda and Miss Edwarda lie there for a moment, in fear, their arms battered, dresses torn, feathers broken in two on the floor. Miss Lucinda is beginning to sniff with fear, but Miss Edwarda is braver. 'We must get out,' she says. And, yes, they must, before the people, small, dirty, half-clothed in the heat, come creeping out from the wrecks of the half-built houses behind the road, the makeshift tents they have erected with sheets over the piles of bricks, and begin chipping, chipping at the carriage, splintering off the gold decorations first, then taking pieces of wood, sawing at the wheels, splintering off the black edges, and then, oh, yes, then, reaching in their hands for the soft leather inside.

And they would use their knives and their rough hands for their hearts.

The Misses Belle-Smyth manage to clamber out, Miss Edwarda pushing up the door, then hoisting herself out and reaching for her sister. 'Don't look,' she says, as she helps her down. 'Don't turn around.' Behind them, the horse is dying – the coachman had not managed to cut it free before the crash – strangled by the rein wrapped around its neck. Around them, people stare. Women with babies, the girls on corners, dirty men holding dark bottles of drink. *Keep walking.*

Miss Edwarda takes her sister's hand and they move forward. But they do not know where they are and they cannot ask. 'Do not tremble,' she hisses. 'Then we will be lost.' As the horse billows, too close to death to scream, they splash through the waste. Miss Edwarda loses a shoe but does not dare bend to find it. And then they reach the end, and it is not a long road, as they had thought, but another small street like the one from which they have come, but this one is worse, overhung by signs that make it so dark that barely anything can be seen. *Walk.*

They stand there, small and afraid, their dresses hot on their backs, and they feel nothing but fear. Going into the darkness would be worse, to return is the same. *We are in hell.*

And then, around the corner, comes a man looking like no one they have seen in this place. He is tall, wearing a black coat and hat, respecting convention rather than heat; he carries himself like a gentleman. They can see little of his face under the drop of his hat, but no matter.

'Forgive me, ladies, but have you lost your way?' His voice is calm above the traffic, and it is like a reed by the side of the river they must both reach out and seize. 'Perhaps you are in need of assistance.'

What luck to him! What fortune. Usually he must travel into town for girls such as this. But here, oh, joy, the Lord has brought them to him.

He holds out his arm to the taller. 'Madam. Let me show you the way.'

I looked down at my hands, clenched in fury and I told myself to stop. *What have you become? Wishing death on other people?* They were right – everybody was right: your family told the truth. *You are evil.* I felt Grace's hand on mine, and I wanted to drop to my knees.

I thought of my uncle standing in line at the pie shop, waiting behind clerks and serving girls and labourers for thick slices from the heavy-armed women at the front. They picked up their papers full of pie and walked off, the men heading towards the docks, filling their mouths with bites of the salty meat, the girls trotting west to the houses in Oxford Street, picking at the soft underside of the crust, the older people with nowhere to go eating more slowly, searching with their tongues for the spots in the pastry where the pig fat had not been quite blended with the flour. All wandering the city, admiring the sun, their minds free of blood. Kind and good, not like me.

I lifted my head to look out of the window. Emily was advancing to the door, her skirts trailing on the stones. She saw me and waved.

'I thought you'd be wanting some help for the evening, miss,' she said, as I pulled off the final chain and tugged open the door. 'Jane still being away.' Her eyes were shining.

'How do you know she has not returned?'

'Anyone could see, miss, that there's no maid here. Anyway, I often passed her on my morning walk to work.'

'Really? Where does she come from?'

'We usually cross ways somewhere around Swan Street. We do not speak.' Her head was high and I felt a twinge for Jane, plainer, younger.

'You are kind to come to offer your assistance, Emily. But I should not take you from your duties.'

'It's not a trouble, miss. It is a pleasure to help a young lady. I used to see you, the odd time you went to the garden. You seemed so pretty and alone.' I looked at her smooth cheeks, and then I thought, Well, if I were a maid in a house as staid as the Kents', where the dust on the clocks is probably the only new thing, ever, I suppose I would watch the girl next door.

She pitched forward to grasp my hand. Her fingers

closed hard and I felt myself recoil. 'Please,' she said. 'Please let me come to you, miss.' Her eyes were on mine. 'It is a living grave there, it is. She stays in her room and he is in his study with goodness knows who. I am young, miss, not meant for a life like that.' She leant back, her cheeks flushed, fear in her face.

'How long have you been with Mrs Kent, Emily?'

'Two years, miss. It's worse since Mr Kent came back. He is always begging her for money, and she cries. Then he paints all day and night, and those girls who come to him are not proper.'

I wanted to touch her hand. 'When my uncle returns, I shall ask him if another maid is possible. But the work here is not as you are used to there. Jane has to clean the house, help wash the clothes, serve our food.' Emily's hands were clean and white, the edges of her nails curved, not jagged and split like Jane's. Her head twitched slightly. The corners of her eyes were blurred with tears. 'I would be most grateful if you could come tomorrow morning.'

'I should best get back, miss.' She stepped away, and it was as if the air were chasing the desperate girl who had clutched at my hands and begged. Her expression smoothed. 'Going out again this evening, miss?'

'I barely leave the house.'

'It seems to me you go out a great deal, miss. I have often seen you leave.' She stood in the doorway, her skirts touching the floor.

'You must be mistaken.'

*

My mother's bedroom was dark. The curtains were closed and there were no candles or other light. I could see nothing, but I thought I would walk to the curtains. My eyes adjusted to the light and the place seemed full of strange shapes and shadows. I touched the wall and wondered how close I was to her large, soft bed. I edged a little further and felt sure that if I made just a few more steps, I could throw myself into it. I did so, and buried my head in the counterpane, smelling her hair and her scent. I turned over and looked at the cornices, which were slowly making themselves out in my vision. And then I heard creaking from near the window. Something was pulling on a beam.

I sat up to see better and that was when I saw.

My mother, hanging from a fur scarf, her hair loose about her shoulders, her head thrown back, her nightdress around her legs, her feet swaying in the breeze. I ran out and screamed for the maids, who came and cut her down, but she would not breathe. I watched behind them until one remembered I was there and bustled me away to my room. They locked the door.

Two days later, my father came to me. His hair was untidy, his eyes shot with blood and shadowed underneath. I jumped for him, but he held out his hand and I knew to sit back.

'I am going to take a sea voyage,' he said. 'I am going to travel. This house will be shut up and sold. You will go to live with your aunt Athelinde in Oxford. That is that. I intend to be away for at least three years. I shall see you when I return. But you will continue to live at Athelinde's. Until you marry.'

He opened the door and left, locking it once more. I threw myself against it and cried for him, but he did not come. Only Emma, who told me to stop the noise, for it would do no good.

They knew. My parents knew. I had dreamt of killing my brother, stabbing him and letting him bleed. And then the chance had come, and I had done it, I had told him to go, so he was lost in the streets. My mother and father saw the evil in my heart. The curse upon me. She died because of me and he ran away. *Your life is mine.*

At Athelinde's, a letter came to say my father had drowned somewhere near Cape Horn. 'He probably wished to die,' said Athelinde. After that, her health began to fail and soon there was nothing for me but Aunt Cross, and then Lavenderfields. And then my uncle's house, where I knew I was never to talk of it. I pretended I had never before visited Spitalfields, and soon I began to believe it myself.

My father, thrown off his sinking ship into chill water, falling with trunks, pans, bottles, sails to the bottom of the sea, becoming a home for the deepest fish.

I could apologize to God for the rest of my life and it would not help. The evil would be there, above me and below me, waiting.

That night I pulled at the buttons and laces on my dress until my fingers were red and sore, and I began to regret not asking Emily to return. Only the thought of my uncle finding me in such disarray spurred me. When

I had finally thrown off my dress and fallen into bed, I lay there, listening to the street quieten, waiting for my uncle's tread on the stairs. He did not come.

I thought Mrs Kent must sleep in the room next to our upper stairwell. She looked as if she had once been pretty, with her greying hair coiled behind her head and a slender frame, but pain was etched over her face, and she clung to her son as she walked, as if she wished to drop to the floor. I wondered if she could hear through the wall.

Mr Kent took her to church every Sunday – St Magnus the Martyr. I supposed she must be very devout. She prayed at night in her room, dreaming of an omnipotent God who could relieve her pain. Renaissance angels would dance in the parlour; a secret cross planted itself at the side of her room. Sometimes, sinfully, she felt nuns taking her in their soft arms. Next door, her son painted, his room strewn with books and pieces of paper, other paintings, stroking with his brush, making art out of thoughts.

I supposed he found the models Emily disliked at the art school. I could not but imagine him flurrying around them, shy of their fine features, hesitant when he told them to move across, so he could achieve the right angle. Behind their coy smiles, they mocked.

I passed the Royal Academy once, years ago, with my father in our carriage, when it occupied the old spot by the Strand. Tall young men sauntered, carrying books and parcels, laughing together. They must think round-faced Mr Kent a man to mock. He might step outside from a lecture and one would call him over and suggest he worked less, for he let down the side with the other chaps. Mr Kent would puff out his pink cheeks. 'I enjoy the work.' He felt only pity for those who did not comprehend the grandeur of Art, saw it only as another step in their life of privilege. The three years at the Academy would change him, turn him turquoise and gold, from a schoolboy into a man creating beauty for the country. So it must be! Art would take him far away from dirty Princes Street and his mother, who always had tears in her eyes. He would reach out with his sharp pencil to tick off each day on the calendar, dreaming of when he could take his own studio somewhere like Great Queen Street, and live in the glow of interested people and the cool of his quiet, arch-windowed rooms.

Please don't.

All the while, I thought, I am here, and the Man of Crows waits in his room. He thinks. He touches the scraps of dresses he collects for his pleasure. He tips the torn pieces of material from hand to hand: uniform blue from Abigail, wine red from Sara Shell, green from Jenny Amber, relishing how the threads fray at the sides. Clever with his hands, he picks up a rudimentary needle and the thick black thread that any man on his own might keep for necessary darning and then he takes the edge of Abigail's blue and places it on Sara's red. He knots the cotton, draws the needle through both pieces, then plunges it back again, stitching small and neat, for he knows that the long ones only fall apart later. At the end of the seam, he doubles over his final stitch, knots the cotton again, and takes up the green, and begins to bind them, so soon they will all be fixed together, tied firmly, like the tails of caged rats, when they have become caught up together and can do nothing but die.

He thinks: The whole nation is afraid of me and here I sit, sewing. I am calm when all around me is frenetic, bloody, afraid.

18. Grace II

I had to make Miss Edwarda need me – and not in that way, for I wasn't so proud as to think there was anything I could do that another girl couldn't, and sometimes I was not sure that my hands were very adept anyway. I had to think of something else. First, I thought it might be tidying. Even when her chamber was in order, the closet was still untidy, summer collars stuffed in with winter scarves and gloves, stockings and shoes bundled together, like the ingredients for a fruit cake piled in a bowl. I left the cook and my duties downstairs – indeed, I was able to do so because they'd hired a new girl called Wheeler – and spent three days in her room. I pulled out the dresses that needed mending or taking up or letting out, and ordered the others by season, then day and evening, and within this, colour and style. She was delighted by my work and said it would remind her to wear the gowns she had forgotten, but soon it was back to the old disorder, and I realized I must think of another way to make her need me.

Yes, hair I could do, but I knew that was not enough. What was there about herself that she did not like? At the first, I hardly noticed when she complained about her looks, so delighted by her that I could not imagine any part of her unbeautiful. But I knew that even though she was pretty, she had – we used to laugh at her in the kitchen – goggling eyes, a bump on her too-wide nose, and ears that stuck out if you did not style her hair correctly. Slowly, carefully, I began to mention them. 'If we put your hair up like this, it will mean that your face looks more open and soft – and your eyes won't stick out so much.' Or I would touch her chest and say, 'I like the neck of that dress. It draws the eye away from your nose.' I said the words with a smile, touching her as I did so. 'That red shawl sets off your complexion, and masks those sallow patches on your forehead.' Each time, I thought she might turn and cry out at me, or perhaps even ram her fist on the dressing-table, but she never did. She always nodded and said, 'Well, perhaps you are right.'

Then I began to push further, to suggest that only I could see how these blemishes might be cured. 'Oh, no, not that dress, miss, no. Can't you see how the decoration at the bosom draws the eye to your nose?' She looked hesitant. 'Yes, yes, I know the style makes your hips look smaller. But face or figure – you need to decide which is important.'

'If only I could have both!'

At that I would sigh, and smile as if such dilemmas were the most miserable faced by humanity.

After a little more of this, I decided the time was right. I got out my red card, my jack, my winner (my father was a card player, lost everything before he left us). *Maquillage.*

Ma, my sisters and I went through so many rooms

after Pa left. The one where we spent the most time was near Seven Dials, in Covent Garden, dirty and leaking when it rained. There were whores upstairs, down and either side. I was excited, of course, by their dress, prettier than Ma would ever wear, and their laughter when they walked up and down the stairs outside my room (they were drunk, yes, but at least they laughed from it rather than crying or screaming like Ma). The two next door – Millie and Tessie – began to let me into their rooms when they were dressing. I sat in the corner and watched. I learnt about hair and most of all about what they called *maquillage*. The whitish fluid they spread over their faces, and the pale powder they dusted on top. They made big smiles and rubbed rouge where it did not crease. Blues and greens they dabbed across their eyes and blended, and then black to rim the lashes. I watched, and marvelled every time at how they made themselves dazzling, and if they turned the right way or the light shone advantageously, they could almost be beautiful. 'You could put less on,' I suggested one day, 'and then people would know you were truly that pretty by yourselves.' They threw back their heads and laughed, cackling like empty bottles. 'No, dear, no! The men want to see it there. They like it!'

Maquillage was for whores, I knew this. But I was sure if I put on just a little less, thinner white paint, pink or peach on the eyelid rather than blue, and paler lips, it would seem as if the girl herself was lovely – and no one would know.

So, after more fussing over necklines and styles, I said,

'I know of some special creams, miss. If you could lend me just a little money, I might be able to think of something.' She gave me two guineas, and I walked out in a quick hour to one of the shops near Seven Dials that sold feather scarves and black gloves without fingers and dresses with no bosom, and spent it all on pots of cream and boxes of powder.

We had a few false starts, of course we did. The first time she looked so overpainted that you'd have thought her a molly. The white went lumpy on the face and the eye powder didn't show up, and she was angry. But I practised on myself, even painted faces on my arms, and soon became deft. She looked in the mirror, turned and threw her arms around me. 'You have made me beautiful!' she said.

'Everyone compliments me,' she said, on so many evenings. 'They say I have finally grown into my looks.' She was exultant, overwhelmed. 'I tell Mother it is rosewater!'

And that was what gave her the idea, I suppose. To turn me to profit.

'I would like you,' she said, after a month or two, 'to meet other girls of my acquaintance. I think you could work wonders.'

One Wednesday afternoon, she told me, she would invite the three richest to tea. They would talk downstairs with her mama, and then go upstairs to look at Miss Edwarda's new dresses. I would do their hair and their *maquillage*. And if they liked it they would pay – her, not me.

That afternoon, I served them at tea and studied her guests. An insipid blonde with dry spots on her face. A girl with pale brown hair and dark smudges under her ordinary eyes. The third had long hair, very thick and black, and her skin was a coppery brown, reminding me of the Malays who used to hang around the docks when we lived at Southwark. Her green dress was so old and ugly that I could hardly credit her being rich. She was looking at her hands, picking at the nails and twitching her shoulder so I could not see her eyes. 'Miss,' I said, bending close to her with the tea tray. She looked up at me and her face was alight with nerves, as if the very fibres were sparking. I touched her shoulder and could almost feel the bone jump.

Later, when I was styling her long hair and Miss Lucinda was talking to the other two, I asked, 'Were you born in London, miss?' I felt her shoulders tense and saw in the mirror that her face was crossed with panic. To save her, I went on, 'Ah, I was, you see. Near the Thames. Mother said she could hear the boats coming in at the very moment I arrived in the world.'

I rattled on until her shoulders softened and her face calmed, and by the time she was easy once more, I had almost finished her *maquillage*. I dusted a little more powder over her face and tapped both shoulders with my hands. 'There! You look lovely.' She thanked me, and then, as she was standing, shuffled awkwardly. As she put her hand into her pocket, I shook my head. 'Oh, no, miss. Miss Edwarda, not me.' She nodded, whispered a thank-you, and went to Miss Edwarda's side of the room. Still, I had seen what she had tried to give me: two guineas.

That evening, Miss Edwarda was a dancing flower. She flung herself on the bed, and threw her shawl on to the table. 'We shall be rich, Grace, you and I,' she sang, bouncing down and kissing me before skipping to her table. 'They loved you!' she said. 'Oh, how clever we are!'

So we were. We continued like that for two months, making up, taking money, and she would give me a little, and then money for supplies. I did dozens of girls, but most often the same few: a redhead with sharp little eyes, the blonde from the first three, and a haughty girl very aware of her fine jawbone. I asked after the black-haired girl once. 'Oh, her!' Miss Edwarda tossed her hand. 'She's too strange.'

I became too certain, that was it. If I felt bored when she touched me, I showed it, rather than pretending sensation, as I had done before: I believed she owed it to me to try to please me. And it seemed to me that if I was beautifying her and her friends, dressing her and tidying her things, as well as my duties in the parlour, she could hardly expect me always to comb back my hair for her and arrange my dress. I suppose I began to think she loved me. And then, at the same time, the girls came less.

One evening in January, I went up as usual. 'Oh, don't worry.' She smiled at me as I stood in the doorway. 'I think you are tired. Why don't you go down and rest?' I shook my head. Rest? If she didn't need me, I would have work in the kitchen. I walked to the bed. 'Oh,' she said, cooing but not touching me, even though I stood right next to her. 'I can see you are weary. Why don't you lie down, then come to me a little later to do my face?'

'But, miss, you cannot dress yourself.'

'Well,' she said, 'you can ask Wheeler to come up for that.' She did not turn as I left the room. I went downstairs and asked Wheeler, and her little brown face lit up with surprise, like a child's. Then I took over her duties for the evening, fetching and carrying and lifting. Every part of me strained to hear them upstairs, the bump of a foot, afraid every moment to hear the break of a sigh. When I went up to paint Miss Edwarda's *maquillage*, her face was calm and, I thought, innocent. Perhaps she had truly thought to rest me.

It was the same for the next two nights. On the third, when I went downstairs to the kitchen, Wheeler was already there. She looked across at me, smiled, brought her finger above her head and proceeded to draw a heart, two bulbous tops and a pointed tip at the end, just at the level of her waist.

So then I knew. And while I was loading the tea tray and talking to Jones and polishing, my mind overturned with white heat and fury. I would not be like Hall! I would tell everyone what she had done to me, expose her to her mother and father. I would set up Wheeler for stealing and she would leave, weeping, and then I would have Miss Edwarda back to myself. But I knew that neither would work – no one would listen to me, and even if her mother dismissed Wheeler, my mistress would only chase down another willing maid. I clanked together the tea things and hated everybody.

'Somebody's cross tonight,' sang Jones. 'I wonder why? Perhaps she is less of a *favourite*.'

An idea formed in my mind, with the smell of old lamb in the kitchen and my hands deep in dirty water. *I would show them all.*

I would find another. I would find another girl like her, who would take me on as a lady's maid – and a little more. And when I had gained all I could from her, I would go to one of her friends.

I wouldn't choose the prettiest or the most energetic. I would have the girl who was shyer and quieter, had the look in her eye of keeping secrets. Miss Edwarda would not say why she had left her school and I had not pursued it. Likewise, I never asked about the suspicions we had in the household – Mrs Belle-Smyth's special doctor, or when the master was out all night. I told myself I would not make the same mistake again. This time, I would prise out her secrets and use them to bind her and her money to me.

I pictured the girls I had met, discounting the sniggering ones with yellow plaits, the girl who read while I worked, the cool one with frizzy hair – Miss Grey, I thought – and the chatterbox Macdonald sisters. And then I remembered the strange girl, rich and dark and terrified of everyone.

Of course! I could almost see myself touching

powder over her dusky cheeks, styling her long black hair and saying to her, 'Tell me about yourself.' And as I began to find out things about her, I would touch her too.

I would go to wherever she lived and make it so she could not exist without me. And when things soured, she would have to give me more money than she could even imagine. There would be no money for dresses, and no more boxes of books or music, or sweet cakes from the baker's, or extra tips to her own maids to fetch her this or that.

In my mind, I touched her dark hair lightly. You are the one, I said. I shall take your secrets. I shall make you pay.

19. Chains

My mind played tricks upon me. I thought it must be the fear. My family, all dead, wandered in my mind. I started with fragments. A seaside holiday.

I suppose I was about seven. My father, mother, Louis and I travelled to Ramsgate in the carriage and took lodgings by the sea, near where the Princess had stayed with her mother. We walked to the sands every day. My mother took the waters for her headaches, and we made castles with Sophy, our nurse. The bathtub in the lodgings was much smaller than ours, and when I put on my shoes in the morning, I found that the wind had blown them full of sand. On the last evening, my father decided that Louis and I could stay up late to dine with them at one of the hotels on the seafront. I cannot recall the actual meal, although I think I see the high white vestibule of the hotel, men in black standing attentive as soldiers. What I remember is our walk from the hotel, the evening still light. Louis and I went ahead, hand in hand, my parents behind. At a road, I stopped and turned and looked straight into my mother's face. She had dropped her head to my father's shoulder, her cheeks flushed red, and she was smiling. My father blew me a kiss.

So we were content, then, the four of us. We made each other so.

I recalled so little of the rest. The birthdays, the other holidays, moving to two new houses, my classmates, and eating cakes with Louis in the tea-room near his school. I had pictures in my mind, but they were still and did not move, and sometimes they changed, so I could not be sure I had not invented them.

I supposed I'd had such memories once, pink and white thoughts that allowed you to say: 'I had a very happy childhood.' But now they had been washed over by the dark room and my brother's cry.

The bang came from Mrs Kent's wall. I woke and lay there but it was quiet. A bell struck a quarter past the hour. I sat up, not wanting to fall back into sleep. I had dreamt I took my manuscript from behind the bureau and every word was altered to her name: Jane Oak.

I gathered my shawl and walked out into the hallway. I held the banister. My uncle was not in the house, I was sure. It did not seem as if even the particles of dust on the stairs had moved. I was alone and my uncle had stayed out all night, risking the crime of the streets.

I pulled on my gown, quickly, so I could tell Emily if she called that I was already dressed, and hurried downstairs to sit at my table in the parlour. If I lived out the day normally, he would return.

But my mind would not stop and I put my head into my hands. There was a knock on the door. Emily, again, I supposed. I pushed my script back behind the bureau and walked to the hall, my head heavy.

'Hello?,' I called. There was no reply. I peered up to the little hole in the door, but no one was there.

I walked back to the parlour. I looked at the table and my heart swelled. My manuscript was on the table, open at the page where I had stopped. The paper was written across, in a large spindly hand I had never seen before.

Write about your maid.

Grace.

The stroke on the *y* was so long that it stretched far under the *m*. I stared at it. Who wrote like that? Who would take up their pen, in my house, and curve their *y* under the *m*?

The front door banged, as if it were closing. I ran to the window, but there was nobody. The men dug at the road, as usual. I looked around the room and tried to enumerate the things: the masks, the table where I wrote. Nothing had changed, except someone had stepped here, put down their hand and *brought their fingers to my paper*. He, it must be a he, had taken out the manuscript, brought down his pen and tipped off the *y* with a flourish. Then he had patted his hand on my papers, walked from the room, touched the doorknob, smiled. I went out to the stairs, then down to the kitchen, putting one foot in front of the other on the dark wood. The pans were neatly stacked, the knives in rows, the warming irons propped on the stove.

Grace had once stood there, rinsing her hands before she put on her cloak, pulled on her outdoor boots and hurried off into the night.

Write about your maid.

There were new pictures throbbing at my head, pushing hard to get in. They were telling me to write about her because she was dead.

She had walked home through dirt and mud and men with sharp eyes – and now she was dead. *Please, Uncle*, I wanted to cry out. *Please come back.*

The wall was shaking, the table too, and I put out a hand to steady myself. I touched the wall – where she had touched. The plate hanging there grew, and the flowers painted on the china surface began to circle and then wind their way off it, as if they would spread over the wall. A smile cut through it, then began to open, and each flower fell in, one, two, three, consumed.

'Stop it!' I shouted, and grasped the door to go. The way her fine hair fell over her forehead, the creases in her dress straining as she bent, her shyness about smiling because a tooth was beginning to blacken and rot at the back of her mouth. My mind burnt up in the fire.

Her face as he seized her.

I touched the sugar cone on the shelf, rough under my finger. It might be a falsehood, meant to make me afraid. But I knew I was right. The flowers were crawling over the plate and she was lying dead somewhere.

You are alone, said the sugar cone. *No one for you.*

Someone is watching you, said the shelf.

I kept my back to the plate, but I knew it was still sending its flowers over the wall, laughing, splitting. *Write about your maid.* Grace was on the muddy ground, her hair full of dirt, birds next to her, the Man of Crows jovial as he walked away. *I should feel fear*, she said.

They were closing on me, the sugar cone, the table and the chairs. They were coming towards me, pressing, and their voices were low and laughing. *Maybe you are next.* Grace put out her cool hand for my hair and spread her light over the room. *Put Starling out of your mind.* My uncle smiled. My mind flashed and turned.

Grace, her hand on my hair, the touch of her finger on my cheek. And now her thin body on the ground, people staring as the magistrates covered her, eyes wide, mouth caught pleading for mercy. Her breast cut open, her hair like a beak, her body torn, for *everyone to see*. The Man of Crows tearing at her heart.

I could not cry out. The leg splintered from the table.

And then there was a crash from above. That set me free. I ran up the stairs, the scream in my heart spreading across my body. 'Uncle!' I cried, for he was stumbling in the hall. 'It's Grace.' He looked up and his face was covered with blood. The redness shone out in the mid-morning light as he fell against the wall and put his hand over his eyes. 'What has happened to you?'

He moved his hand and I saw that his eye was closed, with blood on the lid, and the beginning of a bruise underneath. There were scratches from what looked like fingernails on his cheek.

'Uncle. Come to the parlour.' I held his arm and began to guide him.

He stopped. 'No!' he said. 'No, I cannot.'

'I think Grace might be dead,' I said, and he wrapped

his arm over his face. *You must be brave*, I told myself. I hardly ever saw the blood of others – it only arrived in my dreams. *Courage.* I thought of the kinder nurses at Lavenderfields, talking to us in long, slow sounds.

'Uncle, you must sit. Who did this to you?'

He clenched his fist in his eye. 'Nobody.'

'Did some robbers set upon you?'

He bent to the wall and put his head in his hands. Then he let out a moan.

'What have I done?'

I put my hand on his back. 'You will feel better with an emetic. There is ipecacuanha in the closet.'

He took his hands from his bloody face. I could not stop myself crying out a little. I steeled myself to reach over my hand. 'It will look better when we have cleaned it.' I heard the words come from my mouth as I pretended calm.

He looked down. 'He began attacking me.'

'Who?'

'I could never have thought it.' I looked at his eye, so bloodshot that the red corners were spreading over the iris. 'I can't clean it,' he said. 'It cannot be cleaned.'

'Let me fetch a bowl.'

'No!' His voice was so loud that I jumped. 'Catherine. You do not understand. When I was your age, I thought I could forget my shame by taking a woman or using drink. But doing such things does not give relief. It brings more shame!' He was clutching my hand so hard it hurt and he was almost shouting. 'Then, instead of the shame in one corner of your life, it is everywhere.

Each time you think, you find only ignominy. And when all your thoughts are shame, then that is what you are.' He beat out the final words on my hand and the blood dripped as he did so. Then his voice softened. 'Do you think it is good, my dear, to be purely, simply, one thing? Even if the thing is evil, the integrity is to be cherished, no?'

'Uncle, your mind is rambling.' *Someone has been here!* I wanted to shout. *Grace is dead!*

'Do you remember the sonnet, Niece? "They that have power to hurt and will do none"?'

'No.' Downstairs, the plate was still letting its flowers spread.

'"Lilies that fester smell far worse than weeds"? We read poetry on our outings when you were a child, I am certain.'

'Someone has been here, in the house,' I said quickly.

Then his gaze changed. 'Of course you do not remember. My apologies, Catherine, dear. I suffered a slight shock. Thank you for your assistance. Now, perhaps you might allow me to sit for a while in my study. I assure you, my injuries are less severe than they may appear.' He put his hand on his face. 'I require only a little time to recover. I hope to be well tomorrow, for our visit.'

'Our visit?'

'We are due at the Janissers' for tea.'

'You did not say.'

'I told you very clearly, my dear. Yesterday.'

'You did not.'

He turned away. 'I would consider it a kindness, Niece,

if you might go quietly to your room. If you could let me pass.'

'I think Grace is dead!' I said to his back. I wanted to run after him, tell him I was afraid, that I wanted it to stop. I knew he would not turn.

My room was too hot. I held on to the door and my head was full of red mist. I looked at the dolls and the books, and willed them not to move. *Stay mine.* But then they did. The bed began to sway and a long crack began to cut through the jug. It widened and the pink flowers from either side began to shake. *Stop it.* I threw myself on to the bed and plunged my head into the pillow. *Grace.* I wished Jane would come back from her home. She would be able to help me.

There were footsteps. My uncle was walking past my room and along the corridor. He stepped slowly down the stairs. I lay there and listened. *Do not go to the kitchen!* I wanted to cry. The tables are advancing and the plates breaking and everything is dying. *They that have power to hurt and will do none.*

My mind would not stop now. It curved and took me, and the thoughts fired their own path and would not let me free.

Dead Girls

Oh, you dead girls. You think you can hide from me. Yellow-haired, red-haired, dark, brunette, you are all the same, caring only for who looks at you, not for what you see. You saunter through Oxford Street and St James's, believing – oh, how you believe – that you are kept safe from the evils of the city by the admiring gaze of men and the cushioning of wealth, windows shining like oiled skin piled up with goods from across our great Empire, silks and fruit, minor swirls of sugar to be scattered across the sweet sponge, pink-iced cakes of your tiny pitiful lives.

You lie to yourselves. Such things are empty baubles, and those who believe in them live upon false dreams. And you are not free or happy or able to choose, for because you are here, you are already dead. You give nothing to the world, you simper and think about ribbons, and take a delight in flashing your skirts at men and provoking them to madness. Then, oh, yes, then you cry innocence.

I remark you all as I walk over the city, this city that is my possession and is to you a mirror for your vanities.

I see you.

I wait.

20. Meat Street

The Man of Crows walks back to his lodgings, eyeing people as he goes. How he pities them, those men carrying their tools, women humping laundry, barefoot children selling bits of wood. Their lives are easy, commonplace, and his is great. He has touched the source of life and he has taken it away. He felt the last of the girl's breaths under his hand. He has rid the country of her dirt.

That night, he thinks: *I must discover the next one.* It is exciting, his task, and daunting. The responsibility of finding.

Into the streets the next day and searching for her. He understands that he must not be too ambitious, he must not expect to find her immediately. There are many girls in the city, after all. He must watch them all, search out one with hints of vulnerability. At midday, he stands at the corner of Oxford Street. The girls pass him. Even though he is against the wall, they come so close that it is unbearable. Their smell fills his nostrils. Skirts touch his ankles. Wisps of hair come so close to his face that they burn his cheeks. *Make them go.* Why are there so many?

He cannot look at the bustle in front of him. He walks past a woman with a tray of cakes and a stack of pans and comes to a side road. No quieter. There is a queue of them outside a shop. He supposes it is a cheap food shop, pies or the like. He walks a little towards the red, peeling frontage. They are not simply waiting there, the girls, they are idling. Some of them have their pies, and they are still standing there, talking with the others, tossing back their hair. They are eating the stuff the minute they are out of the shop, cramming the salty mess into their mouths. He thinks of it falling on to their tongues. Three errand boys pass him but he hardly cares.

So many girls, sauntering, eating, laughing, playing with their skirts. He stares at one, small, yellow-haired, brown dress, talking to a redhead. Maidservants, he supposes, playing truant from their duties in Pall Mall or one of the squares. The yellow-haired girl has no manners. In one hand, the newspaper falls open slackly, like a woman's legs; on top of it is the mass of pastry and meat, and she is delving her dirty hand into it and pushing the stuff into her mouth. He moves closer and can see that she is not even swallowing one mouthful before she opens up and puts in another. She must hardly taste a thing, he thinks. She is simply throwing warm grime into her mouth, gristle and fat, meat bulked out with flour. She is eating dirt. The pig poked around the filth-ridden muck-works and bricks outside the city. She was slaughtered by a man who had never washed his hands, and axed quickly so the blood ran into the ground, cut into pieces by the butcher, and the good bits sent to houses in St James's, the rest, fatty legs, the sex organs, sent out to the pie shops. And then, in the kitchen of the shop, the real dirt, when the cook kneaded the dough, and pushed her fingers, spattered in dirt from her female parts, spittle and the stuff from her nose, deep into it. The black of her nails burrowed into the soft flour. She patted it out with her hand, then made up the pies, blood and soil and waste wrapped up together, baked in an oven full of evil.

And now the yellow-haired girl takes up the meat and puts it into her mouth. They feed her in her maiding place, of course they do, but she wants something forbidden, to fritter her little wages, to relish. She has taken her dirty penny from the hot purse in her skirts and passed it over the counter. He moves three steps closer. He wills her to catch his eye, but she sees only her friend. Now he is closer, he sees the truth. She is excessively plain, with pockmarks and lank hair. When she turns to him, her eye is quite dull. She is dead already.

He straightens as he feels his heart drop. He must start once more. And then, in front of him, is another girl. There is a pie, wrapped in paper, hot in her hand.

'Good afternoon, sir.' She gives him a neat bob. He stares at her. Her cheek is a little flushed. She waits for an answer, he sees. 'Do you not know me, sir?'

He must shake his head. No.

'It is Grace, sir. We have met once or twice. When I was a maid, sir.'

So it is. He looks at her and he cannot credit it. 'What do you do here?'

'I am just walking, sir. I no longer have a position.'

His mind soars. 'Will you walk with me?' He looks

down at the pie she holds, the fat glistening under the pastry. In one immediate motion, he has reached down, seized it, and thrust his hand into the meat. It falls into his fingernails. How those old sows must have screamed, when the axe was brought down, their useless bodies quivering, their clotted blood splattering the face of their slaughterman. He smiles at their dirty, desperate snouts as he throws the stuff on to the ground. No doubt some slut would see it and dive down, licking it off the pavement, tasting a mouth of meat and grit as she lay face down, like a sucking worm.

'I saved money for that,' says the girl.

'You will lose your figure. And I shall buy you something better. Come.' He puts his heel in the meat for good measure, so the slut can eat his dirt too, and takes the girl's arm. He feels indignation in the stiffness of her muscles, and he wants to laugh. She does not know his power. She does not understand that he can tread soil into the cobbles, and force her to consume every last scrap of it, and she will be grateful, for at least she is alive.

But when he pulls her closer, she is still aloof, and he understands then what he wishes to do. This one, this pretty one, she is different. He will take her back to his lodgings, and there he will make sport with her. First, he will ask her questions. Then, when she is afraid and confused and begging for it not to happen again, he will take his knife to her. But, unlike the others, he will not kill her immediately. No. Every day, he will cut a little more. And eventually, when she is begging and her cries are nothing but squeaks in her spotted throat, he plunges in the knife. And then he discovers which parts of her flesh wish most for his touch.

My first meeting with Grace was at the house of the Belle-Smyths. Miss Edwarda said that there was a maid who would style our hair. There were some other young ladies there, I believe, a Miss Benn and a Miss Frost, whom I never saw again. I sat on the sofa in Miss Edwarda's room and I looked up as Grace came forward. I waited as she touched the hair of the others, with Miss Edwarda looking on. Then she came to me and laid her hands on my shoulders as she spoke to me. I hardly knew what she said for her words were so soft, and I was dizzied by her touch. Miss Edwarda watched and smiled as Grace began to pull at my hair, put it back into strands, and used pins to hold it. Then she brought her hands to my face, and there were creams on her fingers. When she had finished she gave me a mirror. I saw my reflection and it was beautiful.

'How did you do so?' I asked.

Grace only smiled.

'She is a clever girl, is she not?' said Miss Edwarda. 'Her hands.'

I gave them much of the money from my purse.

The next time I returned, she was not there. I asked after her, and Miss Edwarda said she had other duties. I found myself dreaming of her – until one day I walked into the parlour and she was standing with my uncle.

Our mornings together, in the yellow light, and the nights when the wood of the bureau burnt my hand.

'Come,' she said to me. 'Tell me what they did to you. Tell me everything.' And I did. She fingered my cheeks, then brought her hand down. I saw her face and it shattered into a thousand pieces.

And now she is dead, her hair splayed in the mud, her face open, crows arranged next to her, their sharp feet resting on her breast.

21. Spelman Street

The front door was banging as if it would break. I gathered myself off the bed, ran my hand over my hair, stumbled downstairs and looked through the spyhole. A tallish man, dressed in black. I looked again and saw Constantine Janisser. I called to him that I was coming and began the long process of unlacing the chains.

'Miss Sorgeiul.' He pushed his way in and slammed the door. He was so close to me that our breasts were almost touching. I could smell sharp metal on his breath, and something else, sweet, like drink. I felt as if I was untidy and rumpled, my hair raked, and I was ashamed. In a moment, my uncle might lumber up, blood on his face, and Constantine Janisser would think we were criminals.

'I had to come here,' he said, as I moved away from him. His whole body was radiating heat. In the gloom, he was a rangy tree, swaying as if caught in the wind. 'Something dreadful has happened.'

'My maid, Grace, is dead.' He was a messenger from the real, safe world. The plates would not crack when he was here.

He grasped my hands and I flinched. 'I'm sorry. But you are so isolated, you must know little.' His pupils were close to me, black and wide.

I summoned my composure. 'Would you come into the parlour, Mr Janisser? My uncle is occupied.'

He shook his head. 'I saw him depart. I wished to speak to you without him.'

He had been watching the house.

'I should ask you to leave.'

He seized my arm. 'We have no time for propriety! You must pay attention. Something terrible has happened.'

'Mr Janisser, I beg you to leave. I will cry out, and my uncle then the Kents next door will hear. I will walk to the parlour and scream until you depart.'

'But I am your friend. I wish to tell you just one thing. Miss Grey –'

'I implore you, sir, if you were a friend, you would leave.'

'I have looked at where they are taken. Do you realize? It is like a shape. Hoxton, Swan Street, the docks. It is a shape.'

'I will scream for the watch and they will come to arrest you.' *Where was my uncle?* If our shouting had not roused him, he must be without consciousness.

He pulled me towards him and I was in his arms and close to him. 'You are not safe, Miss Sorgeiul. No one is. I came to tell you.' He let me go and I fell back against the wall. 'You must not be too quick to trust.' He turned and opened the door. 'But it seems as if you are making a sufficient success at that alone. I tell you, I came as a friend.' He threw open the door and went out. The hot air flittered in and his black cape followed him. Then the door fell closed and I was alone, surrounded by the emptiness, like a ghost.

I laced the chains. Abigail in Swan Street, Miss Shell near the church, Jenny Amber by the docks, and the next must be Grace, her face wide to the sky, her hair around her face.

My uncle's coat and stick were still beside the door.

I walked slowly downstairs, listening for sounds. 'Uncle. Are you there?' The kitchen was as I had left it, the cold surfaces clean, no flowers, no splintered table. I closed the door. I was sure I had heard him come downstairs. If I had heard him come downstairs, where was he?

I looked across. The locked door. The door he said had nothing behind it. I stepped forward and hit it with my hand. Then, because there was no one else to hear me, I knocked, so hard that my hand hurt. Still nothing. I ran to the kitchen, reached down a large pan from the shelf, and began battering at the door. Images filled my mind: my uncle sick and dying, covered with blood, holding out his hand for me. I walked upstairs and hauled out the big metal bar that my uncle kept by the front door. I dragged it back, and threw it at the locked door. The wood gave a little, so I threw it again. I hit it once more, and could see the blackness of the room on the other side.

'Uncle?' I could see nothing but the dark side of a heavy piece of furniture. 'Are you there?' I wielded the bar again, and the wood buckled into a small hole. I beat at its sides until it was big enough for me to gather my skirts, breathe deeply and crawl through. I edged forward with my hands, feeling for splinters. I could see nothing but dark. Was there no light?

'Uncle?' I could feel wood beneath my hands. I pulled myself up, clutching at some sort of dresser, but still I could see nothing. I moved my hand along and felt velvet and understood that I could see nothing because there were drapes in front of me. I pushed at the velvet, found the break – and slipped through.

I stood in warm blackness. Lavender, mixed with the coppery tang of burnt metal, hung in the air. I breathed carefully and took a step forward. My eyes grew used to the shadows. A glass bottle with a heavy base bubbled in the centre of the room, blue smoke puffing out from the top, the fire underneath blossoming a powdery light. I stood as if in a dream, wondering at it all. This was my uncle's, surely – but why was it here? All the while, when I had been sitting upstairs, this stuff was bubbling underneath me. The walls were thick with shelves, and some held books, but most were filled with *things* – animal skulls and bones, candles, bottles of all colours and sizes, scraps of stained glass, pieces of wax, metal bowls and saucers, torn papers. Everywhere there were dried flowers, daisies and buttercups in bunches on the shelves, roses on the walls. I thought of my uncle here, with Mr Trelawny, no doubt, running his fingers over the skulls.

There was a burst of flame from the fire under the bottle. I started, and a bitter aniseed smell filled the room. What was this stuff – and where was he? I could not imagine his anger if he found me here. I unclenched my fist, walked forward – and stopped. All along the far wall were strange shrubs. One at the front had a long trunk and yellow leaves. There was a little tree, covered with small red fruits, another with orange fronds like ferns. And then I saw it.

The plant in the far corner was a heavy green stem leading up to large violet flowers that touched the dark wall. Stiff, false-looking petals around garish yellow hearts, the same as the ones painted on our street outside. I reached out, touched a petal – it felt like wax – and edged my fingers over the bumps splaying towards the heart at the centre. I could not help pushing forward and dropping my fingers into the soft heart. I pulled back, and felt a sickness at the sight of the bright stains over the pads of my fingers. The lavender smell intensified. I took a step away.

I tried to imagine them here, my uncle and Mr Trelawny, watering the plants, touching the glass, while Jane bustled in the kitchen and I walked across the floor of the parlour above. The lowest table, next to the bubbling blue stuff, bore a large green scarf that seemed to cover a collection of objects.

I moved closer and saw through the gloom that there were patterns on the floor. I stared at them, trying to focus, and understood they were the star signs, twelve segments of a circle. The paintings were rather beautiful, I thought, a little like a picture I had once seen with my father of the medieval window at the cathedral in Chartres. I moved to the table and saw that it was not a table at all but a large brown book propped on smaller books. I took the green wrap, pulled it up – and my heart lurched.

My things. My things that my uncle had told me the hospital had lost. The silver cross on a chain that my father had given me at my first communion, my brother's school geography book, my favourite pair of blue slippers, my silver bracelet. My uncle, touching them, toying with the cross. Mr Trelawny stroking the silver bracelet. *Do I disturb you?* he had said.

My father had given me the silver bracelet for my tenth birthday. I had felt so grand and grown-up at my birthday meal, finally possessed of a double-figured age. After I had been examined by the doctor, Miss Smith had taken me to a cold room with white walls, and removed the chain from my neck. My hair hung over my face, my eyes stinging as Miss Welsh pulled the bracelet from my arm. 'We will keep them safe for you, never fear,' she said.

One of those girls, Jenny Amber, perhaps, had a bracelet like mine, given to her by her father on a birthday when she was ten or eleven. She could not imagine that she would ever be grown-up, overgrown as her mother, with her greying hair and crêpy eyes. And then when she grew older, and had to deck herself with false-gold bracelets, she had worn her father's gift still. And now she is in a dark room somewhere, not buried yet.

I took them, the cross, the school book, the bracelet. The slippers I would leave for his dirty fingers. I pushed them into my pocket. An impulse made me dip down my hand and bring out the brown book. I pulled open the cover to a wrinkled piece of parchment. I turned to a page of tall craggy script that I did not recognize. I screwed up my eyes to make it out, contemplated moving the bottle of pale liquid closer so I could see. I squinted again, and saw the words *Swan Street*. Then underneath the number '1'.

I scanned down the page. 'Summary of Contents'. There was a series of numbers. Appearance. *Black hair, strong teeth, small nose, large-pupilled eyes, tall shape, small waist, scant bosom*. Every part was detailed, right to the chewed skin around the fingernails. Age: *19*. Class. *Upper*. Education: *Interrupted*. Parents: *Undistinguished*.

Health: *Prone to eye pain, stomach pain, severe (frontal) headaches*. Mental health: *Fragile. Possibility for self-murder*.

I had read so far as if I were dreaming, eyes floating over the paper, but at those words I started to tear through the pages, throwing them over quickly, hitting them back. There were descriptions of people I did not recognize. Someone with curly hair, another with thin ankles. Five was plain with a large nose and a suspected suicide in the family. Six was a young gentleman, with pretensions.

I turned back the pages to the first: *Self-indulgent, prone to vanity. Weak, demanding, preoccupied with self. Seems innocent, pretends a shy heart. Highly likely to injure self and others. Jealous. Cruel. Desires to cause harm*.

I flung the book shut and threw it to the floor. *Desires to cause harm*. Panic scraped across my mind.

When I was a child, I used to pretend to fall out of

bed to have an excuse to trot downstairs and sit with my mother and father. It must have happened once and I had been whisked to the parlour, so after that I began to pretend. I would push myself to the edge of the bed, let myself drop and land on the floor with a bump. Then I would rub my eyes to make them red and stumble downstairs.

I remember the first time I lied. My mother had put down her embroidery and come to pick me up and perch me on her lap in front of the fire, and my father had given me some of his rock cake. On the second, when there were visitors, Mama had sent me to the cook, who gave me a floury hug and promised to make me a mouse with dough. What I could not remember was how they told me to stop. Maybe Mama caught me when I was padding downstairs in my nightdress. Or told me at breakfast or while we were out walking. Then I knew that my excuse to escape into the warm adult world of downstairs was gone and I was to stay in my cold, dark room with the monsters for ever, angry and ashamed.

That was what I wanted more than anything. To be able to pad downstairs, tell my mother I had fallen out of bed and prop myself up on my father's knee, feel warm flames on my face.

22. St Paul's

I leant back against the wall where Constantine Janisser had been twisting my arm. *I will blow at your house*, said the wolf in my storybook as a child.

Preoccupied with self. Jealous. Cruel.

The book careered through my mind. Why would he – for surely it was the work of my uncle – why would he write so? Perhaps he was correct. Perhaps every word was right. *Desires to cause harm.*

I felt as if I were choking. I needed air. I moved to the door. If I was cruel and dangerous, then why was I standing fearful behind the door? *Highly likely to injure self and others.* I reached down and began pulling open the chains, unlacing the lock. I tugged the handle open and looked out over the dirty street.

I took a step and breathed hard against the tightness of my corset. Then I saw Crispin. He was tied to the gatepost with a short piece of string, piteously situated and straining his eyes. I crouched to him, touched his face, and held his stomach with one hand while I unpicked the knots. I stroked his chin. 'Who did this to you?'

He jumped into my lap, buried his head in it and mewed. I carried him inside, not looking at the people on the road.

'There,' I said, when I had pushed the door closed, laced it as much as I could with one hand and taken him to the parlour. I moved my chair to the window, made a nest on the seat with my wrap and tucked him inside it. 'You are safe now,' I told him. I supposed that one of the local children had thought it a joke to tie him up.

I stroked his head and rubbed behind his ears. 'Poor Crispin.' I walked back to the hall to finish locking the door. I was pushing across the final bar when there was a smashing sound from my room. I ran there, pushed open the door and saw glass spattered over the table and floor. Two bricks, roped together, a piece of paper propped between.

One line.

Perhaps you are forgetting.

I flung it to the floor and looked at the smashed window. I thought of how I had run outside alone, and I was suddenly filled with anger. 'Can you see me?' I shouted, to the walls and the empty window. 'You cowards!' The words drifted into the walls. Around here, people shouted and screamed in their houses for any number of reasons, and no one would hear my cries. I picked up a shard of glass and brought it down into the thin skin of my arm, at the curve of my elbow, and touched out a line with the tip. The glass felt gentle, like a friend, and I could not help but roll up my sleeve, hover over the soft skin next to the crease and pierce the flesh. I traced the line, watching the blood blossom. I touched the wound, feeling the freshness of the blood on my finger.

The sound of crashing metal from outside echoed in the room. Perhaps a pedlar had dropped his pans. It brought me to myself. I looked down at my arm and felt sickened that I could do such a thing when poor Crispin was downstairs, alone. I pulled my dress over my arm and hurried to the kitchen.

Crispin had disappeared. My wrap was gone too. The chair was empty. My manuscript was on the table, and it had not been before. It was open at the page I had been writing. But the last four sentences had been inked out, in long, black lines.

Fear clutched at my temples and reached into my heart. There was no sound in the house, save the cracking of the roof in the hot wind.

The man was in here. He had come in here and written the lines in my book. He was here and I could not stay. I tore off the page, threw it on the floor and ran upstairs, not caring if he was there, seized my things and the piece of paper with Mr Trelawny's address from the drawer. I flew downstairs, unlaced the front door and hurried into the street. The men were there but on the other side of the road. I ran in the opposite direction, so I would not pass the flowers on the corner. I saw Mr Kent coming towards me, hid my face in my cape, rushed to the end and hailed a cab. *Perhaps you are forgetting.*

'Hart Street?' The driver turned his head and winked, his ginger beard quivering. 'Might take longer than usual. Some kind of disturbance in town.'

'Could we pass Liverpool Street on the way?'

I flung myself into the musty interior and felt the jolt

as we moved. I sat back and tried to block out the pictures of the magic show, the broken window, the fingers around the wall, my uncle's book.

'Liverpool Street, miss.'

I did not know where it was, Crenaban and Crenaban, Importers. 'Let us go slowly,' I said. 'I will see the house.' We drove through the traffic, watching the road. I passed bankers, lenders, other importers, clerks and lawyers. None looked as if they prospered. I had imagined this road full of clerks hurrying with papers, each firm generating whole worlds of money. But the doors were quiet. The windows of two fine men's shops were boarded over. And then we arrived at another house and we had found it. A sign read 'Crenaban'. But the place looked deserted. There was a wooden bar over the door. The windows were dusty and there were no signs of bustle inside. Whatever he had been doing, he had not been coming here.

'If them owes you money, reckon you're out of luck!' the driver shouted.

'Drive on.' The horses lurched and we moved forward.

The backs of my eyes were pricking. *Let them out*, my mother used to say, when I was very small. *Tears make it better.* But all those times I had cried and cried and only made myself feel more desolate than before – at Lavenderfields, they allowed you to weep, as long as you did so quietly, at night. But crying invited comfort, and there was no one to help me, no brother placing his arm around me, no father to nod affectionately, no mother to stroke my hair. I was alone, my boots thick with dirt from the street, Crispin's fur on my dress, and the eyes of a man I did not know over my belongings. *Tell me*, said Grace. Her hand in mine.

'Nearly there.' I bent forward to see a street of white houses.

'Right, miss. Are you certain that's the one you want?'

Number sixty-five looked as if it had been occupied by thieves. The windows were covered with cheap wood, the door boarded up and fenced with a metal grille.

I pulled my cloak tighter around my face. 'Thank you. I shall descend here.' I handed him too many coins for the fare.

'You don't wish me to wait?'

'No.' I threw him another shilling, which I thought was what he wanted, and stepped out, not looking back.

The street was calm. I could hardly imagine Mr Trelawny here, shuffling along in his dirty overcoat and worn shoes. High white houses flanked both sides of the clean road, ten or twenty years old at most, all polished surfaces and doors, so many windows that their parlours were open like gardens. Two ladies walked by, a governess held the hand of a little girl, and a maid gossiped with a delivery boy outside a gate. And then there was boarded-up number sixty-five, a dirty dead cabbage in an otherwise fine display.

I stood in front of the door. The house looked as if it had been the kind of fresh-painted new property that my uncle scorned. The door was flanked by two ornamental trees, and there was a lamp over the top. I thought of Mr Trelawny creeping back here, late at night, wandering into his own house after padding through ours. His puffy hands touched his keyhole and opened the lock – the same fingers that had flickered over my silver bracelet and tapped the cover of my brother's geography book. The banisters in Princes Street were brushed with fingerprints, curving over each other, my uncle's, Grace's, Constantine Janisser's – and Mr Trelawny's. He had stroked the parlour door frame before he walked in and told me to take care. His rough hands, the nails splayed at the sides, touching my bracelet, tracing the pattern, smiling at me sitting upstairs and having no idea.

I lifted the latch of the gate and walked to one of the boarded windows. I picked at the nail but it stayed in the wood. I walked to another window, free from wood but thick with dust. I brushed at the pane and stared through it into a study of some sort, with a desk and chair. I scrubbed again at the glass. The desk was covered with things, just as my uncle's study had been. I stared again. A hat lay on the table. One I had seen before. Black, with a red band, a diamond-like stone glittering on the front. *I have need of a young person, you see. Let the young lady decide.*

And then, on the wall over it, a sign. The figure of eight, with the dragon's eyes and teeth.

I turned and saw that the two ladies were watching me. Just past them, two men in flapping coats stood talking at a gate. They were looking at me too. The child with her governess, the maid and the boy, and the men who had just appeared, all of them were watching. I gathered my skirts in my hand, as would a normal girl, and began to walk out of the gate. Turning my back to the women, I went towards the end of the street. I turned the corner and wanted to run, but knew I should not. If I did, they would know I was the mouse to be caught.

After the third street, I felt brave enough to turn. Neither the women nor the men were behind me. Instead I saw two girls arm-in-arm, four sailors sauntering, a child clutching his mother's hand. Everyone was accompanied, save a pieman with his tray – and his cookshop was probably around the corner. Only I was alone, wandering in my striped dress, carrying my gloves, walking the streets with no one to claim me.

I have need of a young person.

23. Edwarda

I used to spend hours writing about Improvement. I wrote about plans to put rosewater applications and creams on my face, eat only one egg at breakfast and enhance my personality. Now I do not care about my character for I know goodness is nothing, beauty little, and all that matters is who is in charge. I used to want to be a girl in a painting. I would wear a white dress, my hair around my shoulders, my face so lovely that men might think they could die at the sight of me. I would be like Helen of Troy, begin wars with my loveliness.

Now I make art. I turn people into paintings. You could put them on the wall and stare at them.

My father hates us both for we are not boys, of that I am sure. Ever since I was small, everything I did has disappointed him. Even though I am pretty and my manners are perfect, they say, he thinks nothing of me, and little of Lucinda. Only our cousin Constantine interests him: when that gangly fool walks into the room, you would think that Father had seen his new bride.

Father sent us away to school when I was seven and Lucy five. We cried, that is what I remember, and the other children were cruel to us because we wept so. But, then, it did not take me long to learn that I could have them under my thumb. Then they left Lucy alone because they were afraid of me. My method was simple: I was cruel to a weak girl – fat or bad complexion or, best of all, poor. I knew the first when I saw her: Rosamund Clay. An ugly girl and her apron was cheap. She had a big nose pushed into the middle of her face, and her skin was red and peeling, as if she had been burnt by the sun. I thought her whole body would look the same. I said to the others: You could pull a piece of skin from her back and still there would be more, tearing until the whole looked like some kind of map. 'Couldn't you put some ointment on your skin?' I whispered to her, across the classroom. 'Doesn't it hurt when you rub your hands? What man will marry you?' At the end of the embroidery class, I told everybody I had seen her skin dropping to the canvas, and then she had *sewn it on*. Her two friends, Anna and Sarah, did not take long to desert her. She sat alone at meals and I laughed that her skin would fall into the food, and then she would be *eating herself*.

She left at the end of the tem. I saw her father come in the carriage, tall and handsome, compared to her. If I had smiled out at him with my pretty eyes, he would have wanted me to be his daughter, not her. I supposed he was angry with her for being so plain and such a failure.

I did not need to do it all the time after that. I learnt early that periods of quiet, when I did not touch a soul, made me more feared. I tried Anna, her slow, fat friend, who had thought that turning against Rosamund would give her protection. A new girl with oily hair came on a church scholarship, and we made light work of her.

It all became so easy. Then, in my final year, a new mistress, Miss Smithel, began at the school. She was to teach French. She looked like a child. I supposed she had been a pupil-teacher, and now she was in our school. I thought she was probably a poor girl without parents.

How you find someone to make a picture out of them: look for someone who wishes to be liked. They just desire a friend, you can tell: their eyes beg like those of a dog. In our first French lesson, she entered with a nervous smile and told us she wished to know our names. That was her first mistake. After that, it was not hard. We began with simple things: humming through her lessons, spoiling our work, leaving pins on her chair, stealing her books when she was not looking, dropping ink on her hand as she passed. 'Girls,' she would beg. 'Please.' But she never spoke to Miss Kettering, the headmistress, so we knew she was desperate to stay. I wrote whole essays in my book. 'Smithel *La Bête*'. '*La Stupide*'. We drew pictures. Her wispy hair in its hopeless bun, her quivering little mouth, the thin nose, the flat bosom, we drew them all. I painted her surrounded by men declaring they would never marry her. We continued the game. The more she did not tell another teacher, the more we knew we had won. And then, finally, we came close to plague her. There had been three lessons in which we threw paper balls and flicked ink at her, refused to listen, shouted loudly when she spoke, dropped our books on the floor and refused to pick them up. And then, at the last one, we perfected our plan. We approached her, and as she flapped her hand at us and told us to go away, we moved closer and began picking at her skirt. Alice pulled gently at her hair. Gwendolen fiddled with the back of her bodice. Emmeline touched her cuffs. We were so close we could smell her heat. We began to touch closer to her bosom, and Alice tugged out her hair in earnest. It fell around her face and she screamed, a low cry, pushed at us, and ran from the room.

Winning.

One of the younger girls, Maisie, three years our junior, discovered her. She was lying in the garden, a bottle by her side. Arsenic, they said later. Her hands were black. I looked at her empty, open face and I thought that I had made her truly beautiful.

I had to leave the school, of course, Lucy too, even though she had not an idea of what had happened. My father said that I should stay at home and act as his secretary: then we would see how lucky I had been at school.

So I do – not Lucy, for she is too stupid. I must spend my day with him, listening to him talk and writing it down. Legal material, wills, messages, documents, ships, trades. Every word seems the same to me, and sometimes he grows angry with me and tells me I have confused one line with another. And if I protest and say I wish to be riding or paying calls like other young ladies, he tells me I must stay with him and redress the wrong I have done.

If I am slow and lazy, he makes me write about his hobby of breeding plants. He does not wish to grow them in a garden but to write of plant change and plant breeding, how to make one plant change by using another that is very similar, grown very close. I can bear this least for it is all Latin names and then terms of science, and sometimes I must leave whole sections for pictures. I have no interest in plants, and I hate every name, for I can spell none of them, and he laughs at me. Even worse is when he asks my opinion on the breeding, and I can think of nothing to say. 'Surely,' he says, 'if we breed a plant with one that is very nearly related, the end product will be stronger. The mistake all along with cross-breeding is choosing plants too far apart.' He tells me to write about family trees, and brother plants.

Then, sometimes, he wants to insert sentences on the Queen. Along with the wonder of plants, his favourite subject is her marriage. How wise she was to choose her cousin, what a greater choice the Prince Consort was than the Prince of Orange or one of the Russians, how their blood will be strengthened by their union so their children can marry the offspring of her uncles. Even so, he only allowed me three new gowns for the celebratory wedding balls at the Rooms, which I call cruel. I imagine that he wouldn't have given me more had I been invited to the palace itself. I should visit the palace. I think I would fill the throne better than fat little Victoria.

Most recently, he wishes to write down his thoughts about the Man of Crows. He looks at the newspaper reports and asks me to transcribe short accounts of the victims. He asks my thoughts on the victims and how close they came to death. I tell him I do not find the subject interesting. I lie, I read about the Man of Crows with eagerness too. I think that he must be a most fascinating man.

He takes people, he torments them. I feel sure that if we met, he and I would have much to converse upon. I imagine us sitting together in an expensive hotel, I in my fine green hat and velvet suit. He solicits my opinion on the girls he has touched with his hand. My words are so wise that he is quite struck. Next day, he sends a parcel to my home. I open the fine box and see: he has given me diamonds.

If my father would only let me go out, I might find him.

I miss school, from time to time. It is much harder now I am here to find a person to make into a picture, like Rosamund or Miss Smithel. I can play with my maids, but they are easy prey. I wanted Miss Sorgeiul, not plain but so nervous she twitched every time I saw her. My father told me to leave her alone, said she was too rich, although she does not seem so to me. I only have Lucy, and it is so dreary and familiar with her. She crumbles so easily when I pull her hair, cries when I laugh, and if I tell her she looks plain, she is fiddling with her face all day long. There is no pleasure.

When I go back to my room, if I find a spider or a beetle, I hold up my mirror to any light that remains and reflect it so the thing burns like a hot stone. I wish I could do the same to my father. I think of the plant names that rush through my head and then I remember the names of those girls I drove to leave the school – Rosamund, Elizabeth, Anna, Marianna, Bella – and I know they think of me now with fear, even if Rosamund is no longer so fat and Elizabeth so poor. I often think of finding them again, just to see the fear in their eyes, and to know I am superior. Miss Smithel flits through my mind – someone such as she could never have lived long. Then I call Wheeler to assist me to dress.

24. Maiden Lane

All London lay ahead of me, but I had nowhere to go. I had once so longed for freedom, and now I had it, but nowhere was safe. I could find a library in St James's and sit in the quiet. Or I could stand on Trafalgar Square, watch them building Nelson's Column, then walk to the new National Gallery, with all the art students next door, two years old. No. I would be strange and peculiar, surrounded by ladies in silks of yellow and blue, their hats trimmed with artificial flowers, sketching the lines of a Madonna or listening to a lecturer describe the deposits of paint on a canvas. I would stand there with dirt on my face and dark spots on my skirts, and they would turn from me. And how could I do these things, walk like a tourist through a city, when nothing is the same as it was, so they say, and maybe the gallery is not like that at all, but empty and deserted, the paintings beginning to peel in the heat, the frames cracking, weeds growing through the floor? The library might be the same, the shelves buckling in the sun, the books fallen and splayed on the floor. In this great city of a million or more, of fine houses, ballrooms, work sheds, so many lives going on, and nowhere for me to breathe.

What would happen if I just lay down? If I just dropped on to the road and lay there, in the dirt, as people walked around me and I saw feet and the hems of skirts, and the wheels of carts. I am just resting, I could say. I need sleep. And then I would lie there, and my hair would cushion me as the sky above burnt and it would be as if I were a child, lying in the grass, looking at the flowers around me that trembled in the breeze, wishing they could become fairy houses. I would lie there and hardly notice the odd kick from a foot as a cart boy tripped or an old man wavered. *I am here.* I would close my eyes against the clouds as the crows dipped towards me, beating over on the wind, their feathers touching my eyes, softness dropping to my face. No. I held the wall. I could not die, I knew it. The world would not let me go.

Let the young lady decide.

All over the city, there were women and girls who were useful. The richer ones worked as milliners, dressmakers, shop girls, and the others were servants or street-sellers. They worked and returned to their houses and thought of their sweethearts or clothes or cakes, and life made them happy. But I could do nothing, and my house was full of blood.

'Paper, miss?' A little boy with a dirty face thrust it at me. 'Decent people flee the city, thanks to the crime. Read it here.'

I held out my hand. The front page said it: women were considering leaving. *Not safe for children.* Westminster School had declared that it would begin the September term in a campus near Windsor.

'That's yesterday's date.' I shook him off and began to walk as he shouted behind me.

'Today's news! Only today!'

'Half a penny for old news.'

'It's true. They're leaving, all of them. All the good people.'

He took the coin, and I stood with the news, reading in the street, as no lady would. The foreign writers mock our country for having fallen vulnerable to such a man. The Spanish announce the crisis our responsibility for letting our girls run free. The journalists declare that young female workers push forward our success in industry and we cannot do without them. Rather, blame should be apportioned to the Queen, for hiding in her rooms, huddling with her ladies and Lord Melbourne, and the Prince Consort who thinks of nothing but Germany.

There were flames in my mind. The Man of Crows and then Louis. I dropped the newspaper to the ground, and tried to play over the moment when they had come for my brother. I could not. It would not work. The story I had rehearsed over and over in my mind would not come. Him being taken, me counting, my mother screaming, the carriage home, my father's face. The hat on the table and the sign on the wall.

I had always thought I had made the men come. That's what Mr Gillibrand had said. *You wanted us to come.* The evil in me had dreamt of killing my brother and brought two men to us so he could die. I had made it happen. *You have murdered him*, my mother said. I had believed so, and the blood cut across my mind as I imagined them killing him, and the knife was in my hand. But now the shape was on the wall in Mr Trelawny's house, and my thoughts were not the same.

The fear was a hard ball in my chest, pressing against the bones. I could see the spire of a church over the roofs. A church, the place where people went to be good. I would go there and forget what had happened to me.

I steeled myself and walked to the gates. It was a neat, square building, the large wooden doors flanked by a group of old men warming their hands over a fire. I could sit in the dark on a wooden pew, under the soaring stone of the pulpit and the stained-glass window, and in such a place I would be simple, one thing, and my thoughts would be clear. I pushed the door and made my eyes adjust to the darkness. A man in robes was touching the candle at the side of the altar and two women knelt in prayer. I sat, and felt the marble floor send its coolness through my feet. I would have visited every Sunday, if I had been a girl without sin. I might sit there, weary of my whiskered father and plump mother, in my second-best dress, wondering if the cook had made custard tart or rice pudding for our meal. At the altar, the minister hands communion to good, normal people, with their everyday mistakes.

I would look up at him, wondering if he might press my hand as I left. In the cup is not blood but wine. *Christ's blood*, they say, but the words mean nothing for it is not blood at all. For me, my other, good self in her second-best dress, this is the only blood I ever see or touch, apart from my own. I feel nothing when I drink it, other than relish its sweetness and a sense of transgression. *Drink this.*

The stained glass, the wooden pews, the stone floor are holy, as if they were created by men infused with a kind of angelic light, and all those who step on them are kinder, better than the others outside, awaiting their just reward.

The two women in front of me were still praying, but even if I bowed my head, I would not be able to find God. If I were that virtuous girl, I would be certain that God was always watching over me, prompting me to guilt about little lies and offering me the promise of Heaven.

I could not even say now – such a wicked thing – that I was sure He exists. I knew the answer was that man creates evil, not God, but I could not think Him so helpless. Or perhaps I must believe this, someone like me, for if there is no God or Heaven, then there is no Hell, and that was where I must be destined. I reached out to the curved wooden edge of my pew and touched the smooth underside. I looked up and the man in robes was standing quite close to me, clearing his throat. I supposed he was suggesting I leave, for I was hardly praying. I picked up my cloak and gloves and stood to walk out.

The sun was bright outside. The men caught at my skirts. I leant against the wall. I could not remember it. The story of my brother would not play, and instead all I could think of was the hat on the table and the sign on the wall.

'Good afternoon, miss,' said a small, pale girl standing by the iron fence.

I nodded and made a move to pass her, as if I had somewhere to go. She bobbed her head. 'You were in the church, miss? Some of our young ladies are very fond of praying.'

I stepped forward and she fell in with me. 'Do you know the Society of Friendless Girls, miss?'

I shook my head. Her skin was white, as if it never had bloomed, and her eyes were pale grey. All the colour was in her clothes: a green-striped dress and real flowers on her hat.

'Girls come to London for work. And then their mistresses beat them, make them sleep on the floor like dogs. That is, if they're lucky. Sometimes they're seized for, well, other things.' Her accent made me think of the girls selling cockles by the Thames.

'And factories are no better. The girls end up quite burnt. I am sure you have read in the papers. They come to us because they are friendless, miss, quite alone. They have been made privy to matters that a young lady like you would not be able to imagine.' Her eyelashes and eyebrows were so pale they seemed hardly to be there.

'I am sure it is a charity of great value.' I saw myself dressed as a maid, arriving at the door, declaring myself friendless. She thought me like the Belle-Smyth girls, given a little by their father each month for causes.

'Our house is on Henrietta Street, just nearby. You would be very welcome to visit, miss.'

I shook my head.

'Just for a moment. May I ask your name?'

'Miss Grey. Miranda.' How easily the words came.

'Mine is Ellen Friette. My father was French.'

We turned two corners as she chattered that Covent Garden was a particularly central place for a home, and they ran a tea shop on Sundays, cheaper than anywhere. Some girls, she said, thought that everybody in a place like that might be old, but when they came and saw girls their own age helping, why, then they changed their minds! I nodded, imagining her curving her pale hand around the pot of tea, showing her little teeth as she smiled.

'There is a terrible place, miss.' She pointed at a low-built house with board on the windows. 'Girls make silk flowers, ruining their fingers, twisting the wire in, and the dye they use, it's full of poison.' She clutched my arm as we stood by the wide window. 'That's why I wear fresh stuff in my hat.'

She steered me on and we arrived at another house, fresh-painted, newish. I could see women in easy chairs through the window. She pushed gently at the black door and we were in a narrow hall, with lamps on the walls, and a board covered with notices. 'Our house, miss. This is our parlour, dining room and little library, and on the floor below, we have our kitchens.'

She put her hand on the door to the adjoining room. 'Where would you wish to start, miss? There are young ladies reading in the library. Or practising cleaning and polishing in the kitchens. We train them to be laundresses, ladies' maids, and then our patrons aid them to find a position. Or you might like to see the dormitories.'

'How many girls share a room?'

'Twenty, miss. They each have a trunk for clothes and a box for belongings. You will find a visit very interesting, I assure you.'

The skin on her cheeks was so pale you could see the blood vessels swelling underneath. I would follow her there, and see what? A neat row of beds and boxes. One girl might open her box and show us a doll from her father, a few shawls, some candles, a prayer book. I would have stared into the life of another for no gain at all.

'I am sorry,' I said, words scurrying out of my mouth. 'I have remembered an appointment.' I began backing towards the door. She came after me, saying I could always return another time. 'I am sorry,' I repeated.

Her eyes turned a little flinty then, and I knew that any proper lady would give money. My skirts flurried around my legs and I fished in my purse, found two shillings and placed them on the table. Then, as I moved forward, I realized I could not open the heavy door by myself. So I stood by it, feeling poor and ashamed as she thanked me for the money, unlocked the door, and let me out into the street. All those girls, eating plain bread, darning their dresses, practising curtsies and listening to sermons every Sunday – so they could learn to be good maids and be shown off to people like me, who were lower than they.

I held the corner of the wall of the next street, wishing my heart would still. I felt dizzy and a pain was beginning behind my eye. 'Nice and hot,' said a voice. An old woman, her grey hair gathered into a dirty bonnet, missing three front teeth, was thrusting a basket at me. 'Finest sheeps' trotters. Fresh today.' I looked down and saw the jumble of hoofs, salt crystals just sinking into the flesh. 'Ha'penny each.' I had read that they used the stuff they hollowed from the hoofs for glue and also for blue paint. My dress had stripes of blue, the same colour, perhaps, as the stuff coming from the trotters, a blue that oozed and leaked and ran between the hands of the men painting in Mayfair, making things beautiful. As if there were not sheds in the south-east full of women scraping the hairs off the hoofs, so they could be boiled.

She shook the basket at me and I put my hands in my skirt. I looked down at the basket, and the heaps of little feet, cut halfway, wobbled and became not the feet of animals but devils, as if hundreds had lost their feet at the gates of Hell and watched them thrown into the cauldron for baking. I was about to say no, but she was already retreating, clutching her basket to her bosom. Her eyes had been small and fearful – *of me.*

'You should not be out alone,' said a man's voice behind me. He came to the side, smallish and squat with fair hair. 'Young ladies should not. If I had young ladies under my care, I would send them away.'

I am safe from him because I am evil, I did not even care to say. Such words that had seemed so important were as nothing now.

He came closer and I saw the bumps on his nose. 'You seem very calm, miss. Are you not afraid?'

And that was the worst of it. I was not afraid, and I did not care. I could sense nothing. I could not feel.

'Please excuse me, sir,' I said, dipping my head. 'I must rejoin my mother.'

When I was a very small child, I thought sometimes that I might change entirely when I grew older. Just as my baby teeth had fallen out, I would grow into someone quite new. I always thought of princesses then, or queens, or great ladies, but now I wanted only to be part of the crowd who passed me and did not have to think. I had heard about the market on the Piazza, the stacks of fruits and vegetables like little castles. I could buy my own bunch of flowers, and then become a part of it, making little nosegays, and selling them, like the Irish girls did. And then I would be Catherine Sorgeiul no longer. No sign on the wall. Miss Wood stepped into the box, and smiled.

But the whole market was probably dried and shrivelled in the heat, and there were few women because they had fled to the country. There was little to buy but sick old flowers, brought in on the boat from France or Holland, kept in water all the way, and fruit from other countries with a damp bloom on their skins. And I would be a joke there – no flower girl me, but a draw for men to steal from.

I wished I knew where Jane was. I could go to her, sit by her fire.

My brother was in my mind. My uncle. Grace. *Write about your maid.* The words crept up my back, cold and hard and fearful – and alone. I thought of my uncle and Mr Trelawny looking at the map, and the times when my uncle left the house and I did not know where he was. My uncle. The Man of Crows. And then I shook my head, sent the thought away. Impossible, ridiculous. I had been alone too long. How could I imagine he might do such things? But still it waited there, the thought, hungry.

I took three steps to the right and then began to hurry towards the Piazza. Another road, full of carriages and carts. I stared up at the rush of glossy paint and windows, seeing one man, two women, a family opening a door. And then I heard my name.

25. Fashion Street

'Miss Sorgeiul!' cried a female voice. I looked around and could see only a confusion of wheels. Then again. 'Miss Sorgeiul.' The voice was coming from a large carriage on the other side of the road. The window opened and Miss Lucinda Belle-Smyth's face poked out, her blonde hair quivering. The coachman was staring at me, an eyebrow raised in mild surprise. 'Why are you over there?'

I gathered my cloak and made a pretence of watching the road, so I could walk over to her.

She was at the window. 'Did you receive my note? I sent it two days ago.'

I shook my head. I could not think when I had last seen post at Princes Street.

'Oh? Odd. Well, never mind. How fortunate we encountered you.' The coachman opened the door and gestured for me to step in. 'I cannot credit you are walking there alone, Miss Sorgeiul. You should have written to us.'

I looked at the three of them, mother, two daughters, in the warm carriage and it was as if they were all holding out hands to me. I took a step farther. They were wearing very fine dresses, dark pink for Miss Lucinda and pale violet for Miss Edwarda. Miss Lucinda had piled her hair on top of her head and plaited the strands with ribbons and flowers. I could climb into the carriage with them and be a young lady – and not have to think about my uncle.

Mrs Belle-Smyth leant forward. 'Good afternoon, Miss Sorgeiul. I am so glad you will be accompanying us to the Rooms. How we look forward to the Gordon Dance, every year.'

I had forgotten. The Gordon Dance at the Lilly Rooms, the highlight of our calendars. This year, taking place in the afternoon because the nights were not safe. We were supposed to spend weeks preparing our dresses, visiting the hairdresser, retiring early with violet oil on the skin around our eyes, smoothing rosewater over our lips, forgoing cake, pointing our toes. Miss Edwarda smiled, her hair looped over her ears in a style I could not comprehend. I thought that their efforts at economy had been stilled. Mrs Belle-Smyth's face was crossed, I was sure, with disapproval of my appearance. I was suddenly caught by affection, for I could only undermine their careful, saved-for beauty with my old dress and unkempt hair yet still they had called me over.

'Were it not for the dance, we would take the summer in Switzerland,' said Mrs Belle-Smyth, touching her teeth with ragged nails.

'Come!' said Miss Edwarda. 'We cannot wait for ever.' The coachman came to my side and handed me into the carriage, next to Miss Lucinda, safe. I could say to myself: *I am merely going to a dance and Grace is still alive.*

'My dress is a little – old,' I managed. The carriage lurched and we set off through the thick traffic.

'You look charming,' said Mrs Belle-Smyth. Miss Lucinda was nodding. I glanced at my dirty dress and reddened hands, and thought: *I am a good foil.* My untidiness would make them look more beautiful and seem kind for taking pity on a lost girl.

'Shall Miss Grey be at the dance?'

'I think not,' said Miss Lucinda. 'I did not receive a reply from her, either.' Miss Grey, the other lady in waiting, plainer dress, poorer complexion, no family, another mirror to reflect their glory and gloss, mask the dry patches on their faces, the catches in their gloves.

'She is a very nice young lady.'

'The Janissers are kind to her,' said Mrs Belle-Smyth.

'It is good to take in relations,' I said, looking straight at her.

Mrs Belle-Smyth hissed slightly. Then Miss Edwarda stretched her hand towards my face. 'Will you permit me to arrange your hair?'

I held her eyes in mine. I saw the green spot flutter at the bottom of the iris. 'I would be grateful.'

She moved her hands to my neck. 'Do not try now, sister,' said Miss Lucinda. 'We will wait until the carriage has stopped.'

'Yes,' said Miss Edwarda, and turned to the window. I did the same and saw the Strand cut into the Mall and then towards the palace. The carriage slowed.

Mrs Belle-Smyth jiggled her leg. 'We should have arrived at the dance by now.' Her eyes flickered at the thought of all the fine carriages full of young girls who were arriving before us, girls from Twickenham and Richmond and Chiswick and St James's who had practised their dancing, and forgone cake to whittle their waists and slept with their hair covered with oil, and smoothed rosewater on their lips. *Think of that*, I told myself. *Let Grace still live.*

Miss Edwarda rolled her eyes. 'We were late for the hairdresser, Monsieur Le Toque, at Cross Street. Do you know him?'

I shook my head.

'He is very fine,' she said. She leant towards me and tipped her bonnet back slightly, so I could better see the plaits and curls around her head.

'Very pretty,' I said. This is the world I want for myself. No hands around the corner and *no one in my house.*

'We had to quite beg for an appointment. There was an awful press. Some ladies visited him last night and afterwards had to sleep on wooden shelves, so as not to ruin their style.'

'I am sure.'

'Still,' said Mrs Belle-Smyth, twitching her fingers, 'we could have arrived earlier.'

'Then we would have never met Miss Sorgeiul, Mama,' said Miss Lucinda.

Mrs Belle-Smyth nodded. 'That is true.'

'Miss Sorgeiul would have had to walk alone.'

Mrs Belle-Smyth stared at her daughter, then at me, and turned to the window. 'Indeed.'

We were quiet as the carriage jogged along, taking us closer to the Lilly Rooms. I crossed my hands in my lap.

When I had first arrived with my uncle, he had sent me to a dancing lesson in a hall near Covent Garden on a Wednesday afternoon. When Thomas had left me by the door, I saw that every girl was accompanied, most by mothers, but some by ladies who were surely governesses, a few by fathers. I followed the line, trying to hold my back straight, as if I went to such dances all the time. It was a room with no windows, girls everywhere, a man in a green suit beating the floor with a stick, older women passing behind the girls, touching their waists or hips into position. My nostrils filled with heat, lavender oil and the polish of shoes. The floors were so shiny they were like mirrors. The music grew louder. I felt it move into my ears and stay there.

As a child, I pushed a piece of cotton into my ear, and was too afraid to tell my parents. In the two days before my mother discovered it and took me to a doctor, who edged it out with hot oil and wooden sticks, I could hear hardly anything. It was as if I were under water, waves crashing over my head. I had felt like that again in the dance class. I could not stay. I walked from the hall, holding my skirts. When Thomas took me the following week, I hid in the anteroom and listened to the music. We continued like that until my uncle forgot to ask and I stopped. I wanted those simple days back.

We descended from the carriage, and the man turned the horses away. Miss Lucinda and Miss Edwarda tidied their skirts and turned their faces forward, like soldiers.

We joined the line, entered the door, and removed our bonnets. Miss Edwarda smiled at me and touched the elaborate whorl of hair over her forehead. I was glad there were no mirrors for, as we stepped forward, we were surrounded by girls in pale dresses, their hair arranged around feathers or hairpieces, their eyes bright with expectation. I yearned for Miss Grey and her brown puffed sleeves. Men with swords leant against the walls, and tossed their dark hair at us as we passed – at Miss Edwarda, presumably, and her pink and white smile. I knew I was not seeing straight: that there would be patches of wear on the dresses and dry scales beneath the upsweeps of hair, dirt under the nails and burns on the gloves, and everyone had an ailment, stomach-ache or leg strain, a throb starting in the head, and other diseases that people could not feel or sense, early dropsy in the grey-haired woman by the door, a weak heart tapping inside the handsome man in yellow. All of us, every second, minute, hour, moving closer to being old, unbeautiful, unwanted.

'So many people here,' breathed Miss Edwarda, clutching my arm.

I heard the women were leaving the city, I wanted to say.

But she was in raptures. 'Oh! Look at the table.' She pulled me a little closer. The table was so abundantly filled you would not have believed there were shortages. A large pheasant sat decked with its feathers, a joint of roast beef shone, heavy pies glistened, and the head of a pig sat with an apple in its mouth. There was cheese, glazed, expensive loaves of bread, a large plum pudding and something that looked like a white castle decked with candied fruits, an apple pie and then jellies, six of them, standing sentry at the ends of the table. Miss Edwarda had been caught by an acquaintance, so I walked closer to a red jelly, balanced on a silver plate, surrounded by the knives and forks that would pierce the top, its curved sides trembling with the movements of the floor. The raspberries and strawberries inside looked as if they were floating in the sky. I could be the first to pick up a spoon and slide it in. Our cook used to make jellies when I was a child, mixing the stuff from the calves' feet with sugar, water and fruit, brushing the mould with almond oil, turning it upside down so the waste liquid fell out.

'You are examining the desserts, miss?' A man of about my height with large cheeks and sandy hair was standing next to me. The buttons on his waistcoat seemed almost to burn with his smile. 'I have a sweet tooth myself.'

I knew it was unseemly to talk to a man to whom I had not been introduced, but his eyes seemed so open and his face so cheerfully plain, after all the handsome, unfathomable people, that I wanted to answer him. I thought he would be made happy by feeding ducks, a cricket match, and I bobbed my head. 'I was fond of jellies as a child.'

He gave me a wider smile and I could almost see the cricket-match teas in his pink cheeks. Then fingertips touched my back at the top of my corset.

'Miss Sorgeiul,' said Miss Edwarda, so close that she was almost whispering. 'We thought we had lost you.' The top of her lip was a little split.

I turned to her. 'You will excuse us, sir,' she said to the man, and linked her arm through mine. 'Come. Mother and I have been looking for you.' She brought her finger to the top of my cheek. 'We should address your hair.'

'Oh, I do not think –' I began, but she was already steering me, and I thought that she was probably right: something must be done if I was to stay in a ballroom full of girls wearing diamonds in their hair.

'Let us go to the windows,' she said. 'We shall have light there.' She smiled at me and flicked her skirt as we passed some soldiers in a doorway. We took a few paces further into the corridor, and then she stopped. 'Turn around. Then I shall begin.' She brought her fingers to the base of my neck and I felt her palms on the tiny hairs. Her hand closed around my chignon and began to undo what remained of the style.

'If only I had known,' she said, her voice sing-song, 'I could have brought some pins.' She touched my ear and pulled out a pin just above it. She must shake out her hair and its pins when the maid was taking it down for she was rich and had boxes of them, but with me, she took out each pin and held it in her palm. I could feel them spiking as she moved her fingers. The back part of my hair dropped to my shoulders.

'I do not think you need to worry yourself, Miss Belle-Smyth. I am able to do it myself.'

'Really?' she said smoothly, into my ear. 'Are you sure?'

Girls and men surged past us, and my heart began to beat quickly.

'It is very easy to make mistakes,' she breathed. She touched my neck with a fingernail. 'I once had a maid who arranged my hair. She cut my skin.' I felt her flick one of the bones in my back. 'Careless.'

I looked at the group of girls, arm-in-arm, shaking their heads excitedly and coming towards us.

'Really, Miss Belle-Smyth, I am grateful to you, but I would not wish to keep you from the dance.' My voice had turned high and strained.

'It is no inconvenience,' she said. The last of the people pushed past us as the music began next door, and the corridor was quiet. I felt the draught from the window around my ankles.

I gathered myself to sound brave. 'I think we should find your sister.'

'Stay,' she said, taking another pin from my hair. 'I am close to completion.' Her finger brushed my ear. I tried to think of the man looking at the jellies, the music, the girls in pink– anything to stop my heart crashing so hard at my ribs. I tried to stand still and breathe deeply, ignore her hands on my hair.

'How do you find the dance?'

'Oh, very fine.' The heat was pricking at my skin. Her fingers continued picking at the underside of my hair.

'Yes. But every year there are people I do not know. There are so many people in the city, do you not think, Miss Sorgeiul?'

I could not speak.

'All these young ladies. I should know them, but I do not.'

'I do not know them.' I wished I could see her face. Her blonde curls and slightly upturned nose, the mouth thin and pronounced. Her fingers dropped, and she turned me to face her. I hardly knew her.

'Have you been attending to these murders, Miss Sorgeiul?'

The music was loud in my ears now. 'No.'

'How close they fall to you.'

'I am grateful to you for arranging my hair. But surely we should return to the dance.'

She touched my forehead. 'It will only take a few more minutes. I learnt about hair, you know, by watching my maid Starling. But, as I was saying, these deaths. They seem to be escalating, do they not?'

Her voice was cool, as if she were rounding her tongue in her mouth.

'I do not know.'

I felt her finger twitch over a strand near my ear. 'Your uncle was very interested in Starling. He asked my father to send her to you. I wondered why he wished for her so strongly.'

Three more girls pushed past us and I felt the silk of a sleeve against my back.

'I wonder if she is even still alive. It is a dangerous place you live in. She has disappeared, has she not?'

'I do not know.'

She shrugged. 'Your uncle told my father. He is a

strange one, Mr Crenaban. The way he looks at people. I should be afraid of him.' She touched my hair again. 'I wonder what he said to Grace.'

I wanted to push her hands away, but it was as if my arms and legs were held down and nothing would work.

'So many girls,' she said. 'As many as hairpins.' I stared at her palm and there were six, side by side. 'They break easily, do they not?' She picked one up and bent it slightly out of shape. 'It is so easy to be hurt.' She looked at me again and I felt her hand gripping mine. That was it. I could not bear more. I pulled away, picked up my skirts, turned on my heel and rushed for the main room. I forced my way through the warm bodies in silks at the door and saw the whole gathering, dancing couples, mothers at the side, girls by the food, and then Mrs Belle-Smyth, starting in surprise. I ran straight across the hall, my hair falling around my face, into the corridor, past the men milling at the sides and out of the door.

I stood there, among the men in uniform, and did not know what to do. I took a step forward and saw the row of cabs. I hurried for one, climbed in. And then I knew. I directed him to number thirty St James's Street and listened to him grumble that it was too short a ride. He took me twice around the block, and then we arrived in a street of grand, quiet houses.

I paid him off, descended and pulled on the shiny bell. 'Yes?' said a girl with a French accent, poking out her white-capped head.

'I wish to see Mrs Janisser,' I said, to the white door.

'She does not receive callers in the afternoon.'

I felt her eyes on me and thought of what I must look like to her – my face on fire, my hair wild and undressed, no cloak or bonnet. 'Tell her it is Miss Sorgeiul.'

She cocked her head and opened the door wider so I could stand in the airy hall. The floor tiles were chequered like a chessboard, and there was a heavy sideboard topped with a vase of white flowers.

The door flew open and Mrs Janisser burst through. 'Oh, my dear!' she said. 'I am so sorry you have been waiting.' She caught my hands tightly. 'Come into the parlour.'

She had a little of what looked like flour on her cheek. Her eyes were bright and blue. I thought of her, busy with her house and the menus and the Ladies' Society, visiting her dressmaker for identical navy gowns, and I could not say it to her. *I am lost and everybody is dying.*

'I am sorry,' I managed. 'Is Mr Janisser – your son, is he in?'

'Yes, my dear, but please come through. I would be glad of your company.' She moved her hand up to touch my cheek and tears glistened in her pinkish eyes. 'You received my message?'

I shook my head.

'Miranda – Miss Grey – is missing. She did not return from the Egyptian Hall.'

My stomach turned. I looked down and the tiles on the floor were coming towards me. 'She never returned?'

'Constantine told me that you three became separated after the show. He searched everywhere for you, but finally decided that you had both returned by cab.' Her dry hand folded around mine. 'We were so relieved to hear from him that you were safe.'

'He did not say, when I saw him.' The streets full of people and Miss Grey in brown wandering alone, her face flaming, her eyes full of tears. I had run away and given no thought to her.

'She never wandered. Even as a little girl.'

The wall was shaking. The flowers were growing towards me. There were glasshouses of such flowers somewhere, their yellow stamens reaching up, craving. 'Her parents must be afraid.'

'My dear, they are dead. She has three sisters, at school in Kent with my own dear Sophia.'

'How did they die?'

'Dear, it was a long time ago. Please, come to the parlour. I will call for tea. I had hoped for a visit from the Belle-Smyths. I am so grateful to you, my dear, for otherwise I would sit and worry alone.'

I was about to take her arm when there was a crash and the front door slammed open. Constantine Janisser stood there, his coat open and hair awry.

'Mother!' His sleeve was torn. 'Why is she here?'

He seemed much taller than he had been. I could not take my gaze from him. I heard her fight for words. 'You are rude to our guest, Constantine.'

'Mother, you are a fool.' He pushed his way in and grasped my arm, close up to me. 'Miss Sorgeiul, you must depart. Leave and do not return.'

'Why did you not tell me of Miss Grey?'

'You would hardly let me speak.' He turned to his mother. 'Go to the parlour. I will come to you.' She looked at me, the tears glimmering in her bloodshot eyes, and I thought she might reach out a hand. And then, like a woman used to obeying, she turned away. 'Goodbye, my dear.'

He stared at me as the door closed. 'What are you doing here?'

I returned his gaze. 'Your mother invited me in. I wanted to ask why you came to me.'

'I am telling you, you must go.'

'Have you been looking for Miss Grey? Where is she?'

'Miss Sorgeiul, I am sure we will find her. I beg of you, please leave.'

Footsteps crossed above my head – a maid, I supposed. 'What if I refuse?'

'I will make you leave.'

'I am sorry I sent you away. I was afraid. You were trying to tell me something. Miss Grey – and something else?'

'Please, Miss Sorgeiul, I wish you would leave.'

'I shall not move until you tell me what you came to say.'

'I will make you go.' His hand was tapping his leg, over and over.

I looked at his dark eyes and the long eyelashes, and

I knew what to say to make him let me stay. 'Well, then, I will remain until your father returns. I will ask him.'

He stared back, his face bearing fear. 'No. I will open the door, and you must leave now.'

The anger in his eyes was growing. I stepped out of the door and into the street. I had nowhere to go. My uncle and Mr Trelawny were gone, the Janissers would not receive me, the Belle-Smyths were no friends, and churches had no place for girls like me.

I walked towards Piccadilly, trembling.

Perhaps, I thought, Miss Grey had found Mr Prior – they had forgiven each other after all. But I thought of the times I had been alone, the hands of the men reaching out for me, and I felt the sickness of fear. That evening I had wandered the city, imagining Mr Janisser and she bumping home in their dingy carriage, when all the time she was somewhere else, captured, tormented, afraid.

You must keep your mind calm.

The shop where I had bought my supplies for writing was just across the street. It was closed. I walked to the window, but there was no display of paper, as there had been, and I supposed it must be shut. *Miss Grey visiting me, the green embroidered stems of her dress curving around her waist.* The shops on either side were boarded, but there was a short row of them that looked open, a few yards along. I walked to a window, arranged around a large wedding cake, the exact replica in execution to that of the Queen, according to a small sign, and the side shelves were stacked with more cakes, tottering under the weight of their icing, overdressed courtiers to the great lady in the centre. A boy showed a tray to a group of women. It looked warm and inviting, and I moved to enter – then thought better. A pastry shop was not a place where one could stay for long. I would look strange and odd there, a messenger from another world.

The next shop was a chemist's displaying a brown shelf of glass bottles filled with red, blue and green liquids. A neat set of notices offered cures for everything: headaches, pains in the joints, stinging in the eye. The bells of a church struck half past the hour. I tugged on the dark handle and entered.

A small man burrowed out of a door to stand at the mahogany counter. 'What can I do for you, madam?' I had been given a lifetime of drugs, but I did not think I had ever entered a chemist's. I looked at the large jars of brightly coloured pills and bottles of pink liquid. Under the shelves were polished drawers with gold handles and finely written signs on white card.

'What can I offer you, miss?' he ventured, in his cracked voice. 'Pills for the nerves, perhaps?'

I stared at a concoction of linked glass tubes above him.

'Headaches? Strains in the legs? Young ladies love to dance.'

'I need.' I looked at him and could not say it.

'A cream of rosewater to nourish the face? No. Very wise. You are too young for creams.' He turned his back and pulled out a drawer. 'And I doubt you require hair, for I see you have plenty of your own. But perhaps I might show you, in case you have a friend less – fortunate than yourself.'

He turned and flourished a large drawer at me, crammed to the top with hair: red, yellow, black and all shades of brown. He held it closer and I stared. Slowly, he held up a skein of deep red and rubbed it gently in his hands. 'Some hair can feel rough. This, from the finest of ladies, is so rich it is practically alive.' I wanted to reach out a finger. 'I can see you recognize quality, miss. As well you might, with hair like your own.' I stared at a soft blonde plait. A girl, somewhere, had once combed it, rubbed it with oil, felt it splay over her pillow at night, and this was what made me speak.

'I need a tincture for fear,' I managed. 'You can prevent gout, colds, aches. Surely you can prevent fear too.'

The man smiled and smoothed a hand over his jacket. 'We live in dangerous times. You are not the first to ask, miss. But such a thing is not possible. Melancholy, nerves, yes, but not fear. It is a natural reaction and cannot be quelled.'

'But I need something. I am always afraid.'

'I know a man who can treat fear. He takes a house near Knightsbridge.'

'Is there nothing you can give me?'

'Try Mr Silver. Let me give you his address.'

'I must go.'

'As you wish. Such fine hair. Almost Indian in its lustre and shine. You would not consider selling it, miss?'

I stared at him.

'Of course you would not. A young lady like you. Forgive me.'

I stood for a moment. 'How much would you give me?'

He darted out from behind the counter to stand by me. I held my breath as he reached out a hand and tried not to recoil. His hand brushed the side of my cheek. 'Would you let it down for me?'

I shook my head. 'I do not have time.'

He moved to stand behind me. 'Handsome.'

'How much?'

His voice was almost lost in his throat. 'That would be our arrangement. It is easy for you to grow more. And it is hard without, well, a full assessment of the wares.'

'I shall ask at another shop. I am sure they will tell me.'

In one swift movement, he was close to my side. 'You drive a hard bargain, miss. If it is all of the same quality as the hair that is visible, and if you were to come to me and offer it all – and allow me to cut it, I would offer you eight guineas.'

I fought to control my mouth. I had never seen such money. 'Only that? I have been growing my hair for years.'

'Ten. But there is my final offer. And you must let me take the hair from you.' He held up his forefinger and thumb and rubbed them together. 'I like to cut close.'

'Well, then, I may return. Goodbye, sir.'

I stepped out into the light, the bell jangling behind me.

I passed more shops and Miss Grey ran in my head at every one. The fishing tackle in the country shop made me think of her home in the country, and I wanted to demand brown silk at the haberdashery. Her face reddening as she realized she was alone at the Egyptian Hall, her hands clenching.

The bells struck five. I had no idea what I would do for the night. I walked past the late delivery boys and couples arm-in-arm. The voices coursed in my head as I walked, hardly knowing where I was going. Miss Grey, Grace, my uncle, the patterns on the wall.

After some time, I could not find breath so I stopped and leant against a wall. I took in the smell of the streets and waited for a minute. I did not know where I was. Three women flaunted themselves in pink dresses. I was so craven and desperate that a wink from the tallest felt like a soft embrace. I pulled my shawl around me and began to walk the way they had come, following the same path I had done two nights ago. I continued past a pub, and into the street behind a large church. I walked down past the fences next to the graveyard, trying hard to look around me, hoping to push away the voices in my head. I stared at the graves, the fencing, the few clouds in the steaming sky.

I walked back to the street and trailed my hand over the wet bricks. I pushed my hands on the wall, as if they were becoming part of the stone, and a sharpness began in my wrists.

There was a touch on my shoulder. I stilled for a moment, turned. 'I thought you were dead.'

26. Miss Vine

You think I am beautiful. I look down from the stage and see my reflection in your ordinary eyes. I smile, and everything I do is to please you, for there is misery sufficient at home, you say.

My features matter nothing. You simply need someone to look at, and I will do. Otherwise you would have no one to think over but each other.

I have tasted potatoes from Scotland and meat from Essex and I know the carrots from Wales are the sweetest that can be found. He calls out that he found me in Egypt, but he didn't, not really. I found him. After I ran from the other one, I wandered the streets a little, arrived in Covent Garden, and there I saw a travelling magician turning tricks on a street corner. He had a little dog he patted and made jump. I watched him until he saw me and then we began to speak.

'You should do better things than this,' I told him. 'Dogs and frogs.'

'Could you do better?' He wasn't like most men: the black in his eyes stayed small when he looked at me.

'No, but I could have ideas, and that would be better.'

He laughed and turned away, but still he watched me,

and then he came back and said, 'Well, perhaps I could do with a girl.'

All the time I was showing him how I could dance a little and pose (I knew enough about that) and then we talked of my price. I kept my hands over the beads in my pocket, shining like luck, and the things that meant I could not go back to Pa, Ma, Netty and the rest.

We never made much money until we thought of putting the murders into our show. And it seems an odd one to me, but I was never so popular with the men as I was when I began to pretend to die every night. I have many visitors now. They ask questions about my dress because they want to touch it. Younger ones say, 'Have you ever been on the stage?' and all ages say, 'This is no life for a nice girl like you.' Others tell me that they did not admire my show, in the hope that this will touch me. 'I wonder how you will end,' said one, shaking his head. 'What you will do once your beauty has faded?' He meant to make me afraid, but that is the day I long for.

Sometimes I feel fear when I look out into the great crowd. I think, *He is there, and soon he comes for me.*

So I let them in, those men, after the show, for they are not him.

'I am interested in the way you *walk*,' that man said, round face, little smile, skin like a child's. I suppose he imagined a warm boudoir, draped in velvet, not my damp backstage room, littered with props from a hundred shows before. He did not wish to see my feet cut from dancing, the callouses at the base of my fingers from carrying the boxes. Really, it was not me he wanted at all. He desired to be chosen, that out of all the other men at the show, I would hold out my hand and say, 'You.'

I still have the beads with me, under my pillow.

27. Chicksand Street

Red hair, yellow hair, red hair, yellow hair, brown hair in braids, auburn hair in pigtails, black hair in plaits, a long curl of white hair, blonde hair in a bun.

Hair grows longer after death. Long, long, long, silky on the back.

Red hair, yellow hair, red hair, yellow hair.

28. Sardinia Street

A dirty shaft of sunlight curved over my face. I stared up. I let the colours in front of me meld and blur, and then I saw the sharp cheeks of Constantine Janisser. 'Poor Miss Sorgeiul.'

'What happened to me?' Miss Wood's hair fell over my eyes. Edwarda Belle-Smyth laughed and took out pins from my hair.

'You said something to me and then you fainted. You fell to the floor.'

I could hardly feel my body and my throat was dry with thirst. The ground under me was hard and the sky was bright. 'Where am I?'

'You are where you fell.'

I was in the street. Lying in its midst, people all around me, staring at me, as if I were dead. I was like a victim of the Man of Crows. Anyone could have found me.

'No, no, don't try to sit. You have had a shock.'

The light careered around him. 'I cannot stay here. How long have I been here?'

'Not long, I am sure. A few minutes. There was no one here when I found you.'

I had been fainted there, people everywhere, watching. Even if they had not come close. *What had become of me?*

He was still talking: 'I wanted to find you. I was sorry I sent you away. So I came out but you were nowhere to be seen. I asked at the shops, and that odd little chemist thought you had walked this way.' He patted my hand. 'I am glad I found you. Anything could have happened.'

'The sun is so bright.' It was piercing my eyes, turning me over.

'Do you think you can stand? We should not stay here.'

I closed my eyes and pushed myself to sit upright. The cobbles burnt my legs.

'May I help you?' He took my arm. I tried to stand, three times, but I could not. And then I remembered.

'I saw Miss Vine. She touched my arm.'

'The magician's assistant? But she is dead, Miss Sorgeiul. They found her near the warehouses at Doveton Street. The Man of Crows again, apparently.'

My mind flamed. 'She cannot be dead. I felt a touch on my arm and it was she.' Miss Vine, her hair around her face, dancing onstage, now caught by the Man of Crows.

'She died not long after the show, they think. She must have been caught in the crowd, running away.'

His Cleopatra, dead in Doveton Street. Her beautiful hair.

'It was her!'

'It must have been a girl who looked a little like her. A beggar. We must be grateful she let you alone while you were incapacitated.'

‘But it looked like her. She spoke to me.’ Everything burnt in my mind. ‘How can she be dead? Why can he not stop?’

‘Miss Sorgeiul, we should leave this place. It will soon be evening and we would not wish to be alone. Let me escort you to Princes Street.’

‘I have nowhere to go,’ I said, and then all the words came scrambling out of my mouth. ‘My uncle was attacked and is now gone. I think our maid is dead. I cannot return.’

He bent closer to me. ‘Let me invite you to my lodgings, Miss Sorgeiul. I have taken rooms in Holborn close to my place of work. You will be quite safe there, I assure you. My landlady, Mrs Lamont, is very kind.’

The street was all around him, men, animals, children. His rooms would be dark-panelled, handsome, neat, a building full of men, and the Man of Crows could not come near. My head throbbed. ‘I cannot.’

How can you invite me to your lodgings? I should have said. *How can you treat me in such a way?* But the girl who would speak so would have family and friends and a home and people who considered her reputation, when I had nobody.

And I would still be afraid there. The Man of Crows could still find me, break through the walls, put his hands on me, take me away. ‘I cannot. I have nowhere to go.’

‘Come with me. Miss Sorgeiul, you should not be wandering the streets. There is a murderer at large, you know that.’

His mother and the blooms on her table rushed into my mind. I sat up and remembered. 'Miss Grey. Miss Grey has been missing since the show.'

'I did try to tell you when I came to Princes Street. But now, I assure you, she is safe. It is just that my mother does not know.'

'What do you mean?'

'My mother was not always kind to her. I think Miss Grey took the opportunity to escape. She is with friends. I believe she will return home soon.'

'I did not know she had friends.' Miss Grey, the pearls trembling, her face reddened, in the streets alone.

'But everybody has friends. Now, let us talk of this at my lodgings.'

Miss Grey's plump arms in her brown puffed sleeves. 'I wish I knew where she was.'

'Come, stand.' I got to my feet and looked at the mud on my dress. 'We shall take a carriage.' His hand was on my arm. Miss Wood opened her eyes as they laid her in the box and waited for the touch of knives that would not hurt. Her face as he opened the lid. Miss Grey ran out. Grace put her leg next to mine and smiled. I looked down at his hand. 'No!' His fingers were so slender that I thought I could see the bones under the skin. Under the nails, the blood was flowing, and the lines of white had brief dips in them, like mine. I caught myself then and reminded myself of how much I had detested him when I first saw him. But, still, the hands tapped a little at my mind – and I remembered, *You have no one else.*

'My maid, Grace, is dead. I think she has been killed.'

'Poor Miss Sorgeiul.'

I looked at him, and the street past him, the stall of flowers behind and the maids scrubbing at the front of a house. 'I would like to go to my family home. In Richmond.' Miss Grey ran through the streets alone until he held out his hand to her. 'I have nowhere to go. I cannot go to your lodgings. I want to return to my family home.'

'But you cannot mean so?'

'I do.' I said the words and they were true. 'I wish to return there. I have nowhere else.' The dragons on the wall and the hat. *I have need of a young person.* Mr Trelawny.

'But people would be living there. It was surely sold many years ago.'

'I do not care. I want to see it.' The place where I found the demons first, but then, perhaps, they did not exist.

'The streets are dangerous. Lone journeys are ill advised.'

'If you will not come with me, I shall go alone. I have not been there since I left, when I was a child.'

I watched thoughts cross his face. Then he nodded. 'Come, we shall walk for a carriage. You should be able to find the address?'

And so we set off, through Holborn and Covent Garden. Charing Cross was thick with carts coming to the inns. I stared at the young girls clasping bundles, the men hunched over their knees. Why would you want to come here? This city of evil.

'Tell me of what you think, Miss Sorgeiul.'

'I have a feeling in my mind that I cannot stop. Something terrible will happen. I am sure of it.' There was too much fear in me to isolate a single part.

He shook his head again. 'Nothing terrible will happen.' In one quick movement, he reached over and pushed his coat from one side of the seat to the other. 'There. That is the worst thing that will happen, a coat moved out of place. Miss Sorgeiul, I know Miss Vine was a shock, a dreadful event. But the Man of Crows will soon be stopped, I assure you, and this horror will be over. The authorities are searching for him, and they will have him, I promise you. I am sure Miss Vine died quickly. We must be thankful that she is the only one now for a few days. And I know what occurred to poor Miss Wood was terrible, but they are saying it was a mistake. Something was ill prepared with the trick, a false lid was missing. What we saw was an awful accident, nothing worse than that.' His breath was hot on my face.

'I cannot stop thinking of it' I averted my eyes from his. 'Why did you send me away when I was with your mother?'

'I was afraid of what you might say.'

'I cannot believe that.'

He hung his head. 'It was my father. He had come to an odd idea, about the Man of Crows. He thought that you attracted evil. He had talked so violently that I did not want him to find you.'

I am evil, I had said. And now someone had recognized it. Mr Janisser. I stared from the window at a little line of children walking, hand in hand, voyaging out from school, I supposed.

'Please, Miss Sorgeiul, do not think of it. He was wrong, worried. Forgive him.'

And then the words came out: 'It is all my fault.'

'Do not say that.'

'It is. I began writing about that man, and now he is coming. He took my maid. He knows me.'

'Do not say such things.'

'No. The evil followed me.'

He turned his face. 'I would like to know what it is that a young lady thinks evil. Telling another girl she is plain?'

'I once visited a fortune-teller,' I said then. 'Not long after I arrived at my uncle's. I wondered what someone with the second sight would think of me. She took me into a dark room lit with reddish candles and played with my hands and moved cards around. She said to me that I should stop being so reserved and let other people look after me. There was no one, I wanted to say to her. Because of the wicked thing I had done.'

'I will not listen to this.'

'Please. You see, I always believed I was evil. My brother was killed and I always thought I was responsible, that I had conjured up two men to take him and murder him, and it was my fault. I dreamt of it. But now I am not sure what I think. Perhaps it was not because of me after all. But I began writing about the murderer as I thought he would stop the great sin inside me.'

He pushed back his dark hair. 'This is ludicrous. I refuse to hear it.'

'But now I do not know if I killed my brother at all, and if not, whether I wrote about the Man of Crows when I should not. I thought my evil would protect me from him. But now I think I might be wrong.' I wanted to speak – I would continue even if he did not care to listen, for if I did not speak to him, then there was nobody. I told him of the dreams I had, which had caught me and tormented me.

He was sharp: 'Miss Sorgeiul, all children dream of dying. I should think that dreaming of stabbing your parents means nothing more than that you were afraid of their death.'

I began to talk again of my dreams in which I was cutting my brother and he was dying in my arms and I was happy.

'I should think it not uncommon to dream of destroying a sibling. I am sure the doctors told you this and you have forgotten.'

I carried on, not stopping, letting him say his words but hardly listening. And then I told him of the street, the words rushing quick and relentless. The moment when the man had said, 'So. Which pretty young person shall we have?'

The carriage was quiet, save for the rattling of the wheels.

'Well,' he said finally, 'I would call this a perplexing

story. Your parents died at the shame, you say? I should have thought they would have been grateful to have one child still.'

'Even a child who had sacrificed the other? No. With his death and my evil heart, they felt they had lost everything.'

'I cannot credit it. What of your other relatives?'

'My father's family thought my mother penniless and they cut him off. My mother had no family, except her brother.'

'Mr Crenaban.'

'He brought her up. Their parents died when she was twelve and he seventeen, and he took charge of her. They continued in the same house.' I was speaking louder now. I wanted anybody to hear. 'That is why I was so strange. I was ill because of the things I had done. I had conjured up these men, and my mother said I was lying, that I had simply sent my brother away. But now, I do not know.' I told him about the hat on the desk in the house of Mr Trelawny and the sign of the dragon on the wall.

He put out his hands and held his fingers together at the tips. 'But, Miss Sorgeiul, what makes you think that your brother is dead?'

'Of course he is dead! What else would those men do to him? You did not see their eyes. They were cruel and evil and looking for someone to slaughter.'

'To me, a child like that would be more useful alive. He could infiltrate fine houses with his manners and clothes and steal for them. You could have done so too, but not so well.'

I shook my head. 'They wanted to kill.'

'Miss Sorgeiul. These were two men, you were children. They did what they wished. If you had said, "Take me," or refused to speak, it would have made no difference. They took your brother because boys are stronger and better at stealing.' *Interesting choice*, the man had said to me. *You decided to save yourself.*

'I know he is dead.'

'Well, perhaps you are right. I cannot tell. He could be anywhere. He would be – how old? – seventeen, now? He might be in a thieves' rookery around Bethnal Green, running the younger children. Or he might have come free, found some sort of position. Or he could be dead, as you think.'

'But how do you think they found us? And why did Mr Trelawny have the hat?'

'That I do not know. Perhaps a coincidence. You may not, Miss Sorgeiul, remember the hat very perfectly. And surely there are many like that, with a diamond stone and a red band. But still, apart from that, I find the reaction of your family unfathomable. I do not see why they were so sure you had killed him, merely because you had dreams. I do not understand why they were so eager to see you as guilty.'

'Children can do bad things. A child can abandon her brother in cruel streets.'

'You did not.'

'No. And I do not know about those men, either.'

'Well, clearly it was not your fault. I cannot believe you ever thought it was. You must feel relief now.'

I did not. The idea that I had done evil had been a part of me for so long that I did not know what I was without it.

'But then I wrote about the Man of Crows. And now he is coming.'

'Do not speak like that. I cannot understand it. I have sympathy with your story about your family, of course I do, but I will not listen to these words about the Man of Crows. Yes, he may have caused the death of Miss Vine, and your maid. But that may have been mere coincidence.'

'You know nothing.'

'Miss Sorgeiul. I will listen to no more of this. Perhaps you wish to torment yourself like this. It gives you consequence, I suppose.'

'You believe that?'

'I do not see why you should interject yourself into dreadful events like this. Let us not talk for a while.'

He turned away. I was left to my thoughts, ugly, red and cruel, the same scenes playing one after the other, over and over. Miss Grey in her brown puffed sleeves, her frizzed hair ruffled by the crowd, the red spots on her face painfully bright as she pushed out of the Egyptian Hall.

'We always desired more children,' my father had said, abruptly. 'But I regard our two together and cannot but conclude that we have the perfect size of family.'

'Do not sleep, Miss Sorgeiul.' We were passing wide-spaced villas and gardens. 'We are near the palace where our dear Queen spent her childhood.'

I peered out but could see only a park. 'Our Queen we never see since the murders.'

'She should not have married.'

'Maybe no woman should.' *I thought you were introduced to me as a husband*, I did not say.

'Miss Sorgeuil, you must not go back to your uncle. He cannot have cared for you if he let you believe you had killed your brother.'

'He did not mention it after I came from the hospital.'

'That is little better.'

'Do you ever feel,' I looked at his neat hair and knew he would not understand, but I had to say it. 'Do you ever feel that there is too much living to be done? As if you do not want another day because after it there would be more to bear?'

'Miss Sorgeiul. You must look at life with gratitude.'

I gazed down at my palm and at the lines crossing through the skin. The one that fell around the base of the thumb was the strongest of all, scored angrily into the skin. The other lines – heart, fortune, friendship – were bound up at the edge of my palm. Other people's palms had separate lines, gently marking their soft flesh. Mine were confused with each other. 'But that's good,' said a visitor to our house once, when I was a child. 'Your life is strong, it takes up all the other lines in itself.' I stared at it, thinking it was looking even thicker than it had before. I wished it might slim and fade – and set me free. Grace lay in the soil. *I should feel fear.*

'I am still afraid. I am sure something terrible will happen.' *I have no other friends*, I wanted to say. *Even though I once thought you dull and even sly, and tried to run away from you, now I have no one else.* 'I worry about Miss Grey.'

'I assure you, she is quite well.'

I saw fields, and houses set in fenced gardens. I should have recognized the route, I supposed, but I did not. Then we drove through strips of houses that seemed familiar, but I was not sure. I leant my head against the interior of the carriage and tried not to think of him sitting beside me. The horses turned and we moved to a green adorned with a small church.

'This is Richmond?'

'So I believe.'

We turned into a street of large houses, and every one made me start. The lane where I walked with my mother to my deportment lesson. The church. On the green, we watched cricket matches. Eleanor, a girl I had been friendly with, lived in the large house with a blue door. Then I saw our road.

We were at the house, drawing up to the front, the garden overgrown, weeds tangling over the drive, the gate hanging open. The whole building looked as if it were dead, the front almost entirely covered with ivy and creepers reaching almost to the roof. Slates had fallen and splintered on the dry grass. Flowers had covered the front when I had returned from the family in Cambridge, pinks and blues and yellows, the colours of dresses for dolls. 'I should have thought the neighbours might complain about this mess,' Mr Janisser said, peering.

I could not believe it was as it was. I had imagined a family taking it over, perhaps even pulling it to the ground, making a new story over the old, dreadful one. The grass was so brown it looked as if it had been burnt. 'I thought it had gone to my aunt Cross.'

'You never wondered what happened to the money of your family?'

The horses stopped and the coachman came to the side. 'I did not want to think of it.' I climbed down and stood in the garden, breathing in the smell of dead plants. Birds were fluttering around the roof, perhaps nesting in the chimneys.

The beds were weaving weeds and moss. The bush at the front had flowered, but most of the petals had dropped to the soil in the heat. I touched a brown leaf. 'My brother and I were never allowed in the front garden without our parents. I used to admire this from the window.' The sun heated my hands.

He walked to the front door, turned the handle, and it fell open. As we stepped in, the hall was dark. There had been a chandelier hanging in the hall, once, but I could not see it now. I touched the wall and felt dampness. 'I cannot see a thing.'

Constantine took my hand. 'Let me assist. Take a step forward.' To the side of us was the parlour.

'It must have been a pretty home.' It was only that, with none of the grandeur of St James's.

'Shall we look into these rooms?' There was eagerness in his voice. I nodded and tried to open the parlour door. It stuck, then gave, and dust puffed into my face. One of the shutters was hanging off, so there was light, and I could see that no one had covered the chairs or the table. Dark patches of mould were climbing over the walls. In the fireplace a pottery jug splayed dried flowers. I realized it had been there, filled with lilies, the day my father had left.

'Dreadful smell,' Constantine said at my shoulder.

'Dead flowers.' I looked at the sideboard, where there had once been a glass bowl of beads. As a child, I had spent hours crouching to the same level and eyeing the beads. 'How can it not be there?'

'What?'

'The bowl.'

I was about to take a step when he clasped my arm. 'Don't. There is glass everywhere.'

At first I could see nothing, and then, as my eyes adjusted, I saw he was right and fragments, even whole pieces, were skewed across the floor. 'What has happened?' The shelf that had once held a row of glasses was bare. There were no plates on the wall, and the mirror over the hearth and the heavy vases to either side were all gone. Every item of china and glass had been taken and smashed to the ground. He touched my arm and steered me to the door. 'Let us leave. You may catch your foot on the glass.'

'I do not know if I wish to go upstairs,' I said, when we were in the hall.

'I shall go. You do not have to follow.' He took two steps up and then I knew I did not wish to remain alone. I followed behind him. 'We should take care,' he said. 'Some of the stairs may be unsafe.'

I gave him my hand and we began to walk up, and around the landing, by the large window, which was almost black with dirt. The vase that had been on the shelf by the window was not there. My brother's room was closest, then mine, two spare rooms on the other side, my father's study. At the back was my mother's room. 'I do not want to enter any of them.'

'Are you sure? If the house is condemned or sold, you would not have another chance.'

'My mother died in there. I have not been here since.'

'You could perhaps show me your room.'

I stared at my door. Behind it was everything I had left, my bed, my dolls, the tiny house for which my father had made furniture, the Ark for Noah balanced on the shelf, my books. I had been too afraid to ask my father to allow me to take my things to Aunt Athelinde's. The old Catherine was in there, the child playing with belongings, at home yet.

'Will you let me open the door?' said Constantine.

I had tried so hard not to think of my life in this house, blocking it from my mind, for this was what I had ruined. But the garden was splattered with weeds, the front rooms spoilt with broken glass and maybe it had never been anything more than just bricks and pieces of stone, never really ours.

'You go first.'

There was a cracking sound from downstairs. 'Maybe a fox,' he said, grasping the handle. The door bulged against the frame, then popped. I followed him in. He reached across, pulled at the inner shutter over the window, and there was a shaft of light. The walls were bare. The bed was only a wooden frame and there was no chair or table. The shelves were empty. No dolls, no books, no Ark.

'My father so hated me. He must have thrown it all away.'

'Someone did, certainly. And someone threw glass on the floor downstairs.'

I could not bear it. 'Let us go. Please.'

'Perhaps this was not a good idea.' I was surprised by the tremor in his voice.

He began to move towards the stairs. I started after him – then turned back. My brother's room. I stood in front of the door. 'I want to see inside.'

'Are you certain?'

'Yes, and then I shall never come again. Open it for me.'

The crack came again from downstairs. 'There is probably a whole family of foxes down there.' He opened the door and we walked into the darkness. I clutched the wall as the door swung closed, hearing him breathing behind me.

And then there was the sound of footsteps. The door was thrown wide and then light flooded in.

So,' said my uncle's voice, 'all of us here together. Mr Janisser, my dear Catherine and I.'

29. Park Terrace

My uncle stood in the doorway. His face was covered with more cuts, the eye bleeding, and his cheek flowered a bruise. He was leaning on a walking stick.

'So, Catherine, you return to the home you lost. Has your visit been of assistance?' His voice was so cracked that I could hardly hear the words.

'My brother's room. I had to see it. I do not know if any of the story I believed about him is true.'

'Oh?'

'I went to Mr Trelawny's house and I saw the symbol on the wall. And Mr Janisser told me it was wrong, that no family would blame a child so. Did you not, sir?'

My uncle coughed violently. 'Oh, but you were a special child. All those interesting dreams. You imagined massacring your brother.' He clicked his fingers in front of his face. 'And then, in a puff of smoke, he disappeared.'

'Mr Janisser thinks those dreams meant nothing. You did a cruel thing. Did you take him? What did you do to him?'

'It was strange that you never recognized Mr Trelawny. One would have thought that a man who had exerted so much, well, *change* on your young life could never be forgotten.'

I have need of a young person. The smoke curving up

from his hand. Mr Gillibrand. My uncle smiled. 'Now you recall. It was not long after you came to me that I had contact with Mr Trelawny through business. I learnt our connection and that he had taken your brother. He recognized you. I could hardly credit the coincidence.'

I had to try to speak clearly. 'Where is my brother?'

'Oh, he is dead, my dear. Long dead. He did not have the strength.'

'For what?'

'Mr Trelawny took young men from the streets to assist him in his endeavours.'

'As I thought!' broke in Mr Janisser. 'Child robbers.'

'Mr Trelawny handed them to another. The children were given a good life, enough food, and their only role was to fulfil a few little tasks.'

'Little mercenaries too, I imagine,' said Mr Janisser.

'Killing for money, indeed. But poor Louis never got that far. He could not survive the demands of the life, and the punishments when he tried to escape. He did the matter to himself in the end. With arsenic, I believe. A coward.'

'I sent him to such a fate.' Louis, his face covered in horror, the poison working itself into his heart. His slow death approaching, his body begging to live.

'You dreamt of his death and it came true. How prescient of you.'

'But I think it cruel,' Mr Jannisser broke in. 'It was a kidnapping and could have happened to anyone. Why did her parents blame her? It is a terrible thing to do to a child.'

'They were weak. Very weak. They did not have her strength. No, no, my dear, you do have strength. Just regard how you have become preoccupied by the murders. Most girls would be afraid.'

Mr Janisser moved closer to me. 'I think it cruel. Even if the parents were quite deluded by grief, you were wrong and cruel, sir. You should have taken her from the hospital. And when you met Mr Trelawny, you should have told her she was innocent. Your behaviour has been criminal, sir, criminal.'

'Nothing criminal. Simply fascinating to see a girl with such a delicate mind.'

I was a toy for you, I wanted to say.

'Can you deny the appeal of it all? I admit, at first, I took you, Niece, for someone had to do so. But then, when I met Mr Trelawny, understood the coincidence, the serendipity was too much. I had to see if you might recognize him.'

'How wrong to bring him into the same house,' said Mr Janisser. 'A game for you. And what sort of business would ever have introduced you to such a man? Stolen goods, I presume?'

'Perhaps it was just as well he was not at home in Hart Street when you called, Catherine my dear. What use he might have put you to. He attacked me, could you credit it? A violent man, after all our dealings. He didn't agree with my plans for you, Catherine dear. But still, I do not regret our meetings. There was such a marvellous – well, frisson, when you two met. For me, and him. Perhaps for you too. And then, if all this were not sufficient, you became fascinated by the Man of Crows.'

I wished I could run past him and never see him again. 'I brought the evil closer to me. Grace. He finds me.'

'Oh, my dear, do not look at me in such a fashion. I am not responsible for the murders. Indeed not. Mr Trelawny and I have been following them, but such vulgar methods would not be interesting to us. It was only when you became such an eager follower that I noticed you anew.'

'I wish I had never thought of him.'

'But your writing on him was so very original, my dear. Mr Trelawny and I were following him too, but without your – unique approach. Going out to run and find him, walking through the street.'

'You knew?'

'Of course, my dear. We heard you leave, come back. How very original, we thought. But, most of all, we thought, *she will be next*.'

'Your book.'

'Yes, that is correct! Our book of victims. The milliner, the courtesan, the sailor's wife – and you.'

'Prone to jealousy.

'Indeed. We were so sure you would be next. But you have stayed safe. Odd, do you not think?'

'He takes girls of the working classes, you said.'

'Well, I said this to you, my dear. But it seems as if recently he has expanded his interests.'

'Are you saying,' broke in Mr Janisser, 'that you wished for your niece to be taken in the quest to prove some sort of hypothesis?' My uncle stared back at us. 'You are sinful, sir.'

He shrugged. 'I merely allowed events to take their course.'

'And you do not know the man's identity?'

'No, indeed.' He hesitated.

'Do you?' I begged him.

He shook his head once more. 'No. But he surely lives in Spitalfields. And you are very conspicuous, my dear.' He winked at me. 'If only you would have been more amenable to night walks with me.'

The flowers on the wall. 'You took me out.'

'But of course, my dear. Young ladies should not be alone. But I did not succeed. Indeed, no. I did so well with Starling.'

'Grace. What did you do to her?'

'I did not have to. I simply imagined – and she was gone. How clever of me.'

The bureau behind us shook and began to turn. Flames in my mind spread over his face. 'You sent Grace away into the street and hoped she would be caught.'

'Indeed. I made her remain until late and then sent her out. I wondered what might happen to her. And indeed, I had no further use for her. Belle-Smyth told me she would be a useful informer on you, that she listened. But it seems it was only his daughters she resented. You and she created – a bond.'

'You wished her to die.'

'No, no, my dear. We simply wished to see. And then, after that, it became clear to us: you had not been taken.

Even though the gentleman seems to have a certain attraction to your – circle.'

Mr Janisser broke in: 'Miss Sorgeiul, there is something I have not told you. I gave you falsehoods when we met. My mother does not know. Miss Grey is no longer living. They have found her body near Spitalfields Church. The man must have taken her after the show.'

'No.' My head was burning. 'I do not believe it.'

A tear ran down his cheek. 'I lost her. I lost both of you. I could not find her and he found her instead. I cannot think of how afraid she must have been.' A second tear fell. 'We have to pray that the end came quickly to her.' There was a sound from my uncle, but I could not hear what it was – a laugh, a cough or a sigh.

Miss Grey, her puffed sleeves, the piping at her waist, her face when I asked her about Mr Prior. *I expect they have heard about the murders*, she said to me. Miss Vine, in the Egyptian Hall, beckoning to the people, watching them stare at her, thinking of the men at the end of the evening, wanting to touch her. *I have Miss Grey*. The magician rose up and his face was covered with blood.

Miss Grey, alone, dying, the man with his hands around her neck. The red bumps on her face when she felt emotion. Her warm hand on mine at the show, the pearls at her ears.

'Make it stop.'

In the Janissers' hall, where Miss Grey's feet and skirts had touched, her hands brushing the wall, her hair. Standing there, my dress would have caught some of her dust, mixed with that of Mr Janisser and the maids. I might have her with me. *Deliver us from evil.* I looked to the wall and a fire began there, out of nowhere, spreading towards me, its flames to burn into our hearts. The room shook. *Stop.* I could not bear it.

My uncle was watching me. The shelves at the back of the room jolted as he moved forward.

'You have done criminal things, sir.' Mr Janisser, so convinced that justice would be done.

My uncle smiled. 'Nothing illegal, my dear Mr Janisser. Nothing at all.'

'You watched your niece and hoped she might die at the hands of a murderer.'

'Interest. Mere interest.'

'You wanted me to die.'

'My dear, how can you not be struck by your position? You, the young girl who lost her brother, and the Man of Crows.'

All the time I knew he did not love me, but I did not think he wished for me to die. *You would not have mourned me*, I wanted to say, but I could not. I was nothing more to him than the revelation that he could be right.

'Mr Trelawny and I were so fascinated by crime. We meant to write on it. You, Catherine, would have been our ultimate proof of our belief that people attract evil to themselves. Your tormented soul, your past, your obsession with the Man of Crows, and then your death.'

'I cannot bear it.' I looked at my hands, the thick life line, and Grace and Miss Grey looked back at me.

'You are a criminal, sir.'

'But then, so is your father, Mr Janisser. I acquainted Belle-Smyth and Janisser with my interests. So intrigued.'

Miss Edwarda at the ball. *So many girls. As many as hairpins.*

'What we wanted to know: why does he choose the ones he takes? We thought you could be our guide.' Miss Grey looked out at me, smiled. I had tried to escape her. 'My poor niece, thinking that you imagined nobody knew your story. In reality, it was our amusement.'

So many girls.

'You are cruel, sir. You made her think she was evil. And then you hoped she might die. That is nothing but wickedness, sir.'

He shrugged. 'But without me, where would she have gone? She would be back in Lavenderfields. And, out, what use was there for her? She was hardly going to marry, was she? Not with her history. You did not want her, did you, sir?'

I stared at him. 'My dreams. I always thought I was full of sin.'

'Perhaps they meant nothing, who knows? I imagine there was little different in you from the normal, selfish, grasping child. Only after you thought you were evil came the interest in your character.'

Miss Grey flashed in my mind. My uncle and the Belle-Smyths in their coffee-house, talking and laughing. Mr Trelawny and my uncle patting my things in his hidden room.

'Poor niece,' he said. 'Worrying that you had told

Starling about your family.' He smiled and his teeth were like the fat in meat. 'Everyone knew of the hospital, my dear. And what you had done to your family. It was rather engaging, watching you think you had lied so well.'

'I still do not understand why her parents would think her guilty,' said Mr Janisser.

'Ah, yes. Well. I believe they thought me her father.'

If I watched the shelf for long enough, it might fall and splinter over us all. 'No.'

'I would wish not. Such nervousness of spirit is not part of me. Although, as I said, aspects of your morbidity were fascinating, my dear. It is possible, I admit. I wished your mother to know me, still, again, after the wedding. Your father found out, of course, much later, and so I was banished.'

'No.' My father crying out, forbidding my uncle to visit. My mother's tears. How quick they were to believe I betrayed Louis. *Bad blood*, she said.

He shook his head. 'I had thought you might be interesting. But now I do not wish for my blood to live. There are too many young ladies in the world.' He held out his hand. 'Although, I must say, less so now.'

Miss Grey, her eyes staring out from under the soil. Grace, her heart next to mine.

'Of course, if I am your father, then that is a crime. But who knows? So far, it is true, many matters suggest you are not normal.'

'I am going to leave. I will leave through that door and I will not see you again. You cannot stop us.'

'How can you think of leaving? Such horrors lie waiting for you in this city of crime, my dear. You are surely in danger from him now.'

I shook my head. Grace and Miss Grey were at my mouth and I could not open it.

'I think it cruel,' said Mr Janisser, 'to tell a child she had caused death. Children are innocent.'

'I will leave now.'

'I shall follow you.'

And then there was a cry and a movement. Mr Janisser had grasped a candelabrum and was holding it over my uncle. He brought it down hard and my uncle collapsed as if he were made of leaves.

My mind flared. 'You have killed him.'

'No, no. Look, he breathes. He will return in an hour or so. Now, you must hurry, Miss Sorgeiul, depart. Go somewhere, as far as you can. I will stay here and stop him from leaving when he wakes.'

'But then what will happen?'

'Oh, I can break away. Now go, please. You wish to, do you not?'

'What has happened?' I felt the tears at the sides of my eyes. Louis and I, sweet children together, my father praising his family. All the while, perhaps I was not his.

'You must leave.'

Mr Janisser began pushing me towards the door, away from my uncle. I almost turned to regard my brother's room just once more, but then Mr Janisser's hand was on my back and he helped me down the dirty stairs and into the hall. I looked at him and he gave me a small smile, opened the door, and then reached out to touch my hand. I stepped out, pulled the door shut behind me, and it closed softly, with a click.

30. London Fields

I dragged myself into the road. I knew Mr Janisser was right, that I should run, but I did not know where I might go. I would have to take a cart to Dover and the boat to Europe, but I did not know where. But then, I thought, I could not leave with nothing. I had money and my manuscript in my uncle's house, and I would need them. I ran out into the main road, and hurried along until I found a free cab – there were few about at that early hour. I did not look from the window as we drove.

He let me out in Princes Street, and I walked slowly towards the house. Grace danced through my mind. The early morning sun was beating hard on my face and through my dress. I felt sick and ill and every picture in my mind was darkness. A stab caught my heart and I had to bend to catch my breath.

'Good day, Miss Sorgeiul.'

I looked up into the moon face of Mr Kent. I felt too breathless to speak so I tried to nod. The sky around him was burning white, no clouds near his head.

He raised his hat and touched his pale hair. 'I have not had the pleasure of seeing you recently.'

The fear in my mind flamed and faded. 'Mr Kent,' I began. 'I need to get to –'

He smiled. 'I always drew great satisfaction from seeing you.'

'Yes. But –'

'Sometimes you would be escorted by your uncle. At other times you were writing in your parlour.'

I nodded, then understood I could not walk past him. He was blocking my way.

'I desire to bring similar application to my painting.'

I stared into his round blue eyes. I surely had blood on my face. My hair was matted and my dress untidy. I must have looked like something from another world. And yet still he stood there talking in a high, sing-song voice as if he were reading me a story.

'Forgive me, sir, but I have an urgent appointment.'

He touched my cheek with a dry finger. 'Why did you never come to visit me, Miss Sorgeiul? We were neighbours and you never came.'

I put my hand on the bricks behind me. 'I am sorry, sir. It did not occur to me. I suppose my uncle did not make many calls.'

'My mother was lonely on her own. When you first came, she was hopeful that you might visit her.'

'I am sorry.' I thought of her fragile smile and I knew he was right. 'I did not understand.'

'My poor mother. Alone with our cat.'

'Please give her my kind regards.'

'Would you come now and give her the solace of your company?'

A trickle of hot water dripped over the bricks on to

my back. 'I am sorry, Mr Kent. I must attend my appointment.'

'But what can a young lady have that is so very pressing?' He touched his pale eyebrow. 'Surely you could step in. Just for a moment. It would be so little for you. To my mother, it would be an inestimable pleasure.'

He was correct. I had done so little. I had sat in my house and thought only of myself. I thought of him painting flowers on walls, then telling the Society he wished no more to do with them.

'Is your maid, Emily, at home?'

He passed a hand over his forehead. 'Not today. I wish you would pay my mother a visit.'

I looked into his pale eyes and I felt that to say no would be cruel. 'Well, let us say a brief call. And then I really must depart.' In return, I would feel charity, as if I were a person activated by concern for others, rather than my own selfish preoccupations.

He closed his eyes briefly. 'Thank you, Miss Sorgeiul.'

We walked in silence. The street looked the same as always, the children tumbling a ball near the stables, the workmen labouring on the hole in front of number seventeen. Our key would still be under the stone.

Mr Kent gestured towards his house. His mother was not sitting at the window. He pushed open the heavy door, and we were in cool darkness. I had always imagined their house as blandly laid out, spotlessly clean, but instead there was a heavy cobweb at the corner of the ceiling and the paint was peeling from the walls.

'I think my mother may be upstairs. You might wait in the parlour.'

'Of course.'

He opened the creaky door into a similarly dark room. I thought about how hard Jane must have worked to clean around our objects. This place looked as if it had not been dusted for years.

He closed the door behind me and I smelt damp again. There was a glitter of glass, and then my eyes accustomed and I understood what it was. One wall was stacked high with glass boxes, full of birds. There were two blackbirds on pebbles, a large magpie propped on what looked like imitation grass, and a great gold eagle spreading its wings. I walked closer and saw two boxes of owls, white and brown, their eyes wide. Birds were pinned to the walls too. I was not quite sure what they were – blue tits and chaffinches, perhaps, all of them with sharp little beaks and glass beads for eyes. I turned. A swan hung over the door through which I had entered, its wings spread wide above the frame. Across the other wall a flutter of sparrows had been caught in flight.

There was a creak from upstairs and I supposed Mrs Kent must be coming down. I knew little about birds. I tried to think of their song, but I could think only of the city birds that croaked over Princes Street. I stretched out a finger to one of the sparrows. Their feathers were glossy, their beaks shiny, as if they were new. Someone – perhaps Mr Kent – had travelled into the countryside with a gun and shot them. He brought back their bloody bodies, pulled out their intestines, tugged free their hearts, stuffed cotton into the skin and sewed up the gaping wound. He cut out the tongue, varnished the beak, pulled out the jelly eyes and placed glass beads in the raw, red holes. Perhaps he did it here, his hands covered with blood, feathers across the table.

The door opened. 'My mother descends. So, Miss Sorgeuil, have you been well? I have not seen you since the magic show.'

'Yes. A terrible event. My –' I thought better of it. 'The death.'

'I should think it was accidental. Those panels give way easily. Still, he will hang.' His eyes were bright in the shadows. 'Indeed. But, tell me, Miss Sorgeiul, how progresses your writing?'

'Well, but it was nothing, sir. Just a few thoughts about the passing day.'

'He was a great traveller, your uncle, was he not?'

'Indeed.'

'I would like to travel, to Europe and the East. I am sure I would see places and buildings that would assist my artistic endeavours. I have seen little more than London and the Kent countryside.'

'Is your mother unwell, sir?' I was still standing and the wings of the swan at the corner of the room were shifting slightly in my vision.

'Would you like to see my studio?'

I wanted to take a step away from him. 'I am sorry, Mr Kent, I really do not have long.'

'My mother is just arriving.'

'Perhaps I should depart. I will return tomorrow.'

'But I am not sure you will. You lead such an occupied life, Miss Sorgeiul. Unlike my poor mother.'

The sparrows were fluttering. 'I have an appointment.'

'You walk to so many places, do you not?' He moved closer to me and I smelt mint. 'A young lady out alone.' He tapped my cheek and my heart seized. He brought the other hand to my hair.

The owls opened their beaks and turned their heads. *How could you not have seen?*

'I wear gloves when out walking,' he said.

I put my hand on my chest in the hope that it would stop my heart beating so. Surely not. It could not be. It was.

'My current painting is of ladies as fairies, just near a cave. Do you have an interest in art, Miss Sorgeiul?'

'Not today.' I was trying to edge past him.

'Young ladies seem to have no interest in art. It is a male pleasure. Solitary. The young ladies I ask to model are often reluctant.'

'Why –' I began, but could not finish.

'I see you have been admiring my birds, Miss Sorgeiul. They are so free, are they not? Would you not like to be a bird?' He took my hand in his plump palm. 'Your hair is dark but a blackbird is too coarse. You are delicate like a thrush, but they are bolder than you. And yet birds live in groups. You are solitary.'

'No.'

'I saw that one girl visit you. Frizzed hair, patterned dress.'

'I was wrong ever to have friends.' Grace and Miss Grey looked out at me from under the ground, their faces covered with soil.

'What were we talking of? Oh, yes – painting. I wished for a composition of ladies as fairies. But it would not come. Alive, you know, they will not be beautiful. They must keep talking.' He dropped his head. 'And now I have no heart to continue.'

How clever I had thought I was, with my pen and paper, writing about the Man. *No time for books*, said Miss Grey. The fronds spread out from her dress and wrapped themselves around my heart.

'I must confess that I have become distracted,' he said. 'Such pretty hair. I am glad you always refused your uncle's suggestions to have it cut.'

Let me go. Outside the door, the cobbles would be under my feet and I could turn my face to the sun.

'I have been raised, Miss Sorgeuil, to consider human life essential. I only meant to hurt her a little, you see. I did not know she would fall so easily. I was afraid, truly. But then nothing happened and no one came after me, and I was not stopped. So I tried it one more time. And I was not caught again. And then those reports appeared in the newspapers. I thought – shall I tell you? I thought: They want me to continue. I am like a play to them, and they wish for more crime. Like that show, do you not think? Acting out fatalities for public delectation is surely a sin.'

I bowed my head. 'Abigail, Sara, Jenny, Grace. All of them.'

'Do not forget Miss Vine. And perhaps Miss Wood was me too. And you never seemed to worry over your maid Jane. You were so preoccupied by Grace that you quite omitted her. I was sorry to see my work so unappreciated. I painted flowers on walls for you, and still you did not attend to me. But now I am weary of being a story. I wish to desist.' He held out his hands to me. 'I wish you would help me.'

I forced myself to hold my voice steady. 'I am sure that if you simply abstain, you shall lose the desire to continue.'

'No, no. That is akin to relinquishing the taste for sweet things or wine. You stop consuming them in the knowledge that you could do so again, if you desired. This is quite different. I must never do it again.'

'Yes.'

'How can I desist?' His eyes were wide.

'I could go to research the matter in books and find a solution for you.'

'I had forgotten your love of books. I am grateful to that key under the stone. I found it of excellent utility. You two would go out and leave me your house.'

I stared at him, my heart clutching.

'I was so happy when I first entered. And yet I found so many doors locked. Yours was open, Miss Sorgeiul, and the parlour's.'

Write about your maid.

'You have so few possessions – half a dozen dresses, no jewellery, no letters. So instead, you made a story for yourself! It was all very interesting. In fact, I became rather intent on reading the next instalment. I felt such disappointment when I arrived and found you had not progressed.' He wagged a forefinger at me. 'Authoresses are supposed to entertain their public, madam.'

There was a creak from upstairs. 'I thought you became a little melodramatic at times. And I wearied of your descriptions of your unhappiness. But I must give you credit, some of your speculations were very near. I enjoyed your assessment of the culpable man's motivations.'

I was in his prison of words and he was simply going to throw more at me, and when he had finished, he would do as he wished with me.

'And you liked my gift to you? The cat? You called him Crispin, I believe. I knew he would bring you to me.'

'Yes.' The magpie eyes glittered over my head.

'You know, Miss Sorgeiul, there were aspects missing in your account. I wished you might show the Man of Crows returning to the scene and pondering his crime. And I felt you did not explore the need for society to project evil on to such a man.' He turned and patted a brown-paper parcel on the table.

Miss Grey stared up at me and joined hands with Grace, somewhere I could not reach.

He took a step closer to me. 'I once thought that you could help me. You could complete your story, write that I was seized by repentance, and then I would be so. I would no longer wish to continue.' He held a finger to my cheek. 'Would you do that for me?'

I forced myself to speak. 'I would be pleased to.'

'I would also wish you could make something else

happen. There was a girl, some time ago, whom I used as one of my models. And then she disappeared. I tried others to no avail. Could you write that she apologized, and returned to me?'

'I shall do so.'

'See over there?' He gestured to a shuttered desk. I walked to it and touched the wooden lid. 'Turn the key.' I did so, my fingers slipping on the metal. I opened the lid and found a pile of expensive cream paper and a pen.

'I have prepared it all for you. Do be seated.'

He pulled out the chair for me and I smelt lavender. I gathered my skirts and sat. Then his voice was behind me, at my neck. 'Shall we begin?'

The crow overhead opened its beak.

'But then, Miss Sorgeiul, you have been a little slow of late. There is nothing on Miss Vine or any of the others. Perhaps you might not be sufficiently quick at writing.' His tone was doleful. 'I am a very exacting reader. I may keep asking you to revise until it is to my taste. You may have to stay here for some time.' He touched my hair.

And then the door fell open. Mrs Kent stood there in her nightgown, her grey hair hanging loose around her face. I saw the wrinkled skin of her hands as she raised them. Her gown was netted with holes, a giant spider's web. She was like a child's version of a Greek goddess, Hecate, perhaps, with leaves in her hair.

'Mother!'

'You should let Miss Sorgeiul leave,' she said, her voice as strangely high as his. 'I think she would like to go.'

And those were my words. As if the strength came from the air, I threw off Mr Kent's arm and his hand, pushed him from my way. I snatched the brown-paper parcel, touched her hand and ran for the front door. I threw myself on to the street and rushed around three corners to Bishopsgate. I made myself slow to a walk, alongside the labourers and sellers, women carrying their children, serving maids on errands, pretending I was just another person, passing through the day. I heard his voice in my mind: *Shall we begin?*

I felt water on my forehead. I looked up and there were heavy clouds in the sky.

'Rain?' said a woman next to me.

I put out my hand and the damp struck my palm. I looked down and there were spots on my dress. And then the clouds opened and rain began to pour. It pattered on the ground, dripped on to my hair. I put my face to the sky and felt water cover my mouth. The sky tumbled with clouds, crashed, and the street turned blue.

31. Models

He tells me to walk up the back stairs, remove my dress and put on the outfit he has decided I should wear. Then I assume my pose, arm stretched out, one leg bent sideways, my hair untied. I must wait like this until he comes. I do not know how long I stand, for there are no clocks, even if I could tell time.

When he first found me, we worked in Great Queen Street, but now we must come here, where it is cold and dark, even in summer, and the streets are noisy with sick animals and crying babies. I cannot see why a gentleman like him would want to live here. He says his mother is downstairs, but I see nobody in this dark house but him.

He found me when I was tying violets with Netty. Pa bought us a job lot from the market and sent us off with ribbons to bunch them up and sell them to gentlemen clerks in the City. We took them up the church steps, for there was no use round the house for big useless girls like us, and tied until our fingers were red. I felt as if I would be sick from the smell of violets. Then we had to run after the gentlemen – but not into another girl's patch, or we might get a slap.

I was shy at thrusting them into faces and would do anything not to – tighten my boots or look for a ribbon or say I had a pain. As the sky was dusking, Netty grew a little wild with me. 'If we go back with even a single one, Pa will beat us.'

'Perhaps that will not be necessary,' said a man's voice behind us, calm as you like. He was a little man, wearing his hat against the sun.

'Thruppence a bunch,' said Netty, pushing them at his face.

'Three. Wait, I shall take them all.'

'But, sir –' Even Netty was without words and that was a feat.

'I have one condition.' He turned to me. 'What is your name, miss?'

'Jessamy.' Pa likes long names.

'My condition is that Miss Jessamy accompanies me to my rooms.' He reached out a finger. 'You have remarkable eyes, my dear.'

'Pa will be expecting us home.'

'I could accompany you and discuss matters with your father.'

'He won't like it.'

'But if you refuse, you will have to take the violets home with you, and surely he will not be pleased then. I am planning a composition of fairies and Miss Jessamy has every feature I require.' He held out shillings on his palm. 'I shall pay.'

The thought of him back in our rooms with Ma red-faced over the washing and the little 'uns screaming and then all the neighbours asking what was a man like him doing paying a call and thinking that we might be in some wider money trouble than we were already. That decided me.

'I will come with you, sir.' Netty was about to speak and I shook my head at her. 'How can it be of harm?' I whispered. 'And anyway, whatever happens, I shall return with the money.'

'I will come with you.' Poor Netty, holding to our virtue and trying to show our family as respectable, imagining Pa's fury, when really, if he saw the coins, his eyes would light up like a mirror of them and he would send me and anyone else, even the little 'uns, to do what the gentleman pleased.

And so I walked back with the gentleman to Great Queen Street, and when he was done with me, he gave me the guinea and pennies for a pie on the way home and asked me to come back next day. And here I am, every morning, putting out my arm, pretending to be a fairy, taking his money at the end of it. If I were a magic being, I would wear a dress that covered my bosom, not this piece of white stuff, which would be no good even as a bride's veil. And I don't care if some say it's not honest work, for what else might I do? Drag washing between houses, like Ma, and work myself to the bone scrubbing at other people's dirty lives?

It was my hair won him to me, that's what he says. He is always coming to me to try new styles, gathered at the side, mounted, loose or plaited. His hands are dry when he touches me, and I wish he would let me do it myself. He brings pins and ribbons to put in it, but his favourite is a comb with a feather. It must have cost him, for it has silver on it and pieces of the inside of a green and blue shell. He says he saw it in a shop near the Strand and thought of me. I would wear it home, but someone would steal it.

He tells me he plans a painting of fairies dancing in a cave. 'I had once thought I would take different models. But I have decided I shall simply paint you and vary the features a little. Would you not like to be different fairies?'

I do not think I look much of a fairy. They are little baby things with fluttery wings whereas I am quite normal height with thin legs like Pa's and I would not suit wings at all. But he says I have the wrong idea of fairies, and actually they are just beautiful. Even though I had never seen myself in a mirror before I met him, I could have guessed that I had looks from the men outside the Prince William, who, once I turned twelve, dropped their eyes past Milly Sands, who has bosoms like big flowers, and looked at me.

It did not take him long to demand that I remove the dress. He said he could not paint the lines and some such words, but I did not hear them because I had expected it – who pays all that money for a girl just to stand there? So sometimes I was naked as the day I was born, on others he had me put a veil around my waist and tie it, and all the time, over and over, I jumped and danced and put out my legs, ignoring the glittery look in his eyes that every man got staring at me, even Pa.

He says after he has finished this painting of the cave, we will try another. I am like Titania of the fairies, he says, and he will make me look like a queen, all my hair around my shoulders. I nod and smile but I do not think I want to be with him then. I grow weary of listening to him rambling all day, talking of the girls in the street. I should be out there, showing myself.

'I wish there could be times when I might go out and there would be no females there. I would be so much more content.'

I want to say, Why paint us, then?

'I can hear what they think, those girls. They are thinking words of hate.'

Today he is all dissatisfaction about the sand and the cave and he makes me move a little to the right, then the left, turn my hand, then something else. I think only of when he will go down for his meal, leaving me to my pie.

'The comb matches your eyes. It makes you so pretty. But with you, it is not only an appealing appearance. You have beauty of thought. Do you ever feel you are too good for the world, Miss Jessamy?'

'I do not know, sir.'

'Would you not wish to be preserved as you are, in proper youth and innocence?'

'I look forward to growing older, sir,' I lie – the only thing I think of is having money so I don't have to stand in dingy rooms like this wearing not a stitch.

'I am conserving you in my picture. But in life you will go on to change.'

'I try not to, sir.'

He reaches out and puts a hand just above my bosom.

'I wish that would not happen.' He begins to walk to the door. 'Wait for me, just a moment. I will return.'

He closes the door behind him and then it comes to me. I do not wish to be here when he returns. I hurry to the back room, pull on my dress – and then I stop. I hurry to the other end of the room, jump out of the doorway, into the hall, and across the way is a door that is closed. His. I walk into the other room, and it is a lady's, untidy like a cookpot, with bedclothes strewn about. I see the wooden box sitting on a table next to the mirror and I go to it, pull open the lid, and there is what I want: pearls and gold bracelets and a necklace of violet stones. I pull them into my hands, not caring if anyone can hear, then run along the corridor to the studio, where he still is not. My heart is leaping with the excitement and wickedness of what I am doing, and how daring I have been. I gather up my shawl – not that I couldn't buy myself the finest silk shawl from India now – put my hands over the jewels and rattle down the back stairs. As I leave, the wind crosses the fire and sends it dead.

I reach the bottom of the road and I walk more quickly. I do not stop until I reach Liverpool Street, and then I can slow. He cannot find me here. I stand by the Fox and Grapes and I pull out the comb that he has pushed into my hair, hold it up to the light and throw it on to the street. Hopefully, some girl will find it, a pretty thing she could not afford, even if she saved up weeks of wages, good to please a sweetheart. I see it lying on the ground, shining between two stones. Perhaps, I think,

I shall try a new type of job, one where I might really be a magic being. A girl on stage.

I look at the people around me – the old men, the children, the women – and I smile. Then I begin to run.

32. Sand

In the darkness, I name my children. As a little girl, I thought of what I might I call my own infants: Agnes, Helen, Pearl, Beatrice, May. They were names I thought better, more perfect, than my own. I suppose that what I was doing was not naming fresh, separate people but conjuring revised versions of myself, free from history. They rise up now, new figures, small babies with shiny hair, their bodies immaterial. Their souls are untouched and pure, the chance to start again.

There is so much darkness here, even though it is a hot country and, indeed, greatly hotter than I had ever expected. I suppose I thought of the scenery in terms of the painting on my uncle's parlour wall: desert that stretched to the horizon, a temple and a Nubian guard in colourful dress. On the ship over, I had thought of the clutter of objects in the Egyptian Hall, the sphinxes on the walls, the false mummies and strips of hieroglyphs. I could not square such things with a real country, a place where people bought food and ate and walked along the street.

Although there are sandy wastes, there are not the colours I expected: the women dress in black or blue and the men are plain in brown. The colonial balls in the evening are different, I am told, a riot of girls in pink and yellow, like semi-precious stones. I hear the trill of violins playing Liszt and Mozart. It mixes with the sound of the pipe players who sit outside the tea shops and make me think of the banjo man who used to play in Princes Street, late at night. I listen to the music of the balls, but I do not attend. I am not of the right class, a teacher now, no better than a governess. And although most of the families here are French or Italian, I do not think it would be wise to be so public.

I spend my evenings in darkness, after school ends and the sun burns itself to its birth in the corner of the sky. I take a room from the same woman who rented to Mademoiselle Meypert, my predecessor at the school. Madame Selden lives downstairs, with mementoes of her dead husband, and we see each other in passing in the morning and evening, and that suits us well. We dined together initially, but it was awkward and cool. Now, using the excuse that she prefers to eat earlier, she lays out my meal on a tray in the evening and I eat alone, reading the history or geography I must teach the girls the following day. I suppose she thinks me stiff and cold, as northern Europeans are supposed to be. My landlady misses Mademoiselle Meypert. 'She was always so gay!' she told me sadly, as we watched the clock at meals. Well, now she is bright and laughing in the French countryside with a soldier who was similarly charmed by her toothy smile, and in her place Madame Selden has me, cold and dry, hardly speaking. I wonder if I can capture a little of Mademoiselle Meypert's happiness by touching the walls.

In the evenings, I think of what I could hear from my room in Princes Street – the bells ringing at Christ Church, the talk of women, the shrieking of cats. Here I listen to the square. It will be my life now, for I can never go back. I must live here, alone, in the darkness, afraid. I suspect my uncle is still there, in Princes Street, and perhaps Mr Kent is still next door. I wonder if my uncle feels remorse, or if he is still convinced of the excellence of his plans. Perhaps he believes that I was wilful and wrongheaded, and rues the time he wasted on me. Or – as strikes me with fear, late at night, when I feel most alone – he still plans for me and would come for me if he could. I cannot rely on being far from England to be safe. I am always listening, watching the other teachers for a change in behaviour towards me. I sit through interminable prayers every morning and watch faces from under half-closed eyes. When I think of him, fear holds me and I hear him say: *I shall follow you.*

Only six months ago, I was fleeing from Mr Kent. In Bishopsgate, the heavens opened and rain poured over the roofs, and streams ran in the streets. We all stared at the water – the carters, the children, the men carrying bricks – and the woman next to me wept. And then the people began to hurry from their houses, carrying pails and barrels and saucepans and even cups, fighting over the water, even though it was never ending. I held my hands to my face and the tears were no longer there. I picked up my skirts and hurried onward. I remembered my way to St James's and the chemist's shop. He was still there, the old man, picking at his drawers. I hurried through the door in a sheet of raindrops and thrust myself in front of him.

'Buy my hair, sir?' The rain had battered it out of style and whole strands were hanging around my face. He came out from the desk, behind me, and put his hand to the back of my head. 'I am sorry it is wet,' I managed.

'I prefer it wet,' he said. 'Easier to cut and to judge the length. Would you let it down, or shall I?'

My hands slipped and fumbled over the strands as I felt his hot breath on my neck behind me. I lost pins and knew I should slow my hands to complete the task properly but my mind ran wild with Mr Kent and my uncle and Miss Grey, Grace in the soil. It was as if those images controlled my hands.

'Do not worry,' he said. 'We have time. Hours. I could lock the door to ensure our privacy.'

'Do not. I will manage.'

It fell sodden over my back. I heard him bringing out the blade. 'Hold still,' he said. And then I felt the knife cut into my hair, just as the one held by Miss Smith had at Lavenderfields. He cut again and, unlike her, he spoke to me. 'Do not be afraid. It will not hurt. What lovely hair. How soon it will grow back.' I felt his hand inch around and the back of my neck trembled. The hair was dropping into his hand, the stuff touched by my uncle, then Miss Edwarda putting in the pins, and finally Mr Kent, with his dry, cold fingers.

'Many young ladies shed a tear.'

'Not me.'

He had the black mass collected in his hands. 'Now let me neaten the edges for you. I will ensure it grows back evenly.'

And then I had the guineas in my hand, and I was hurrying outside, back into the rain. I almost fell into a man holding a barrel above his head to catch the drops, but carried on, as if I was not the same person and all the hands that had been on me had been taken away, with my hair.

Within a day, I was on a packet to Calais with a purse of money and false papers I had bought from a man who made his trade known by the docks. My name was that of someone's dead daughter, Mary White. On the boat, an Englishwoman befriended me and I told her I was fleeing a forced marriage. She thought Paris was not far enough and I should travel to Egypt, the cheapest of all the distant passages. And here I am, made once more anew, with the name of Miss Elka Svenson, a young lady, recently orphaned, from Sweden, of strictly virtuous and restrained character.

When I arrived in Cairo, I expected that I would have to become the companion of an old lady, but a woman at an office told me of Madame Maréchal's *école* for young ladies. And I was fortunate: Madame was in urgent need of an *institutrice* for Mademoiselle Meypert had departed abruptly. I told Madame I had been a teacher in Stockholm and wished to travel to aid my grief. She told me that many came to Egypt to forget, and two days later I became a teacher for her. That was the one time I saw her humanity. Then I saw the other Madame Maréchal, stern in the corridor, keys at her side. Even the parents are nervous of her.

So I, who have seen so much blood, have been put in charge of the bodies and minds of young girls. I teach English, a little history and geography, and look respectable. Most of the families send their daughters to Paris to school. We take pupils whose merchant fathers are too poor to do so, or dabble in less legal trades, and hope that we will teach them to be good wives. Or those whose families simply cannot let them go. I have a large classroom, with wide windows that catch the sun in the afternoons, and a wall on which there are paintings of the French countryside. I found the girls knew so little that it was easy to pretend I had great scholarship, as they write down facts about wars and plagues and the great rivers of the New World. Madame Maréchal appears to be pleased, or at least not dissatisfied. What rendered me unpopular as a child makes me useful to her as a teacher, it seems: my lack of conversation. I sometimes talk in the mornings with Mademoiselle Titine, who teaches embroidery, but I avoid Mademoiselle Séverine, whose family lost their great fortune in the Terror. She and Mademoiselle Rousson whisper together and go about arm-in-arm.

From time to time, a student and her parents ask if I ever visited London during the spate of recent murders.

I have perfected a look that suggests it is distasteful to mention such a thing to a guardian of the pure souls of young ladies. Then they are quiet, even the fathers keen to explain to a young teacher about the scandals.

I tell myself that Mr Kent has stopped. Most of our newspapers are French or Italian, but I have seen a few copies of *The Times* and the *Morning Chronicle* and the news is not of him. There is discussion of the thick snow and difficult winter weather, the excessive bias of the Queen towards the Whig Party, the progress of the tiny new Princess Royal, the stiffness of Sir Robert Peel, the Prince Consort holding dinners. Surely Mr Kent takes no more victims, if this is all our news. There is no word of further crises of trade so perhaps the country is recovering and the crime is gone.

I think of writing a letter, sent without my name, to the Home Office to tell them of Mr Kent. But I doubt they would believe it, and if they visited him, they would find nothing more than a student fond of stuffed birds. I think about him and I cannot comprehend his motivation. I imagined a man suffused with hatred, thought I would know him the minute I saw him, but it was Mr Kent, my neighbour, with his wide, simple face, killing girls with handsome hair, dreaming of his lost model.

And then I think of Miss Grey and Grace, and my heart burns. The flowers on Miss Grey's dress curve around my face, and Grace is touching my hair. All of them dead, at his hand, when I am still alive. *Why did he let me live? Why take them and not me?* The funeral of Miss Grey, the Janissers standing over the grave as her coffin is lowered into the ground. Her face smiling at the magic show, her arm in mine. If she had never visited, he would never have seen her.

When I first arrived, I kept my hair cropped to my head, but I have begun to let it grow once more. The hair I have now is completely new, not related to the stuff my uncle touched and Mr Kent admired. But still it is the same thickness and colour, and otherwise I look the same, although my face is a little thinner, and my cheeks are a touch browner. I am sure it does not matter. No one would match Miss Svenson, orphan, with Catherine Sorgeiul. After death, I have learnt, the Egyptians believe that the parts of the body take on their own lives and the name survives for ever. Catherine Sorgeiul survives, but in London, and I do not know her.

My uncle will not find me here. He would never think I might come to Egypt. He probably believes I am somewhere in the countryside outside London. I am sure he could not imagine me living alone. I tell myself that late at night when my mind throws blackness at me. My uncle-father. That thought I cannot bear, and when it comes, it sets my mind rambling in terror through it all – Tyburn, the place where we lost my brother, my mother's cries, her body hanging from the beam, my father drowning. The amusement of Mr Trelawny, the two of them reading my book. His hope that I might die. And then there are the new thoughts: as Mr Kent had not killed me, my uncle might have found another way to prove his hypothesis. *Intriguing*, he might say.

I wished your mother to know me.

How pleased he and Mr Trelawny must have been with themselves. I imagine them, Belle-Smyth, Janisser and Trelawny, my uncle and maybe others, sitting in a coffee-house in St James's, exchanging their ideas. So brave, so clever, they must have thought themselves, so ingenious. *Let us see how she dies*, says my uncle. He thought of his book with Mr Trelawny, and how he would be celebrated for his great science and observation. *Why some are killed and some survive.* I would have been their best example, in my grave.

I know I should hope to forgive him, but I can think of him with nothing but anger. He wanted to make us all his playthings, for amusement.

When I first arrived in Cairo, I thought of Louis always. I thought of myself in Lavenderfields, and him afraid, in the hovel of Mr Trelawny, thinking we had all deserted him. 'There is nothing for you but me,' I imagined Mr Trelawny saying.

I want to cry out to Louis, *Wait for me! I come.* Instead, he stole arsenic, and took it before they could catch him, his face pulled apart by the poison eating into his bones. *Stop!* I must teach myself not to think so for it leads to nothing but pain. Mrs Janisser weeping in her parlour, Mrs Kent watching from her window.

I say I hate my uncle, but I share his blood. I am his, whether niece or daughter, after all, and my fear is that I cannot escape entirely. I wrote about the murders, and drew them closer to me. And I thought, at that moment in Richmond, that I could have hit him with the candelabrum, and if I had attempted to ensure his death, could I really say I was better than him? And I cannot be entirely good if I am alive, when so many others are dead.

I find myself worrying that my uncle or his friends might pay closer attention to one of the Misses Belle-Smyth, Miss Edwarda, perhaps, for she knew about cruelty. They would wish that she is taken by Mr Kent. I have to hope that Constantine Janisser will watch for them. I tell myself that it has not already occurred, that Miss Edwarda is not already dead by the hand of the Man of Crows, his last victim maybe. But the more I say this to myself, the more I think that it may have happened so.

So many girls.

I have to hope that what I carry around with me will become a story, a series of events, not a core of pain as it is now. In my dreams, I see my brother, Miss Grey, my parents coming for me, alive, set free.

I look at my gay pupils, who believe books obstacles to their lives. I admire their contentment and wonder if it is better for happiness not to read or write past what is necessary. They come to the classroom scattering endearments, *chère* and *chérie*, names which mean nothing to them for everyone is dear. The little ones are still children and the older ones bold with the certainty of making lives different from their mothers'. I prefer those of fourteen and fifteen who are no longer children, not yet young ladies. Other teachers dread them, but I watch these midpoint girls, too much sometimes. I wish I could return there myself and make my life different. I want their unconcern and faith.

I enjoy every instance of behaviour that infuriates

Madame Maréchal. It amuses me that Delphine Eglet is dancing when I arrive to take the lesson, and I smile at the girls who play with each other's hair. Even Marie-Claire France – who is always demanding why I have no fiancé – amuses me. In all of them, there is a turning to the light, a kind of expansion that I think will be torn down by the world, sooner or later.

Not long after I arrived, I began to notice a small girl at the side, her dark hair always tied in a large bow. Aimée de Guillory was not as eager to laugh and call out as the other girls, and she was often set apart from them. What appealed to me was her alertness. She made me think of a small animal, eyes bright, always watching. Her work was solidly average, but spectacularly neat. It was almost as if she was being excessively orderly to cover her real thoughts on Shakespeare or the reign of Childéric. I stared at her essays, looking for those real thoughts hiding under the words. In lessons, her dark eyes tracked mine.

Once, she arrived early to class and sat there upright, her uniform carefully pinned. I asked her about herself and she told me in smart, clipped answers that she had grown up on her family's plantation in Guadeloupe and they had moved to Cairo last year. They expected to return to the plantation, she said, perhaps in the next five years. I asked where she saw her fate, and she ducked her head. Over the next few months I asked her more questions. I drew pictures in my mind of her home: tall trees, lush grass down to the sea, bowers of red and pink flowers over a squat, white house. And around it, the slaves planting for sugar and later harvesting the cane and dragging it to be burnt and boiled down. *Do you not think it cruel?* I wanted to ask. I had read the stories of the abolitionists, the branded slaves, women forced to give up their babies, children maimed and dying, so many of them.

'Can owning people be fair?'

She looked at me, her face calm. 'It was my family, Madame. Their choice.' I was about to speak again, but saw she wished to continue. 'My father said he was tormented, the first time he saw the markets. But then he decided that if God had not wished us to use people so, He would have given us a sign.'

Living people bought, even born, to pursue the purpose of others. Like dolls.

'Do you prefer life in Cairo?'

'I do not know yet, Madame.' She dropped her eyes to her hands and I returned to the books on my desk.

In September, Madame Maréchal asked me to escort the middle year of girls to the house of a doctor so they might take a few lessons in chemistry, in the hope that a wider curriculum might prevent parents sending their girls abroad. I sat at the back and regarded while little Docteur Le Christophe declared he would demonstrate the different properties of chemicals. He held up various powders: salt, iron ore, and another whose name I did not recognize. After telling the girls at the front to lean away, for fear of hurting their eyes, he took a small heap of whitish stuff and dropped it into a bowl of water. It began to skate across the surface and, within a few moments, started to burn, the sparks flying and brief flames shooting into the air.

'You might think that the compounds I have shown you are always so,' he said. 'Instead, when you mix them, their properties change.' He showed us, by adding a little of the white stuff to salt, how that too could dance around the surface and refuse to dissolve.

'I hope I am not teaching you young ladies to wreck your cook's store cupboard. What do you think, Mademoiselle Svenson?'

I nodded, smiled. He divided the girls into pairs, so they could burn compounds. 'You know, young ladies, everything can be changed. Indeed, we should better see the whole world we live in as always in alteration. Nothing will be the same at the end of today as it was in the morning. And every time we use something, it differs. It is rather like a word. When we say it, we make it slightly our own.'

I turned to watch the more careless girls, hoping that none of them would spill anything. I looked over Geneviève de Sagnier and Delphine Eglet's shoulders, then saw Émilie Jesse catch her finger, but my attention was not with them. Surely, I thought, if piles of powder can change and leave their old versions behind, then the same can be true for feelings and people. Hearts can transform and be new. I must believe this.

I used to believe that time flew as a straight arrow. I thought that my life would progress neatly, things would be mapped out for me. I believed in destiny. Now I know that does not exist. All I have done so far, it seems, is to escape the desires of others, and now I hide from them in a country on the other side of the world.

My girls are educated here primarily, it seems, to raise the desire in men to marry them. But that is a kind of incarceration they wish for. To live truly you must, in a sense, be restricted and imprisoned, for you cannot love without submitting thus. I am free, but not loved or loving, and I suppose that is how I shall continue.

After I have finished this last page of my manuscript, I shall no longer write. For there are prisons in words too. Even though these pages were for me, I have written them for others. Mr Kent read my words, my uncle, and Mr Trelawny, probably Mr Belle-Smyth and Mr Janisser senior, too. They smiled, turned the pages, mocked. I was so proud of myself, so sure I saw into hearts, and instead I did not see a single thing. I started writing about evil because I thought I would know it, and instead I found that evil was not a thing in itself but can be created by fortune and moment, and those who do evil may believe they are acting rightly. It cannot be found or located as a whole thing, but exists in the movement of time. All I did in writing was to bring the evil closer to me.

I have been copying out every line on to new paper, so that I can dispose of the pages touched by my uncle and Mr Kent. But still, when I look at my manuscript, it seems that whatever I wrote, the words had already been used by someone around me: every line has on it the taint of my uncle, or the hospital, even Mr Kent. I thought writing a way of getting free of the hands of others, but instead it has entwined me with them just as tightly as I ever was.

Yesterday afternoon I escorted the third-year girls to the house of the father of Rose du Jacquette, a younger girl to whom I had taught history once or twice. He had offered to show them his collection of butterflies. A tall, dark man whose skin had been much burnt by the sun, he welcomed us into his parlour and told us he had settled in Cairo after working as an officer on map-making projects in South America and Africa. He said that his travels had enabled him to pursue his passion for butterflies and he had returned with many handsome specimens. He had, he told us, gone to great effort to create the atmosphere of the Brazilian rainforest in the little glasshouse next door.

He led us through his parlour and we passed through double doors, walked into thick green leaves. Steam wound up from stone birdbaths and wooden tables were piled with chopped apricots and fruit. 'That is where my gentlemen feed,' he said. 'They use their probosces.' I realized that what I had taken for flowers, on the leaves, were butterflies, fluttering and settling. One slipped past me, landed on the wooden table and began poking his proboscis into a piece of date. He had closed his wings so all I could see was the brown pattern on the outside, the two eyes on either side. The girls were wandering on, and Monsieur du Jacquette was with them, while I stayed behind, watching the creature extend his long brown prong into the fruit. To the side, there was another, with wings that seemed not solid but a mere gossamer skeleton. We had had butterflies in Richmond but they were tiny angels, primrose yellow or delicate blue. These were large, long-winged, powerful.

'Any difficulties, ladies?' called back Monsieur du Jacquette. There had been concern that one of the more nervous girls might be distressed by the heat and the fluttering, and fall into hysterics if one of the insects was to brush her with his wings. There was a happy chorus of denial and I returned my eyes to the large one feeding on the date.

'It is very beautiful.' Aimée de Guillory was standing at my shoulder. 'I wish he would open out.'

'I think his wings are blue and green,' I said.

And then, as if it had been listening to us, the butterfly splayed into the air and a riot of green, yellow and violet fluttered around us. Aimée looked up and held out her hand. He landed on her bosom, perching on the pale folds of her gown.

'It likes me,' she said, delighted. He shifted slightly and began to sweep his proboscis over her dress, fluttering his wings.

'It does not want to move.' She held a finger towards the wings. Over her head, more butterflies danced.

'Let me take my gentleman from you.' Monsieur du

Jacquette had come up behind us. 'Once they are nested on the body, they are hard to extract.' He moved his index finger to touch the butterfly's leg. We watched it recoil, then flutter to the table.

'Are you enjoying the visit, Mademoiselle?'

I smelt tobacco and heat. 'Very much.'

'How interesting to meet a lady from Sweden. Quite a rarity in these parts. I hear you are from Stockholm. You must miss it.'

'Very much, Monsieur. The cold weather.' I told my heart to still. Aimée was gazing at the butterfly, paying no attention to us.

'I have visited the city. Where did you live?'

'My parents had a house near the old town. Olgar Street.'

'Then you will know my friends, the Linds in Ladugårdslandet?'

'Possibly. My parents did not spend much time in society.'

He smiled, but his eyes did not. 'They do not seem to know you.'

I looked at the tree above. Every one of its leaves had been gnawed into holes. 'I kept myself rather quiet.'

'What a coincidence.' He turned to me and raised his hat. I stared and my stomach lurched, for I saw the face of the man who had come to visit my uncle so soon after I had come to live with him, offering the South American mine.

'I too am reserved. However, I do like to keep up

with events in the newspapers. So many intriguing things occur, in the modern world. Fortunately, we all have family.' He blinked.

I could say nothing.

'Do you not agree, Mademoiselle?'

'I do not read newspapers.' And then a red butterfly flittered over his head and the answer came to me. 'I understand that many significant crimes are not reported to the newspapers. Not murder, of course, but quieter evils, theft and fraud.'

He touched his hair. 'That is true, Mademoiselle.'

'We must rejoin the young ladies, sir. We are grateful to you for entertaining us with your impressive collection.'

'The visit has been an honour. I discovered many beauties in South America.' He bowed. 'I hope we meet again.'

'I think that unlikely, sir. I seldom leave the school.'

I shall not. I will continue at Madame Maréchal's and teach my girls and no one will find me. On the way here, I considered becoming a nun, and that is the way I shall live. I shall stay retired, undiscovered. It is the bargain I make to be free.

I watch him retreat. In a hundred years' time, none of us will be here, and different people will stand where we once did, wearing strange clothes and using tools we can hardly imagine. They will remember nothing of our lives and what we did, and they will not care. They will interest themselves in kings, queens and wars, not people going through their days. I will become one of those forgotten lives, not remembered, unseen.

The red butterfly hovered over Aimée's head. I held out my hand. 'Come along, Miss de Guillory,' I said to her. 'The rest are almost at the other side.' She grasped my palm with her thin fingers and together we walked forward, through the coils of steam and the dark shrubs. In front of us, the sun glittered over the heads of the girls. Their hair shone in the late afternoon light.

Historical Note

The Pleasures of Men is a work of fiction, and although historical events have been used, licence has been taken. There was no serial killer in 1840 who murdered young women in the fashion of the Man of Crows. In fact, although murder was rife in early-nineteenth-century Britain, most killings were a consequence of domestic disputes, battles between workmates, spurned lovers or other aggrieved parties exacting revenge. In contrast to the ways in which we normally perceive murder today, group or serial killings were attributed to gangs.

Nowadays, when repeated murders are discovered, we imagine a lone killer, wandering the streets. To us, the serial killer is such an evil figure that he must be acting alone. In the nineteenth century, people found it impossible to imagine such crimes being perpetrated by an individual. The growing belief in the individual serial killer was heavily influenced by the literature of murder, such as the work of Arthur Conan Doyle. Perhaps the greatest influences on our perceptions of murder were books about split characters – most notably Robert Louis Stevenson's *Dr Jekyll and Mr Hyde* (1886). Such books were vital when women began to be found in east London in 1888 with their throats cut. Although initial theories believed the murders were committed by gangs, public opinion soon became convinced that the culprit was an individual. A letter written to the Central News Agency signed 'Jack the Ripper' gave him a name, although the letter was probably a hoax. The hunt was on for a killer – and many were convinced he had a split personality and led a respectable life during the daytime. Indeed, an actor playing Mr Hyde was briefly arrested – suspected because he was so convincing in the role. The murders were never solved, and the number of victims is a subject of furious debate. One thing is certain: after Jack, serial killers had to be seen as acting alone.

The Man of Crows, thus, is a product of my imagination – but Spitalfields in 1840 was an area which he could have wandered. The streets around Princes Street had lost much of their wealth, as the silk manufacturers moved out to the countryside. Although some way from the extreme poverty of the late nineteenth century, it was an area that respectable people were increasingly nervous of visiting. Social reformers as well as sensational journalists rued the poverty, crime and despair of the inhabitants. As the *Illustrated London News* declared in 1863, it was 'one painful and monotonous round of vice, filth, and poverty, huddled in dark cellars, ruined garrets, bare and blackened rooms, teeming with disease and death'.

Britain in 1840 was suffering a severe economic downturn. Poor winters and a series of bad harvests, combined with the aftermath of the depressions caused by the end of the Napoleonic wars, had a severe impact on the poor. Britain was becoming, as Benjamin Disraeli suggested in *Sybil*, two nations: the rich and the poor. People fled an increasingly impoverished countryside to the cities – and found themselves living in squalor. The average life expectancy was thirty, less for the poor, and many children died before the age of ten. The Chartists demanded further representation and terrible riots seemed possible. As the political diarist Charles Greville wrote, 'Parties are violent, government weak, everybody wondering what will happen.' Poverty in Britain had a direct impact on the rest of the world – notably the great 1837 Panic in America. And yet faith in the stock market remained, as in the case of the Railway Mania of the 1840s. People invested wildly in railway stock – until the bubble burst.

Depression, poverty and economic uncertainty all breed crime – and terror. Many accept urban isolation, poverty and struggle. Some can only assuage their demons by punishing, dominating and killing others. Such is the killer in this novel: inconspicuous, seemingly innocuous and murderous.

Mr Kent is loosely based on the famous fairy painter, Richard Dadd (b. 1817), who moved from Kent to London to study at the Royal Academy. In 1842, he accompanied Sir Thomas Phillips, formerly Mayor of London, on a tour through Europe to the Middle East – ending in Egypt. The tour was too much for his delicate mind and he returned convinced he was controlled by the god Osiris. Dadd killed his father a few months after his return in 1843. Many have speculated on what occurred during his trip to Egypt to so unbalance his mind. In my imagination, thus, Catherine is not quite as safe as she believes at the close . . .

I have long studied the Victorian era and, as such, I am grateful to all those intrepid nineteenth-century reporters and diarists from whose work the voices of our ancestors speak still. I am indebted to scholars whose invaluable work on London, Spitalfields, the poor, art, travel, crime, servants, prisons, women and daily life I have used in *The Pleasures of Men*. Among the most useful have been Peter Guillory, *The Small House in Eighteenth Century London* (Yale, 2004); *Victorian Pubs* by Mark Girouard (Yale, 1984); *Victorian Babylon: People, Streets and Images in Nineteenth-century London* by Lynda Nead (Yale, 2000); *Sin, Organized Charity and the Poor Law in Victorian England* by Robert Humphries (Macmillan, 1995); *Capital Offences: Geographies of Class and Crime in Victorian England* by Simon Joyce (University of Virginia Press, 1993); *The East End: Four Centuries of London Life* by Alan Palmer (Murray, 1989); *Victorian Crime, Madness and Sensation*, ed. by Andrew Maunder and Grace Moore (Ashgate, 2004); *Inventing the Victorians* by Matthew Sweet (Faber, 2001); *Thackeray* by D. J. Taylor (Chatto, 1999); *The Rise and Fall of the Victorian Domestic Servant* by Pamela Horn (Macmillan, 1975); *The Victorians* by A. N. Wilson (Hutchinson, 2002); *The Invention of Murder* by Judith Flanders (Harper Press, 2011), *Consuming Passions* (2006) and *The Victorian House: Domestic Life from Childbirth to Deathbed* (Harper Press, 2003); *The Blackest Streets: The Life of a Victorian Slum* by Sarah Wise

(Bodley Head, 2003) and *The Italian Boy* (Cape, 2004); *The Victorian Household* by Shirley Nicolson (Stroud, 1994), *Street Life in London* by J. Thomson (1877), *The Worst Street in London* by Fiona Rule (Allan, 2008); *An Account of the Historical Benefactions Belonging to the Parish of Christ Church, Spitalfields* by Sumerset J Hyam (1866); *The Dens of London and the Poor of Spitalfields* by H. R. Williams (1850); *An Appeal to the Public in Defence of the Spitalfields Act* by William Hale, Silk Merchant (1822); *Criminal Life: Reminiscences of Forty-Two Years as Police Officer* by James Bent (1891); *The Wilds of London* by James Greenwood (1867); *Ragged London in 1861* by John Hollingshead (1861).

Also vital were *Florence Nightingale* by Mark Bostridge (Viking, 2008); *Death in the Victorian Family* by Pat Jelland (Oxford University Press, 1996); *Girls Growing Up in Late Victorian and Edwardian England* by Carol Dyhouse (Routledge,1981); *Household Gods: The British and their Possessions* by Deborah Cohen (Yale, 2009); *Middle Class Culture in the Nineteenth Century* by Linda Young (Macmillan, 2003); *Music and British Culture, 1785–1914*, ed. by Christina Bashford and Lianne Langley (Oxford University Press, 2000); *Nineteenth-Century Media and the Construction of Identities*, ed. by Laurel Brake *et al* (Macmillan, 2000); *Victorian Newspapers* by Lucy Brown (Oxford, 1985); *Jack the Ripper and the London Press* by L. Perry Curtis (Yale, 2003); *Crime and Society in England, 1750–1900* by Clive Emsley (Longman, 1987); *Child Murder and British Culture, 1720–1900* by Josephine McDonagh (Cambridge University Press, 2003); *Women,*

Crime and Custody in Victorian England by Lucia Zedner (Clarendon Press, 1991); *Illegitimate Theatre in London* by Jane Moody (Cambridge University Press, 2000); *Popular Culture and Performance in the Victorian City* by Peter Bailey (Cambridge University Press, 1998); *Public Purity, Private Shame* by Ronald Pearsall (Weidenfeld, 1976); *Hospital and Asylum Architecture in England, 1840–1914* by Jeremy Taylor (Mansell, 1991); *Mental Disability in Victorian England* by David Wright (Oxford, 2001); *Lunatic Hospitals in Georgian England* by Leonard Smith (Routledge, 2007); *The Secret History of Georgian London* by Dan Cruickshank (Random House, 2009); *City of Dreadful Delight* by Judith Walkowitz (Virago, 1992); *Charles Dickens and the House of Fallen Women* by Jenny Hartley (Methuen, 2008); *The Victorian Celebration of Death* by James Stevens Curl (David & Charles, 1972); *Necropolis London and its Dead* by Catharine Arnold (Simon & Schuster, 2006); *Behind Closed Doors* by Amanda Vickery (Yale, 2009); *Public Lives, Women, Family and Society in Victorian Britain* by Eleanor Gordon and Gwyneth Nair (Yale, 2003); *The Victorian Undertaker* by Trevor May (Shire, 2006).

I also found of great assistance *Victorian Fairy Painting* by Charlotte Gere *et al* (Merrell, 1997); *Richard Dadd: The Artist and the Asylum* by Nicolas Tromans (Tate, 2011); *The Late Richard Dadd, 1817–1866* by Patricia Allderidge (Tate, 1974); *Fairies in Victorian Art* by Christopher Wood (Antique Collectors, 2000); and *Sketches by Boz* by Charles Dickens (1836); *Dickens Dictionary of London* by Charles Dickens Jr (1879); *Life and Labour of the People* by Charles Booth (1889); *Britain's Work in Egypt by an Englishman in the Egyptian Service* (1892); *The Nile* by E. A. W. Budge (1892); *Chronicles of a Journey, 1839–40* by Mary and Tom Beswick, ed. by Tom Beswick (Filey, 1997); *Diary of a Tour in Greece, Turkey, Egypt* by Mary Dawson Damer (1842); *Egypt in the Nineteenth Century* by D. A. Cameron (1898); *Egypt under the Khedives, 1805–1879* by Robert Hunter (University of Pittsburgh Press, 1984); *The Englishwoman in Egypt*, ed. by Azzah Kararah (University of Cairo Press, 2003); *The Future of Egypt* by E. Dicey (1898); *Letters From Egypt* by Florence Nightingale (reissue, 1987); *Notes on Nursing* by Florence Nightingale (1859) and, of course, *London Labour and the London Poor* by Henry Mayhew (3 vols, 1851), fourth volume 1861.

I am indebted to the marvellous collections of nineteenth-century maps, broadsides, pamphlets, wills, letters and civic documents in the London Metropolitan Archives, the Guildhall Library, the National Archives and particularly the British Library.

Acknowledgements

I wrote much of this book while living in a rented flat in Paris in 2008. I lived by the Seine and found the streets surprisingly deserted late at night, and unlit. To me, wandering around at night, some of the darker streets seemed just as they would have done centuries earlier. I began to think about London and how the streets would have appeared to someone who did not know them at all. Very soon, Catherine and the Man of Crows came to my head – and then I could not put down my pen.

I refined and completed this book while studying my MA in Creative Writing at Royal Holloway, London. I am deeply grateful to all those tutors and students who read and gave me invaluable feedback on my work, especially Andrew Motion, who has been a great supporter, Susanna Jones, Preti Taneja, and thank you to Eley Williams. I am also grateful to Sam Mills for her reading and thoughts, and Joe Stretch for very helpful criticism. Dan Cruikshank, the expert on eighteenth and nineteenth-century Spitalfields has been of great assistance. I am grateful to the staff of the London Library, the Bodleian Library, the Guildhall Library, the London Metropolitan Archives and the National Archives and particularly the British Library.

Mary Flanagan and the students on the Creative

Writing Workshop at City Lit read a very early version of this work in 2006, and gave me invaluable criticism, particularly Zoë Deleiul, Belinda Burns and Emma Jacobs. My very first creative writing teacher, Clare Morgan at Oxford, inspired me to take my work seriously.

Thank you to Simon Trewin for making the journey of the book so marvellous. Thank you to Ariella Feiner, Zoë Ross, Jessica Craig and Jane Wills at United Agents, to my careful and thoughtful editor, Mari Evans at Penguin, and Louise Moore, Tom Weldon, Celine Kelly, Francesca Russell, Ruth Spencer, Sarah Hulbert and Hazel Orme; Elisabeth Dyssegaard and Sam Brown in the US, Iris Tupholme in Canada, and also to all of those in the media who have let me talk about the Victorians on their programme. Marcus Gipps had read this book perhaps a hundred times, and has been unfailingly full of patience and inspiration. I am very grateful.

Reading Group Questions

1) Catherine is an unusual girl with a strange and dark past. What were your first impressions of Catherine as a character? Did your view of her change over the course of the novel?
2) *The Pleasures of Men* is set in London's East End in 1840. In what way do you think the setting of the novel adds to the atmosphere of the story?
3) We discover quite quickly that Catherine is rather isolated living in her uncle's house. How far do you think this isolation contributes to her sense of fear and fascination with what's going on outside on the streets of London? Do you think her decision to write about the girls murdered by the Man of Crows contributes to her sense of hysteria around these murders?
4) *The Pleasures of Men* is told primarily through the eyes of Catherine but in chapters nine and seventeen we get to see the story from Grace's point of view. What do these chapters add to the novel? How important is Grace's character to the book?
5) Catherine's strange nature has made it difficult for her to establish friendships with other ladies of her standing, making the one she strikes up with Miss Grey quite unusual. Does Catherine's

friendship with Miss Grey show a different side to her character?

6) Because of the wicked thing Catherine believes herself to have done the night her brother is taken, she holds herself responsible for all of the terrible events that follow. How much of a victim do you think Catherine is? How far do you think her belief that she is evil affects her actions?
7) We meet Mr Kent several times over the course of the novel. What were your impressions of him on each occasion and to what extent did your impression of him change?
8) The story ends in a very different setting to the streets of London's East End. What did you think of the novel's ending? Have you any thoughts on what might happen next to Catherine?